The Collected Supernatural and Weird Fiction of Vincent O'Sullivan

The Collected Supernatural and Weird Fiction of Vincent O'Sullivan

Twenty-Seven Short Stories and Poems and One Novella of the Strange and Unusual Including 'The Burned House,' 'The Abigail Sheriff Memorial,' 'When I Was Dead,' 'The Houses of Sin,' 'The Next Room,' and 'Verschoyle's House'

Vincent O'Sullivan

LEONAUR

The Collected
Supernatural and Weird
Fiction of
Vincent O'Sullivan
Twenty-Seven Short Stories and Poems and One Novella of the Strange and Unusual
Including 'The Burned House,' 'The Abigail Sheriff Memorial,' 'When I Was Dead,'
'The Houses of Sin,' 'The Next Room,' and 'Verschoyle's House'
by Vincent O'Sullivan

Leonaur is an imprint of Oakpast Ltd

Copyright in this form © 2023 Oakpast Ltd

ISBN: 978-1-916535-70-1 (hardcover)
ISBN: 978-1-916535-71-8 (softcover)

http://www.leonaur.com

Publisher's Notes

The views expressed in this book are not necessarily
those of the publisher.

Contents

A Study in Murder

As I got out of a cab at Piccadilly Circus, I was hailed by Gladwin.

"Just the man I was looking for!" he cried. "Let us go somewhere and have a drink."

At that moment a glass of brandy happened to be the thing I wanted; so, I followed Gladwin to the Criterion readily enough. Besides, he was excited: and people are always interesting when they are excited.

"A man feels strange," said Gladwin, sitting down by a table, "when he looks around this place and thinks that everybody in it will outlive him."

"Do you feel like that, by any chance?" I asked, lighting a cigarette.

"Yes, I do. Let me tell you this, my friend," he went on, in his earnest, impulsive way, which was wont to become a little wearisome: "You know that I'm not much better than a pauper. Well! I'm sick of slaving away for a wretched paltry salary, and I'm going to end it all, I've thought about it for a long time, and something that happened today has quite settled it.—By the way, do you think I'm mad?"

"Oh Lord, no!" says I.

"Because I'm not. Now, you know as well as I do, that all this time, since luck has taken to using me as a football, I've been kept together by the thought of Margaret. I thought, that somehow or other, if I only pegged on, I might—Well! I have seen her today. She was kind enough to state that she could never marry me, and that her father didn't want her to see me again. She was also so good as to mention that it would be insane, considering my position, for her to marry against her father's wishes. Then she spoke of you.—Hullo! you've upset your glass! Waiter, another soda and brandy here!—As I was saying, she spoke of you. She said that her father was most anxious to have her married to you, and was doing his utmost to bring about the match. I suppose you never did have any feeling in that way for Margaret?"

"My *dear* fellow!"

"I thought not; and I told her so. Besides, I said that you were too good a friend of mine to try to step into my shoes. But she only shook her head, and went out of the room weeping. And so, tonight I'm going to end it all! In your company I'm going to do everything that makes a man's life bright and merry; and then I'm going to blow the soul out of my body somewhere by the river.—You'll come with me?"

"Yes—of course!" I said, with a slight hesitation, "But what are these things that make a man's life bright and merry? Only the usual stupidities—dining, a theatre or music hall, and all that!"

"But it is these very *banalities* that I want!" exclaimed Gladwin. "I have done them so often when I was fairly happy, that I am anxious to learn what they seem like on the night when I'm going to die. Meet me for dinner at the Berkeley at half-past seven."

As I drove home to dress, I took this letter from my pocket and read it again:—

I write to you because I know that you are such a true friend to us both, and have so much influence with my father. I need not protest that I love Mr. Gladwin with all my heart; but how can I tell him so, when my father will not even speak to him! Please, please try to do us good, to make our lives content. Perhaps you will think it a fine and great thing, to serve two creatures who can never repay you.—Margaret.

"How odd it is," says Gladwin, as we strolled towards the Empire, "that all this stir and bustle which I am in the midst of tonight, will be going on just the same tomorrow night, as though I had never existed."

"Yes," I replied; "how proud you must feel as you move amongst this commonplace throng! Dr. Johnson said, that when a man has resolved to kill himself, he may go and take the king of Prussia by the nose, at the head of his army. It is a fair question whether a man has not a right to take leave of life when it ceases to charm—to be beautiful."

"If you are so much in love with suicide," says Gladwin, rather irritably for him, "why on earth don't you do it yourself?"

"Oh! I have a great many reasons. The chief of them is, that so many people depend on my life. Take my valet, for instance. That young man supports his mother and three sisters. Now if I were to die, I should be a cause of misfortune to all of them. No; I cannot commit suicide, because of my valet."

"Of course, you are right," said Gladwin, as we turned into the theatre; "and I am a fool!"

"Are you under sentence of death?" a woman asked Gladwin in the *promenade*, as it is called, of the Empire.

She laughed, and disappeared in the crowd. I turned to inspect Gladwin: and indeed, he had a low look. His face was pale and wet: there was nervousness, fatigue, even fear, in his demeanour. Seeing these things, I led the way to the bar.

"My friend, when I look around this place, with all its light and joy, it almost tempts me to give up the game," said Gladwin, with a glass of brandy in his shaking hand.

"How few people there are in the world who have the courage to give life the slip!" I murmured, as if in a study. "Men talk glibly about death being preferable to the smallest evils of our lot: but it is when people come face to face with death that they wave the white feather in a vehement and degrading fashion. There are but two sets of heroes in the world—the Anarchists and the Suicides!"

"You don't mean to say I'm a coward?" Gladwin rapped out with a flush,

"Really, I was hardly thinking of you. I have concluded that you intend to go back to your drudgery; to see Margaret——"

"You think wrong," interrupted Gladwin. "Let us get out of this damned hole—it stifles me!"

"When Margaret wept today," remarked Gladwin, as we sat to supper in the *Hôtel Continental*, "do you know I—that is, it just occurred to me, that she might love me after all!" "One is usually deceived in these cases," I said, drawing on the table-cloth with a fork. "You *wish* her to love you, and naturally twist every unmeaning thing to your advantage."

"You know best," answered Gladwin, filling his glass. "If she loved me, you would be first to notice it. Margaret has a beautiful mind," he added after a bit, "I hope she may never be unhappy." And with that he put his hands to his face—to hide his tears, I think; because he laughed so loud the next moment. Notwithstanding this merriment, I thought it wise to purchase a small flask of brandy as we left the hotel.

"If I think of the time when I was a lad, it just takes the heart out of me!" declared Gladwin, as we walked, through quiet streets, arm-in-arm to the river. "My people were always so good to me; and the dear old place——"

9

He choked. "Try a little of this stuff," I said, offering my flask.

He took a long drink; and then we went on for a while in silence.

"I know I wasn't born to end like this!" he broke out suddenly. "I'm not clever, and I'm not much good any way; but I've never lied, I've never cheated, and I don't think I've ever spoken a bad word of anyone. By God, I haven't! And now nobody cares for me, and I'm being paid out like a hanged dog!"

We had come to the Embankment by this time, so I turned on him with great indignation.

"And do you think I would stand idly by and watch this performance," I exclaimed, "save that I am sure you can never continue your mean life! I am sure, too, that you could never bear the thought of Margaret in another man's arms; but from what I've heard——"

"Please don't add the last straw," he screamed out in a sort of agony; "let me die without knowing that!—You are the best friend I have ever had," he said, taking my hand, "the best friend that any fellow ever had,"

I pressed his hand, with real feeling. Then I looked around, and noting that we were free from observation, I said:—

"I think I will stop here, while you go on to the bridge. Never fear, old chap, I shall see the last of you,—'tis all I can do!"

"Goodbye," said Gladwin; "God bless you, my friend!"

He went forward a little; then, much to my annoyance (for I dreaded lest some should find us in company), he came back again, shewing a ghastly, twitching face.

"If I thought that Margaret loved me——" he mumbled in his throat.

"She shall hear of your death," I murmured, "and she will be sorry for you!"

He nodded his head twice, as if satisfied, and went to the bridge. There he climbed upon the parapet, exploded a pistol at his face, and fell forward into the water.

"Did you see that suicide?" says I to the policeman who came running up.

"Yes, sir," answered the man, fumbling for his whistle.

"I had nothing to do with it, had I?"

He stopped short and looked at me narrowly. I fell to examining my cigarette to see if it was burning well. He was a young man, new to the police service, I should think. Doubtless I impressed him—in my favour, I mean: I do so impress people sometimes.

'You, sir!" he exclaimed, and shook his head. "Oh, dear no, sir!"

"*That's* all right," I said. And then I laughed.

Hugo Raven's Hand

1

The girl had always been an annoyance to Hugo Raven. Even when their relations had been most intimate, he had found her petulant, wayward, at times a little morose; and now, although he had not seen her for nearly a year, the recollection of her vaguely troubled him. She had letters of his, for instance—eager, passionate letters, written in warm and unwary moments—which he regretted; and these letters, exposed just at this point of his career, might prove disastrous. "What a bother she is, that Grace Casket," he said to himself.

He sat to breakfast, one Sunday morning in summer, in his chambers in the Temple. The rooms were light and charming: a drowsy peace had settled on everything. Through the open windows the breath of the lime trees in King's Bench Walk floated in, and a humming bee would now and then hover above a bowl of wet, amber-coloured roses. He had the *Morning Post* of yesterday propped up before him, so ordered, that he could with ease read this advertisement:—

A marriage has been arranged, and will shortly take place between Hugo Raven, Esq., of the Inner Temple, barrister-at-law, and Hilda, only daughter of Sir Matthew Chancel, Bart., of 12, Walpole Street, Mayfair, and The Priory, Little Maddon, Dorset.

He read this advertisement so often, that he noted how one of the letters in his name was a little out of place—printed higher than the others, and he was irritated. But he thought that the advertisement, on the whole, ran very well. He leaned back in his chair, stroking his beard with his large, powerful hand, on which he wore two rings, and stared at the ceiling. Yes! certainly he had done well for himself in the world; had now, in his thirty-fifth year, reached the "home-stretch," as people say.

He had been only an ordinary passman at Oxford; but when he

13

came to town he discovered in the law, which has the reputation of being so dry, matter which for him was not dry at all. Well! just this interest of his in his subject, taken with his somewhat arrogant, over-bearing (could it have been what is called *browbeating?*) manner, was found most valuable in his practice at the Bar. After a while he became accustomed, and began to be talked about; he was said to be a safe man to have on your side. Then he went a great deal into London so-ciety, with the purpose of discovering some woman who had money enough to be his wife.

This girl, Hilda Chancel, he had now found. He was rather a fa-vourite with people. Sometimes he engaged a little with the fine arts. He painted tiny pictures of fields, and farmhouses, and sunsets, in water-colours. He said he adored music; and in a box, at an opera of Wagner, would pass a pleasant hour in conversation. When there was nobody to talk to, he yawned and looked horribly "bored," then he told you, afterwards, how the music had charmed him.

He despised men of letters, whom he called "writing chaps," and had the illusion (like many another!) that if he could only spare an hour or two a week for trifling, he could produce great books. Indeed, he used to write sugary little verses for the albums of ladies—verses about "flowers" and "showers," "heart" and "part," "kiss" and "bliss." He would read these verses to his friends, and he called them his "po-ems." He had met Grace Casket, who was an assistant in a milliner's shop in Regent Street, by accident, and he had made her—a girl of this class—his mistress on principle; his principle being, that an adven-ture which is bought is not worth having.

Hugo put his hands in his pockets, and sauntered lazily to the window. The sun gleamed on the buildings of the Temple; and all about was the stillness which makes Sunday a festival in that quiet neighbourhood. Below the window, on the gravel, some pigeons gur-gled and coo'd—that strange sound of pigeons! which reminds one, in some subtle fashion, of the soft feel of warm milk. Hugo watched one of them that had gone apart from the others, strutting and prun-ing itself, with idle concentration; then, quite naturally, his eyes fell on Crown Office Row, and the form of a woman at the far end.

He started wildly; a sick feeling came all about his heart, as if a hand had grasped him and tightened there. Then he fell to reasoning with himself. The figure in the distance had, certainly, a look of Grace Casket; but in our lives people did not appear in that way, just when you were thinking of them, as they did in silly novels and stories. He was one of those men who, having never had a taste of the marvellous, their use is, not to stand in doubt, but to deny strenuously that marvels happen. He watched the woman as she came slowly along, swinging her parasol, and stopping now and then to look over the gardens towards the river. An old gate-keeper, in his coat with brass buttons, hobbled by: she spoke to him, and he seemed to be indicating this very house. After that she came straight for the entrance.

"How absurd!" thought Hugo. "There are other men on the staircase besides myself."

He heard her slow, rather heavy step on the wooden stairs, and the hush of her dress. She knocked at his door. It was Grace Casket, sure enough. What a misfortune!

He thought of resting still, so that she might conclude he was out. She knocked again. Ah, curse her! She was sure to go to Whitcomb's rooms opposite, and ask about him. He walked with quick, hard steps, and unlocked the door.

"Oh, Hugo!"

"Come in, come in! somebody may see you."

When she entered the room, the first thing she did was to cross over and bury her face in the cool roses. Hugo thought that was rather pretty of her. She was tall and fair-formed; of the English type of prettiness—of beauty, if you will!—with her scarlet lips, her cheeks cream and red, and her waving, bronze-coloured hair. Her hands were large and covered with black gloves; when she sat down, she let her hands fall together in her lap, and Hugo perceived that there was a hole in the finger of a glove. There was a note of the provinces in her speech: it came like the odour of fields in a dusty street on a hot day. Sometimes she neglected to give the letter h its full value; and when she observed that she had done so, she became confused, and added the letter to the next word in her mouth which began with a vowel. This habit lent a quaint effect to her talk, and it greatly annoyed Hugo Raven. "How different she is from Hilda Chancel," he thought.

She sat looking at Hugo, who was standing. "Won't you talk to me, Hugo?" asked the girl at last, a little plaintively.

"Oh, yes, of course I'll talk to you. I suppose you came here to talk," he answered, roughly. "Why *did* you come here? Will you be good enough to tell me that?"

"Hugo, dear, please don't be angry with me—I can't stand your anger!" She stood up and stretched out her arms, then drew them in and clasped her hands on her breast—a graceful, unconscious action.

15

"I read in the paper yesterday that you are engaged to be married. I didn't know where to find you before. Oh, you can't think what I've suffered this last year! For six weeks I was so ill that I couldn't work, and I had no one to turn to. Then this morning I came here. I met an old man outside—I think he belongs here—and he shewed me the house. He seemed to know you."

"Very likely! "Hugo answered abruptly. "Now then, what do you want?"

"What do I want? Oh, Hugo dearest, don't talk to me like that—you kill me! Why I want you, dear—you—you—you! You are everything in the world to me! Don't marry this other girl! No matter how nice she is, she can't love you as I do. Don't marry her—marry me!"

"Marry you? Marry a girl out of a bonnet shop? You must be mad!" he exclaimed brutally. "Great heavens! that would be a fine ending of my career. Upon my word, I congratulate you on your inspiration!"

Possibly, to endure his brutality had become a habit with her; for she went on as though he had not spoken.

"Or don't marry me, if you don't like. Only let me be near you always, never go away from you, I will be so quiet and good, and I'll try hard to improve, indeed I will. Oh, my God, how much I love you!" she cried, and began to sob.

There fell a silence. A warm air glided softly into the room and stirred the curtains. The flutter of the pigeons sounded far off. Stealthily, the sun had crept to the bowl of roses, and was drying them. In a sharp, hard tone, a clock struck the quarter.

"I suppose you are thinking," she said, wearily, "that it would be as well if I was dead,"

As a matter of fact, he had been thinking of nothing whatever. He started now, and looked up.

"You know I have always liked you, Gracie," he murmured, taking a pen from the table and playing with it.

She heard him call her "Gracie," and her eyes cleared.

"Oh, Hugo, let us forget all that has happened. Let us forget this dreadful last year. Let us go on as we used to, and have our own love, I've got all your letters, and I read them sometimes and think how sweet you were. Do you remember?"

"Yes; I remember."

"Let us begin again all the dear old things—our long nights together, our walks."

"I was going to propose a walk somewhere," Hugo said. "You

know Acton Green where we used to walk; we shall go there. Can you come tomorrow?"

"Ah! not tomorrow. But Tuesday—"

"Very well! on Tuesday. I will meet you there about five o'clock; I can't get away before, but the days are long, you know. And now," he added, looking at his watch, "I'm afraid I must ask you to leave me. I have two or three people coming to see me about some business matter, and I should not like them to find you here."

"Kiss me before I go, Hugo dear," she said. "You have not kissed me for so long!" He kissed her, tenderly enough. "You do love me, don't you?" she cried, clinging to him.

"You know I love you," he answered slowly.

He watched her as she went down the stairs. At the end of the first flight, she paused as if taking thought.

"On Tuesday, remember, you will be sure to come?" she called.

"On Tuesday; have I not said Tuesday?" said Hugo, with an impatient laugh, and banged his door.

2

It had become a custom with Hugo, since his engagement, to dine at Sir Matthew Chancel's house on Sunday evenings. On this Sunday, after his interview with Grace Casket, he talked a great deal. Hilda Chancel thought he was brilliant and wonderful.

Just at that time, the evening papers were packed with details of an atrocious murder. In the drawing-room, after dinner, they talked of murders. Miss Chancel loved them. She would like to know a murderer; she said murderers were adorable creatures.

"Hilda!" cried her mother.

Hilda Chancel was tall and thin, of a remarkable appearance. She had an easy temperament, a temperament which inclined her towards letting things go loosely by. She made rash little speeches, either because she thought they were clever, or because she did not think at all.

Now she laughed. "Oh, Hugo, you must help me!" she exclaimed. "Don't you simply worship murderers?"

"Ah! I am afraid I can't help you in this," he said gravely. "A murderer sins deeply against his fellowmen. I wonder how he can live after the act, how he can endure the remorse. If I were to commit a murder, I should see only one way out of the misery, and that way would be suicide."

Everybody thought that this was extremely well said. Hilda, who

17

took her morals from him, let the topic fall. Shortly after Hugo went away.

As he was walking rapidly to his club, he was hailed in a thick and jovial voice.

"Why, Raven t old chap, I haven't seen you for an age! How d'ye do, old bird? You're not so great that you can't notice a fellow."

Hugo knew who had stopped him. "How are you, Scarford?" he said frigidly, and was for going on.

This Scarford was a doctor; a man of parts, yet a hopeless failure. He had taken a good degree in science with half of his strength, and had been, at one time, an enthusiastic scholar. Of a sudden he had become gross, and slovenly, a railer at decorum; and now he went through life unshorn and sodden-eyed. He frequented the houses of call in the Strand, consorting with second-rate actors; and knew a barmaid at every inn between Trafalgar Square and Ludgate Circus. He and Raven had been at Harrow together, where he had often done Raven's Latin for him. During the past five years, whenever Raven sighted him in the distance, he thought it his duty to cross the street to avoid a meeting with him.

"I am in a hurry, Scarford," he said now, trying to brush past.

But the other was too quick for him, and grasped his arm. "Let us have a drink together," he stammered.

A thought shot through Hugo's head. "Where are you living now?" he asked.

"Oh, somewhere in the forest of South Kensington—you know it is a forest," says Scarford, with a loud laugh.

Hugo just smiled. "Have you a surgery there, and drugs, and all that?" he went on, to make sure that he would not be wasting his time with a sot.

"Oh yes, I suppose they are all there, unless somebody has run away with them. I say, old chap, you're much too sober, and so am I. Let us go and have a drink."

For a full hour, Hugo sat on a high stool, before a bar, drinking whisky; and was introduced to people whom he devoutly wished never to meet with again. There was a girl behind the bar, with a look remote from innocence, in whom Scarford was interested. Could it be the curious chemistry of her hair? Hugo wondered.

When, at last, they came into the open air, the doctor turned very drunk. Hugo proposed to drive home with him, and they went off in a hansom.

At his house Scarford produced more whisky; and they sat in the "surgery" drinking, and talking together. Hugo spoke of poisons. He had been reading some cases of strange, subtle poisonings lately; and he remembered one affair, in particular, which had come under his notice when he was last on circuit. He contradicted the doctor on some points, and the latter grew angry.

"You shall see for yourself!" he cried. He got up, and fetched three jars. "I've got some stuff here that will kill a horse in less than five minutes."

"How very interesting!" says Hugo, smelling at the jars. "Dear me! I had no idea. May I take a little of this? I—you see, I am a little of a chemist myself, and I should like to analyse this at my leisure."

"You may take the whole blooming lot if you like!" said Scarford, slapping his legs and laughing. "Only don't ask me to pay the undertaker. I'll go as chief mourner. To see me as chief mourner at old Raven's funeral!"—and he roared, and hiccoughed, brushing the tears from his face.

Hugo went back to his chambers very gaily; and all the next day he carried a light heart. On Tuesday he was busy; and it was after six o'clock when he arrived at Acton Green. Grace Casket was waiting for him.

"How late you are!"

"How could I get here before?" he asked crossly.

Then he subdued the irritation which this girl always caused him, and went on quietly: "I came as soon as I could. I was engaged all day."

'Yes, I know, dear. I was stupid to say that!"

"Have you been here long?" he asked, not because he cared, but because he could think of nothing else to make conversation.

"Since four o'clock. I know you said five, but I had an idea that I might miss you, and I have something important to say," She looked as if she had been crying.

"Well! won't you say it now?"

"Not yet, please! I would rather wait awhile."

They walked on through the strange, pretty village—strange, because it is like a toy, or model, village, set down in the midst of one of the ugliest parts of London—till they came to a stile, on the other side of which was a path which led over the fields to Willesden. It was very still. Overhead, the leaves of the trees intermingling looked like patterns of Brussels lace. The sun having hung in the sky for some time, like a plate of red-hot metal, suddenly dropped down; and night was there.

"Tell me your important thing, Grade."

"Not yet! not yet!—oh, I can't yet!"

She was only playing on him in her old silly way, he thought. It was her troublesome, tortuous method again, and it maddened him.

They climbed the stile, and walked some yards till they came to a clump of bushes. Hugo looked all around.

"Why won't you tell me?"

"Hugo dearest, you did not kiss me when we met; and I feel so tired. You have not kissed me today."

"No, by God! but I'll kiss you now!" and with that he drove a knife into her neck, behind the ear.

She gave a deep groan, and Hugo put his hand over her mouth to stifle her. She caught his hand between her teeth and bit it. Then they fell on the ground together, and Hugo saw her eyes staring up at him full of hate or love—he could not tell which; only recognised a great longing for the power of speech—to say one word—in them. She dug her fingers into the earth, and stretched out straight—stiff and straight. She was dead.

He bound his bleeding hand with his handkerchief, and fled from the corpse, leaving the knife—a common one, not easily to be recognised—in the neck. As he sped over the field, he had but one thought. "She is dead! I shall not have to marry her. No exposure! She is dead. Marry a girl like that, who could hardly spell! and her rough hands! No! a thousand times, no!"

He ran, and this thought ran in his company, till he came face to face with a man whom he took to be a tramp. By one of those uncontrollable impulses, which impel us at times to do just what we would not, he was moved to accost the man and ask the way to Willesden. The man told him civilly enough; and then begged. Hugo gave him two shillings, and started off again. How mad of him to speak to the tramp. The man must have noted, even in the dusk, his disturbed air. And to give him two shillings—a ridiculously large sum! It was like hush-money. So, he came to Willesden.

Little jets of gas were springing up in the streets. Before a flaring public-house he paused, and then went in. Inside there were a number of rough-looking men, who kept their eyes fixed on Hugo. He asked for the best brandy, and remained, drinking deeply, for half an hour. He was not the philosophic murderer, careless and indurated: he was appalled, and his heart was oppressed by the horrible deed he had done; and he drank because he wanted to forget that white thing lying away there among the bushes.

After a while he began to talk to the men, and treated some of them. They grew familiar.

"Give every man in the place a drink at my expense!" cried Hugo, and started to sing a catch.

"I don't know so much about that!" says the barman, truculently—putting his thumbs in his waistcoat; "I think you've had about enough. What's the matter with that there hand o' yours?"

The blood had soaked through the handkerchief, and a red stain shewed. Hugo explained that he had fallen on the steps of the *Underground Railway.*

"I think after this one you'd better get home," the man said, when he had served the drinks. "Soon you won't know where you are. You've got a tidy lot inside you already."

"My good friend," exclaimed Hugo, "my dear and good friend—I knew you were my friend the moment I saw you—as you say, and as I say, home is the place. Now, I'll go home—if you can get me a cab."

"Cab, sir? I'll get you a cab," said a thin, red-haired fellow by the door. He darted out, and returned in a few minutes with a cabman at his heels.

"'Ere's a four-wheeler, sin I got 'im for you, sir,"

"Is that what you want me to drive?" cried the cabman in great disgust. "I thought as you said a toph. E're, you Jimmy! Do you want me to drive 'im? That ain't no toph. Why, look at 'is eyes! He's a-trying to laugh, and he's just green afraid o' somethin'!"

"Come now, don't give us any of that!" said the man behind the bar, who was anxious to be rid of Hugo. "If you don't want to drive the gentleman, somebody else will. He's stood drinks to every man in the place, and he'll give you one, too, if you want it. What'll ye have?"

"Why, if 'e's got the money, then that's all right," answered the cabman, on whom this speech had taken effect. "If 'e pays my fare, it's no business o' mine; and I asks his parding if I've said what's a bit off. I ain't perticler who I drive, nor nobody ever said it o' me neither."

He took his drink; and, going outside, held the cab door open while Hugo stumbled into the cab. Then he climbed on the box, and the cab rattled away.

In the cab the thought of the murdered girl came once more to Hugo. He saw her face, her dress, the hands he had despised so much; in especial, he saw that last lingering look in the eyes, ere the life died out of them for ever. He beat his hands and rubbed his face—the thought was still present. He put his head out of the window; the dead face grinned at him in the darkness.

As the cab jolted along the quiet roads, he heard a hoarse voice singing a ditty which was popular at the time:—

But all the same, it is a shame
To leave a pretty maidie,
When every little gentleman
Walks home with a little lady.

It was the cabman, who was thus endeavouring to make the hour go lightly. Hugo knew the song, and bawled out the next *stanza*:—

At four a.m. we cuddle them,
As through the streets we're going;
'Tis ten to one we see the sun,
And hear the cocks a-crowing!
That drunken loon, the bare-faced moon,
Leaves useful corners shady,—
When every little gentleman
Walks home with a little lady.

The cab began to go slower, and then it stopped. The cabman got off the box and shoved his red, pimpled face through the open window.

"Look 'ere, guv'nor!" he said, "just drop it, will you? I don't know who you are, nor where you come from; and I don't want to. But I sing this 'ere song on Sundays to my missus and the kids, and I don't want to think when I'm singin' it, maybe next Sunday, that you've been a-singin' of it too. You may be balmy, or you may 'ave taken an extra drop—but, any'ow, I don't like you, that's all! If you don't take what I say, I'll set you down 'ere—it's all one to me!"

Hugo smiled greyly. "Very well! Very well!" says he. "I'll do anything you want. Only get on! For the love of God," he cried, the terror which was in his soul leaping to his eyes for a moment, "get on! get on! Drive away from this cursed place. Here, I know you are a good chap—shake hands!" and he held out his hand wrapped in the stained handkerchief.

"No; I don't want any of yer blood," replied the cabman roughly: "but I suppose I'll drive you." He climbed on his box, and the cab rumbled on again.

Early on Thursday afternoon, Hugo Raven sat in his chambers in the Temple. He was very serene. The long, choking agony which had come on the heels of the murder, had given place to a sense of relief: and now he only thought what a benefit it was to have no more of the girl. He had eagerly scanned the papers to see if the body had been discovered: but the matter was not mentioned by any of them. It was very hot. Not a leaf stirred on the trees outside his windows, and the hum and murmur of the busy crowd beneath lulled and soothed him. How fortunate he was! He was waiting for Lady Chancel and her daughter, who had gone to see someone or other in the city, and were to pick him up on their way back. He was going to take them to a "private view," in Bond Street, of the works of a painter. He dozed. Yes: how fortunate he was!

There was a knock at the door, and Hilda and her mother entered, Hugo was immediately alert and attentive, pushing up comfortable chairs, and offering iced drinks. Hilda looked deliciously fresh and cool in a dress of some white, clinging stuff, and a large hat with drooping flowers. She drew off one of her gloves, and her thin hand reminded him of the women in Rossetti's pictures: not that he liked Rossetti's pictures; but he liked hands of that kind. They were so different from—well, no matter!

"We have just come from that horrid city," said Miss Chancel; "and it is so nice of you to give us something with ice in it, Hugo! I wonder there is any smoke left in the other parts of London: the people in the city look as if they absorbed it all."

"They *are* black, poor dears!" murmured Lady Chancel; "and they seem in such a hurry."

"On a day like this," the girl went on, "one ought to sit on a rock without clothes, like the people we shall probably see in the pictures in a few minutes, sucking cold drinks through a straw."

"My dearest Hilda!" exclaimed her mother, whose life had, by this time, become one long protest against her daughter's talk, and one long submission to her daughter's will.

"But the pictures do not suggest the whole truth," said Hugo smiling, and bending forward. "You see, there might come a time of storm."

"Yes!" sighed the girl; "I suppose one would have to keep one's clothes to provide against a storm. I don't like storms."

There came a rap at the door. "What a bother!" cried Hugo. "Pardon me a moment till I see who it is."

Two men stood in the passage. "Mr. Hugo Raven?" says one.
"Yes."

"Thank you, sir. I come from Scotland Yard. We want to see you about a girl named Grace Casket, who was found murdered on Wednesday morning in the fields near Acton."

Before Hugo could stop them, they had shoved past him into the room.

One was a tall man with an authoritative manner; the other was low-sized, with sandy hair and beard, and stupid, fish-like eyes.

"Good afternoon, ladies," said the big man.

Hugo followed them, a little pale, but perfectly tranquil. He put his right hand, which was almost healed, into the pocket of his trousers.

"This is Lady Chancel and her daughter," he explained; "I am engaged with them. Can't you come some other time?"

"Or we can go, it you have business, Hugo," said Hilda, rising.

"I think I like the ladies to remain," says the little man.

"Yes!" added the other; "the ladies might remain. I think you said you knew this Grace Casket?" he went on, turning sharp on Hugo.

"I said nothing of the kind."

"Did you know her?"

Hugo got rather confused: the presence of Hilda and her mother was against him. "I did not," he answered.

"That's very odd!" said the little man; "because there was a letter found on her addressed to you!"

"Let us go, mother!" cried Hilda, rising again decisively.

"If you will please to stay, madam," said one of the men. "You sha'n't be kept long."

"This is monstrous!" Hugo broke out; "perfectly monstrous to keep the ladies here against their will!" He did not say more, however, lest he should have the appearance of being guilty.

"Suppose you read that letter for the gentleman, William," observed the big man.

So, the little man read it, slowly, haltingly, in his squeaky voice.

My own Hugo,
If I have not the courage to say what I want to tonight, I am going to send you this letter. Somehow, I don't think I shall speak to you before we part tonight. Oh, it is so hard to say I But I thought you were a little cold to me when I saw you on

Sunday. But it may be my imagination, Hugo, darling, I don't know how to say it right, but if you really love this other girl more than me, take her, dear, and I shall never see you or trouble you again. I will send back all your letters if you want them, but I should like to keep them. They will be all I have of you. My own Hugo, I hope you will be always happy. Think of me sometimes. My heart is breaking.

With all my love.

Gracie.

Hugo sat by the table, shading his face with his left hand. Then this was the important thing she had wanted to say! She had made her great renunciation, she had yielded of her own accord, and the murder was useless, after all! He felt a spasm of pity for the poor dead face; was it already beginning to rot and grow shapeless? He turned his eyes. Hilda was very white, and Lady Chancel looked old, and wrinkled, and yellow.

"Of course, you did know this girl, Mr. Raven," said the detective.

"She was my mistress for three years. I had not seen her for a year. She came here on Sunday and made a scene, and to pacify her, I promised to meet her on Tuesday. I did not keep that appointment."

"Well now, that's strange!" remarked the big man. "A gentleman answering to your description spent about an hour in the *Stag of Ten* public at Willesden on Tuesday night."

"I was not the man," Hugo said, low and doggedly.

"Not? Then this gentleman, whoever he was, took a four-wheeler as far as the Marble Arch. There he discharged the four-wheeler, and took a hansom. The driver of the four-wheeler didn't like the looks of his fare, so he took the number of the hansom. The driver of the hansom has been found, and remembers perfectly driving a gentleman to the Temple from the Marble Arch, on Tuesday night. He says the gentleman was drunk. He says, too, that he heard the gate-porter say: 'Goodnight, Mr. Raven,' as you—that is, as the gentleman went in."

All this time the little man was edging over to the table, on the right side of Hugo. Now he knocked over, as if by chance, a valuable porcelain vase. Instinctively, Hugo plucked his hand from his pocket to save it. The little man grasped him by the wrist.

"How dare you seize my hand! you scoundrel!" yelled Hugo, losing all control. "Let go my hand."

But the little man held him with a grip like steel. "Look at the wound on this hand, ladies, please!" he called; "I want you to see this hand before it heals. The dead woman had blood in her mouth. She bit the man that murdered her."

There was a close silence. Then Hugo rose.

"Of course, if you want to make evidence out of this bruise on my hand," he said, calmly, "I am naturally powerless. There is one thing, however, which will throw great light on this matter. It is in my bedroom. Let me go there: I shall return at once."

The detectives, knowing that he could not escape, agreed.

What followed passed so quickly, that no one had time to interfere, Hugo Raven came back into the room, laid his hand on the table, and then, drawing a small axe from under his coat, he sent it through his wrist. It fell with a dull thud.

"If you think my hand is such a valuable piece of evidence, gentlemen, there it is for you!" and he tossed it into the empty grate.

He gave a groan, and staggered over to the mantelpiece. "Scarford knows something, after all!" he muttered.

"He has poisoned himself," said the little man, who had been in the bedroom, "he did it well, too! He can't live more than a minute."

His eyes grew larger and larger; they seemed to start from the sockets. His tongue shot out, all black and furred. Still, he did not fall. The blood from the stump fell—*drip*—*drip*—*drip*—on the carpet.

The Burned House

One night at the end of dinner, the last time I crossed the Atlantic, somebody in our group remarked that we were just passing over the spot where the Lusitania had gone down. Whether this were the case or not, the thought of it was enough to make us rather grave, and we dropped into some more or less serious discussion about the emotions of men and women who see all hope gone, and realise that they are going to sink with the vessel.

From that the talk wandered to the fate of the drowned. Was not theirs, after all, a fortunate end? Somebody related details from the narratives of those who had been all-but drowned in the accident of the war. A Scotch lady inquired fancifully if the ghosts of those who are lost at sea ever appear above the waters and come aboard ships. Would there be danger of seeing one when the light was turned out in her cabin? This put an end to all seriousness, and most of us laughed. But a little, tight-faced man, bleak and iron-grey, who had been listening attentively, did not laugh. The lady noticed his decorum, and appealed to him for support.

"You are like me—you believe in ghosts!" she asked lightly.

He hesitated, thinking it over.

"In ghosts?" he repeated slowly. "N-no, I don't know as I do. I've never had any personal experience that way. I've never seen the ghost of anyone I knew. Has anybody here?"

No one replied. Instead, most of us laughed again—a little uneasily, perhaps.

"All the same, strange enough things happen in life," resumed the man, "even if you leave out ghosts, that you can't clear up by laughing. You laugh till you've had some experience big enough to shock you, and then you don't laugh any more. It's like being thrown out of a car—"

At this moment there was a blast on the whistle, and everybody rushed up on deck. As it turned out, we had only entered into a belt of fog. On the upper deck I fell in again with the little man, smoking a cigar and walking up and down. We took a few turns together, and he referred to the conversation at dinner. Our laughter evidently rankled in his mind.

"So many strange things happen in life that you can't account for," he protested. "You go on laughing at faith-healing, and at dreams, and this and that, and then something comes along that you just can't explain. You have got to throw up your hands and allow that it doesn't answer to any tests our experience has provided us with. Now, I'm as matter-of-fact a man as any of those folks down there; but once I had an experience which I had to conclude was out of the ordinary. Whether other people believe it or not, or whether they think they can explain it, don't matter. It happened to me, and I could no more doubt it than I could doubt having had a tooth pulled after the dentist had done it. If you will sit down here with me in this corner, out of the wind, I'll tell you how it was.

"Some years ago, I had to be for several months in the North of England. I was before the courts; it does not signify now what for, and it is all forgotten by this time. But it was a long and worrying case, and it aged me by twenty years. Well, sir, all through the trial, in that grimy Manchester court-room, I kept thinking and thinking of a fresh little place I knew in the Lake district, and it helped to get through the hours by thinking that if things went well with me, I'd go there at once. And so it was that on the very next morning after I was acquitted, I boarded the north-bound train.

"It was the early autumn; the days were closing in, and it was night and cold when I arrived. The village was very dark and deserted; they don't go out much after dark in those parts, anyhow, and the keen mountain wind was enough to quell any lingering desire. The hotel was not one of those modern places which are equipped and upholstered like the great city hotels. It was one of the real old-fashioned taverns, about as uncomfortable places as there are on earth, where the idea is to show the traveller that travelling is a penitential state, and that, morally and physically, the best place for him is home. The landlord brought me a kind of supper, with his hat on and a pipe in his mouth. The room was chilly, but when I asked for a fire, he said he guessed he couldn't go out to the woodshed till morning. There was nothing else to do, when I had eaten my supper, but to go outside, both to get the smell of the lamp out of my nose and to warm myself by a short walk.

"As I did not know the country well, I did not mean to go far. But although it was an overcast night, with a high north-east wind and an occasional flurry of rain, the moon was up, and, even concealed by clouds as it was, it yet lit the night with a kind of twilight grey—not vivid, like the open moonlight, but good enough to see some distance. On account of this, I prolonged my stroll, and kept walking on and on till I was a considerable way from the village, and in a region as lonely as anywhere in the country. Great trees and shrubs bordered the road, and many feet below was a mountain stream. What with the passion of the wind pouring through the high trees and the shout of the water racing among the boulders, it seemed to me sometimes like the noise of a crowd of people. Sometimes the branches of the trees became so thick that I was walking as if in a black pit, unable to see my hand close to my face. Then, coming out from the tunnel of branches, I would step once more into a grey clearness which opened the road and surrounding country a good way on all sides.

"I suppose it might be some three-quarters of an hour I had been walking when I came to a fork of the road. One branch ran downward, getting almost on a level with the bed of the torrent; the other mounted in a steep hill, and this, after a little idle debating, I decided to follow. After I had climbed for more than half a mile, thinking that if I should happen to lose track of one of the landmarks, I should be very badly lost, the path—for it was now no more than that—curved, and I came out on a broad plateau. There, to my astonishment, I saw a house. It was a good-sized house, three storeys high, with a verandah round two sides of it, and from the elevation on which it stood it commanded a far stretch of country.

"There were a few great trees at a little distance from the house, and behind it, a stone's-throw away, was a clump of bushes. Still, it looked lonely and stark, offering its four sides unprotected to the winds. For all that, I was very glad to see it. 'It does not matter now,' I thought, 'whether I have lost my way or not. The people in the house will set me right.'

"But when I came up to it I found that it was, to all appearance, uninhabited. The shutters were closed on all the windows; there was not a spark of light anywhere. There was something about it, something sinister and barren, that gave me the kind of shiver you have at the door of a room where you know that a dead man lies inside, or if you get thinking hard about dropping over the rail into that black waste of waters out there. This feeling, you know, isn't altogether unpleasant; you relish all the better your present security. It was the same with me standing before that house.

I was not really frightened. I was alone up there, miles from any kind of help, at the mercy of whoever might be lurking behind the shutters of that sullen house; but I felt that by all the chances I was perfectly alone and safe. My sensation of the uncanny was due to the effect on the nerves produced by wild scenery and the unexpected sight of a house in such a very lonely situation. Thus, I reasoned, and, instead of following the road farther, I walked over the grass till I came to a stone wall, perhaps two hundred and fifty yards in front of the house, and rested my arms on it, looking forth at the scene.

"On the crests of the hills far away a strange light lingered, like the first touch of dawn in the sky on a rainy morning or the last glimpse of twilight before night comes. Between me and the hills was a wide stretch of open country. On my right hand was an apple orchard, and I observed that a stile had been made in the wall of piled stones to enable the house people to go back and forth.

"Now, after I had been there leaning on the wall some considerable time, I saw a man coming towards me through the orchard. He was walking with a good, free stride, and as he drew nearer, I could see that he was a tall, sinewy fellow between twenty-five and thirty, with a shaven face, wearing a slouch hat, a dark woollen shirt, and gaiters. When he reached the stile and began climbing over it I bade him goodnight in neighbourly fashion. He made no reply, but he looked me straight in the face, and the look gave me a qualm.

"Not that it was an evil face, mind you—it was a handsome, serious face—but it was ravaged by some terrible passion: stealth was on it, ruthlessness, and a deadly resolution, and at the same time such a look as a man driven by some uncontrollable power might throw on surrounding things, asking for comprehension and mercy. It was impossible for me to resent his churlishness, his thoughts were so certainly elsewhere. I doubt if he even saw me.

"He could not have gone by more than a quarter of a minute when I turned to look after him. He had disappeared. The plateau lay bare before me, and it seemed impossible that, even if he had sprinted like an athlete, he could have got inside the house in so little time. But I have always made it a rule to attribute what I cannot understand to natural causes that I have failed to observe. I said to myself that no doubt the man had gone back into the orchard by some other opening in the wall lower down, or there might be some flaw in my vision owing to the uncertain and distorting light.

"But even as I continued to look towards the house, leaning my back now against the wall, I noticed that there were lights springing up in the windows behind the shutters. They were flickering lights, now bright—now dim, and had a ruddy glow like firelight. Before I had looked long, I became convinced that it was indeed firelight—the house was on fire. Black smoke began to pour from the roof; the red sparks flew in the wind. Then at a window above the roof of the verandah the shutters were thrown open, and I heard a woman shriek. I ran towards the house as hard as I could, and when I drew near, I could see her plainly.

"She was a young woman; her hair fell in disorder over her white nightgown. She stretched out her bare arms, screaming. I saw a man come behind and seize her. But they were caught in a trap. The flames were licking round the windows, and the smoke was killing them. Even now the part of the house where they stood was caving in.

"Appalled by this horrible tragedy which had thus suddenly risen before me, I made my way still nearer the house, thinking that if the two could struggle to the side of the house not bounded by the verandah they might jump, and I might break the fall. I was shouting this at them; I was right up close to the fire; and then I was struck by—I noticed for the first time an astonishing thing—the flames had no heat in them!

"I was standing near enough to the fire to be singed by it, and yet I felt no heat. The sparks were flying about my head; some fell on my hands, and they did not burn. And now I perceived that, although the smoke was rolling in columns, I was not choked by the smoke, and that there had been no smell of smoke since the fire broke out. Neither was there any glare against the sky.

"As I stood there stupefied, wondering how these things could be, the whole house was swept by a very tornado of flame, and crashed down in a red ruin.

"Stricken to the heart by this abominable catastrophe, I made my way uncertainly down the hill, shouting for help. As I came to a little wooden bridge spanning the torrent, just beyond where the roads forked, I saw what appeared to be a rope in loose coils lying there. I saw that part of it was fastened to the railing of the bridge and hung outside, and I looked over. There was a man's body swinging by the neck between the road and the stream. I leaned over still farther, and then I recognised him as the man I had seen coming out of the orchard. His hat had fallen off, and the toes of his boots just touched the water.

"It seemed hardly possible, and yet it was certain. That was the man, and he was hanging there. I scrambled down at the side of the bridge, and put out my hand to seize the body, so that I might lift it up and relieve the weight on the rope. I succeeded in clutching hold of his loose shirt, and for a second, I thought that it had come away in my hand. Then I found that my hand had closed on nothing, I had clutched nothing but air. And yet the figure swung by the neck before my eyes!

"I was suffocated with such horror that I feared for a moment I must lose consciousness. The next minute I was running and stumbling along that dark road in mortal anxiety, my one idea being to rouse the town, and bring men to the bridge. That, I say, was my intention; but the fact is that when I came at last in sight of the village I slowed down instinctively and began to reflect. After all, I was unknown there; I had just gone through a disagreeable trial in Manchester, and rural people were notoriously given to groundless suspicion. I had had enough of the law, and of arrests without sufficient evidence. The wisest thing would be to drop a hint or two before the landlord, and judge by his demeanour whether to proceed.

"I found him sitting where I had left him, smoking, in his shirtsleeves, with his hat on.

"'Well,' he said slowly, 'I didn't know where you had got to.'

"I told him I had been taking a walk. I went on to mention casually the fork in the road, the hill, and the plateau.

"'And who lives in that house?' I asked with a good show of indifference, 'on top of the hill?'

"He stared.

"'House? There ain't no house up there,' he said positively. 'Old Joe Snedeker, who owns the land, says he's going to build a house up there for his son to live in when he gets married; but he ain't begun yet, and some folks reckon he never will.'

"'I feel sure I saw a house,' I protested feebly. But I was thinking— no heat in the fire, no substance in the body. I had not the courage to dispute.

"The landlord looked at me not unkindly. 'You seem sort of done up,' he remarked. 'What you want is to go to bed.'"

The man who was telling me the story paused, and for a moment we sat silent, listening to the pant of the machinery, the thrumming of the wind in the wire stays, and the lash of the sea. Some voices were singing on the deck below. I considered him with the shade of contemptuous superiority we feel, as a rule, towards those who tell us their dreams or what some fortune-teller has predicted.

"Hallucinations," I said at last, with reassuring indulgence. "Trick of the vision, toxic ophthalmia. After the long strain of your trial your nerves were shattered."

"That's what I thought myself," he replied shortly, "especially after I had been out to the plateau the next morning, and saw no sign that a house had ever stood there."

"And no corpse at the bridge?" I said; and laughed.

"And no corpse at the bridge."

He tried to get a light for another cigar. This took him some little time, and when at last he managed it, he got out of his chair and stood looking down at me.

"Now listen. I told you that the thing happened several years ago. I'd got almost to forget it; if you can only persuade yourself that a thing is a freak of imagination, it pretty soon gets dim inside your head. Delusions have no staying power once it is realised that they are delusions. Whenever it did come back to me, I used to think how near I had once been to going out of my mind. That was all.

"Well, last year, being up north, I went up to that village again. I went to the same hotel, and found the same landlord. He remembered me at once as 'the feller who stayed with him and thought he saw a house,' 'I believe you had the jim-jams,' he said.

"We laughed, and the landlord went on:

"'There's been a house there since, though.'

"'Has there?'

"'Yes; an' it ha' been as well if there never had been. Old Snedeker built it for his son, a fine big house with a verandah on two sides. The son, young Joe, got courting Mabel Elting from Windermere. She'd gone down to work in a shop somewhere in Liverpool. Well, sir, she used to get carrying on with another young feller 'bout here, Jim Travers, and Jim was wild about her; used to save up his wages to go down to see her. But she chucked him in the end, and married Joe; I suppose because Joe had the house, and the old man's money to expect. Well, poor Jim must ha' gone quite mad. What do you think he did? The very first night the new-wed pair spent in that house he burned it down. Burned the two of them in their bed, and he was as nice and quiet a feller as you want to see. He may ha' been full of whisky at the time.'

"'No, he wasn't,' I said.

"The landlord looked surprised.

"'You've heard about it?'

"'No; go on.'

"'Yes, sir, he burned them in their bed. And then what do you think he did? He hung himself at the little bridge half a mile below. Do you remember where the road divides? Well, it was there. I saw his body hanging there myself the next morning. The toes of his boots were just touching the water.'"

My Enemy and Myself

In the garden, when I was a child, I used to stare for hours at the white roses. In these there was for me a certain strangeness, which was yet quite human; for I know that I was full of sorrow if I found the petals strewn over the hushed grass. I had a terror of great waters, wild and lonely; I saw an austere dignity in the moon shining on a flat sea; things, cordage and broken spars, cast ashore by the ocean, told me wonderful, sad tales. And because my head was thick with thoughts, I had little speech; and for this I was laughed at and called stupid: "He was always a dull child," murmured my mother, bending over me, when I, in the crisis of a fever, was on the point of embarking for a vague land.

As I grew older, I still dwelt within my soul, a satisfied prisoner: the complaint of huge trees in a storm; the lash and surge of breakers on an iron coast; the sound of certain words; the sight of dim colours which blend sometimes in grey sunsets; the heavy scent of some exquisite poisonous flower; a contemplation of youthful forms engaged in an unruly game;—ah! in these things also I found perfect sensation and ecstasy. Still, my tongue held to its old stubbornness: I was ever delayed by a habit of commonplace speech, a shame at exposing my thoughts. In time I won a cloud of easy acquaintance; but my awkwardness in conversation, my tendency to be maladroit—call it what you like! always stepped between when I was about to make a friend. Then, at last, came Jacquette.

I remember that she was playing a composition by Chopin, a curious black-coloured thing, when I first came into her company; and now, even as I write, when our love is over, I hear that sombre music again. But the important matter is, that here was the person I had been seeking so long; here was the mind to meet with my mind; with her I could, at length, get out of myself (as we now say); become free. All the dear thoughts which had for years dwelt with me in close privateness,

I gave to her; all my desires, all my mean hopes.

Ah! the merry airs we had then: her bright laughter which, as wind, drove glumness, as foam, before it! I think I tired her of my enthusiasms and decisions; but it was so sweet to have someone to listen and understand, and she never would admit that she was tired. Nay! one morning in the apple-orchard, when the wind was turning her hair to the sunshine, she kissed me very prettily on the mouth.

After that, I forget how long it was till I came in one night and found my enemy sitting with her at the fireside. He was not my enemy then, mind you: indeed, I thought him a nice, pleasant creature, with a mighty handsome face. We became familiar: he seemed to like me, and I was sure I had gained another friend. The months glided by, and we three came to sitting together late of nights: he and Jacquette, the wise people, silent, gazing at each other; I, the fool, in the middle, talking in a youthful, impassioned way.

Once I paused suddenly, and looked up, and caught a somewhat contemptuous smile peeping from the corners of Jacquette's mouth and dancing in her eyes; while he, for an answer, fell a-laughing into her face. Of course, I must have wearied them both, *bored them* (as we say) to desperation; but I was a very young man, with all the warmth and admiration of the young; and in the time of youth, a woman is always older than a man. Besides, I loved her so much, and I had such strange pleasure in loving her, that I think it was rather cruel of her to laugh.

"Why did you laugh at me?" I asked, when I was twisting a garland of wild roses for her hair.

"Oh, I didn't laugh!" she exclaimed. "Or if I did," she added, looking down with a tooth on her lip, "it must have been because I was so pleased to hear you saying beautiful words to us—poor ignorant things!"

The next day I had an affair of great importance in the town where I lived, so I told Jacquette that on account of this affair I could not go down, as my custom was, to her cottage by the sea, that night. But as the day waned, and the night closed in, I became the thrall of a longing to hear her singing voice, to play fantastic music with her delightfully. Thus, it came about that it was nearly eleven o'clock when I reached the shore, and hearkened to the calling sea. There was a note of melancholy, almost a sob, in the noise of it tonight: and that, taken with a monstrous depression, filled me strangely with a desire to die—to give up life at this point!

I saw a light in Jacquette's bedroom, but the rest of the little house was dark; and I was turning away, when my hand chanced to strike the door-handle, which I pushed, and found the door not locked. Let me go in! (thinks I): I shall sit awhile and dream of Jacquette, and a few chords touched softly on the piano will tell my love I am dreaming of her. Here (perhaps you will say!) I was wrong: but I was ready to welcome a servant's company, or, in spite of his growing offensiveness, my enemy's, should I find him there, rather than be alone with my saddening thoughts.

The room I chose to sit in, because there was a dying fire in it, was just under Jacquette's bedroom; and ere I had sat a minute, I became conscious of voices in the room above. As soon as I made out the man's voice, a thousand serpents seemed literally to eat their way into my brain, turning my vision red; and I lay for an hour, maybe, on the carpet, fainting, and stricken, and dazed. Now, at last, after an hour I was myself, or rather more than myself, with every nerve tight as a fiddle-string, still seeing red, as I unclasped the long jack-knife, which the Greek sailor had given me, and laid it in the hollow of my hand.

I knew that it would dawn by three o'clock, so I stood quite still, only moving my tongue over my dry lips, and shaking my head to keep a sweat from running into my eyes. A cat cried in the road, and the breakers thundered against the rocks.

A little before dawn, while it was yet dark, I heard a murmur of low voices—her voice and my enemy's; and then the man came down the stairs.

"Goodnight, my sweet love!" said Jacquette.

"O my darling, goodnight!" came from my enemy, and so he banged the door behind him.

One moment I paused to peer through the window, and make sure of my man. Then I fetched a run, and was on him like a panther, holding him close, with his hot breath scorching my face. Coming on him from behind, as I did, the middle finger of my left hand struck his eye, and now, as I pressed, the eye bulged out.

"My friend," he groaned, "for Christ's sake, have pity!"

"To hell with your friendship!" I said. "Much pity you had for my honour!" says I, and with that I let him have the knife in his throat, and the blood spurted over my hands hot and sticky. As soon as I could get free of his clutch, I looked up at Jacquette's bedroom window, and there she was, sure enough! in her nightdress, with the blind in her hand, gazing out. Straight up to her room I went, and flung open the door. She turned to me grey and whingeing.

"My little love ——," she began.

I put my hands on my hips and spat hard into her face. Then I tramped downstairs and out of the lonely cottage.

I had not the least fear of detection: the servants slept in an outhouse, and the place was too desolate for any chance passenger.

I stood triumphing by the corpse of my enemy; but even as I looked the moon shewed from a rift of cloud, lighting the blood, and the hue left by violent death in the features, and I ran for my life from that hideous one-eyed thing.

I came to the town, and to a house where I lay constantly, about four o'clock, in a curious trembling fit. I bathed my head and hands, however, in a heavy perfume, and then became strangely calm, and fell to thinking of the rightness of the deed. Just there was the consoling thought: certainly, I had done a murder, but in doing it I had delivered punishment to a traitress and her paramour. Now that the thing was over, it was clearly my duty to forget all about it as soon as possible; and this I set myself to do, aided by a cigarette and a novel of the ingenious Miss Jane Austen. I had succeeded in my aim, I was clear-minded and very serene, when of a sudden something heavy fell against the door of my room.

"At this hour?" I murmured in surprise, and went to the door.

A body that nearly knocked me down, the dead body of a man, fell into the room, and lay, face downward, on the carpet. Then I did the one act I shall never cease to regret: From a movement of kindness, pity, curiosity, what you will! I bent down and turned over the corpse. Slowly the thing got to its feet; and my enemy, with a dry gaping wound in his throat, and his eye hanging from its socket by a bit of skin, stood before me, face to face.

"O God, have mercy!" I screamed, and beat on the wall with my hands; and again and again:—"God, have mercy!"

"You do well to ask God for mercy," says my enemy; "for you will not get much from men." He stood by the fireplace.

"I beg of you," I said, in a low, passionate voice, "I beg of you, by all you find dear, for the sake of our old friendship, to leave this place, to let me go free,"

He shook his head. "For Jacquette's sake?" He laughed harshly.

"My friend," I said to my enemy, "for Christ's sake, have pity!"

"Pity you?" says he, in a jeer. "You!"

As I looked at him, I was stung into strong fury. My eyes clung to the wound in his throat, and my fingers ached to close in it—to misuse it, to maul it.

But as I sprang at him, he gave a shriek that woke the town; a shriek of fear too, let me think it at this last, like to that of a lost soul when the gates of hell have closed behind forever: and when the people of the house rushed in, they found mc kneeling by his dead body, with my knife in my enemy's throat, and his new blood, bright and wet, on my hands.

★★★★★★★★★★★★★★★★

They will hang me because I loved Jacquette,

The Abigail Sheriff Memorial

Liddy the *mulatto* girl at Mrs Wasman's room house opened my door noisily "Say are you awake?"

"No."

"Well, here's some mail for you."

"Alright, put it there," I mumbled with my head under the bed-clothes. "What time is it?"

"'Bout half-past three. The sun's been shining just lovely all day. Listen why don't you go out in the sun once in a while. 'Pears to me that what you kinda need 'stead of laying there in bed and staying out all night. Mrs Wasman's getting real mad, yes sir."

"Tell her I was in as early as four o'clock, this morning, that will console her."

The *mulatto* gave a good-humoured laugh.

I heard her singing and banging with the brush outside on the stairs. I was furious at being woke up when I might have had two or three hours more of unconsciousness. With my eyes closed I tried to think of nothing but it was no use. The awakening, the most hideous hour of the twenty-four had to be faced. I pulled over the chair, on which my clothes had been thrown and went through the pockets. Four cents, a subway ticket, a half empty packet of cigarettes and a small 'taken while you wait' photograph of a girl.

Where had I got that? Oh yes, it was that girl who said she was a model. Her shoulders had been painted by, who did she say had painted her shoulders? She had been on the covers of two magazines. I tore up the photograph and threw the pieces on the floor, and then looked for the letter which the *mulatto* had brought in.

Who could it be from? I hardly ever got letters nowadays. I glanced at the envelope but when I saw the business address of Abner the picture dealer in the corner, I flung it away in disgust and lay down again and pulled the bedclothes over my head. It was of course, another request from Abner to give him some work that would cover the advance he had made six months ago. What a rotten life I thought, soon it would be a year since I had touched a brush or drawn a pencil. I had the beginnings of a sort of renown among certain groups.

A few articles had even been written about me in little hole in corner magazines, but now there was nothing I was more sick of than art and the chatter of art. Art I hardly gave a thought to it I would gladly have put my boot through any picture ever painted if the act would have brought me enough for one really big trail of fortune. I had the conviction of the reason my luck had been so invariably bad of late it was that the stakes I was obliged to play were too paltry and also too vital. When you're staking your food and shelter you are so nervous that your judgement is no longer trustworthy.

That is how it had been with me for seven or eight months. One glorious night I won twenty times as much as I ever got for a picture. But of late sums I had to put up were so small that I used sometimes to go in terror lest they would refuse me at the door. One night they did refuse me. They said I was a broken-down bum. I walked along a street of private houses wondering what I could do. I was suffering the torments of the damned, I would have taken my vest and shirt off and pawned them, but it was too late to pawn.

I would have gone to Abner gone down on my knees to him entered into any contract he liked. But it was too late for him too. What was I to do? It was a hard cold night. But although I was thinly clad and not eaten anything to speak of for the last two days, I scarcely felt the cold. I must have had fever for I was shaking and burning all over. I felt sure that if I could get back there, just once for only five minutes the luck would come flowing my way.

I could not go back to where I lived. I thought with horror of the bare room and the flaring gas jet. I'll go in the river I thought, sooner than go back to my bedroom tonight. Just ahead of me a motorcar stopped, a footman jumped off and opened the door and a lady stepped out. It was no decision of mine I had no time for decision. I was driven by instinct to go up to her.

"You couldn't help a poor fellow this cold night?"

"Ugh you get out," shouted the footman. "Beat it you dirty beggar."

But the lady turned and seeing a shabby looking man without an overcoat being hustled by her fur-clad servant she may have thought that things were not altogether as they ought to be. Anyhow she paused as she was entering the house. "I'm so sorry for you," she said to me. "Please take this," and she handed me a bill.

It was as well she did, if she had refused, I might have plucked her rich coat off her back and made a run for it. I'm telling you I was desperate.

"*Madame's* too good to the like of you," said the footman. "If you don't clear off, I'll call a policeman."

I turned into the avenue and by the advantage of a street lamp I looked at the note in my hand. It was probably a dollar, but it might be two, it was *ten*. Whether it had been given by goodwill or in mistake there it was and it brought luck that night. I did well. With the proceeds I furbished myself up somewhat. Heaven knows I hesitated about doing this but it was necessary. If I presented a fairly decent appearance where I went to play, they would not be so ready to insult me and throw me out. That was the only reason I bought clothes, for I had gradually cut adrift from all acquaintances.

And as for the art world that lives in expensive studios and gives receptions and wears dress clothes and looks after its health, I had nothing to do with it. It was always a question with me when I had a dollar whether it would be safe to go without food or not. Once I had a kind of fit in that place where we play and it made things very unpleasant for me. They were afraid I might die in the house and then the police would come in. So, to prevent a recurrence of the fainting fit I began to eat more regularly.

Sometimes I would take what might be called a good dinner, two or three dishes, then I would give myself some advice and go immediately back to my room and resolve to stay in all night. But if you have only one room the worst hours to be in it, I think are the early hours of the night. For if you have only a cheap room to depend on for shelter and hold that precariously you have surely had horrible thoughts in it at one time or another. And they are all over the wall.

If you find yourself in your room at nine or ten o'clock in the evening, a time when you might have a respite these haggard thoughts come down from the wall, and crowd round you and the anguish is such that only the most heroic experience can bare it. I never could. The voices in the streets, the lights and noise called me out of that place of torment. In the streets you have the illusion of sharing the torment with others. It all seems strange to me when I look back on that time now. That life has become so grey and indifferent I ask myself could that really have been me? I hardly existed 'til five or six at night. It all depended upon the awakening. If I regained consciousness upon the pleasant thoughts that I had recovered a good sum from the night before I might go out even if the sun was shining, stroll in the park, buy myself a decent meal.

In the opposite case, I would lay there supinely prolonging a co-matose state as much as I could so as not to face the blank merciless day with all the shifts and expedients and scrapings and humiliations. As for work, drawing and painting, are you laughing at me? I tried it once or twice to do what is called commercial work, pictures for ad-vertisements. Even with that kind of thing I could make no headway. I stared at the paper for an hour at a time but I was developing a new system of play a flawless system which was bound to succeed.

Well, this day that the letter had come from Abner I found that I had four cents and a subway ticket curse it all. It was late in October, but my vest would have to go to the pawnshop, also the silver cigarette case which I kept for desperate emergencies. I could no longer recall the number of times it had been pawned and redeemed. It had been a good friend to me that cigarette case since that woman gave it to me with her name "Maggie" reproduced in facsimile of her writing across the cover.

I suppose she thought I should always carry it next to my heart. She did not foresee the coarse jokes of pawnbroker's assistants about "Maggie" at which I used to smile in the hope of putting them in the humour to advance me a little more. I heard the cuckoo clock in Mrs Wasman's parlour pipe out five and decided to get up, but I lay 'til about half-past five. Then I dressed, wrapped my vest in a piece of newspaper and slipped the cigarette case into my pocket. My hat was really too big, somebody had sat on it last night.

As I was studying it absentmindedly, my eyes fell on Abner's letter on the floor near the torn photograph of the girl. Perhaps I had better see what he had to say. Then I thought it would be only giving myself useless pain to read the letter and I went out leaving it on the floor. I had to go up town and then across to reach the pawnshop I accus-tomed. Near Maddison Avenue, going toward Fifth whom should I run upon but Abner himself? I kept my eyes down and was shuffling by.

But he hailed me. "Hello, is that the way you treat your friends? Didn't you get my letter?"

His tone was cordial. He seemed to be safe and to mean well. I could see no sign in his eyes of the dollars he had lent me.

"You look more than usually prosperous Abner. The picture business must be booming."

"Yes, I've struck a good line lately, modern Meltons, Ensor, Van Megans. Rick Wundas. Well what are you going to do about it?"

"About what?"

"Why about what I said in my letter."

"The fact is Abner, I forgot to read your letter."

"Well, there it is. I said when I was dictating it that very likely you wouldn't read it. You'll come in for a million someday and never know it. Look here," he said good humouredly, and he took my arm. "Just stroll up Fifth Avenue with me and I'll tell you about the business."

As we walked along, he explained that a lawyer had come to see him last week on behalf of a friend who lived in a remote town in New England. The friend had presented a library to his native place, and desired he wanted to hang a portrait of himself and also of his wife in the reading room.

"I thought of you," said Abner. "Like a flash you came into my head. I said to myself 'I'll send him up there,' you're just the man and it will do you good."

"Why this unaccustomed philanthropy?" I enquired. "I don't want to leave New York, besides I am not the kind of man they're looking for. If there's money in it, and no doubt there is seeing as you've taken on the deal. Why don't you get one of those men with the well-advertised names in expensive studios?"

"Just because they have the expensive studios," Abner drawled. "There's money in this commission as you justly remarked, but not enough money for gilt-edged ornaments of art. Do you know that you can't walk into the expensive studios nowadays and say you want a thing done at once. Damned if they don't pull out their engagement books like dentists. No! No, you're the man I want. You've got talent enough and, of course, you are much cheaper."

We now come to the Square of the interims to Central Park, he pointed to one of the hotels which stand there.

"Down there, come in here with me and have a drink we'll make arrangements and I will give you some money at once. You don't want to leave New York? Why the very thing for you I speak as a friend. You look suffering and exhausted, I suppose you can paint still can't you? How long is it since you tried?"

"Of course, as I have no money, I am not a free agent, I am a slave," I said, "like most other paupers. Still, I don't like to have my life mapped out for me by somebody else. Once more I won't. Let us hear what are your terms? If they are not tempting you will have to find somebody else to paint your citizens Abner."

He swallowed the cocktail he had ordered. Then he mentioned the fee which was much higher than I had expected.

"I'll give you a hundred dollars right now," he said, and he pulled out his cheque book.

The project after all began to take a fairer light. I thought of my mean room with horror and of Mrs Wasman with her shrill or tearful demands for rent. Unless I want to rely upon the product of the cigarette case and my vest, I should be driven to sell the pawn ticket and after that I should be utterly on my beam ends. In any case this portrait painting would not be for long and the chance of walking out of this restaurant with a hundred dollars instead of just my vest wrapped in a newspaper to depend on was too sweet to resist.

"Very well," I said. "Hand over the hundred."

"You'll go tomorrow certainly," he asked as he tore the cheque out of his book. "No mistake?"

"Haven't you any ready money?"

He gave me four dollars.

"Just write me a line when you get up there. I'm sending them a telegram tonight, and they will expect you tomorrow."

He added a few directions which I wrote down. Then we had another drink and parted.

I felt rather dazed. I had eaten very little for some days and the spirits I had taken went to my head. I found myself about eight o'clock in the crowd on Broadway still carrying my vest. A man and a woman got out of a motorcar in front of the restaurant and I heard my name called. It was Ginny Graham the girl who had given me her photograph the night before.

"Gee you look ghastly," she said. "Listen come and be introduced to my friend." She pointed to a man in dress clothes who was standing a few paces away. "Then you can dine with us he's sure to ask you, I'll make him."

"I have a word for you," I said abruptly. "That photograph you gave me last night, it came to grief, I haven't got it anymore."

But she continued to look at me kindly. "Gee, I'm sorry for you, and there's no help for it."

"No help for what?"

"You're so unhappy," she cried. "So unhappy, I don't believe there's

46

another man as unhappy as you. You don't know yourself how unhappy you are."

I felt in my coat pockets for Abner's cheque. "Do me a favour," I said. "Keep this for me tonight and send it down to me tomorrow morning about ten," and I gave her my address.

From the door of the restaurant, she turned and glanced back at me. She still seemed to be saying in her voice made husky by too many cigarettes, "So unhappy, so unhappy."

She sent the cheque before nine in the morning. I had come in very late and had thrown myself dressed on the bed. I went out at once to cash the cheque and came back and paid Mrs Wasman. That done I sat in my room with the rest of the money in my hands. I had that peculiar feeling of contentment, which comes over a man who is constantly threatened with having the bed plucked from under him when he has secured himself a shelter for some time ahead.

Mrs Wasman would leave me in peace now for several weeks. Why go away? The sum of money I held was by no means large but it was enough with which to try certain combinations bound to win. I could see them working out before my eyes. On the other hand, if I should lose, I should lose too all the fee that was to come from Abner. He would get somebody else. There was a struggle, three times I went downstairs and out into the street and back. The last time I decided I would not make the journey.

Two minutes later I seized my hat and ran downstairs and made for a streetcar. In the car I arranged that I would give myself only a minute to catch the train, there should be people blocking the way to the ticket window, I would be too late and there was not another train all day. Accordingly, I hung about the streets neighbouring the station then lounged in at the last minute. The ticket window was clear. I bordered the train just as it was moving out.

In the train I sat feeling as if I were drowned, there was a thin whining in my ears. I could think of nothing, the struggle had spent me. The first clear thought I had, came in about an hour. And it was that I had not told Mrs Wasman I was leaving. Such few things as I owned were still in that square, dismal room. Abner's letter and the torn photograph were still lying on the floor.

Out of town where I had to wait over an hour to connect with another train, I thought I had better buy a few necessary things I should have to walk in on those people with a paper parcel for baggage. But it could not be helped, besides I did not care.

They lived in a good-sized house standing well back from a little street bordered with trees. Something unfriendly and depressing emanated from the house as soon as you crossed the threshold. If I were a practiced writer, I suppose I could bring this sensation home to you. But as it is it baffles me to realise it on paper. It was not so much as a sensation of mystery as of secrecy. Those who had died in that house in the seventy years or more it had been standing had not quite gone away.

Something of them remained in the still rooms. At mealtimes there always seemed to be some other presence or presences at the table, besides the master and mistress of the house. The word for them is subdued. They were subdued to the atmosphere of their house, to their traditions, to the naïve furniture they sat among. This unprotesting acquiescence and the unlovely was of course to be expected given the locality. The tradition was the same as that of the British small treatment non-conformist and religion and politics.

The stock they originated from dreary and unpicturesque religion had no doubt in the first place inspired the dreary and unpicturesque surroundings. In a community which had never opened its eyes to any of the arts except literature and to that only on an unartistic side the absence of any testimony to its aesthetic needs was not surprising.

What did surprise, as when glanced about other than the lack of any personal touch became more and more distressing was that they had conceded so far to an unfamiliar spirit as to have their portraits painted. Certainly, they were the very first of their family to make this concession. That first night neither of them affected me beyond the consciousness that they were there, and that I was their guest.

It is true that I felt sick and desperate and sorry to my heart that I had come there. And I was unable to study them accurately. But in the days that followed when I had become more resigned and clearheaded, they remain so anti-pathetic and irritating that I used to invent all sorts of excuses to be as little with them as I could manage.

David Sheriff was null he struck me as one of the innumerable men who live out their lives without ever realising themselves. He was president of the local bank, as his father had been before him and had by the report of the town much money, though beyond whatever pleasure came from the consciousness that he was rich, he got no pleasure or profit of any kind that I could see out of his wealth.

In our intercourse he always remembered he was paying me. He was very far indeed from that stage of civilisation which breeds the patron of artists who fields himself less obliger than the obliged. He was perhaps fifty-five with a lot of loose black hair parted in the middle over a square forehead protruding at the top, and a plump face. One of the most usual types of American. He had suffered a stroke of palsy two or three years ago and now and then his hands trembled violently and his head nodded a little.

It was easy to see that the gift of this library to his native town he regarded as the central end of his career. It was never long out of his conversation, he had not yet got over his astonishment at his own generosity. It seemed even that he was not quite at his ease about this. For he kept talking to justify himself to prove to himself he was right, that he had not thrown away money on a toy.

"Was it your own notion?" I asked one day, when I was painting him. From the moment I had set eyes on him I had decided upon the kind of thing I was going to turn out. Something after the manner the John S. Sargent official portrait. It was weary work, I had no heart for it, and I was often on the point of kicking my easel across the room. I took a long pull at the coffee I had standing by me. "Did you think of it all out of your own head?" I asked him insolently enough.

"Well, no," he hesitated. "It was more my wife's idea."

"But your wife's name is Miriam, isn't it? Why do you call the library The Abigail Sheriff Memorial? Was Abigail Sheriff your daughter?"

I was feeling all the time that I should like to throttle some of his money out of him. And besides the plan of his ridiculous library filled me with contempt. But although I put my crude questions roughly, he showed no resentment, on the contrary he seemed to smile for some reason or other in a deprecating way and looked a little confused.

"The fact is Abigail Sheriff was my wife's sister. She was my first wife. She died—painful memories," he ended with a mutter. "It was my wife's idea," he said again.

I did not feel any active rancour towards this for it was mere exasperation. I hardly remembered him when I was not in his presence. But his wife Miriam Sheriff I disliked intensely with that kind of dislike which makes one hate the thought of some persons. She was tall and thin and dark and looked considerably younger than her husband. Her thin lips pressed close together indicated a life spent in self-repression and a long habit of silence.

When you saw her what struck you first was an impression of gauntness. The gauntness noticeable one suffers from consumption especially when they are tall and next in a secondary way an impression of flame and so to speak of frigid rage as if she moved among the contingencies of life warily, and resented that she had so to move. Withal she was handsome with a kind of handsomeness which repelled rather than attracted. Indeed, made no effort to attract.

She had extraordinary brown eyes under long lashes, which I could not help looking at, which nobody such was their magnetism could help looking at. Although they were wary and veiled and somehow quaint whether from looking out on tedious days or constant weeping. A mole on the cheek near the lips added to the peculiar fascination of the face by relieving the bitter expression of the mouth.

You thought as you looked at her "Here's a woman who has suffered much. Whose spirit has been outraged and perhaps mortally wounded." You thought that I say but you felt no compassion. I even went so far as to fancy that the fine tragic face was an accident of nature covering nothing more than a soul as shallow and peevish as any of her neighbours. She was often in fits of black silence which nobody dared to interrupt. Brooding, despondent and as I thought almost torpid.

When she did talk it was invariably of the town and the people round about. Some of her characterisations were Syrian and grotesque. From her husband I learnt that the inhabitants of the town disliked her and were dreadfully afraid of her. Me, she seemed to make a point of ignoring as much as she could. She would talk past me to her husband when we were all three together. Even when I looked at her, she always looked away quickly.

From something she said I gathered that she disapproved of the pursuit of art.

"All those boys and girls in New York and Boston who are studying painting want an excuse not to do any real work," she said once in her bitter way.

"I know nothing about art," she said another time.

"You are like me," I said "in that."

"You? You live by it don't you?"

"No, I can't live by it, for sure I ain't got enough punch."

"You are not serious?" she murmured, and she fell into one of her abstracted fits, twining and untwining her slim fingers in her lap while she stared with her dark frown at a point on the floor.

I had begun to paint her now, and accordingly she was obliged to speak to me more than she had hitherto. My intention had been to brush out her portrait of her in exactly the same style as the one I had done of her husband but I had been more and more struck by that fugitive look in her eyes. That unwillingness to meet my gaze of the behind the eyes were a hunted soul seeking madly for refuge. This look so much in contrast to the hard composure of the face always interested me.

Especially soon as I noticed that I was the only person who called it forth. At her husband and at everybody else she looked steadily with impatient tolerance, and it was their eyes which shifted before hers. It weighed with me so much that after the first sittings I threw aside my canvas and began again in an altogether different style. I thought to paint something phantom like, swooning and imprecise after the manner of Eugène Carrière. Thus, it seemed to me I had the best chance of catching the soul. And it was the soul lurking behind those eyes I wanted to draw forth.

Now after I had been working at this for some days, I was puzzled and disturbed by an inexplicable alteration in the picture. I was satisfied with my work, which I scarcely ever am and during the sittings, while Mrs Sheriff was in front of me it seemed to me that I was doing just what I had set out to do, drawing forth her soul. But one morning when the picture was beginning to take its final shape, I could not believe the report of my eyes when I examined it.

This was not a portrait of Mrs Sheriff I was doing it was a portrait of somebody else. Somebody I had never seen before. It was as if you were to see after you had written a letter, a letter in your handwriting but on a subject altogether different from what you thought you had written. Upon a subject in fact of which you had no cognisms. I was extremely frightened. I feared I was going out of my mind. I looked still more attentively at the canvas and I think that I saw a brief look of Ginny Graham, the girl back there in New York.

Yes, there was a vague suggestion of what I can only call the forgiveness of her face I painted.

"That's it," I thought furiously. "The delusions are beginning."

They were bound to begin. Why did I ever come to this damned hole? I had not a sitting with Mrs Sheriff that morning because she had to go to a funeral. I was very glad of it. I was all to give up the work and start for New York. The husband's portrait was finished. Abner would have to find somebody else to do the wife. Somebody who had not suffered from strain and hardship and disappointment whose vision was unimpaired.

51

I went out of doors about one. It was a clear autumn day with a soft and humid air stirring. There was a wood spreading over many miles beyond the town, where I was used to walk or just to lie on my back among the leaves. There the air was dying like a lovelorn queen yielding herself passionately to death. And I took comfort in those woods and the dreamy dappled light that was shed there.

My mood changed, in truth that land there is like a woman, it embraces you with all its colour and softness, and entrances and lulls like a lost filter. Lying caressed under its golden crimson, plunged in its ever-changing ever-offering beauty time is no more. You want nothing of the naïve and unwise turmoil of the market place, content to let the days slip through your fingers like the various coloured beads of a rosary that is all to lie close to nature, very close, seeing nothing of the spacious day or soft low brows of the night.

It was all I wanted now. I was bewitched by the land. It looked at me with all its entrenchments so reproachingly. How can you go away? That life back there of a month ago, Mrs Wasman, the *mulatto*, the dingy bedroom, the foul air and the grinding anxiety. What a hideous dream. But also, what a state I had fallen into to paint my portrait like that. It was not that I had lost my skill because as I recalled the picture out here in the woods, it seemed to me that I had never done anything so good. But it was a portrait of somebody I had never seen, and yet the husband's portrait had come out alright.

It was an honest workmanlike portrait, entirely an original, a shameless pastiche of Sargent which any public body would be glad to accept as a feat of mine. But when I thought of the other, I shuddered with horror and I began to blame the model, that horrible Mrs Sheriff. My feeling for her now was hatred. I spent the afternoon in the woods, towards evening I came upon an opening which came upon a bay, an arm of the sea.

I had been trying to recall as I walked anything special about Mrs Sheriff. Up to this point I had taken no interest in her. But now I had the vivid interest we feel in anything we hate or dread. I remember that on the second night that I was there I had asked David Sheriff how old his house was. And upon hearing his reply I had said as a flourish that in every house which had been standing that long a corpse lies under the hearthstone.

He received this with the usual chuckle which he uttered when anything amused him. But his wife had seemed extremely angry and spoke hardly another word during the evening. This was plainly the whim of a stupid provincial woman, who looked on any kind of plain speaking as bad manners.

What else was there? I could not remember anything. Oh, yes, there was this night it was blowing so hard, and in an excess of boredom I had said inanely that I wondered the entrance door was not blown open. The wind was really pounding on the windows, but Mrs Sheriff had evidently taken my remark as an insult to her house, and rose abruptly from the table, we were at dinner and did not appear again. Her husband apologised for her, a little awkwardly I thought.

The next day when I saw Mrs Sheriff, I excused myself and explained that I had not meant to imply that her house was not sound, but she brushed my excuses aside as of no consequence in her frigid way. "What a disagreeable woman," I said to myself for the hundredth time.

I was thinking that now as I stood facing the bay, looking seaward about two miles away to the west were the capes. Between them the breakers always tumbling, just there, were gleaming and behind them the sun was going down. The sky was a blaze of harmonies, wilder lights, such ineffable beauty I had not seen beyond that ending day.

It seemed as if the light were poring through a gorge which led on and on to the end of the world, and to eternity. It was the gate of Heaven. It was sheer nature untarnished by any touch of man. Thus, and no otherwise must the scene have lain before the eyes of lonely Indian when on this day and at this hour, six hundred years ago, he stood on this spot and stared at the sunset. Nothing, absolutely nothing was there to indicate the presence of man. That is, looking far out to sea as I was doing.

But as my gaze shortened, there appeared on an elevation of the ground, a space clear of trees, a hundred yards or more in front of me. A woman's figure standing solitary in black in the intensely clear light of the sunset tide. I knew her at once, both by her unusual tallness, and also by something special on her baring. It was Mrs Sheriff. She was as I said clad all in black, she must have come straight here from the funeral. She had her back to me looking toward the sunset, and even as I saw her, she stretched out her arms and drew them into her breast. A gesture of yearning and embrace.

Then I saw her drop on her knees, and she bowed down 'til her head touched the ground. She must have remained nearly a minute, in that position. I know it was long enough for me to fear she had died. At last, she rose and walked a little unsteadily nearer to where I lingered, 'til she came to a tall tree which stood solitary with its russet leaves touched to something exquisite by the sunset.

She stood gazing for a time at this tree and then suddenly she flung her arms about the trunk and pressed her lips to the rugged bark.

"She is a mad woman," I thought. I determined to slip away, if possible, without letting her see me, but to strike a path I had to move toward where she stood, and the leaves and dead twigs rustled and crackled under my feet. She turned and saw me. She started violently and stood resting one hand on the tree and the other held over her heart. She was evidently astonished to see anybody in this lone place. But in a moment, she had recovered herself, she had recognised me and she came forward without hesitation or reluctance as it seemed, though she still wavered in her walk.

I have already described her in a picture of her as repellent, certainly, that is how she had impressed me. But as she came toward me now, in the sunset, I thought I had never seen anybody so beautiful. It was an unearthly beauty, a radiance encircled her. Her face was transfigured. About her lips and in her eyes was a smile, tender and welcoming, such as I had never seen before. It was clear that she did not at all resent my presence. I felt that she was even glad I was there.

"You saw me at my devotions?"

Now that she was close by, I perceived that her eyes were dilated and that she was panting a little from some strange emotion which was too strong for her sorely labouring hard.

I muttered ungraciously that I had only just caught a glimpse of her as I was searching for the path.

"We own these woods," she said. "Nobody ever comes here, except in the middle of summer, and very few at any time."

Then as if unable any longer to bear these trivialities of convention she impulsively seized my hand.

"Oh, I am so glad you have come. I have always wished to see you in this place because I am natural here. I am myself. I know you will understand me. I felt the very first night you came that you understood me, and I could never look at you afterwards because I knew you were reading my soul." She paused, coughed a little and touched her lips with a handkerchief.

I thought I saw a bloodstain on it, but it may have been the uncertain light.

"I knew you would sympathise with me," she said.

"Yes, but how did you know?"

"Because you are so unhappy, so unhappy," she cried out in a kind of transport. "We understand each other by that. I love you. I love you because you are so unhappy."

I plucked away my hand. Her words brought Ginny Graham to my mind, and I remembered the vague likeness to Ginny Graham in my unfortunate portrait. I had Ginny Graham on the brain. She was beginning to haunt me apparently as the Sheriff's repetition of Ginny Graham's words vexed me beyond control. I moved a few paces away, but she came up to me and seized my hand again, and put her face so close to mine that I felt her breath warm on my cheek.

"Listen, you will understand me sometimes I think I am hanging to that tree yonder. That tree I love, nailed to it with two burning nails through the palms of my hands, and my face to the west looking down the bay toward the sunset. Tell me, do you ever think that?" Her eyes were wide and imploring. There was agony in the broken sound of her voice.

"She is mad," I thought again. "You are a sun-worshipper," I said tolerantly for the sake of saying something.

She looked at me as if she did not quite understand what I said. Then her expression changed to something like ecstasy. "Oh, the sun I love the sun. Yes, I worship if that is the right word. I kneel to it most of all or when it is setting. I think when it is going this should be the last time, I should ever see it, if I should die before tomorrow, and then I think that to die means to be emerged into all that glory and it is the greatest happiness. You are not angry because I say these things to you? Not angry at all? I've always lived here. I've never been anywhere else. I love the sea and the leaves on the trees now, I love them they're beautiful things.

"Beautiful for themselves alone. Nobody sees them, they grow more beautiful and beautiful and then they die, and nobody has seen them. Sometimes I think they are a little lonesome, that is why I kiss and comfort them. But most times I think that, that is the way to be beautiful only for yourself to create beauty only for yourself and care not at all whether it is praised or not. Tell me what you think. I think so much about myself all day long. All day and often all night I don't know whether my thoughts are right or not. But you can tell me because you sympathise with me. You see my soul."

I stared at her, lost in wonder, this spirit so absorbed in a passion for beauty. A far stronger passion than I had myself. Perhaps stronger and more disinterested than the passion of any artist living. How it must have starved. What a power of self-repression. What an iron will she had shown to go on living her life in stagnant ugliness. The deliberate elimination of the charm and existence. I thought of her house, how her confined soul must have beaten against those walls.

"Your trees are the depths of the souls themselves true aristocrats," I said for the sake of an answer. I was not thinking of what I said. She looked at the ground with a frown she always had when she was in one of her reveries.

"All my life I have loved beauty," she said slowly at last. "Beauty and love those are all I care for. I've only been able to find them in nature. I've never been away or seen things. Tell me should I have found a greater love than the beauty in the trees here and the sea and the sunset and the first star?"

"No," I answered positively. "As for love I cannot speak, but for beauty you would have found no greater beauty because the world has no greater beauty to give."

"Do you think they do not love us?"

"I do not know. You perhaps are nearer to them than I am. I think they are indifferent."

She pondered this again in the same way staring at the ground.

"Let us go home," she said at length.

We walked side by side in silence. I was not inclined to talk, and even if I had been it was impossible to talk the vulgar gossip that brought life to this woman. After we had gone about a quarter if a mile, we came to the trunk of a fallen tree lying across the path.

"Sit down here," she said.

I placed myself beside her on the log and she threw her arm lightly around my shoulders. Nothing this extraordinary woman did could startle me now. In what way exactly she regarded me I could not tell. But she had established in her mind some kind of comradeship between us. It would soon be dusk. The far shore veils glowing crimson and orange with the trees in a black closed mass like a span of velvet below. One star gleamed in the serene air. Far off in the woods a little owl began to cry.

In the gathering shadows, she turned on me her face which I could see was quivering with anguish. "You are so unhappy, so unutterably unhappy. Tell me have you ever committed a crime?"

I tried to laugh, "Ha yes, numbers," I said uncomfortably.

"Oh, I don't mean faults, sins. They are of no importance."

"You mean sins, don't you?"

"But I mean a crime. A great crime. You understand what I mean?"

"Yes, I think I do."

"And have you?"

"No."

"Aah."

I do not know what that sigh that rose from the depths of her bosom signified, whether relief or shocking as it may sound, disappointment. Her arm dropped from my shoulders. After a moment she spoke again.

"What did you mean when you said that night, you know the second or third night you were here that in every house which has been standing many years a corpse lies under the hearthstone? Do you remember? It struck me very much, what did you mean?"

"What did I mean? I don't know what I meant. I spoke just to—I meant nothing."

"Listen shall I tell you what I think you meant? You meant that people do things perhaps without thinking that kill other people. Is that it?"

"Yes, something like that."

"You mean there are many more people who have killed other people than are known?"

"Yes, or than know it themselves even. We are very lucky if we can get through life without killing anybody. Have those who lived in your house before you never killed anybody? Just think a minute. Have they never discharged a dependent unfairly or in a fit of anger? Perhaps that act eventually killed the dependent either by rendering him or her helpless, or in some other way. Did they never leave a man or woman in despair? Did they never nag or humiliate or take unjust advantage? Did they never bear false witness? Did they never put the law in motion to extract the last penny from the poor? The mere letters that kill, a thousand things that kill. Oh, yes, we are very lucky if we get through life without killing somebody"

"Or being killed?" she asked in a whisper.

"There are those that don't kill."

"Is it kill or be killed?"

"No, not that."

She jumped up from the log and stood before me in the unreal light, looking taller than ever in her black mourning gown. She stretched out her arms fully her slender hands loosely open.

"I want you to kill me," she said.

I shall never forget how she said it. If she had been asking me to love her, to kiss her, she could not have looked at me with greater sorcery.

"Kill me!" she repeated breathlessly. "No, don't interrupt, hear me out. You will do it I know because I love you. I've been waiting for you to come so long, and when you came, I know you saw my soul, and I said to myself 'When I tell him all, when I explain he will kill me'. Listen it will be quite safe. I have a private fortune I will leave it all to you. We shall settle the details. Oh, I want to die. Only those who want to die cannot die. That woman whose funeral I was at today, she wanted to live. I want to die and I have not the courage to kill myself. But you will kill me my friend."

I sat there motionless under some evil spell.

"You will do it?" she cried and on her face which she bent down close to mine was a smile, wild rapture.

I shuddered. I felt like something terrible and yet lovely was brooding over me. Then I pulled myself together and rose sharply to my feet.

"What strange things you say Mrs Sheriff. You have everything to live for, money and comfort. Your husband will be wondering what has become of you. Let us hurry back."

We walked the rest of the way without speaking another word. I was very much shaken. I was convinced she was irresponsible. She was plainly ill, and in agonies of wretchedness. I thought I heard her sob in the darkness.

But at dinner she was as still and frigid as usual. She spoke hardly at all to me, but she no longer avoided my eyes. Two or three times she gazed at me, so long and intently that I thought her husband would remark it. I must have had some sympathy with her she said for although I had seen so much misery from poverty and had endured so much misery myself from the same cause that I had little pity for miseries which did not arise from lack of money, or were not accompanied by opinionary. Yet I found myself pitying Mrs Sheriff.

I even went so far as to point out to David Sheriff when we were alone together that same evening that his wife's health needed care.

"Oh, she's alright," he mumbled. "She's been like that for years. There's nothing the matter with her."

The next morning when she came as usual to sit to me for an hour in the loft, which I had chosen on account of the light to work in, she greeted me hardly at all. And seemed more absorbed and restrained and withdrawn from the life around her than ever. Does she even remember how she had been in the wood the day before? It was quite possible she did not, such outbursts of emotion I thought are often followed by a blank. The exhausted spirit can bear no more.

Still watching her as she sat there listless, I regarded her otherwise than I had done on other mornings. I knew now that there were certain subjects she would respond to. Up to this it had never occurred to me to ask her opinion any more than the opinion of her husband about my work. David Sheriff it is true had shown some interest in his own portrait.

What he was anxious about was the likeness. He wanted something that the boys would recognise. He used to stand a while sometimes looking over my shoulder like children do about a painter who is painting out of doors. But she never showed the slightest curiosity. She had never glanced at either picture. She submitted to be painted, but I remembered this morning that the impression which a woman with a sense of beauty so developed took from a picture would be worth having. I said something like this to her. She started, roused out of her dream.

"My sense of beauty?" she murmured with a wry little smile. "Poor me."

I turned round her husband's portrait from the wall and held it up before her. She looked hard at it for a little, not at all like a connoisseur of the fine arts, but as one trying rather to gather some fact or facts from it, as if she were reading a letter. Then she sighed.

"This is very good," she said. "Very like, it is also very cruel. You were angry when you painted it. You did it against your will did you not? As for beauty it is not beautiful at all. Beauty is not hard like that. There is more peace and repose and, what do you call it—detachment in beauty, I think. That is not beautiful like a tree or a flower, it is ugly like a man at a tea party in a small town. Our town here."

I was a little nettled, perhaps because what she said struck home.

"I am afraid you are too classic for me," I scoffed. "You are akin to Lessing and Goethe. I hardly dare to show you what I have done with yourself."

The picture was resting on the easel, covered with a cloth.

"You will bear in mind," I continued, "that it is not quite finished. A strange thing has happened to me with it. I've been trying to paint you, what I saw in you, but what has come out is not you. It's as a portrait of somebody I never saw, and yet I saw her in you. I've been ill and miserable and poor, perhaps my vision has become affected. But you can judge for yourself. Look!"

And I drew away the cloth. I have said that I was trying to paint my picture in the style of Eugène Carrière, that great artist's power of bringing the body to the very confines of life, of catching the twilight between the temporal and the spiritual. Of seizing the human frame when it is swooning away in the ghost emerging. I thought of when I set out to paint this strange Miriam Sheriff but my work was not a poor imitation of Carrière, that I swear it was the best picture I had ever painted, or can ever hope now to paint.

Mrs Sheriff seemed at first unwilling to look at it. Then visibly putting some constraint on herself, she turned towards the picture resolutely. She gave a low cry and pressed her left hand against her side with her habitual gesture. I thought she was going to fall, but she turned away and hurried from the room. Almost before I had time to be astonished, I heard her light foot on the stairs coming up again. She put a photograph in my hands.

"Is that the face you saw?" she asked.

It was the photograph of a young woman dressed after the fashion of fifteen or twenty years ago. She had a handsome face, very unusual, and it was this face I had painted. But in the photograph face there was something sensual, defiant, even solemn. Whereas in my picture it was as if the same woman had passed through some purgatory and come forth a thousand times purified.

"It is my sister, Abigail," said Mrs Sheriff. "I have never seen her like that photograph I always see her just behind my eyes with that look of forgiving as she is in your picture. That is how she looked a few minutes before she died."

She paused and then added quietly, "I murdered her"

"For Heaven's sake don't say such a terrible thing."

"That face is what you saw in *me*, as you said just now. I knew all the time you were seeing it and drawing it out of me. I made up my mind several days ago to tell you all about it. I'm going to tell you."

"Not, here in this house?"

She glanced carelessly round the walls, "Well no, perhaps not in the house. I would rather be out in the open. You remember that tree where you saw me yesterday? Go there this afternoon."

I was first at the tryst by a good hour it looked as if she were not coming, and I felt infinitely relieved. I ought to have resisted her impulse to make me her *confidente*. If she had a tragedy in her life, why should I burden myself with it? Surely, I had enough already to weigh me down. That portrait, what flaw in eye or brain what casting off from the world was the life and voyaging into the unpassed seas of the invisible world, did that portend?

But when at last I sighted her in the distance the forebodings that had been so heavy upon me since morning, suddenly appeared idle. Perhaps the reason was that she was not garbed in black as she had been yesterday but wore the many-coloured costume of a woman who lives in the country and is much out of doors. These healthy clothes, the soft hat she had on, her bright muffler, her rough gloves and her walking stick took her out of the isolation in which I had been seeing her, and established a relation between her and ordinary average women of common place existence.

Her appearance now was so inconsistent with the vision of her making that appalling confession in the morning, that I remind myself once more that she must be suffering from hallucinations, and that she had perhaps forgotten by this time why she had brought me there. But when she was drawing near, a little breathless, as if she had hurried, I saw the countenance cold and indifferent and repelling any advance of attempt at intimacy which she kept for the town, vanish really. As if she had cast off a mask. And there came into her haunted eye a look of even more intense anguish than I had seen yesterday.

"You won't be able to worship the sun this afternoon," I said in a trivial tone, attempting to start the conversation.

It was indeed a dull soundless day, with low hanging clouds ever and *anon*, the sun concealed by clouds sent forth a shaft of light which was not sunshine. The bay lay glassy smooth the colour of slate. The leaves had lost their colour and looked dead and shrivelled on the branches ready to fall. While I had been sitting still there, I had actually heard them dying. A strange dim crackling noise which began and then ceased and began once more.

I had spoken to her as I say in jest but in her reply was a great solemnity.

"I don't think I shall ever be able to look at the sun again, not since I saw what I saw this morning."

She meant my picture.

"You make too much of it," I said to soothe her.

"Abigail, my sister, and I used to come to this place when we were quite little," she went on dreamily. "She used to stand with her back against that tree over there to see if she was taller than I was. How strange that seems after all this time. She always wanted to be taller than I was. David Sheriff, who is my husband now, used to measure us. He used to cut notches in the tree. I wonder if they are there still. I never thought to look 'til now. He was our cousin but much older than we were. I loved David when I was a little girl, and when I grew up, I loved him. He loved Abigail but she cared nothing at all for him.

"We had not much money then. David's father was well to do but Abigail and I lived with our mother who was a widow. Then sister made up her mind to go to Boston and take up business there. It was the best thing she could do if she would not marry David. She was always quarrelsome with mother, with me too. I don't know just what she did in Boston. Mother used to send her money sometimes. She was cashier in some large store, she got mixed up with a man who was also employed in the store and he persuaded her to steal money for him. It must have been for him. Then they found her out and arrested her.

"David was going to marry me. I was so glad, and so was mother. But when this news came, he hurried to Boston. He stood up in court and said he had always loved her and that if they would let her go, he would marry her and pay back the money she had taken. They did let her go on these terms and sister married him at once. That was like a knife in my side. I had begun to get my *trousseau* together. Now there was no more hope. What made it worse was that the very first night they came home I saw that Abigail hated David, though he was crazy about her. She only loved the man for whom she had stolen, and he had disappeared. She was surly and hard and defiant.

"She looked as she looks in that photograph, I showed you. It was taken a few days after they came home. She was unwell she had a cold when she arrived and coughed a good deal. She didn't seem to care, soon she had to stay in bed. I went over from mother's to nurse her. Sister was terribly querulous and unkind to everybody, but especially to David. She accused him of forcing her into marriage and declared that she would never be a wife to him. She got worse and the thought came to me from outside my head. I remember that quite well. It seemed to enter my head from outside, if she was to die David would be free.

"Then one evening the doctor came and said she was much better. She looked better, she was not going to die after all. And a terrible thing came into my head. It was something the doctor said that suggested it. It was a rough winter night with a terrific gale, I don't think I have ever heard the wind blow so loud since. The doctor gave sister

62

a sleeping powder, and said she must be kept warm. If she gets through this night well, he told us, she will mend quickly.

"Then he said as he was going that he hoped the windows and doors were strong or the wind might blow them in. I was to sit up all night with sister. When the clock struck one, I looked at her she was sleeping well with her head on her arm. She was very warm and her skin was moist. We were in that room you have now. You know it almost faces the stairs and the street door. We padded the cracks in the door to keep out the drafts, but the bed was near the door and it had not been possible to move it. I stole downstairs and opened the street door.

"Then I went back upstairs and left the bedroom door open and drew the blankets off sister. The icy wind came streaming into the room. I opened the window to make more of a draft and sat there shivering hoping it would kill me too. I did not want to live. I only wanted David to be free from the unhappy life before him with sister. After a while she stirred and began to cough, but she did not wake up. Cough, cough, cough, I hear that often but she never woke up. About half-past four I went down and shut the door.

"If anybody had passed and seen the door open, they would have thought it was the gale, but nobody passed. I came upstairs again and closed the bedroom door and the window. Then something terrible happened. I heard steps coming slowly upstairs, heavy, deliberate steps like an old man's. Then there came three loud knocks at the door. I jumped into the bed beside sister and covered my head with the blanket. I wondered I did not die from terror. I waited to hear the steps go away from the door, but they did not go away. It was Death that had come. Sister woke up and began to cry. She was much worse. When David was up, he went for the doctor, but sister Abigail died toward nightfall."

We had been standing all this time, there was a distorted smile about her mouth, and she pressed her fingers to her breast, and turned round and stood with her back to me.

"Perhaps it was not that," I said at last uneasily in a low voice.

"Yes, it was that. The doctor said she must have got a sudden chill."

We were silent again for a long time. I could think of nothing to say. At last, wanting to say something I stammered "You—you have your husband, the man you love."

She turned round quickly. Her eyes were quite dry, the imploring smile had gone from her face.

"Yes, I have him," she replied in a hard voice. "You see what he is, that is my punishment."

Then she looked at me intently, straight into the eyes. "Now you hate me," she said.

"Hate you? Oh, you poor creature."

"Then kiss me," she said. "If you cannot hate me."

I took her head between my hands and kissed her on the forehead.

"Will you kill me now?" she whispered insidiously.

"Oh my God! No!"

"But you were sent for that. That is what the picture means."

"I don't know what it means, but not that, never think it."

"Then goodbye and forever my friend, my brother."

She walked quickly away in the dusk and I did not follow her.

She did not appear at dinner that evening. She had a headache her husband said. About nine o'clock I went up to the loft and cut my picture into strips. I felt as if I were stabbing a living creature. I burned the strips in the stove which was there. Then I came down and told David Sheriff that I had fulfilled the contract for his own portrait but that I found I could make no headway with the portrait of Mrs Sheriff, and so I was going away in the morning.

"Call yourself a painter?" he said. "Why she ought to be easier than me. She can sit still I know that." He chuckled but he was evidently put out.

"I dare say Mr Abner can find you someone else."

"Well, no, I guess not. I guess it's my picture the folks want to see down in that library."

He added that he used to do some drawing himself in his young days.

"Over there in woods near the bay I used to draw my cousins. I used to stand them against a tree and cut notches on it to mark their height."

A few months later Abner showed me a newspaper which he had received from David Sheriff. It was a local paper and it gave a full account of the opening of The Abigail Sheriff Memorial Library. My portrait of David Sheriff had been much praised by the orators. There was no mention of a portrait of Mrs Sheriff, and it was said that she herself had been absent from the ceremony owing to illness.

Original Sin

Sans cesse à mes côtés s'agite le Demon,
Il nage autour de moi comme un air impalpable;
Je l'avale, et le sens qui brule mon poumon
Et Templit d'un désir éternel et coupable.
> —*Les Flairs du Mai.*

When Alphonse D'Aubert had laid down his book for the fifth time, having taken it up five times in his wrestle with his thoughts, he decided that *even L'Ennemi des Lois* could not distract him, and so, at four o'clock in the morning, he went into the streets. As he crossed the deserted *Boulevard*, a little boy drew near with a plaintive cry: "*Charité Monsieur!*" and Alphonse, who was almost morbidly good-natured, gave him an alms, and paused for a few minutes of pleasant talk.

When he fell to his walk again, he began to consider, with a sort of sick wonder, why the child who lived in his mind to such fell purpose, could not become to him as this child he had just left: as all other children,—exquisite, helpless, piteous things, craving for love and protection. Thus, it was always with him: after his blackest nights he was ever in the morning at his penitentials: and when the dawn was creeping over the roofs of the houses, he forgot how feverishly he had yearned in the darkness to press his long fingers on the soft throat of a child.

Whether Alphonse was in love with Madame Dantonel or not, it may be said that she was the creature he cared most for on earth. Certainly, on her side, she looked for nothing more tender than a friendship with this somewhat strange young man, whom, in a way of motherly tenderness, she regarded, with his *bizarreries*, his exclusiveness, his superior silences, as a rather terrible child, spoilt by his excellent fortune in the world.

At her house in the *Champs-Elysées* he found himself most readily at his ease: and this fact led him by the hand to the opinion, that he was never in the least happy when he was not there. She was the widow of a man who had been engaged with politics: Alphonse never troubled to inquire how engaged; only recognised the death of the political person as a relief, and as a period to the slight embarrassment with which he was wont to listen to the patriotics—an embarrassment which all forms of activity brought to his contemplative and somewhat melancholy spirit. And after that, he was never so serene, so nearly joyous, as when he was in the company of Madame Dantonel and the little Clotilde, her only child, who was now four years old.

It was on a day when he was most delightful, when he was taking life gaily, that, looking at the little girl as she played on the floor, the stunning desire came to him to take her by the throat and squeeze out her life. He took his leave in manifest disturbance; and fled into the street. He was shaking with horror: of a truth he loved this child, next to its mother, supremely; and yet, amid his disgust, he could not stifle a lust to murder her—a thrilling satisfaction, as he thought of the life ebbing from her face while he crushed her soft round throat with his fingers. That was the first bad night of the many bad nights to come.

On the following afternoon he went to the house again, to try himself—to see how he would "get on"; but within five minutes he departed, grinding his teeth and biting at his nails to keep down his passion, which was driving him to rush back to the house and slay the child before its mother's face. But after a ghastly night of torture, and sweat, and weeping, he found himself, in the morning, suddenly recovered!

All his old affection for the child once more lived in his heart: the devil, it seemed, had been worsted: and it was in this glad condition that he lived for a few weeks. He had given Clotilde many presents before; but now he spent hours in the toyshops, finding a certain piety in thus eagerly buying, as though he were making good a case with his conscience. Ah, those few excellent days! How brilliant he was; how he dealt with the sunshine; how airily he tossed a salute to the passengers in the street!

But it was on a dreary afternoon, when the rain was whipping through the court-yard, as Alphonse stood talking lightly to Madame Dantonel and the child, that he suddenly knew himself to be the slave of his old passion. Oh, to crush that satin throat! He made one tremendous, straining effort, and so beat himself; but the effort was too much for his physical strength, and he fell on the floor as if dead.

When he began to get his senses, he found Madame Dantonel

bending over him with a look of sharp anxiety.

"Ah, my poor friend!" she exclaimed, "but you have been very ill!"

"I have been ill, but now I am well," says Alphonse, in a thick voice. "I am going away—far away from Paris."

"Going away!" And when she got over her surprise: "But why?"

"Because I do no good here," he said, getting on his feet. "Because I find my life too narrow. I go to the *café*, I chat, I smoke cigarettes. Good. I dine, I go to the opera, to a *soirée*. My God!" he cries out, "do you call that a life? Please, my dearest friend, do not prevent me. I am going away."

She took his hand very kindly. "Go, if you wish it," she said; "but remember that you have always two friends here. Is it not so, Clotilde?"

Alphonse was taken with a hard shudder as he went out.

He decided to go to England; with an ultimate thought, perhaps, of America. He crossed the channel in wintry and boisterous weather, and when he came to Dover, he was well content to lie there: postponing, gratefully enough, his arrival at London till the next day. Tired with his tossing journey, he took to his bed early; and at once fell into the profound sleep of fatigue, from which he awoke, about two o'clock, hot and trembling. The figure of the child was before him in the darkness of the room; the full throat, above all was apparent and particular. He rolled on the bed, and tore and bit the pillows: not before had he longed with this violent frenzy to see the child stretched at his feet, looking solidly white and dead.

Damp and shaking, he put on his clothes and went down to talk with the night-porter—a desperate chance under the best conditions; for a foreigner, hopeless! as he found. So, he returned to his room, and opened his windows to the raining night. A strong salt wind was singing up channel; and Alphonse let it get into his hair and eyes, finding respite in this way, and a certain peace. Thus, he spent the night, till the dawn came to shew the grey, uneasy sea, and the grey sky. He departed, when morning had come, on board the earliest packet-boat, and that evening he found himself again in Paris.

Things having come to this point, you may ask fairly: Why did he not turn to the obvious remedy—self-destruction? Yes! But upon reflection it does not seem so likely. Indeed, upon reflection it would appear, that when a man has a desire, a fierce lust to satisfy, he prefers, however the powers of his soul may rebel, to live for the gratification of that desire, that fierce lust. Be that as it will, the man I am writing about did not contemplate suicide; did not, for a moment, glance along that road of escape. But he gave a dainty supper, to which he invited some of his male acquaintance, and a few ladies of generous virtue.

There sat by him a superb creature, with gleaming shoulders and snapping black eyes; and as the mirth grew more disordered, he laid his hand on her swelling throat and tried to tempt himself to kill her in the sight of the revellers. Anyone rather than the child! But even as he thought it, the child floated before his eyes; the remembrance of the strange satiety he would feel when he had choked out her life, which he would not feel at all were he to kill this woman, caused his hand to fall listlessly to his side; and pleading a sudden dizziness, he left the merrymakers to themselves.

So, on the next afternoon, we find him once more repairing to the *Champs-Elysées* and the house of Madame Dantonel. He was feeling easier today; and he discovered at Madame Dantonel's, one visitor who helped to soothe his irritated nerves. This was an old military officer: and Alphonse found his cheerfulness and honest geniality of character very pleasant. He had sat for about twenty minutes, when Madame Dantonel exclaimed:—

"My poor little Clotilde! She has a cold, a slight sore throat, and this is the time when the *bonne* goes downstairs, so she will be quite alone. Forgive me if I go to her."

The time had come. "Permit me!" said Alphonse, on his feet in an instant. It was as though a stranger were talking: he could no more help the words than he could help breathing. "Pray do not deprive *Monsieur* of your company. I will go to Clotilde; it will delight me to see her, and I know the room quite well."

He hardly waited for the murmured pleasure, but ran, trembling with eagerness, up the stairs. The little girl was in bed playing with her doll, and she greeted him with a smile and a glad cry. He clenched his teeth, and squeezed and crushed her throat till the pretty tiny face became black and swollen, and the poor little frame, after a shake and a quiver, lay quite still.

As he came down, he heard Madame Dantonel say goodbye to the visitor, and the hush of her dress as she passed through the hall.

"*Mon Dieu!* how pale you look!" she cried, raising both hands. "Is anything the matter with Clotilde?"

"Clotilde is very well," says Alphonse. "But I think the room was too hot for me, and I am going away now."

"Really! so soon?" she said, genuinely sorry. And she held out her hand.

"No! please don't shake hands with me, I am not worthy!" cries Alphonse, with a wan smile, passing the matter off as a jest. "You will find Clotilde very well," he said again.

The door closed behind him. As the mother went upstairs to her child, he took his way to a chemist's shop which he knew of in the neighbourhood.

The Bargain of Rupert Orange

1

The marvel is, that the memory of Rupert Orange, whose name was a signal for chatter amongst people both in Europe and America not many years ago, has now almost died out. Even in New York where he was born, and where the facts of his secret and mysterious life were most discussed, he is quite forgotten. At times, indeed, some old lady will whisper to you at dinner, that a certain young man reminds her of Rupert Orange, only he is not so handsome; but she is one of those who keep the mere incidents of their past much more brightly polished than the important things of their present. The men who worshipped him, who copied his clothes, his walk, his mode of pronouncing words, and his manner of saying things, stare vaguely when he is mentioned.

And the other day at a well-known club I was having some general talk with a man whose black hair is shot with white, when he exclaimed somewhat suddenly: "How little one hears about Rupert Orange now!" and then added: "I wonder what became of him?" As to the first part of this speech I kept my mouth resolutely shut; for how could I deny his saying, since I had lately seen a weed-covered grave with the early moss growing into the letters on the headstone? As to the second part, it is now my business to set forth the answer to that: and I think when the fire begins to blaze it will lighten certain recollections which have become dark. Of course, there are numberless people who never heard the story of Rupert Orange; but there are also crowds of men and women who followed his brilliant life with intense interest, while his shameful death will be in many a one's remembrance.

The knowledge of this case I got over a year ago; and I would have written then, had my hands been free. But there has recently died at Vienna the Countess de Volnay, whose notorious connection with

Orange was at one time the subject of every man's bruit. Her I met two years since in Paris, where she was living like a work-woman, I learned that she had sold her house, and her goods she had given to the poor. She was still a remarkable woman, though her great beauty had faded, and despite a restless, terrified manner, which gave one the monstrous idea that she always felt the devil looking over her shoulder. Her hair was white as paper, and yet she was far from the age when women cease to grin in ball-rooms. A great fear seemed to have sprung to her face and been paralyzed there: a fear which could be detected in her shaking voice. It was from her that I learned certain primary facts of this narration; and she cried to me not to publish them till I heard of her death—as a man on the gallows sometimes asks the hangman not to adjust the noose too tight round his neck. I am altogether sure that what Orange himself told her, he never told anyone else. I wish I had her running tongue instead of my slow pen, and then I would not be writing slovenly and clumsily, doubtless, for the relation; vainly, I am afraid, for the moral.

Now Rupert Orange lived with his aunt in New York till he was twenty-four years old, and when she died, leaving her entire estate to him, a furious contest arose over the will. Principal in the contest was Mrs. Annice, the wife of a discarded nephew; and she prosecuted the cause with the pertinacity and virulence which we often find in women of thirty. So good a pursuivant did she prove, that she and her husband leaped suddenly from indigence to great wealth: for the Court declared that the old lady had died lunatic; that she had been unduly influenced; and, that consequently her testament was void. But this decision, which raised them up, brought Rupert to the ground.

There is no worse fall than the fall of a man from opulence to poverty; and Rupert, after his luxurious rearing, had to undergo this fall. Yet he had the vigour and confidence of the young. His little verses and sonnets had been praised when he was an amateur; now he undertook to make his pen a breadwinner—with the direst results. At first, nothing would do him but the great magazines; and from these, week after week, he received back his really clever articles, accompanied by cold refusals. Then for months he hung about the offices of every outcast paper, waiting for the editor.

When at length the editor did come, he generally told Rupert that he had promised all his outlying work to some bar-room acquaintance. So, push by push he was brought to his knees; and finally he dared not walk out till nightfall, for fear some of those who knew him in prosperity might witness his destitution.

One night early in December, about six o'clock, he left the mean flat-house on the west side of the city in which he occupied one room, and started (as they say in New York) "up town." The snow had frozen in lumps, and the gas lamps gleamed warmly on it for the man who had not seen a fire in months. When he reached Fifty-ninth Street, he turned east and skirted Central Park till he came to the Fifth Avenue. And here a sudden fancy seized him to walk this street, which shame and pride had kept him off since his downfall. He had not proceeded far, when he was stopped by an old man. "Can you tell me, sir," says the old man, politely, "if this street runs on further than Central Park?"

"Oh, yes," answered Rupert, scraping at his throat; for he had not spoken to a soul for five days, and the phlegm had gathered.

"It goes up a considerable distance from here."

"You'll forgive me asking you," went on the ancient. "I am only passing through the city, and I want to find out all I can."

"You're quite welcome," said Orange.

"That," he added, pointing, "is St. Luke's Hospital."

They spoke a few more sentences, then as the stranger turned "down town," Rupert fell in with his walk. He did this partly because he was craving for fellowship; partly, too, from that feeling which certain men have—men who have never done anything for themselves in this world, and never will do anything—that distant relations, and even total strangers, are apt at any moment to fling fortunes into their hands.

As they proceeded along the avenue, Orange turned to survey his companion. A shrewd wind was blowing, and it tossed the old gentleman's long beard over his shoulder, and ruffled the white hair under his soft hat. His clothes were plain, even shabby; and he had an odd trick of planting his feet on the ground without bending his knees, as though his legs were broomsticks. Orange thought, bitterly enough! how short a time had passed since the days when he would have taken poison as an alternative to walking down the Fifth Avenue with such an associate. Now they were equal: or indeed the old man was the better off of the two: for if he wore impossible broad-toed boots, Orange had to stamp his feet to keep the cold from striking through his worn-out shoes.

What cared he for the criticism of the smart, well-fed "Society" now, when numbers of that far greater society, of which he was one, were starving in garrets! As he thought these things, a late afternoon reception began to pour out its crowds, and a young man and a girl, who had known Rupert in the days of his prosperity, came forth and glared with contempt at the two mean passengers. Not a muscle in Rupert's face quivered: he even afforded those two the tribute of a sneer.

When the pair of walkers reached Thirty-Fourth Street they switched into Broadway. A silence had fallen between them, and it was in silence they paraded the thoroughfare. Here all was garish light and glare; carriages darted to and fro, restaurants were thronged, theatres ablaze, women smiling: everything told of a great city starting a night of pleasure. Besides the love of pleasure which was his main characteristic, Orange was distinctly gregarious; and the sight of all this joy, which he had once revelled in himself, struck like a knife into his hungry, lonely heart. At that moment he thought he would give his very soul to get some money,

"All these people seem happy," says the old man, suddenly.

"Yes," replied Orange. "*They* are happy enough!"

The old man caught the reply, and noticed the sour twang in it. He looked up quickly and saw that Rupert's eyes watered.

"Why, man," he exclaimed, "I believe you're crying! or perhaps you're cold! Come in here, come right in to the Hoffman House!" he went on, tugging at Rupert's coat,

Rupert hesitated. The sensitiveness of one who had never taken a favour which he could not repay, held him back. But the desire for warmth and sympathy prevailed, so he entered. The usual crowd of loafers was about the bar, and those who composed it looked scoffingly at Orange's shiny overcoat and time-eaten trousers. Believe me, the man in rags is not half so pitiable as the poor creature who tries to maintain the appearance of a gentleman: the man who inks seams by night which grow all white by day; who keeps his fingers close pressed to his palm lest the rents in his glove be seen; who walks with his arm across his breast for fear his coat should fly open and proclaim its lack of buttons.

Even the waiters looked disparagingly at Orange; and a waiter's jibes, or any flunkey's, are, perhaps, the sorest of all. But the old man, without noticing, sat down at a table and ordered a bottle of champagne. When the wine was brought, the two sat together some time in a muse. Then, of a sudden, the greybeard broke out.

"Wealth!" he cried, staring into Rupert's eyes, "wealth is the only thing worth striving for in this world! Your tub-philosophers may laugh at it, but they only laugh to keep away from themselves a cankering envy and desire which would be more bitter than their present lack. Let any man whom you call a genius arrive at this hotel tonight, and let a millionaire arrive at the same moment, and I'll bet you the millionaire gets the attention every time! A millionaire travels round the earth, and he gets respect everywhere he goes—why? Because he buys it. That's the way to get respect in the nineteenth century—buy it! Do the fine works of art which are sold each year go to the pauper student who worships them? No, sir, they go to the man who has the money, and who shells out the biggest price. I repeat, my young friend, that what's there "(and he slapped his pocket) "is what counts in the struggle of life."

"I agree with you," answered Orange, "that money counts for a great deal."

"A great deal!" repeated the other, scornfully, being now, perhaps, somewhat warmed with wine. "A great deal! what have you to offer instead? Religion? Ministers are the parasites of rich men. Art? Go into the studio of any friend of yours tomorrow, and see whom he'll speak to first—you, or the man with a cheque in his hand. Why, if a poor man had the brains of Shakespeare, or our Emerson, and was mud-splashed by the carriage wheels of a wealthy woman, the only answer to his protests would be a policeman's 'move on!'"

"I know it! I know it!" cried Orange, in anguish. "I know it fifty times better than you do! I tell you I would sell my whole life now, for one year's perfect enjoyment of riches."

"Not one year," said the greybeard, leaning over the table and speaking so intensely that Rupert could hardly follow him. His old face had become ghastly and looked livid in contrast to the white hair. "Not one year, my boy, but five years! Think, only think, of the gloriousness of it all! This evening a despised pauper, tomorrow a rich man! Take courage, make up your mind to yield your life at the end of five years, and in return I will promise you, pledge you, that tomorrow morning you shall be in as sound a financial position as any man in New York."

Now it is strange that this outrageous proposal, made in the barroom of an hotel situate in one of the most prosaic cities in the world, did not strike Rupert Orange as at all preposterous. Probably on account of his mystical, dreaming mind, he never took thought to doubt the speaker's sincereness, but at once fell to balancing the advantages and drawbacks of the scheme.

Five years! Before his young eyes they stretched out like fifty years. It did not occur to him (it rarely occurs to any young man) to hark back to the five preceding years and note how few and swift were the strides which brought him over them to this very day he was living. Five years! They lay before him all silver with sunshine, as he looked out from his present want and darkness. This was his point of view; and let us never forget this point of view when we are passing judgment on him. No doubt, if the matter had been placed before a man of wealth, he would have denied it even momentary consideration: but the smell of cooking is only disgusting to one who has dined; it is the vagrant who sniffs eagerly the air of the kitchen through the iron grating on the street.

For Rupert, at this moment, money meant all the world. He was a man who hated to face the bitter things of life: and money included release from insolent creditors, from snubs and flouts, from a small, cold, dark room, and, chief of all! release from that horror which he saw drawing nearer and nearer: the gaol.

"There is one more word to be said," observed the old man, smoothly. "Leaving aside the contingency of your starving to death—which, by the way, I think very likely—there is a chance of your being run over by a cart when you leave this hotel. There is an even chance of your contracting some disease during the winter. How would you like to die in a pauper hospital, where the nurses sing as they close a dead man's eyes? Now, what I propose is, that you shall be free from any physical pain for five years."

"If I should accept," said Orange, swirling the wine round in his glass till it creamed and foamed, "I'd desire some slight ills to take the very sweetness out of life." Probably he meant, for fear that when his time came, he should hate to die.

He thought again. He was like to a man who arrives suddenly at a mountain village on the feast of the Blessed Sacrament, and loitering in the street with his eyes enchanted by the tawdry decorations and festoons of the houses, forgets to look beyond at the awful mountain standing against the sky, with menacing thunder clouds about its breast. Before Orange's mind a gay and tempting pageant denied. He thought of the travels he would be able to make, of luxurious palaces, of exquisite banquets, of priceless wines, of laughing, rapturous women.

He thought, too, for he was far from being a merely sensuous man, of the first editions he could buy, of the rare gems, of dainty bindings. Sweetest of all were the thoughts, that he would be at his ease to do the best work that it was in him to do, and that he would be powerful enough to wreak his vengeance on his enemies very slowly, inch by inch. With that, like the crack of a rifle shot, came the thought of Mrs. Annice.

He sprang to his feet. "Listen!" he cried, in such a voice that the idlers at the bar turned round for a moment; but observing that no row was in progress to divert them, they fell once more to their drinking. "Listen!" cried Rupert Orange again, gripping the side of the table with one hand and pointing a shaking finger at the old man. "There is one woman alive in this city tonight who has brought me to the degradation which you witness now. She flung me to the ground, she covered me with dust, she crushed me beneath her merciless heel! Give her to me that I may lower her pride! let me see her as abject and despised as the poorest trull that walks the streets, and I swear by God Most High to make the bargain!"

The old man grasped Rupert's cold hand, and pressed it between his own feverishly hot palms. "It is an unusual taste," he murmured, glancing into Rupert's eyes, and smiling faintly.

2

Orange started "up town" with a song in his heart. Curiously enough, he had not the slightest doubt about the genuineness of the contract, nor had he the least sorrow for what he had done. It mattered little about snubs and side looks tonight: tomorrow men and women would joyfully begin pawing him and fawning. So happy was he, his blood danced through his veins so merrily, that he ran for three or four *blocks*; and once he laughed a loud laugh, which caused a policeman to menace him with a club. But this only brought him more merriment; tomorrow, if he liked, he could laugh from Central Park to Madison Square without molestation.

When he reached the mean flat-house on the west side, there was, as usual, no light in the entrance, and he saw a postman groping among the bells.

"Say, young feller!" began the postman, "do you know if any one by the name of Orange is kickin' around this blamed house?"

"I am he," said Rupert Grange, and held out his hand for the letter.

"*Yes*, you are!" answered the postman, derisively. "Now then, come off the roof and shew us the bell."

Rupert indicated the place, and, as soon as the postman had dropped the letter, he whipped out his key, and to the postman's surprise unlocked the box and put the letter in his pocket.

"Well! you see my business is to deliver letters, not to give them away," said the postman, making an official distinction. "When you said you was the man, how was I to know you wasn't givin' me a steer?"

"Oh, that's all right!" replied Rupert. "Goodnight, my friend."

He went upstairs to his freezing little room, and sat down to think. He would not open the letter yet: his mind was too crowded to admit any new emotion. So, for two hours he remained dreaming brilliant and fantastic dreams. Then he tore open the envelope. He was so poor that the gas had been turned off from his room, but by the light of a match he read a communication from Messrs. Daroll and Kettel, the lawyers, setting forth that a distant relative of his had recently died in a town in one of the Southern States, and had left him a fortune of nearly a million dollars But Rupert knew that this million dollars was only nominal, that money would remain with him as long as he could call life his own.

The charwoman who came into his room next morning, found him asleep in the chair, with the letter open on his knee, and a smile lighting his face. But he was only a pauper, in arrears for his rent, so she struck him smartly between the shoulders with her broom,

"I believe I've been asleep," said Rupert, starting and rubbing his eyes. The woman looked at him sourly, thinking that he would have to take his next sleep in one of the parks. She began to sweep the dust in his direction till he coughed violently.

"You have been very good to me since I've been here, Mrs. Spill," Rupert continued; and, I think, without irony: he had not much idea of irony. He took from his pocket the last five-dollar bill he had in the world and gave it to her. "Please take that for your trouble."

The woman stared at him, as she would have stared had he cut his throat before her eyes. But Orange clapped on his hat and rushed out. He had not even the five cents necessary to travel down town in a *horse-car*, so he walked the distance to the office of Messrs. Daroll and Kettel, in Pine Street. He approached a fat clerk (who, decked as he was with doubtful jewellery, looked as if he were honouring the office by being in it at all), and asked if Mr. Kettel was within.

Now it is something worthy of note, that I have often called on men occupied with difficult texts; or painting pictures; or writing novels; and each one had been able to let go his work at once: while, on the other hand, it is your part to await the pleasure of a clerk, till he has finished his enthralling occupation. True to his breed, the fat man kept Rupert standing before him for about three minutes, till he had elaborately finished a copy of a bill of details; and then looking up, and seeing only a shabby fellow, he asked sharply:—

"Eh? What do you say?"

Rupert repeated his question.

"Yes, I guess he's in, but this is his busy day. You just sit right down there, young man, and he'll see you when he gets good and ready."

The hard knocks which Rupert had received in his contest with the world had taken out of him the self-assertion that goes with wealth: so, he sat for half an hour, knowing well, meanwhile, that his clothes were a cause for laughter to the underbred and badly trained clerks. At length he somewhat timidly went over to the desk again.

"Perhaps if you would be kind enough to take my name in to Mr. Kettel—"

"Oh, look here, you make me tired!" exclaimed the fat clerk, irritably. "Didn't I tell you that he was busy? Now, I don't want to see you monkeying round this desk anymore! If you don't want to wait, why the walking's pretty good!—— This young man says he wants to see you," he added, as Mr, Kettel came out of his private room.

"Well, sir, what do you want today?" asked Mr. Kettel, with that most offensive tone and air which some misguided men imagine will impress the spectator as a manner for the man of great affairs. "You had better call round some other time; we're not able to attend—" he was going on, when he happened to look narrowly into Rupert's face, and his manner changed in a second. "Why, my dear boy, how are you! it's so long since I've seen you, that I didn't know you at first. And, how you've changed!" he went on, and could not help a glance at Rupert's shabby dress; for he was quite ignoble. Then this remark seeming of questionable taste even to him, he cried heartily; "But come into my private room, and we can have a good long chat!"

And in he went, with Rupert at his heels, leaving the fat clerk at gaze.

In a week Rupert was once more dawdling about clubs, and attending those social functions which go to make up what is called "a Season." Above all, he was listening to an appalling variety of apologetic lies. To the average man who said: "We didn't know when on earth you were coming back from Europe, my dear fellow; how did you like it over there?" he could answer with a grave face; but the women were different. One particular afternoon he was at a reception, when he heard a lady near him remark in clear accents to her friend: "You can't think how we missed that dear Mr. Orange while he was away in Africa!" and this struck Rupert as so grotesque that he apparently laughed.

Amid this social intercourse, however, he avoided sedulously a meeting with Mrs. Annice; he had decided not to see her for a while. Indeed, it was not till an evening late in February, after dinner, that he took a cab to her house near Washington Square. He found her at home, and had not waited a minute before she came into the room. She was a tall woman, and wonderfully handsome by gaslight; but she had that tiresome habit, which many women have, of talking intensely—in *italics*, as it were: a habit found generally in women ill brought up—women without control of their feelings, or command of the expression of them.

"My dear, dear Rupert, how glad I am to see you," she exclaimed, throwing a white fluffy cloak off her bare shoulders, and holding out both hands as she glided towards him. "It is so long, that I really thought we were never going to see you again. But I am *so* glad. And how very fortunate that legacy was for you—just when I suppose you were working fearfully hard. I was quite delighted when I heard of it, and my husband too. He would have been so pleased to have seen you, but he is dining out tonight."

There was a tone of too much hypocrisy about all this, and Rupert made full allowance for it. He chatted in his easy way about his good fortune, and recited some details.

"I suppose there is not the slightest possibility of a flaw in the will?" says Mrs. Annice, regarding him keenly. The lines round her mouth had become hard, but she kept on smiling: she had some traits like Macbeth's wife.

Orange laughed his bright, merry laugh which so few could resist. "Oh no, I think it's all right this time!" he said, and looked at her steadfastly with his fine eyes.

Mrs. Annice suddenly flushed, and then shuddered. Her heart began to throb, her head to whirl. What was the matter with her? What was this cursed sensation which was mastering her? She, with her self-poise, her deliberateness, her calculation, was, in the flash of an eye, brought to feel towards this man, whom but a moment ago she had hated more than anyone in the world, as she had never felt towards man before.

It was not love, this wretched thraldom, it was not even admiration; it was a wild desire to abnegate herself, annihilate herself, in this man's personality; to become his bond-woman, the slave of his controlling will. She drove the nails into her palms, and crushed her lips between her teeth, as she rose to her feet and made one desperate try for victory.

"I was just going to the opera when you came in, Rupert," she said; "won't you come in my box?"—and her voice had so changed, there was such a note of tenderness and desire in it, that it seemed as if she had exposed her soul. But even in her disorganised state she was conscious that there would be a certain distinction in appearing at the opera with the re-edified Rupert Orange.

Rupert murmured something about the opera being such a bore, and at that moment the footman announced the carriage.

"Won't you come?" asked Mrs. Annice, standing with her white hand resting on the back of a chair.

"I think not," answered Rupert, with a smile.

She dismissed the carriage. As soon as the servant had gone, she tried to make some trivial remark, and, half turning, looked at Orange, who rose. For an instant those two stood gazing into each other's eyes with God knows what hell in their hearts, and then, with a little cry, that was half a sob, she flung her arms about his neck, and pressed her kisses on his lips.

3

Yesterday afternoon I took from amongst my books a novel of Rupert Orange, and as I turned over the leaves, I fell to pondering how difficult it is to obtain any of his works today, while but a few years ago all the world was reading them; and to lose myself in amaze at our former rapturous and enthusiastic admiration of his literary art, his wit, his pathos. For in truth his art is a very tawdry art to my present liking; his wit is rather stale, his pathos a little vulgar. And the charm has likewise gone out of his poetry: even his *Chaunt of the Storm-Witch*, which we were used to think so melodious and sonorous, now fails to please.

To explain the precise effect which his poetry has upon me now, I am forced to resort to a somewhat unhappy figure; I am forced to say that his poetry has an effect on me like *sifted ashes*! I cannot in the least explain this figure; and if it fail to convey any idea to the reader,

I am afraid the failure must be set down to my clumsy writing. And yet what praise we all bestowed on these works of Rupert Orange! How eagerly we watched for them to appear; how we prized them; with what zeal we studied the newspapers for details of his interesting and successful life!

A particular account of that brilliant and successful life it would ill become me to chronicle, even if I were so minded: it was with no purpose of relating his social and literary triumphs, his continual victories during five years in the two fields he had chosen to conquer, that I started to write. But in dwelling on his life, we must not forget to take account of these triumphs. They were very rare, very proud, very precious triumphs, both in Europe and in the United States; triumphs that few men ever enjoy; triumphs which were potent enough to deaden the pallid thought of the curious limits of his life, except on three sombre occasions.

It was on the first night of a new opera at Covent Garden. Orange was in a box with a notable company, and was on the point of leaning over to whisper something amusing to the beautiful Countess of Heston, when of a sudden he shot white, and the smile left his face as if he had received a blow. On the stage a chorus had commenced in a very low tone of passionate entreaty; by degrees it swelled louder and louder, till it burst forth into a tremendous agonized prayer for pity and pardon. As Orange listened, such a dreary sense of the littleness of life, such an awful fear of death, sang through his brain, that he grew sick, and shivered in a cold sweat.

"Why, I'm afraid Mr. Orange is ill!" exclaimed the countess.

"No, no!" muttered Orange, groping for his hat. "Only a little faint; want some air!—I tell you I want some air!" he broke out in a voice that was like a frightened cry, as he fumbled with the door of the box.

A certain man with a kind heart followed him into the *foyer*.

"Can I do anything for you, old chap?"

"Yes; in the name of God leave me alone!" replied Orange; and he said it in such a tone, and with a face so frightfully contorted, that those standing about fell back feeling queer, and the questioner returned to the box very gravely, and thought on his soul for the rest of the evening.

But Orange rushed out, and he hailed a hansom, and he drove till the cabman refused to drive anymore; and then he walked; and it was not till he found himself on Putney Heath in his evening dress, at half-past twelve the next day, that the devil left him. About two years after this occurrence, he was wandering one Sunday evening in Chelsea, and hearing a church bell ring for the usual service, he decided to enter. As he sat waiting, a little girl of four or five, with her mother, came in and sat by him: and Rupert talked to the child in his quaint, winning way, and so won her, that when the service began, she continued to cling to his hand.

After a while the sermon commenced, and the preacher, taking for his text the words; "*And he died*" from the fifth chapter of Genesis, tried to set forth the suddenness and unwelcomeness of death, even to the long-lived patriarchs, and its increased suddenness and unwelcomeness to most of us. The sermon I suppose, was dull and commonplace enough, but if the speaker had verily seen into the mind of one of his listeners, the effect could not have been more disastrous.

Orange waited till the torture became unbearable, till he could actually feel the horrid, stifling weight of earth pressing him down in his coffin, and keeping him there for ages and ages: then with a heavy groan he started up, and rushed forth with such vehemence, that he knocked down and trampled on the little girl, in his haste to get out of sight of the white faces of people scared at his face, and the child's sad cry was borne to him out in the dark street. The third occasion on which this sense of despair and loss oppressed him, was at a time when he was near a rugged coast. One stormy day he rode to a certain promontory, and came suddenly in sight of the great sea.

As he stood watching a lonely gull, that strained, and swooped, and dipped in the surge, while the rain drizzled, and the wind whined through the long grass, the futility of his life stung him, and he hid his face in his horse's mane and wept.

But sorest of all was the thought that he might really have won a certain fame, an easy fortune, without taking on his back the fardel which, as the months went by, became so heavy. He knew that he had done some work which would have surely gained him distinction, had he but waited. Why did you not have patience? his outraged spirit and maimed life seemed to moan; a little more patience!

I must not let you think, however, that he was unhappy. In every detail the promise of the old man was punctiliously carried out. The very maladies which Orange had desired, were twisted to his advantage. Thus, when he was laid up with a sprained ankle at an hotel at Aix-les-Bains, he formed his notorious connection with Gabrielle de Volnay. It was when he was kept for a day in the house by a cold that he wrote his little comedy, *Her Ladyship's Dinner*—a comedy which, at one time, we were all so forward to praise.

And on the night upon which his cab was overturned in the Sixth Avenue, New York, and he was badly cut about the head, did he not recognise in the drunken prostitute who cursed him, the erewhile brilliant Mrs. Annice? Did he not forget his pain in the exquisite knowledge that her curses were of no avail, and flout her jeeringly, brutally? Nay! when an epidemic disease broke out in a certain part of the Riviera, and the foreign population presently fled, he used his immunity from death to hold his ground and tend the sick, and so gave cause to the newspapers to proclaim the courage and devotion of Mr. Orange. And all these fortunate incidents were suddenly brought to completeness by one singular event.

It was on a winter morning, about three o'clock, that he found himself in the district of Kilburn, and noticed a crimson stain on the sky. More from indolence than from anything else he went towards the fire; but when he came in sight of it, he was startled by a somewhat strange thing. For there at a window high up in the blazing house, stood a woman with a baby in her arms, who had clearly been left to a hideous fate on account of the fierceness of the flames. With an abrupt gesture Orange flung off his cloak,

"Where can I find the chief?" he asked a man standing near, "because I'm going up!"

The fellow turned, and seeing Rupert in his evening suit, laughed derisively.

"I say, Bill!" he sings out to his mate, "this 'ere bloke says as 'ow he's goin' up!" and the other's scoffing reply struck Rupert's ears as he pushed through the crowd.

By a letter which he carried with him, or some such authority, Orange gained his request; and the next thing that the people saw was a ladder rigged, and the figure of a man ascending through clouds of smoke. Higher and higher he went, while the flames licked and sizzled around him and seared his flesh: higher and higher till he had almost reached the window, and a wild cheer burst from the crowd for such a deed of heroism. But at that moment a long tongue of flame leaped into the sky, the building tottered and then crashed down, and Orange was safely caught by some strong arms, while the woman and child met death within the ruins. Of course this affair was noised abroad the next day; and for some weeks Orange, with his hand in a sling, was a picturesque figure in several London drawing-rooms.

Now, which one of us shall say that Orange, with the tested knowledge of his exemption from death, and strong in that knowledge, deliberately did this heroic act to improve his fame, to exalt his honour? I have stated before that we must be cautious in passing judgment on him, and I must again insist on this caution. As for myself, I should be sorry to think that there is no beautiful, merciful, Spirit to note an unselfish impulse, which took no thought of glory or advertisement, and count it to the man for honesty.

But the time ran, and the years sped, until was come the last month of that fifth year, which meant the end of years for Orange. When in the days of his happiness and strength, he had dwelt on this time at all, he had planned to seek out, on the last day of the year, some mountain crag in Switzerland, and there meet death, coming in the train of the rising sun, with calm and steady eyes.

Alas! now to his anguish he felt a desire, which was stronger than his will, tearing at his heart to visit once more the scene of his hardships, to look again on the place where his bargain was concluded. I make certain, from a letter of his which I have seen, that in taking passage for New York, Rupert had no idea of turning aside his doom. The *Cambria*, on which he sailed, was due to arrive at New York a full week before the end of the year; but she encountered baffling winds and seas, and it was not till the evening of the thirty-first of December that she sighted the light on Fire Island.

As the steamer went at speed towards Sandy Hook, Orange stood alone on the deck, watching the smoke from her funnel rolling seaward: of a sudden he saw rise out of the cloud, the presentment, grim and menacing, of God the Father.

4

As the *Cambria* moved up towards the city, on the morning of New Year's day, a certain frenzy which was half insane, and a fierce loathing of familiar sights—Castle Garden, the spire of Trinity Church—took hold of Orange. He passionately cursed himself for not staying in Europe; he cursed the hour he was born; he cursed, above all! the hour in which he had made that fatal bargain. As soon as the vessel was made fast to the dock, he hastened ashore; and leaving his servant to look after his luggage, he sprang into a *hack*, and directed the driver to go "up town."

"Where to, boss?" inquired the man, looking at him curiously.

"The Hoffman House," replied Orange, before he thought. Then he cursed himself again, but he did not change the order.

I have said that the driver looked at Orange curiously; and in truth he was a strange sight. All the dignity of his demeanour was gone: his eyes were bloodshot, and his complexion a dirty yellow: he was unshorn, his tie was loose, and his collar open. His terror grew as he passed along the well-known streets: he screamed out hateful, obscene things, rolling about in the vehicle, while foam came from his mouth; and as he arrived at the hotel, in his distraction he drove his hand through the window glass, which cut him into the bone.

"An accident," he panted hoarsely to the porter who opened the door: "a slight accident! God damn you!" he yelled, "can't you see it was an accident?" and he went up the hall to the office, leaving behind him a trail of blood. The clerk at the desk, seeing his disorder, was on the point of refusing him a room; but when Orange wrote his name in the visitor's book, he smirked, and ordered the best set of apartments in the house to be made ready. To these apartments Orange retired, and sat all day in a sort of dull horror. For a sudden death he had in a measure prepared himself: he had made his bargain, he had bought his freedom from the cares which are the burthen of all men, and he knew that he must pay the debt: but for some uncertain, treacherous calamity he had not prepared.

He was not fool enough to dream that the one to whom the debt was owed would relent; but before his creditor's method of exacting payment, he was at a stand. He thought and thought, rubbing his face in his hands, till his head was near bursting: in a sudden spasm he fell off the chair to the floor; and that night he was lying stricken by typhoid fever.

And for weeks he lay with a fiery forehead and lazing eyes, finding the lightest covering too heavy and ice too hot. Even when the known disease seemed to have been subdued; certain strange complications arose which puzzled the physicians: amongst these a painful vomiting which racked the man's frame and left an exhaustion akin to death, and a curious loathly decay of the flesh. This last was so venomous an evil, that one of the nurses having touched the sick man in her ministrations, and neglected to immediately purify herself, within a few hours incontinently deceased.

After a while, to assist these enemies of Orange, there came pneumonia. It would seem as though he were experiencing all the maladies from which he had been free during the past five years; for besides his corporal ills he had become lunatic, and he was raving. Those who tended him, used as they were to outrageous scenes, shuddered and held each other's hands when they heard him shriek his curses, and realised his abject fear of death. At times, too, they would hear him weeping softly, and whispering the broken little prayers he had learned in childhood: praying God to save him in this dark hour from the wiles of the devil.

At length, one evening towards the end of March, the mental clearness of Orange somewhat revived, and he felt himself compelled to get up and put on his clothes. The nurse, thinking that the patient was resting quietly, and fearing the shine of the lamp might distress him, had turned it low and gone away for a little: so, it was without interruption, although reeling from giddiness, and scorched with fever, that Rupert groped about till he found some garments, and his evening suit. Clad in these, and throwing a cloak over his shoulders, he went downstairs. Those whom he met, that recognised him, looked at him wonderingly and with a vague dread; but he appeared to have his understanding as well as they, and so he passed through the hall without being stopped; and going into the bar, he called for brandy.

The bar-tender, to whom he was known, exclaimed in astonishment; but he got no reply from Orange, who, pouring himself out a large quantity of the fiery liquor, found it colder than the coldest iced water in his burning frame. When he had taken the brandy, he went into the street. It was a bleak seasonable night, and a bitter frost-rain was falling: but Orange went through it, as if the bitter weather was a not unwelcome coolness, although he shuddered in an ague-fit. As he stood on the corner of Twenty-Third Street, his cloak thrown open, the sleet sowing down on his shirt, and the slush which covered his ankles soaking through his thin shoes, a member of his club came by and spoke to him.

"Why, good God! Orange, you don't mean to say you're out on a night like this! You must be much better—eh?" he broke off, for Orange had given him a grey look, with eyes in which there was no speculation; and the man hurried away scared and rather aghast. "These poet chaps are always queer fishes," he muttered uneasily, as he turned into the Fifth Avenue Hotel.

Of the events of terror and horror which happened on that awful night, when a human soul was paying the price of an astounding violation of the order of the universe, no man shall ever tell. Blurred, hideous, and enormous visions of *dives*, of hells where the worst scum of the town consorted, of a man who spat on him, of a woman who struck him across the face with her umbrella, calling him the foulest of names—visions such as these, and more hateful than these, presented themselves to Orange, when he found himself, at three o'clock in the morning, standing under a lamp-post in that strange district of New York called "The Village,"

The rain had given way to a steady fall of snow: and as he stood there, a squalid harlot, an outcast amongst outcasts, approached, and solicited him in the usual manner.

"Come along—do!" she said, shivering: "We can get a drink at my place."

Receiving no answer, she peered into his face, and gave a cry of loathing and fear.

"Oh, look here!" she said, roughly, coughing down her disgust: "You've been drinking too much, and you've got a load. Come ahead with me and you can have a good sleep."

At that word Orange turned, and gazed at her with a vacant, dreary, silly smile. He raised his hand, and when she shrank away—"Are you afraid of me?" he said, not coarsely, but quietly, even gently, like a man talking in his sleep. Then they went on together, till they came to a dilapidated house close by the river. They entered, and turned into a dirty room lit by a flaring jet of gas.

"Now, dear; let's have some money," says the woman, "and I'll get you a nice drink."

Still no answer from Orange: only that same vacant smile, which was beginning to be horrible.

"Give me some money: do you hear!" cried the woman, stridently. Then she seized him, and went through his pockets in an accustomed style, and found three cents.

"What the hell do you mean by coming here with only this!" bellowed the woman, holding out the mean coins to Orange. She struck him; but she was very frightened, and went to the stairs.

"Say! Tom—Tommy," she called; "you'd better come down and put this loafer out!"

A great hulking man came down the stairs, and gazed for an instant at Rupert—standing under the gas-jet, with the woman plucking the studs from his shirt. For an instant the man stood, feeling sick and in a sweat; and then, by a great effort, he approached Orange, and seized him by the collar.

"Here, out you go!" he said. "We don't want none of your sort around here! "The man dragged Orange to the street door, and gave the wretch such a powerful shove, that he fell on the pavement, and rolled into the gutter.

And later in the morning, one who passed by the way found him there: dead before the squalid harlot's door.

The Business of Madame Jahn

How we all stared, how frightened we all were, how we passed opinions, on that morning when Gustave Herbout was found swinging by the neck from the ceiling of his bedroom! The whole *Faubourg*, even the ancient folk who had not felt a street under them for years, turned out and stood gaping at the house with amazement and loud conjecture. For why should Gustave Herbout, of all men, take to the rope? Only last week he had inherited all the money of his aunt, Madame Jahn, together with her house and the shop with the five assistants, and life looked fair enough for him. No; clearly it was not wise of Gustave to hang himself!

Besides, his aunt's death had happened at a time when Gustave was in sore straits for money. To be sure, he had his salary from the bank in which he worked; but what is a mere salary to one who (like Gustave) threw off the clerkly habit when working hours were over, to assume the dress and lounge of the accustomed *boulevardier*: while he would relate to obsequious friends vague but satisfactory stories of a Russian prince who was his uncle, and of an extremely rich English lady to whose death he looked forward with hope.

Alas! with a clerk's salary one cannot make much of a figure in Paris. It took all of that, and more, to maintain the renown he had gained amongst his acquaintance of having to his own a certain little lady with yellow hair, who danced divinely. So, he was forced to depend on the presents which Madame Jahn gave him from to time to time; and for those presents he had to pay his aunt a most sedulous and irksome attention. At times, when he was almost sick from his craving for the *boulevard*, the *café*, the theatre, he would have to repair, as the day grew to an end, to our *Faubourg*, and the house behind the shop, where he would sit to an old-fashioned supper with his aunt, and listen with a sort of dull impatience while she asked him when he had last been at Confession, and told him long, dreary stories of his dead father and mother.

Punctually at nine o'clock the deaf servant, who was the only person besides Madame Jahn that lived in the house, would let in the fat old priest, who came for his game of dominoes, and betake herself to bed. Then the dominoes would begin, and with them the old man's prattle, which Gustave knew so well: about his daily work, about the uselessness of all things here on earth, and the happiness and glory of the Kingdom of Heaven: and, of course, our *boulevardier* noticed, with the usual cheap sneer of the modern, that whilst the priest talked of the Kingdom of Heaven, he yet shewed the greatest anxiety if he had symptoms of a cold, or any other petty malady. However, Gustave would sit there, with a hypocrite's grin and inwardly raging, till the clock chimed eleven.

At that hour Madame Jahn would rise, and, if she was pleased with her nephew, would go over to her writing-desk and give him, with a rather pretty air of concealment from the priest, perhaps fifty or a hundred *francs*. Whereupon Gustave would bid her a manifestly affectionate goodnight! and depart in the company of the priest. As soon as he could get rid of the priest, he would hasten to his favourite *cafés*, to discover that all the people worth seeing had long since grown tired of waiting, and had departed on their own affairs. The money, indeed, was a kind of consolation; but then there were nights when he did not get a *sou*. Ah! they amuse themselves in Paris, but not in this way—this is not amusing.

One cannot live a proper life upon a salary, and an occasional gift of fifty or a hundred *francs*. And it is not entertaining to tell men that your uncle, the Prince at Moscow, is in sorry case, and even now lies a-dying, or that the rich English lady is in the grip of a vile consumption and is momently expected to succumb, if these men only shove up their shoulders, wink at one another, and continue to present their bills. Further, the little *Mademoiselle*, with yellow hair, had lately shewn signs of a very pretty temper, because her usual flowers and *bon-bons* were not apparent.

So, since things were come to this dismal pass, Gustave fell to attending the race-meetings at Chantilly, During the first week Gustave won largely for that is sometimes the way with ignorant men: during that week, too, the little *Mademoiselle* was charming, for she had her *bouquets* and boxes of *bon-bons*. But the next week Gustave lost heavily, for that is also very often the way with ignorant men: and he was thrown into the blackest despair, when one night at a place where he was used to sup, *Mademoiselle* took the arm of a great fellow, whom he much suspected to be a German, and tossed him a little scornful nod, as she went off.

On the evening after this had happened, he was standing, between five and six o'clock, in the *Place de la Madeleine*, blowing on his fingers and trying to plan his next move, when he heard his name called by a familiar voice, and turned to face his aunt's adviser, the priest.

"Ah! Gustave, my friend, I have just been to see a colleague of mine here!" cried the old man, pointing to the great church. "And are you going to your good aunt tonight?" he added, with a look at Gustave's neat dress.

Gustave was in a flame that the priest should have detected him in his gay clothes, for he always made a point of appearing at Madame Jahn's clad staidly in black; but he answered pleasantly enough.

"No, my Father, I'm afraid I can't tonight. You see I'm a little behind with my office-work, and I have to stay at home and catch up.

"Well! well!" said the priest, with half a sigh, "I suppose young men will always be the same, I myself can only be with her till nine o'clock tonight, because I must see a sick parishioner. But let me give you one bit of advice, my friend," he went on, taking hold of a button on Gustave's coat: "don't neglect your aunt; for, mark my words, one day everything of Madame Jahn's will be yours!" And the omnibus he was waiting for happening to swing by at that moment, he departed without another word.

Gustave strolled along the *Boulevard des Capucines* in a study. Yes; it was certain that the house, and the shop with the five assistants, would one day be his; for the priest knew all his aunt's affairs. But how soon would they be his? Madame Jahn was now hardly sixty; her mother had lived to be ninety; when she was ninety, he would be—. And meanwhile, what about the numerous bills; what (above all!) about the little lady with yellow hair? He paused and struck his heel on the pavement with such force, that two men passing nudged one another and smiled. Then he made certain purchases, and set about wasting time till nine o'clock.

It is curious to consider, that although when he started out at nine o'clock, Gustave was perfectly clear as to what he meant to do, yet he was chiefly troubled by the fear that the priest had told his aunt about his fine clothes. But when he had passed through the deserted Faubourg, and had come to the house behind the shop, he found his aunt only very pleased to see him, and a little surprised. So, he sat with her, and listened to her gentle, homely stories, and told lies about himself and his manner of life, till the clock struck eleven. Then he rose, and Madame Jahn rose too, and went to her writing-desk and opened a small drawer.

"You have been very kind to a lonely old woman tonight, my Gustave," said Madame Jahn, smiling.

"How sweet of you to say that, dearest aunt!" replied Gustave. He went over and passed his arm caressingly across her shoulders, and stabbed her in the heart.

For a full five minutes after the murder, he stood still; as men often do in a great crisis when they know that any movement means decisive action. Then he started, laid hold of his hat, and made for the door. But there the stinging knowledge of his crime came to him for the first time; and he turned back into the room. Madame Jahn's bedroom candle was on a table: he lit it, and passed through a door which led from the house into the shop. Crouching below the counters covered with white sheets, lest a streak of light on the windows might attract the observation of some passenger, he proceeded to a side entrance to the shop, unbarred and unlocked the door, and put the key in his pocket.

Then, in the same crouching way, he returned to the room, and started to ransack the small drawer. The notes he scattered about the floor; but two small bags of coin went into his coat. Then he took the candle and dropped some wax on the face and hands and dress of the corpse; he spilt wax, too, over the carpet, and then he broke the candle and ground it under his foot. He even tore with long nervous fingers at the dead woman's bodice till her breasts lay exposed; and plucked out a handful of her hair and threw it on the floor to stick to the wax.

When all these things had been accomplished, he went to the house door and listened. The *Faubourg* is always very quiet about twelve o'clock, and a single footstep falls on the night with a great sound. He could not hear the least noise: so, he darted out and ran lightly till he came to a turning. There he fell into a sauntering walk, lit a cigarette, and hailing a passing *fiacre*, directed the man to drive to the *Pont Saint-Michel*. At the bridge he alighted, and noting that he was not eyed, he threw the key of the shop into the river. Then assuming the swagger and assurance of a half-drunken man, he marched up the *Boulevard* and entered the *Café d'Harcourt*.

The place was filled with the usual crowd of men and women of the *Quartier Latin*. Gustave looked round, and observing a young student with a flushed face who was talking eagerly about the rights of man, he sat down by him. It was his part to act quickly: so, before the student had quite finished a sentence for his ear, the murderer gave him the lie. The student, however, was not so ready for a fight as Gustave had supposed; and when he began to argue again, Gustave seized a glass full of brandy and water and threw the stuff in his face. Then indeed there was a row, till the *gendarmes* interfered, and haled Gustave to the station.

At the police-station he bitterly lamented his misdeed, which he attributed to an extra glass of absinthe, and he begged the authorities to carry word of his plight to his good aunt, Madame Jahn, in our *Faubourg*. So, to the house behind the shop they went, and there they found her—sitting with her breasts hanging out, her poor head clotted with blood, and a knife in her heart.

The next morning, Gustave was set free. A man and a woman, two of the five assistants in the shop, had been charged with the murder. The woman had been severely reprimanded by Madame Jahn on the day before, and the man was known to be the girl's *paramour*. It was the duty of the man to close at night all the entrances into the shop, save the main entrance, which was closed by Madame Jahn and her deaf servant: and the police had formed a theory (worked out with the amazing zeal and skill which cause the Paris police so often to overreach themselves!) that the man had failed to bolt one of the side doors, and had, by subtilty, got possession of the key, whereby he and his accomplice re-entered the place about midnight.

Working on this theory, the police had woven a web round the two unfortunates with threads of steel; and there was little doubt, that both of them would stretch their necks under the guillotine, with full consent of press and public. At least, this was Gustave's opinion; and Gustave's opinion now went for a great deal in the *Faubourg*. Of course, there were a few who murmured, that it was a good thing poor Madame Jahn had not lived to see her nephew arrested for a drunken brawler; but with full remembrance of who owned the house and shop, we were most of us inclined to say, after the priest: That if the brave Gustave had been with his aunt, the shocking affair could never have occurred.

And, indeed, what had we more inspiring than the inconsolable grief he shewed? Why! on the day of the funeral, when he heard the earth clatter down on the coffin-lid in *Père la Chaise*, he even swooned to the ground, and had to be carried out of the midst of the mourners.

"Oh, yes, (quoth the gossips), Gustave Herbout loved his aunt passing well!"

On the night after the funeral, Gustave was sitting alone before the fire in Madame Jahn's room, smoking and making his plans. He thought, that when all this wretched mock grief and pretence of decorum was over, he would again visit the *cafés* which he greatly savoured, and the little *Mademoiselle* with yellow hair would once more smile on him delicious smiles, with a gleaming regard. Thus, he was thinking when the clock on the mantel-piece tinkled eleven; and at that moment a very singular thing happened.

The door was suddenly opened: a girl came in, walked straight over to the writing-desk, pulled out the small drawer, and then sat staring at the man by the fire. She was distinctly beautiful; although there was a certain old-fashionedness in her peculiar silken dress, and the manner of wearing her hair. Not once did it occur to Gustave, as he gazed in terror, that he was gazing on a mortal woman: the doors were too well bolted to allow any one from outside to enter, and besides, there was a strange baffling familiarity in the face and mien of the intruder.

It might have been an hour that he sat there; and then, the silence becoming too horrible, by a supreme effort of his wonderful courage he rushed out of the room and upstairs to get his hat. There in his murdered aunt's bedroom—there, smiling at him from the wall—was a vivid presentment of the dread vision that sat below: a portrait of Madame Jahn as a young girl. He fled into the street, and walked, perhaps two miles, before he thought at all. But when he did think, he found that he was drawn against his will back to the house to see if *it* was still there: just as the police here believe a murderer is drawn to the *Morgue* to view the body of his victim. Yes; the girl was there still, with her great reproachless eyes; and throughout that solemn night Gustave, haggard and mute, sat glaring at her. Towards dawn he fell into an uneasy doze; and when he awoke with a scream, he found that the girl was gone.

At noon the next day, Gustave, heartened by several glasses of brandy, and cheered by the sunshine in the *Champs-Elysées*, endeavoured to make light of the affair. He would gladly have arranged not to go back to the house: but then people would talk so much, and he could not afford to lose any custom out of the shop. Moreover, the whole matter was only an hallucination— the effect of jaded nerves. He dined well, and went to see a musical comedy; and so contrived, that he did not return to the house till after two o'clock.

There was someone waiting for him, sitting at the desk with the small drawer open: not the girl of last night, but a somewhat older woman—and the same reproachless eyes. So great was the fascination of those eyes, that, although he left the house at once, with an iron resolution not to go back, he found himself drawn under them again, and he sat through that night as he had sat through the night before, sobbing and stupidly glaring.

And all day long he crouched by the fire shuddering; and all the night till eleven o'clock; and then a figure of his aunt came to him again, but always a little older and more withered. And this went on for five days; the figure that sat with him becoming older and older as the days ran, till on the sixth night he gazed through the hours at his aunt as she was on the night, he killed her. On these nights he was used sometimes to start up and make for the street, swearing never to return; but always he would be dragged back to the eyes. The policemen came to know him from these night walks, and people began to notice his bad looks: these could not spring from grief, folk said, and so they thought he was leading a wild life.

On the seventh night there was a delay of about five minutes after the clock had rung eleven, before the door opened. And then—then, merciful God! the body of a woman in grave-clothes came into the room, as if borne by unseen men, and lay in the air across the writing-desk, while the small drawer flew open of its own accord. Yes; there was the shroud of the brown scapular, the prim white cap, the hands folded on the shrunken breast. Grey from slimy horror, Gustave raised himself up, and went over to look for the eyes. When he saw them pressed down with pennies, he reeled back and vomited into the grate. And blind, and sick, and loathing, he stumbled upstairs.

But as he passed by Madame Jahn's bedroom the corpse came out to meet him, with the eyes closed and the pennies pressing them down. Then, at last, reeking and dabbled with sweat, with his tongue lolling out, and the spittle running down his beard, Gustave breathed:—

"Are you alive?"

"No, no!" wailed the *thing*, with a burst of awful weeping; "I have been dead many days."

Master of Fallen Years

Several years ago, I was intimately acquainted with a young man named Augustus Barber. He was employed in a paper-box manufacturer's business in the city of London. I never heard what his father was. His mother was a widow and lived, I think, at Godalming; but of this I am not sure. It is odd enough that I should have forgotten where she lived, for my friend was always talking about her. Sometimes he seemed immensely fond of her; at other times almost to hate her; but whichever it was, he never left her long out of his conversation. I believe the reason I forget is that he talked so much about her that I failed at last to pay attention to what he said.

He was a stocky young man, with light-coloured hair and a pale, rather blotchy complexion. There was nothing at all extraordinary about him on either the material or spiritual side. He had rather a weakness for gaudy ties and socks and jewellery. His manners were a little boisterous; his conversation, altogether personal. He had received some training at a commercial school. He read little else than the newspapers. The only book I ever knew him to read was a novel of Stevenson's, which he said was "too hot for blisters."

Where, then, in this very commonplace young man, were hidden the elements of the extraordinary actions and happenings I am about to relate? Various theories offer; it is hard to decide. Doctors, psychologists whom I have consulted, have given different opinions; but upon one point they have all agreed—that I am not able to supply enough information about his ancestry. And, in fact, I know hardly anything about that.

This is not, either, because he was uncommunicative. As I say, he used to talk a lot about his mother. But he did not really inspire enough interest for anybody to take an interest in his affairs. He was there; he was a pleasant enough fellow; but when he had gone you were finished with him till the next time. If he did not look you up, it would never occur to you to go and see him. And as to what became of him when he was out of sight, or how he lived—all that, somehow, never troubled our heads.

What illustrates this is that when he had a severe illness a few years after I came to know him, so little impression did it make on anyone that I cannot now say, and nobody else seems able to remember, what the nature of the illness was. But I remember that he was very ill indeed; and one day, meeting one of his fellow clerks in Cheapside, he told me that Barber's death was only a question of hours. But he recovered, after being, as I heard, for a long time in a state of lethargy which looked mortal.

It was when he was out again that I—and not only myself but others—noticed for the first time that his character was changing. He had always been a laughing, undecided sort of person; he had a facile laugh for everything; he would meet you and begin laughing before there was anything to laugh at. This was certainly harmless, and he had a deserved reputation for good humour.

But his manners now became subject to strange fluctuations, which were very objectionable while they lasted. He would be overtaken with fits of sullenness in company; at times he was violent. He took to rambling in strange places at night, and more than once he appeared at his office in a very battered condition. It is difficult not to think that he provoked the rows he got into himself. One good thing was that the impulses which drove him to do such actions were violent rather than enduring; in fact, I often thought that if the force and emotion of these bouts ever came to last longer, he would be a very dangerous character. This was not only my opinion; it was the opinion of a number of respectable people who knew him as well as I did.

I recollect that one evening, as three or four of us were coming out of a music hall, Barber offered some freedom to a lady which the gentleman with her—a member of Parliament, I was told—thought fit to resent. He turned fiercely on Barber with his hand raised—and then suddenly grew troubled, stepped back, lost countenance. This could not have been physical fear, for he was a strongly built, handsome man—a giant compared to the insignificant Barber. But Barber was looking at him, and there was something not only in his face, but so to speak, *encompassing* him—I can't well describe it—a sort of abstract right—an uncontrolled power—a command of the issues of life and death, which made one quail.

Everybody standing near felt it; I could see that from their looks.

Only for a moment it lasted, and then the spell was broken—really as if some formidable spectacle had been swept away from before our eyes; and there was Barber, a most ordinary looking young man, quiet and respectable, and so dazed that he scarcely heeded the cuff which the gentleman managed to get in before we could drag our friend off—

It was about this time that he began to show occasionally the strangest interest in questions of art—I mean, strange in him whom we had never known interested in anything of the kind. I am told, however, that this is not so very remarkable, since not a few cases have been observed of men and women, after some shock or illness, developing hitherto unsuspected aptitude for painting or poetry or music. But in such cases the impulse lasts continuously for a year or two, and now and then for life.

With Barber the crisis was just momentary, never lasting more than half an hour, often much less. In the midst of his emphatic and pretentious talk, he would break off suddenly, remain for a minute lost and dreaming, and then, after spying at us suspiciously to see if we had noticed anything strange, he would give an undecided laugh and repeat a joke he had read in some comic paper.

His talk on these art subjects was without sense or connection, so far as I could discover. Sometimes he spoke of painting, but when we put to him the names of famous painters, he had never heard of them, and I don't believe he had ever been in an art gallery in his life. More often he spoke of theatrical matters. Coming back from a theatre, he would sometimes fall to abusing the actors, and show the strongest jealousy, pointing out how the parts should have been played, and claiming roundly that he could have played them better. Of course, there were other times—most times—when he was alike indifferent to plays and players, or summed them up like the rest of us, as just "ripping" or "rotten." It was only when the play had much excited him that he became critical, and at such times none of us seemed willing to dispute with him, though we hardly ever agreed with what he was saying.

Sometimes, too, he would talk of his travels, telling obvious lies, for we all knew well enough that he had never been outside the home counties, except once on a weekend trip to Boulogne-sur-Mer. On one occasion he put me to some confusion and annoyed me considerably before a gentleman whom I had thoughtlessly brought him with me to visit. This gentleman had long resided in Rome as agent for an English hosiery firm, and he and his wife were kindly showing us some photographs, picture post-cards, and the like, when, at the sight of a certain view, Barber bent over the picture and became absorbed.

"I have been there," he said.

The others looked at him with polite curiosity and a little wonder. To pass it off I began to mock.

"No," he persisted, "I have seen it."

"Yes, at the moving-pictures."

But he began to talk rapidly and explain. I could see that the gentleman and his wife were interested and quite puzzled. It would seem that the place he described—Naples, I think it was—resembled broadly the place they knew, but with so many differences of detail as to be almost unrecognisable. It was, as Mrs. W. said afterward, "like a city perceived in a dream—all the topsy-turvydom, all the mingling of fantasy and reality."

After outbursts of this kind, he was generally ill—at least he kept his bed and slept much. As a consequence, he was often away from the office; and whenever I thought of him in those days, I used to wonder how he managed to keep his employment.

One foggy evening in January, about eight o'clock, I happened to be walking with Barber in the West End. We passed before a concert hall, brilliantly lighted, with a great crowd of people gathered about the doors, and I read on a poster that a concert of classical music was forward at which certain renowned artists were to appear. I really cannot give any sort of reason why I took it into my head to go in. I am rather fond of music, even of the kind which requires a distinct intellectual effort; but I was not anxious to hear music that night, and in any case, Barber was about the last man in the world I should have chosen to hear it with. When I proposed that we should take tickets, he strongly objected.

"Just look me over," he said. "I ain't done anything to you that you want to take my life, have I? I know the kind of merry-go-round that goes on in there, and I'm not having any."

I suppose it was his opposition which made me stick to the project, for I could not genuinely have cared very much, and there was nothing to be gained by dragging Barber to a concert against his will. Finally, seeing I was determined, he yielded, though most ungraciously.

"It'll be the chance of a lifetime for an hour's nap," he said as we took our seats, "if they only keep the trombone quiet."

I repeat his trivial sayings to show how little there was about him in manner or speech to prepare me for what followed.

I remember that the first number on the programme was Beethoven's Seventh Symphony. This work, as is well known, is rather long, and so, at the end of the third movement, I turned and looked at Barber to see if he was asleep. But his eyes were wide open, feverish, almost glaring; he was twining and untwining his fingers and muttering excitedly. Throughout the fourth movement he continued to talk incoherently.

"Shut up!" I whispered fiercely. "Just see if you can't keep quiet, or we shall be put out."

I was indeed very much annoyed, and some people nearby were turning in their chairs and frowning.—

I do not know whether he heard what I said: I had no chance to talk to him. The applause had hardly died away at the end of the symphony when a singer appeared on the stage. Who he was, or what music he sang, I am utterly unable to say; but if he is still alive it is impossible that he should have forgotten what I relate. If I do not remember him, it is because all else is swallowed up for me in that extraordinary event.

Scarcely had the orchestra ceased preluding and the singer brought out the first notes of his song, than Barber slowly rose from his seat.

"That man is not an artist," he said in a loud and perfectly final voice, "I will sing myself."

"Sit down, for God's sake!—The management—the police"—

Some words like these I gasped, foreseeing the terrible scandal which would ensue, and I caught him by the arm. But he shook himself free without any difficulty, without even a glance at me, and walked up the aisle and across the front of the house toward the little stairs at the side which led up to the platform. By this time the entire audience was aware that something untoward was happening. There were a few cries of "Sit down! Put him out!" An usher hastened up as Barber was about to mount the steps.

Then a strange thing happened.

As the usher drew near, crying out angrily, I saw Barber turn and look at him. It was not, as I remember, a fixed look or a determined look; it was the kind of untroubled careless glance a man might cast over his shoulder who heard a dog bark. I saw the usher pause, grow pale and shamefaced feel like a servant who has made a mistake; he made a profound bow and then—yes, he actually dropped on his knees. All the people saw that. They saw Barber mount the platform, the musicians cease, the singer and the conductor give way before him. But never a word was said—there was a perfect hush. And yet, so far as my stunned senses would allow me to perceive, the people were not wrathful or even curious; they were just silent and collected as people generally are at some solemn ceremonial. Nobody but me seemed to realize the outrageousness and monstrosity of the vulgar-looking, insignificant Barber there on the platform, holding up the show, stopping the excellent music we had all paid to hear.

And in truth I myself was rapidly falling into the strangest confusion. For a certain time—I cannot quite say how long—I lost my hold on realities. The London concert hall, with its staid, rather sad-looking audience, vanished, and I was in a great white place inundated with sun—some vast luminous scene. Under a wide caressing blue sky, in the dry and limpid atmosphere, the white marble of the buildings and the white-clad people appeared as against a background of an immense blue veil shot with silver. It was the hour just before twilight, that rapid hour when the colours of the air have a supreme brilliance and serenity, and a whole people, impelled by some indisputable social obligation, seemed to be reverently witnessing the performance of one magnificent man of uncontrollable power, of high and solitary grandeur.—

Barber began to sing.

Of what he sang I can give no account. The words seemed to me here and there to be Greek, but I do not know Greek well, and in such words as I thought I recognised, his pronunciation was so different from what I had been taught that I may well have been mistaken.

I was so muddled, and, as it were, transported, that I cannot say even if he sang well. Criticism did not occur to me; he was there singing and we were bound to listen. As I try to hear it, now, it was a carefully trained voice. A sound of harps seemed to accompany the singing; perhaps the harpists in the orchestra touched their instruments.—

How long did it last? I have no idea. But it did not appear long before all began to waver. The spell began to break; the power by which he was compelling us to listen to him was giving out. It was exactly as if something, a mantle or the like, was falling from Barber.

The absurdity of the whole thing began to dawn on me. There was Barber, an obscure little Londoner, daring to interrupt a great musical performance so that the audience might listen to him instead! Probably because I was the only one on the spot personally acquainted with Barber, I was perceiving the trick put upon us sooner than the rest of the audience; but they, too, were becoming a little restless, and it would not be long ere they fully awoke. One thing I saw with perfect clearness and some terror, and that was that Barber himself realized that his power was dying within him. He appeared to be dwindling, shrinking down; in his eyes were suffering and a terrible panic—the distress of a beaten man appealing for mercy. The catastrophe must fall in a minute—

With some difficulty I rose from my place and made for the nearest exit. My difficulty came, not from the crowd or anything like that, but from an inexplicable sensation that I was committing some crime by stirring while Barber was on the stage, and even risking my life.

Outside it was raining.

I walked away rapidly, for although I was, to a certain extent, under the influence of the impression I have just described, some remains of common sense urged me to put a long distance between myself and the concert hall as soon as possible. I knew that the hoots and yells of fury and derision had already broken loose back there. Perhaps Barber would be taken to the police station. I did not want to be mixed up in the affair—

But suddenly I heard the steps of one running behind me. As I say, it was a wet night, and at that hour the street was pretty empty. Barber ran up against me and caught my arm. He was panting and trembling violently.

"You fool!" I cried furiously. "Oh, you fool!" I shook myself free of his hold. "How did you get out?"

"I don't know," he panted. "They let me go—that is, as soon as I saw that I was standing up there before them all, I jumped off the stage and bolted. Whatever made me do it? My God, what made me do it? I heard a shout. I think they are after me."

I hailed a passing cab and shoved Barber inside, and then got in myself. I gave the cabman a fictitious address in Kensington.

"Yes," I said fiercely. "What made you do it?"

He was bunched in a corner of the cab, shuddering like a man who has just had some great shock, or who has been acting under the influence of a drug which has evaporated and left him helpless. His words came in gasps.

"If you can tell me that!—God, I'm frightened! I'm frightened! I must be crazy. Whatever made me do it? If they hear of it at the office, I'll lose my job."

"They'll hear of it right enough, my boy," I sneered, "and a good many other people too. You can't do these little games with impunity."

I caught sight of the clock at Hyde Park corner. It was near a quarter to ten.

"Why," I said, "you must have been up there over twenty minutes. Think of that!"

"Don't be so hard on me," said Barber miserably. "I couldn't help it."

And he added in a low voice: "It was the *Other.*"

I paid off the cab, and we took a 'bus which passed by the street where Barber lived. All the way I continued to reproach him. It was not enough for him to play the fool on his own account, but he must get me into a mess, too. I might lose my work through him.

I walked with him to his door. He looked extremely ill. His hand trembled so badly that he could not fit his latchkey. I opened the door for him.

"Come up and sit with a fellow," he ventured.

"Why?"

"I'm frightened.—"

"I believe," I said roughly, "that you've been drinking—or drugging."

I shoved him inside the house, pulled the door closed, and walked away down the street. I was very angry and disturbed, but I felt also the need to treat Barber with contempt so as to keep myself alive to the fact that he was really a mere nothing, a little scum on the surface of London, of no more importance than a piece of paper on the pavement. For—shall I confess it?—I was even yet so much under the emotion of the scene back there in the concert hall that I could not help regarding him still with some mixture of respect and—yes, absurd as it may sound, of fear.

It was nearly a year before I saw Barber again. I heard that he had lost his place at his office. The cashier there, who told me this, said that although the young man was generally docile and a fair worker, he had in the last year become very irregular, and was often quarrelsome and impudent. He added that Barber could now and then influence the management—"when he was not himself," as the cashier put it—or they would not have tolerated him so long.

"But this was only momentary," said the cashier. "He was more often weak and feeble, and they took a good opportunity to get rid of him. He was uncanny," ended the cashier significantly.

I cannot imagine how Barber existed after he lost his place. Perhaps his mother was able to help a little. On the day I met him, by mere chance in the street, he looked sick and miserable; his sallow face was more blotchy than ever. Whether he saw me or not I don't know, but he was certainly making as if to go by when I stopped him. I told him he looked weak and unwell.

"Trust you to pass a cheery remark!" And he continued irritably:

"How can you expect a chap to look well if he has something inside him stronger than himself forcing him to do the silliest things? It *must* wear him out. I never know when it will take me next. I'm here in London looking for a job today, but even if I find one, I'm sure to do some tom-fool thing that will get me the sack."

He passed his hand across his face. "I'd rather not think about it."

I took pity on him, he looked so harassed, and I asked him to come on to a Lyons restaurant with me and have a bit of lunch. As we walked through the streets, we fell in with a great crowd, and then I remembered that some royal visitors were to proceed in great state to the Mansion House. I proposed to Barber that we should go and look at the procession, and he agreed more readily than I expected.

In fact, after a while, the crowd, and the rumour, and stirring of troops as they fell into position, evidently wrought on him to a remarkable degree. He began to talk loud and rather haughtily, to study his gestures; there was infinite superiority and disdain in the looks he cast on the people. He attracted the attention and, I thought, the derision of those close to us, and I became rather ashamed and impatient of those ridiculous airs. Yet I could not help feeling sorry for him. The poor creature evidently suffered from megalomania—that was the only way to account for his pretentious notions of his own importance, seeing that he was just a needy little clerk out of work.—

The place from which we were watching the procession was a corner of Piccadilly Circus. The street lay before our eyes bleached in the sun, wide and empty, looking about three times as large as usual, bordered with a line of soldiers and mounted police, and the black crowd massed behind. In a few minutes the procession of princes would sweep by. There was a hush over all the people.

What followed happened so quickly that I can hardly separate the progressive steps. Barber continued to talk excitedly, but all my attention being on the scene before me, I took no heed of what he said. Neither could I hear him very plainly. But it must have been the ceasing of his voice which made me look around, when I saw he was no longer by my side.

How he managed, at that moment, to get out there I never knew, but suddenly in the broad vacant space, fringed by police and soldiery, I saw Barber walking alone in the sight of all the people.

I was thunderstruck. What a madman! I expected to hear the crowd roar at him, to see the police ride up and drag him away.

But nobody moved; there was a great stillness; and before I knew it my own feelings blended with the crowd's. It seemed to me that Barber was in his right place there: this mean shabby man, walking solitary, was what we had all come to see. For his passage the street had been cleared, the guards deployed, the houses decked.

It all sounds wild, I know, but the whole scene made so deep an impression on my mind that I am perfectly certain as to what I felt while Barber was walking there. He walked slowly, with no trace of his usual shuffling uncertain gait, but with a balanced cadenced step, and as he turned his head calmly from side to side his face seemed transfigured. It was the face of a genius, an evil genius, unjust and ruthless—a brutal god. I felt, and no doubt everyone in the crowd felt, that between us and that lonely man there was some immense difference and distance of outlook and will and desire.

I could follow his progress for several yards. Then I lost sight of him. Almost immediately afterward I heard a tumult—shouts and uproar—

Then the royal procession swept by.

I said to Mr. G.M., "Whether he was arrested that day, or knocked down by the cavalry and taken to a hospital, I don't know. I have not seen or heard of him till I got that letter on Wednesday."

Mr. G.M., who is now one of the managers of a well-known tobacconist firm, had been in the same office as Barber, and notwithstanding the disparity of age and position, had always shown a kindly interest in him and befriended him when he could. Accordingly, when I received a letter from Barber begging in very lamentable terms to visit him at an address in Kent, I thought it prudent to consult this gentleman before sending any reply. He proposed very amiably that we should meet at Charing Cross Station on the following Saturday afternoon and travel in to Kent together. In the train we discussed Barber's case. I related all I knew of the young man and we compared our observations.

"Certainly," said Mr. G.M., "what you tell me is rather astonishing. But the explanation is simple as far as poor Barber is concerned. You say he has been often ill lately? Naturally, this has affected his brain and spirits. What is a little more difficult to explain is the impression left by his acts on you and other spectators. But the anger you always experienced may have clouded your faculties for the time being. Have you inquired of anybody else who was present on these occasions?"

I replied that I had not. I had shrunk from being identified in any way with Barber. I had to think of my wife and children. I could not afford to lose my post.

"No," rejoined Mr. G.M., "I can quite understand that. I should probably have acted myself as you did. Still, the effect his performances have had on you, and apparently on others, is the strangest element in Barber's case. Otherwise, I don't see that it offers anything inexplicable. You say that Barber acts against his will—against his better judgment. We all do that. All men and women who look back over their lives must perceive the number of things they have done which they had no intention of doing. We obey some secret command; we sail under sealed orders. We pass by without noticing it some tiny fact which, years later, perhaps, influences the rest of our lives. And for all our thinking, we seldom can trace this tiny fact. I myself cannot tell to this day why I did not become a Baptist minister. It seems to me I always intended to do this, but one fine afternoon I found I had ended my first day's work in a house of business.

"Much of our life is unconscious; even the most wide-awake of us pass much of our lives in dreams. Several hours out of every twenty-four we pass in a dream state we cannot help carrying some of those happy or sinister adventures into our waking hours. It is really as much our habit to dream as to be awake. Perhaps we are always dreaming. Haven't you ever for a moment, under some powerful exterior shock, become half-conscious that you should be doing something else from what you are actually doing? But with us this does not last; and as life goes on such intimations become dimmer and dimmer. With subjects like Barber, on the other hand, the intimations become stronger and stronger, till at last they attempt to carry their dreams into action. That is the way I explain this case."

"Perhaps you are right."

The house where Barber was lodging stood high up on the side of a hill. We reached it after a rather breathless climb in the rain. It was a shepherd's cottage, standing quite lonely. Far down below the village could be seen with the smoke above the red roofs.

The woman told us that Barber was in, but she thought he might be asleep. He slept a lot.

"I don't know how he lives," she said. "He pays us scarce anything. We can't keep him much longer."

He was fast asleep, lying back in a chair with his mouth half open, wrapped in a shabby overcoat. He looked very mean; and when he awoke it was only one long wail on his hard luck. He couldn't get any work. People had a prejudice against him; they looked at him askance. He had a great desire for sleep—couldn't somehow keep awake.

"If I could tell you the dreams I have!" he cried fretfully. "Silliest rotten stuff. I try to tell 'em to the woman here or her husband sometimes, but they won't listen. Shouldn't be surprised if they think I'm a bit off. They say I'm always talking to myself. I'm sure I'm not.—I wish I could get out of here. Can't you get me a job?" he asked, turning to Mr. G.M.

"Well, Gus, I'll see. I'll do my best."

"Lummy!" exclaimed Barber excitedly, "you ought to see the things I dream. I can't think where the bloomin' pictures come from. And yet I've seen it all before. I know all those faces. They are not all white. Some are brown like Egyptians, and some are quite black. I've seen them somewhere. Those long terraces and statues and fountains and marble courts, and the blue sky and the sun, and those dancing girls with the nails of their hands and feet stained red, and the boy in whose hair I wipe my fingers, and the slave I struck dead last night—"

His eyes were delirious, terrible to see.

"Ah," he cried hoarsely, "I am stifling here. Let us go into the air."

And indeed, he was changing so much—not essentially in his person, though his face had become broader, intolerant, domineering and cruel—but there was pouring from him so great an emanation of power that it seemed to crack and break down the poor little room. Mr. G.M. and myself had no desire to thwart him, and it never occurred to us to do so. We should as soon have thought of stopping a thunderstorm. We followed him outside on to the space of level ground before the house and listened humbly while he spoke.

As well as I can recollect, he was lamenting some hindrance to his impulses, some flaw in his power. "To have the instincts of the ruler and no slaves to carry out my will. To wish to reward and punish and to be deprived of the means. To be the master of the world, but only in my own breast—Oh, fury! The ploughboy there is happy, for he has no longings outside of his simple round life. While I—if I had the earth in my hand, I should want a star. Misery! Misery!"

He leaned upon a low stonewall and looked down on the town,

over the pastures blurred with rain.

"And those wretches down there," he pronounced slowly, "who jeer at me when I pass and insult me with impunity, whose heads should be struck off, and I cannot strike them off! I loathe that town. How ugly it is! It offends my eyes."

He turned and looked us full in the face and our hearts became as water.

"Burn it," he said.

Then he turned away again and bowed his head in his arms on the wall.

I don't remember anything clearly till a long time afterward, when I found myself walking with Mr. G.M. in the wet night on a deserted road on the outskirts of the town. We were carrying some inflammable things, flax, tar, matches, etc., which we must have purchased.

Mr. G.M. stopped and looked at me. It was exactly like coming out of a fainting fit.

"What are we doing with this gear?" he said in a low voice.

"I don't know."

"Better chuck it over a hedge.—"

We made our way to the station in silence. I was thinking of that desolate figure up there on the hill, leaning over the wall in the dark and the rain.

We caught the last train to London. In the carriage Mr. G.M. began to shiver as though he were cold.

"Brrr! that fellow got on my nerves," he said; and we made no further allusion to the matter.

But as the train, moving slowly, passed a gap which brought us again in sight of the town, we saw a tongue of flame stream into the sky.

The Dancer at the Opera

1

The dancer at the opera
Had the calm eyes and mystic grace
Of grey-clad holy nuns, but ah!
Her soul reflected not her face.

Her soul lay drunken with the vaunts
She tolled, like maddened bee, from lips
That gave her wondrous body chaunts—
White cloud which made her soul's eclipse.

And as one who drinks thirstily
Out of a cold and crystal well,
Is stricken at its depths to see
The slimy poisoned fungus dwell;

So, at rare times the youth who dies
Her sweets with slow kiss to explore,
Sees her soul weep behind her eyes,
Then pass and leave her as before.

2

One night the dancer was elate,
A night when stars made cold their beams,
A monarch was to hear in state
The best of Wagner's music dreams.

Before her mirror she prepared
(The thought just added to her bloom)
To win a triumph no one shared.
Her loveliness filled all the room.

The church-bells spoke the clock at six,
When throughout Paris at the tolls

Folk kneel before the crucifix,
And say "Hail Mary" for their souls

Wrapped in her furs she seeks the stairs,
And then descending gay of heart,
Humming light operatic airs—
Why does she pause and wildly start?

Four men of grave and sombre mien,
Four men in funeral array
Bearing a coffin in between,
Are coming up and bar her way.

Imperiously her questions ring:
"What messenger for you has sped?
For whom do you this coffin bring?
Who in this house is lying dead?

"Answer!"—One hastens to obey:
"We bring this coffin here for a
Mademoiselle who died today:
The dancer at the opera."

"Liars!" She springs from where she stands,
With face of ice and breast in flame,
To drag away the sable bands:
Upon the lid she reads her name.

She gains the street in blinding woe:
Think you she seeks the garish hall
Where the lights vie with gems? —ah no!
She kneels at a confessional.

3

Where the king sits the music sobs
With passion too acute for tears,
Then bursts forth in triumphant throbs
Till the stars tremble in their spheres.

He, listening to the mighty surge
Of sound, hears strangely mingling in
Some wild harp-notes: The devil's dirge
For sinners who have ceased to sin.

Verschoyle's House

—*En, quo discordia cives*
Perduxit miseros! En, quis consevimus agros!

Sir John Holdershaw, living retired in Paris in the year 1689, went one day to the *Comédie*, where was acted a piece by Boursault with which he was much discontented. When he had returned to his lodgings, he wrote in his note-book, after violently censuring the play, what follows:

"In the first act, before I went asleep, there was a part (but 'tis true writ here by "Mons. Borsalte in a vein of fooling) which minded me (though far enough off), and my countryman Mr Amcotts too, of a story told in our country of old Mr, Verschoyle, in King Charles and Oliver Protector's time: And I did promise a gentleman last night I would write it down for him; but what with watchings and silly healths my fingers and head tremble woundily of a morning."

Sometime later he composed his differences with King William's government, and returned to live quietly on his estates. His life in the country seemed to weigh heavily upon him, and it was, as he said:

"To tear myself from my chagrins, and the slow hours, and the thoughts of poisonous devouring rascals who have drawn me in, and now undermine me in the country, that I have undertook to reach down some bright pictures hanging in my mind, which soon must fade otherwise."

Accordingly, he wrote out various pieces concerning the adventures of his life, and also three or four tales he had picked up here and there; among them the one he had been reminded of at Paris. It is chiefly from Sir John's narrative that the ensuing pages have been taken.

1

In the early part of 1645, on a cold dull morning, King Charles, walking slowly, against his wont, in the Christ Church meadow at Oxford, read carefully some papers he had taken out with him. Two gentlemen in attendance, Mr. William Legge of the Bedchamber and a certain lord, loitered a few paces behind. After a while, the king paused, and half turning looked at the lord, who hastened forward.

"Here is a report that concerns your country, my lord", said the king, and he put his finger on a closely written paper.

The nobleman, who was short-sighted, bent over to see better, and then he smiled in spite of himself. "It is old Mr. Verschoyle," he said.

But the king was in no laughing humour. "He is little better than a traitor!" he exclaimed warmly. "Nay, I think him worse. He claims to be loyal and well-affected, and yet, though it appears he has a great estate, he has lent neither money nor any comfort in these troubles, nor shewn any affection to me or my cause save by vain words. He deserves to be disjusticed, and his house beset, I tell you truly, my lord, the carriage of this Mr. Verschoyle and men like him, who will not declare themselves freely, but float up and down with the tide of the war, has given me as much grief as almost any misfortune since this damnable rebellion. Yes, men who act as this man, I tell you, would be glad of my ruin. They go all ways in the world to destroy their king. For what is that they do, but making a common cause, giving countenance, and taking hands with the rotten-hearted villains who go about seducing the honest tenantry of the country from their devotion? — Has this man any excuse? Is he hampered? Has he compounded? The report says not."

"Sir, he is old", answered the nobleman, who was of the Privy Council, and had himself suffered many thousand pounds' loss for the king. "He is all but seventy; some say more. He was at court in the queen's time, and continued there some years after your royal father came into England. I have heard he was much noticed by the Lord Chancellor Bacon, at whose house he pried curiously in crucibles, and alembics, and the arts of nigromancers; searching spells, the philosopher's stone, and the principle of life. He married but a few years ago in his old age the young daughter of Sir Thomas Foulkes, who went to Italy long before our troubles began, and who, returning to England to marry his daughter, died suddenly on the wedding night, having been, as they say, slain by Verschoyle with his wizardries.

"His daughter, a great heiress, had been betrothed from her young age to her cousin Sir Edward Morvan, now or lately with Sir Richard Byron at Newark, and a very true servant of Your Majesty; but her father was so besotted by old Verschoyle's charmings (for it could be nothing else) that she was forced to the old man's bed. Where her fortune now is", continued the lord, seeing that the king listened, "or what enjoyment she has of it, none can say. As for Mr. Verschoyle himself, when I taxed him with his passiveness in regards Your Majesty's service, going to his house myself to that end, he burst forth in a thousand excuses and reasons to shew why he could not further the cause: as that his tenants were sullen and unruly, that he had a great charge of servants for his lady's needs, and was put to it to maintain the tenants in their holdings.

"And in truth, Sir, for these four or five years he has lived in a mean poor way, his family ill-clad, and keeping but two old horses in his stable. Some maintain he has great sums bestowed in the Low Countries, and with merchants at Genoa. In truth", concluded the nobleman, who had his own reasons for wishing that part of the country to remain free of soldiery, "I humbly think that to despatch a troop for the harrying and wasting of his house and lands would do Your Majesty small service—no, not now, nor any time later."

As he listened, the king kept rapping impatiently on the papers he held. "Has he discovered himself?" he now inquired. "Has he ever told out boldly in any company what side he is on in these struggles?"

"Sir", returned the nobleman, with some change in his demeanour, "I have been shewn a little tract which, though he did not put his name, 'tis certain he wrote, and the title was, if I remember right: *Problems necessary to be Determined by All that have or have not taken Part on Either Side in this Unnatural War.*"

At this the king stared for an instant with amazed and angry eyes, and then almost against his will, as it were, smiled out at his attendant. "Yes", pursued that one, smiling now himself, "and the inside was as dark and double-dealing as the title, the writing being so close and folded no man could tell what foot the writer stood upon. Nevertheless, that he has some agreements with the Roundheads I know well, from a sure hand; but (added the speaker with a serious want of tact) he claims to be uxorious and governed by his wife, whose cousins are deeply engaged on that side. —If he were harried and his house fired", said the lord, again reverting to his anxiety, "the cause would be little better off; for if he were killed his tenants would rebel and surely would not pay, and if he escaped, seeing his monies lie abroad, he could doubtless without difficulty, by the strict relations he has maintained in London, obtain a pass from the Parliament to go beyond seas."

"And a good ending too", said the king vehemently; "a most desirable ending, to rid this distracted kingdom of him and all like him. He is worse in my sight than a declared rebel. A strange time", quoth the king somewhat bitterly, "a strange bad time with no blessing on it, when men can fence and argue and try all means to find out how little they can do for their lawful sovereign. When I see", he continued graciously, "what you, My Lord, and other loyal subjects suffer in my cause even here in this town; packed together, living coarse and meanly, with only the sad spectacle of war and sickness; while it consoles and cheers me in these trials, yet it does incense me the more against base wretches even as this man who use cunning and tricks to lie snug at home."

He had, however, notwithstanding his indignation, evidently taken notice of his attendant's hint as to the inexpediency of dragooning Mr. Verschoyle in his house; and he had besides more important affairs to engage him than that gentleman's contumacy. And therefore, it was that after a pause he merely said, with that mixture of melancholy and dignity which was his greatest charm and enabled him to pass grandly through the most galling situations, frequent enough since the war began, wherein circumstances compelled him to forego his most cherished desires—well, perceiving something like that to be the situation now, he deliberately quenched his anger and only said, looking meanwhile afar off vaguely at the bare trees and spectral river, where the morning mist still hung, as if he watched a scene enacting there, —"Whensoever it shall please God", said the king slowly, "to enable me to look upon my friends like a king, they shall thank God for the pains they have spent in my cause." And having said that, he drew forth another paper and fell to talking of a different matter.

But if the king, at the time he was comminating Mr. Verschoyle, had been suddenly transported from Oxford to Mr. Verschoyle's house, his wrath, instead of dropping, must have sensibly increased.

It chanced to be the day that Mr. Verschoyle gathered in his rents; and there were the tenants coming up to the door quietly, and laying on the table in the panelled hall where Mr. Verschoyle himself sat by a rousing fire—not, as you might fancy, just half or a quarter of what they owed, which in those troubled times, when most of the great estates were disorganised, and the tenants froward and demoralised, many landlords would have been glad to get—but, wonderfully enough! the full amount as ever and that without sulks, or murmuring, or making the disturbed state of the country an excuse for their unwillingness to pay.

It is true that these peasants, when they came out from the dark house blinking into the daylight, bore a look of astonishment and relief as though they had just passed safely through a danger, and some of them replaced curious rustic charms and amulets which they had kept in their hands while they were indoors carefully back in their clothes; but their uneasiness was not provoked by parting with a sum of money. On the contrary, they rejoiced that they had got that business over: now they might sleep another year without affliction, or terror of marauding, burning troops, the rumour of whose wild doings elsewhere had reached them vaguely; or worse still! of those witches and devils who come by night in the country places, laying waste the land, tearing the careful thatch from roofs, and leaving in their train strange languors and wasting diseases among the strong men and the cattle, and slowness, palenesses and faintings among the unmarried girls.

The truth is, Mr. Verschoyle's reputation as a wizard pervaded the countryside; to encounter him at night would kill a child in the mother's womb; if he entered your house, it was an omen of the most deadly; to affront him was more than the boldest dared to do. Better to eat grass and bitter herbs, and lie cold at night, than to see old Verschoyle at your door asking for his rent. Had not the daughter of Will Lees, off there in the fen, whose father had withstood the esquire to his face that his thin undrained land yielded not the rent put upon it, from a fine buxom girl fallen suddenly into such a decay and consumption that her flesh took on the colour of blue and her bones rattled; —being vexed with no natural sickness, but undeniably by magical art, as was proved the night she died.

For her mother sitting by her, the girl fell to groaning that one was pulling her out of bed by the feet, and upon the mother asking who was pulling her, says the poor creature: "'Tis Squire Verschoyle who has sat this hour at the foot of the bed." Yes, and when the corpse was borne to the churchyard, and the grave was found to be too short, all were convinced that the wizard had distorted the thin body so that it might not lie easily in its place of burial.

Still, though there were reasonable terrors for every hour under Mr. Verschoyle, there were immense advantages also. It was owing to his magic power, people thought, that there was so little sickness on the land, and that since the war broke out, they had lived unharassed by soldiery. Indeed, so important seemed these advantages to Mr. Verschoyle's tenants, that although they did not love him at all, and trembled in his presence, they would not have exchanged him for any other landlord in England. Little they cared for king or Parliament! In the struggle which was now devastating the country they were not partisans; or rather, owing to their master's skilful training, they were solely partisans of Mr. Verschoyle.

He had already induced in them that temper which later blazed out generally in the South and West, when the peasantry, or "Clubmen" as they were called, banded themselves together to drive both armies impartially from their neighbourhood. This temper which, as we know, was roused in the "Clubmen" by plundering and ruthless exactions, Mr. Verschoyle called up, so to speak, in advance by descriptions of these miseries, and threats, kept purposely vague, of their imminence, and the consequent withdrawal of his protection; so that his tenants were at last determined to chase from their fields the troops of either side.

It was not, however, that they seriously feared invasion: the king no doubt was great, and the Parliament great too, but what were they against the powers of the unseen world? Under the government of those incalculable powers whose weapons their squire, old Mr. Verschoyle, possessed and occasionally brandished, they did, no doubt, live in a perpetual tremor; but that was alleviated after all by the genuine advantages already mentioned. And these advantages, these striking immunities, were certainly solid enough, considering the time, to make people who enjoyed them put up with a great deal, though the causes of them of course were to be looked for elsewhere than the common people imagined.

That the estate had escaped invasion from the contending armies, and demands for free quarters, was largely sheer luck. It lay remote from the theatre of war, one boundary of it being desolate coast; it was not a good country wherein to manoeuvre squadrons; and, perhaps chief of all, there were no fortified or garrisoned houses anywhere near to attract attention. The northern boundary of Mr. Verschoyle's estate touched a tract of land which had belonged to his father-in-law, lately dead, and was now merged in his own; while his only neighbour was Sir Edward Morvan, whose house stood about fifteen miles away to the west.

He was therefore free from local influences and a neighbouring gentry who might from one reason or another have driven him to take action in the war, as happened in other parts of the country where the conflict, during the first years of it at any rate, was greatly embittered by little local provincial jealousies and quarrels, men taking that fair opportunity to pay off old rancours which had been gathering for years before the war, and which had nothing to do with the high matters they were ostensibly fighting for. Furthermore, he was careful even now, but especially a little later on—say, just after Naseby, when affairs took an unmistakable turn against the king, he was careful to pay with scrupulous regularity the monies exacted by assessment from the land.

These seem to be the chief causes why Mr. Verschoyle and his tenants had dwelt hitherto unmolested, and it will be seen he had himself done hardly anything to bring this happy condition about, though of course like many others he had taken the trouble to get Protections both from the king and the Parliament, upon which however he was too shrewd to depend. But on the other hand, that his people had been so little afflicted by that terrible fever and ague which was always lurking in the cottages up and down England, may fairly be put down to his credit.

For a man of that age he took an extraordinary interest in drainage and sanitation, the importance of which he probably understood from the valetudinary Bacon, in whose house he had spent so much time; and when after the death of King James he came into the country for good, he set himself to overhaul the dwelling-houses on his estate— not, it must be confessed, from any genial feeling for the welfare of his tenants, but simply from a scientific concern to have things as they should be.

No; magic had doubtless nothing to do with the unusual prosperity of Mr. Verschoyle and his tenants; and yet as they saw him this day and every day that he took his rents, it is no wonder that the stoutest quailed. The hall where he sat, panelled to the ceiling with black oak, was gloomy enough, and the gloom was thickened by the stained glass which filled the high windows. Watching Mr. Verschoyle as he sat there taking money, none could doubt that he knew his reputation and condescended to the lowest tricks to maintain it. He had never changed from the dress of King James's reign; but his daily costume, all but the deep ruff, was at this moment concealed by a black cloak stained with crimson, cast about his shoulders, while on his head he had placed a kind of mitre scrolled with cabalistic signs.

At the table, covered with large books heavily bound and clasped, was seated near him a one-eyed rascally-looking man, devoted soul and body to Verschoyle, who served as his steward, and might well be taken for his familiar in unholy rites. And as the brief afternoon waned, and the night seemed gradually to advance in veritable wafts of blackness across the chamber, where the fire now glowed redly through the twilight, those who had been late in leaving home and had unwisely tarried till this hour, found something terrific and portentous in those two figures.

Neither spared any shameful mummery to strike terror into the simple peasants who stood before them awestricken. Old Verschoyle would clutch the money they tendered with his huge hands and mumble over it certain charms and spells, and then pass it along to the steward who, while pretending to go through the like indecency, would diligently count the pieces.

Nor did the old man shrink from the poorest antics of the mountebank. It happened, to give one instance, in the course of the afternoon that a man who had brought his wife with him actually ventured to complain, whereupon Mr. Verschoyle, noting that the hall was pretty full and a performance would not be wasted, picked up some grains of a powder he had carefully laid by him, cast them into a glass of water, and spreading his great hands over it as the liquid turned red, cried out in a terrible voice, "Blood, Blood!"—upon which the one-eyed droll with horrible contortions began to drink it. The woman, who was with child, was taken with a trembling fit, and she and her husband passed haggardly away, all present shrinking from those blighted ones.

It would seem as if Nature, foreseeing the part he was to play in his old age, had carefully prepared for him an adequate appearance; every wrinkle on that extraordinary visage seeming to be laid there to produce a duly calculated effect. Towards the end of 1636, upon one of his visits to London, becoming as time went on rarer and rarer, he was seen at some gathering by the painter Van Dyck who, after considering him for a little, holding meanwhile his under lip between his thumb and finger as his manner was when he was taking in a subject, drew near at last, and accosting Mr. Verschoyle with much civility offered to make his portrait.

This portrait still exists in the possession of my worthy friend, Nicolas Ursal, Esquire, of Fraynes, and anyone who examines it carefully can see that Van Dyck welcomed here a genuine subject, coming to him perhaps as a relief amid the endless round of fashionable portraits apt to become insipid in the long run even for a man so enamoured of elegance and the dainty fragile things of life as he was—and painted this one happily, "with his heart", as people say.

With what force and inspiration, with what indescribable *brio*, the great bald skull, the beaked predatory nose, the long beard, beneath which you divine the firm pitiless mouth, even to the old-fashioned vesture of the last reign—yes, with what conviction all these are rendered; leaping out as it were from a picture of which the dominant tone, nevertheless, is sombre.

But what perhaps shews most of all that Van Dyck was interested in this work, is the certainty we have, that instead of falling back, as was his languid, somewhat insolent wont, upon the hired models with well-shaped hands he kept by him to supply delicate hands to his troop of sitters, here he has rendered Mr. Verschoyle's hands just as he found them: thick, broken-nailed, knotty, cruel— "Grand hands of a strangler", said the artist to himself, smiling admiringly, as he painted them in with gusto. Nor are the very height and clumsy massiveness of the model's frame evaded or attenuated to gentler proportions in the picture.

Mr. Verschoyle's conversation, too, Van Dyck must have found a distraction from that of the people he usually dealt with. Verschoyle's coarse abusive wit, his command of vituperation and the large phrase, entertaining as it sometimes was, he shared however with some others; notably with his friend Sir Kenelm Digby. But what was piquant in his character was the conjunction of baseness—an ignoble occupation with the meanest and most sordid things—and a strange idealism, dreamy, yet coldly speculative rather than enthusiastic. In his youth he had been a hard-drinking, hard-fighting, unscrupulous scoundrel.

One of his maxims had been that if you start by refusing to say "By your leave" to the world, the world will end by saying it to you. He had played a thousand pranks: he is said to have accompanied Sir Walter Raleigh on his wild voyage to the Oroonoko. Later, when he was almost middle-aged, he had been entertained, as we have already learned, for some time at Gorhambury; accepted, we may be sure, by the subtle, refining owner of the place, to whom all other gifts save mental ones seemed almost negligible, for some gift, keenly descried, which separated him plainly from the crowd.

But in his studies, pursued untiringly at that beautiful seat, he had felt himself bound to follow the system of learning advocated by his entertainer, which implied a contemptuous intolerance of the fantastical and unnecessary, and a grave impatience of such speculations as by their nature were not susceptible of logical demonstration, excepting only (possibly from other than religious promptings, and perhaps on the whole, less sincerely than he would have it appear) the mysteries of the Christian faith—well, Mr. Verschoyle followed in all that but a certain distance, and had then boldly struck off into a path of his own; devoting himself with passionate intensity to uncertain, godless, ill-reputed studies: the arts of the nigromancer, spells, witchcraft, the nota-tion of omens, alchymical divinings, the transmutation of base metals, the present resurrection of the dead; with curious wayward medita-tions upon the influence the spirits of those we have known in life have after their death for good or ill upon the fortunes of the living.

Even by jealous professional operators he was acknowledged to be at this time the most excellent proficient in England, and perhaps in Europe, for resolving horary questions; and beyond that, he was reported so well versed in the Black Art as to practise the circular way of invoking spirits with a success to which none other could pretend. Neither did his master expressly discourage him in these pur-suits, watched him rather with a kind of bantering scepticism: such studies were mazy and confused, he thought, and ended, it was to be anticipated, nowhere, nor could anyone declare certainly how much of them was verity and how much vanity.

Besides, either from deep policy, or—with that baffling tortuous mind who can tell?—perhaps from genuine piety, he let it be known that he considered "similar" enquiries must be bounded by religion or else they "would be subject to deceit and delusion"; and how far amid these magical labyrinths could one travel without encounter-ing Sathanas himself, and tendering a hand for his powerful yet fatal aid as he prowled there in his congeries? So at least men should be encouraged to think; and all means and figures, even fables and old wives' tales, should be employed to prevent the world from wandering vaguely after high and vaporous imaginations to the manifest injury of a laborious and sober inquiry of truth.

For such imaginations begat hopes and beliefs of strange and im-possible shapes, and therefore (Verschoyle often heard him say it with his fine meaning smile, using almost the very words he had written, as they sat pleasantly at table, where the sweet breath of the flowers came and went through the windows "like the warbling of music")—therefore it was to be noted in those sciences which held so much of imagination and belief as magic, alchemy, astrology, and the like, that in their propositions the description of the means was ever more monstrous than the pretence or end.

And these frivolous experiments, he was wont to add a little scornfully, were as far differing in truth of nature from such a knowledge as we require, as the story of King Arthur of Britain or Hugh of Bordeaux differed from Caesar's *Commentaries* in truth of story.

But furthermore, it was for Mr. Verschoyle and experimenters like him to observe, that however entrancing these occult studies, these dizzying voyages through the uncharted seas of knowledge, harrowed by tempests and lit by ruddy flames—even Hell-fire itself!—beating above, around, what do I say? on the very hands and face of the desperate navigator, whereof one might concede, if you wished, that the gains would be so well worth the hazards once the headlands passed, the haven won—ah yes, however exciting and bewildering these quests which enhanced the discreet enthusiasm of the scholar with something of the passionate intention of the gamester, there were other studies, in effect, so much more real, so much more worthwhile: kingcraft, statecraft, the law even, which had the reputation of being so dry, but which, as people knew, he himself had shewn at various times, and notably in his Charge upon the poisoning of Sir Thomas Overbury, could be rendered on due occasion vivid, flexible, entertaining as a romance.

And had you not the arts (though this appeal Mr. Verschoyle, who was unfamiliar with the fine arts, might not be expected to take in, any more than, coarse and full-feeding himself, he could understand that delicacy of the senses which induced in the Lord Keeper a sickness and faintness if a servant came into his presence shod in neat's leather —but had you not the arts which came pleasantly to the spirits: poetry, the falls of low music in bowers on a moonlit night, sculpture, the cadences of rhetoric? Nor were these mere toys, as men of weak judgment might conceive, but all related among themselves and to the great order of the world. Consider for example the trope of music to avoid or slide from the close or cadence—well, was not that common with the trope of rhetoric? Again; is not the delight (as he wrote so charmingly and truly) of the quavering upon a stop of music, the same with the playing of light upon the water?

By some such reasonings did the illustrious sage endeavour to draw his guest to honourable learning, albeit lightly and intermittently, as one who cared little whether his arguments took effect or no. After all, the broad placid river of learning was fed by innumerable rills, and it might be unwise to divert or dam up even the most apparently turbid.

So too perhaps he had reasoned when he seemed willing to examine seriously the "Sympathetick Powder" of the youthful Kenelm Digby, that wonderful salve which was vouched to heal though a man were bleeding to death at a distance of thirty miles, and consequently made such a heavy demand upon human credulity; —going so far, they say, in his complaisance as a willingness to register the drug among the observations he proposed adding, had he lived, by way of appendix to his Natural History.

And yet the compound itself, both in its constituent parts—moss of a dead man's head, man's grease, and the rest, and in the odd method of utilising it—never touching (as one might anticipate according to the practice of the craftiest chirurgeons) the wound itself with the salve, but dressing and anointing instead each morning the weapon wherewith the wound was given; only laying at the same time upon the wound a linen cloth wet in the patient's urine:—ah, what else could all that be but one of those gross attempts to block and darken true science of which he wrote so sternly:

"The impostor is prized, and the man of virtue taxed. Nay, we see the weakness and credulity of men is such, as they will often prefer a mountebank or witch before a learned physician."

But when the "Powder of Sympathy" was put before the world he was old, and perhaps more tired than he seemed; he had fallen from extraordinary glory and had drunk his full of gall and humiliation; all the powers and honours he had so feverishly struggled and schemed for all his life may now, tardily, have taken on a dun and uncertain look; and noting that, he may have disposed himself to regard all things else with an ironical tolerance. And of that tolerance Mr. Verschoyle, for one, reaped the benefit. This last, for his part, the large, sanguine, sophistical projector, had been taken with a veritable enthusiasm for the "Powder of Sympathy"; and when not long after he made the acquaintance of the man who had promulgated its virtues, he found him congenial and they became friends.

That romantic figure, buccaneer, swashbuckler, duellist, braggart, alchymist, poet, architect, courtier, theologian—what else? who passes to and fro so vividly and gallantly across the stage of the seventeenth century, generally feared, always admired, though never quite respected or trusted—"a teller of things strange", as Evelyn calls him good-humouredly; who constantly vapoured and hectored, but with such an air that men dared not laugh at the one or resent the other; —how could he fail to attract one of Mr. Verschoyle's nature and intellect?

For this was the man who would be found in years to come declaring himself a Cavalier and Catholic, and yet managing the amazingly dexterous exploit of keeping a foot at once in the court of Cromwell and in that of the widow of the late king: a man, who was completely untroubled, it would seem, by moral principles, or scruples, or restraints, and who seriously believed and acted upon what he wrote, "That no man is to be lamented for finding any means, whatsoever it be, to please and gratify himself", which however did not prevent him from discussing doctrinal points of a religion he held apparently with no ardour, and so little of the spirit that one is led to believe he joined the Church of Rome for little else than the pleasure of flaunting in the face of the world the paradox of a man taking immense risks for what he did not care a straw about.

Sir Kenelm's notion of friends was that "those are to "be esteemed good that are the least ill"; and he found Mr. Verschoyle, although many years older than himself, a man so young, so eager, so curious, so loud too and turbulent on occasion, so indifferent to other men's censures, that he lived much with him, and took great delight in his qualities and conversation. The very bulk and size of the two men, and their tendency to domineer, made them appropriate companions. After Sir Kenelm's return from his piratical cruise in the Mediterranean, but especially after the death of his wife, when he retired to Gresham College to pursue the study of chemistry, and to divert his melancholy by learned discoursings, he was often to be seen in Mr. Verschoyle's company, clad in the sad-coloured clothes he now affected which, like the straggling beard he had grown since his bereavement, matched congruously enough with the other's presence.

As for Verschoyle, that part of his nature which had been least valued at Gorhambury, the gross and coarse part, which was on the whole the strongest part, he was not at the trouble of modifying to please Digby, who had indeed himself the same proclivities, though, if you will, more interrupted and softened. But though all that was very saliently there, still intellectual curiosities, a passion, never at rest in either, for rending the veil which hid the secrets of Nature, had almost as much to do with their friendship. Many discourses did they have together of rare chemical secrets, of antimonial cups, of unheard-of medicines. They watched the stars, and cast horoscopes.

With the help of one Evans who lived in Gunpowder-alley, a most horrid wizard, reputed to be the familiar of the dark angel Salmon, they called up a spirit; and they being all within the body of the circle, after powerful invocation it came first in the shape of a toad, speaking high and shrilly, which proved it to be not Gabriel or Michael or any blessed Heavenly angel, who when they do speak, says one of the wisest masters and operators, "it is like the Irish, much in the throat". But when Verschoyle undaunted, and to the great fear of the adept, who though he had taken some cups to hearten him was in a sad trembling state, commanded the fiend in a terrible voice to leave off his tricks and come forth, there was heard a very dismal groan, and a thing dreadful, unformed, rolling at Verschoyle's feet worshipped him as its Master, and Lord of the Powers of Hell.

So, we are told; but be that as it may, there can be no doubt that Sir Kenelm Digby had at one time, whatever he may have thought later, a great respect for Mr. Verschoyle's parts and curious learning. There is still extant a letter of his addressed to Verschoyle wherein, after equalling his friend for deep knowledge and high speculations to "a Brachman of "India" he had met with in Spain, and protesting in his large way that Verschoyle "had ravished the secrets of Nature, and made the lodestone a thing "of no wonder", he goes on —

"Persuaded of those conferrings, that I say will come drily to yourself which it freshens me to witness. Sir, I have seen you do that by magical arts which would blast the eyes of ignorant vulgars and analphabetes to behold."

And in a letter to another correspondent, written from Paris, he speaks ungrudgingly in a like strain, and quotes with seeming approval a saying of Verschoyle's to the effect, that a system of philosophy or religion should be like to a coat whereof the cloth is strong and good, so that the shape can be changed many times to accommodate the needs of the body.

Later, some years before the war, they fell apart, and gradually ceased even to correspond. Whether they quarrelled, or whether Sir Kenelm's public acceptance of the doctrines of the Church of Rome, however wide and untrammelled that acceptance might be, and though Sir Kenelm seems to have held to the old distinction between the Church of Rome and the Court of Rome, considering himself bound only to the first—whether that made intercourse undesirable, or what else it was that put an end to their friendship, cannot now be determined. Certainly Mr. Verschoyle, for his part, who as he grew older became more than ever unwilling to compromise himself for trifles, as he deemed opinions and disputes about religion, would have steered clear of Sir Kenelm Digby after his appeal to the English

Catholics for funds on the queen's behalf had been discovered by the Parliament.

If Verschoyle had ever had it, he had lost long ago that generosity of mind which was so constant a trait in Sir Kenelm's character. The wise man, he considered, was he who professed the religion of the dominant party in the State, and did as little as he could, without offending that party, to harass the minority.

For himself, privately, he inclined to the doctrine of those old curious subtilisers of ethics whose aim has been to distinguish acts from being, what we do from what we are, pronouncing the last alone pleasing and interesting to the gods: a doctrine which he was to find roughly adopted, and urged somewhat crudely as the effect of knowledge and the Spirit of God, by the sects called Ranters and Seekers of his own time; though, unlike him, the sectaries sheltered their equivocal teaching under the name of Christ—calling to men to hearken to Christ within them, and maintaining that all impulses of nature, even towards things commonly forbidden, were the workings of Christ in humanity; thus in their turn curiously arriving—but by what different roads!—at almost the same landing-place as the *Illuminati* of Spain, or the believers in the revelation of Anthony Buckuet in France.

But it must not be understood that he was foolish enough to advertise his indifference in matters of religion: on the contrary he assumed at one time what may fairly be called, considering the personage and the way he took himself, an appalling piety, carrying his insincere mummery so far as to deceive the eminent and judicious Bishop Juxon; the prelate regarding this penitent, whose scandals and ill-practices had been the talk of two courts, with great contentment.

It remained for the good Mr. Nicholas Ferrar, to whose conventlike house, the Hall at Gidden, or Gidding, in Northamptonshire, Verschoyle in his fervour, pretending the need to search his conscience, had asked leave to make a visit, and was thereupon graciously welcomed—it needed Mr. Ferrar with his saintly eyes to discern the genuine nature, the rank nature, the bias to sin underlying the mockery of this conversion which had duped the bishop and other men of the world.

On the second evening since his arrival, after evening prayers, which as it was an extreme cold winter night had been recited in the parlour where there was a fire burning instead of in the church, as was the ordinary use of that family, Mr. Ferrar takes Verschoyle and gently draws him before a table of brass placed on the wall of the room by the venerable Mrs. Mary Ferrar, which bore an inscription upon it composed perhaps by Herbert of Bemerton, and smiling always lays his finger on these words which made part of it:—

"He" who any ways goes about to disturb us in that which is and ought to be amongst Christians (though it be "not usual in the world), is a burthen whilst he stays, and shall bear his judgment, whosoever he be."

He did this, however, not pointedly, but rather laid his hand on the tablet as if by chance, talking meanwhile of his mother who had set it up there, and her quiet life; for he was very sensitive and gentle, and would not hurt the feelings of his guest. But it would have been all one had he been harsh and blunt: Mr. Verschoyle was not sick of that disease called tenderness of conscience, and never took an affront save when it suited his convenience; and now, not at all disconcerted, and apparently indifferent to this rebuke—if that be not too rough a word for what was done so dreamily—he lingered on a day or two more, howling at night over his sins, claiming to see his sweet Jesus, and raving out other blasphemous and hypocritical indecencies too odious to repeat.

When at length he took himself away, the family offered up special purifying orisons: had they been as Popishly disposed as many fancied, they would certainly have exorcised their dwelling-place with consecrated water. As it was, for days following there was an uneasiness, an indescribable *malaise* in the house, an unwonted sluggishness and untowardness troubling its calm and sedateness, as though the Father of all Evil had in reality passed there.

Yes, the base part of Mr. Verschoyle's nature was by far the strongest, and it was that which as he grew old, coagulating into avarice, had most to do with his retirement into the country.

And yet, just as in his youth it was a mixture of dreaming and rapacity which had sent him voyaging to the other side of the earth with Sir Walter Raleigh in search of gold, so now in his old age, mingled curiously with the habits of the miser which led him to reside constantly on his estate for the purpose of grinding money out of his tenants, there was also something of the temper of the fastidious builder of visions—visions of Heaven or Hell, of sweet faces or places, of fantastical nether worlds, what matters it? —who prefers to live solitary, to sacrifice many sympathies, and adopts an unfriendly and repellent attitude towards mankind, simply from the fear that others may do or say that which would disturb the rhythmic life he has so carefully organised; even as a shriek tearing through a happy dream awakens the sleeper to the trifling of fools or the desolation of tears.

But to gain high and worthy ends, he never thought of making the sacrifices or going to the trouble and inconveniences he did to gain bad; and the bad of course predominated. All his life he had been able at any moment to relinquish his favourite studies and intellectual pursuits, but he had never been able—anyhow he had never cared to abjure rapine, lust, riot, all of which, now that he was old, had rolled themselves into avarice, not so much from the love of money itself, as because that was the only field open at last for the exercise of the undying instincts of the bird of prey, the robber and marauder, the overbearing tyrant.

This eagerness to gain treasure, to wrench from others their property, which in the Middle Age would have sent him pillaging and ravaging the land with a horde at his back, and which he had never been quite free of even in those early years when the harsher vices sit unnaturally on a man; those hard propensities which led him, for example, as it was currently told, so far as to perjure himself early in the present reign in his desperate efforts to escape the fine imposed on him for declining the obligatory honour of knighthood, increased as he became aged and rose up about him like a ruining tide, drowning as it were all else except what was indeed akin, his passion for domination, which, in its turn he gratified, not arrogantly, but rather by stealthy covered ways and serpentine windings gaming his ends, bringing people to his mind.

The scandal of his marriage, a business in which he enthralled and intimidated the already dying Sir Thomas Foulkes, and tore the young heiress almost from the very arms of her lover to share his unholy bed, was the crowning instance of his predatory capacities. After that, saving his pride in his house which he cherished and dealt with as a jewel, all his mental powers seemed willingly abandoned to the poorest sort of men's dealings with each other, tricks of bailiffs, usurers, lawyers, which had not even boldness to lend them glamour.

But his house was indeed worthy of the sedulous care he bestowed on it. Built in the time of Henry the Seventh, and enlarged by Mr. Verschoyle's father during the early years of Elizabeth, it was now become a captivating example of the middle-sized Tudor dwelling. Time, with his hand of grey, touching the stones had happily moulded them, and the storms of over a century, extremely violent in that coastward region, confusing various early crudities of the building, had but enhanced its mellowness of tone.

At the end of a long summer day, when the gardens drowsily breathed a thousand sweets, and the voices of labourers ending their work in the fields might be heard faintly on the long terraces—in those flying lights the house took on a wonderful dignity and charm; so much indeed that its young mistress, in her first lonely and unhappy summers there, was fain to linger out of doors till night fell suddenly, scarfing up the outlines, and leaving only a dark mass, grim and somehow terrifying, premonitory of the wafts of blackness to be encountered inside.

But not only summer, the breath of all the seasons lingered there wooingly, increasing the singular charm of the house; and it was probably to be seen at its best towards sunset on a windless day of autumn, when a chill was in the air urging to swift movement out of doors, and that vague odour of burning wood and leaves which pervades the country in fine autumn weather suggested agreeably the bright fire on the hearth to greet one returning.

Then in the changing afternoon the house stood out clearly, with the smoke rising straight from its chimneys, and behind it the sun waning amid the wild colours of a sky orange, crimson, golden; while even as one gazed came swimming into all that glory, lucid, serene, spiritual, bringing an unutterable conviction of termination and requiem, the evening star. Yes, the sky thickened, it was almost night; now truly "the labourer's task was over"; the mill ceased, birds nested, the sheep were folded; but for the call of a crow winging homeward, the far cry of a teamster to his horses, a watchdog's bark at some distant farm, the land already reposed.

Ah—as one mournfully watching the house through her tears in a kind of ecstasy would think—could death but come in the evening as easily and sweetly, quieting the turmoil of hearts and consciences, as the fields were stilled at the rising of yon star! —But, in effect, in all conditions, whether under snow or beaten by rain, the house offered itself seductively to the imagination. From the windows could be heard the muffled beat of the surf, and the great clamour of the sea as the tide came in. Strange birds driven ashore by the hard weather would whirl with anxious cries about the chimneys, or perch on the jutting stonework under the roof.

And on all sides rolled away and away to the horizon the plain, its level interrupted only by church-tower, or windmill, or cottage, widely dispersed, so that you could follow for miles with the eye the course of a road lying like an idly thrown piece of white tape among the fields. At the opening of the drive, opposite the entrance gate, stood the parish church, with the dead lying around it just off the high-road, who might be thought, not too fancifully! to have part and interest still in the small noise of the countryside and the few passengers who went by the way. The living was now vacant, the last incumbent having been so harassed by Mr. Verschoyle that the sexton coming to the church one morning at dawn found the body of the vicar swinging by the neck from a pillar in the gloomy aisle.

Not the least comely feature of the place were the gardens, planted at the side of the house and running far back in the rear. Mr. Verschoyle had always cherished these gardens; he had desired the celebrated John Tradescant to control the ordering of them and to embellish them with his fancies: and indeed they were very stately, and of great curiosity and beauty. Contrived with so much skill that even in that bleak clime they offered somewhat of refreshment at all seasons, it was here the young mistress of the place loved best to spend her long pale days, tending by preference the sadder flowers which she watered, as one might surmise, with her tears.

Apparently free to wander whither she chose, yet her movements in reality strictly confined to the gardens and terraces, she reminded herself in her great longing for the free air of the outer lands, and in her narrow imprisonment there, of a cart she had once seen in an Italian city conveying prisoners condemned to the galleys through the streets. The cart, although covered over, had an air-hole on the top, and through this hole appeared—so significantly, so poignantly! —a pair of coarse grimy hands waving aimlessly, as if the hopeless wretch within was thus blindly trying to identify himself, to take a last contact with the lovely freedom of the streets.

Like those hands, from the same mad longing, her eyes, as she leant on the balustrade of the terrace on a calm evening, not seldom reverted to a certain far away point on the coast; there, it was said, the smugglers, coming from the Low Countries on fine dark nights, were wont to run in their contraband goods. Well, might not those men, desperate as they were, be persuaded by the gift of the few jewels she had left to land her on the shores of the Continent; and then, somehow—never mind how—would come Italy, help, freedom! So, dreaming, she would remain for an hour at a time with her elbow on the stone, resting her chin in her hand; till the mere sight of Mr. Verschoyle passing in the distance sufficed to remind her despairingly how futile it was to struggle against his will, how she was helpless as a young fluttering bird in his big hand. Nay, those very smugglers—with whom, moreover, in all likelihood he had dealings—would even they have the hardihood to oppose him?

Whenever she thought of freedom, she thought with passionate longing of Italy. As a young girl she had lived much at Genoa in the family of the Duchess Paola Adorno Brignole-Sale whose name she bore, and whom she was thought to resemble. However that might be, in the English Paola, at any rate, what you saw was a young woman's face which indicated that however unusual and terrible the griefs she might have to suffer in her life, she would never meet them with large tragic utterance and demeanour, but rather in the spirit of a rebuked child, pouting and surprised, and quite ready to laugh through her tears at the first intimation that the storm was over.

There was in her face a sort of distressed notification that she was not being caressed—the action she could understand best; and a sort of wonder that it was omitted. She was not a tall woman, and her face would have been conventionally pretty had it not been for a look one would call it high-bred, save that undeniably high-bred people constantly do such abject things—but at all events a nobleness of mien which assured you that on any trying occasion she would not be found trivial and common. Yes, that; and furthermore, a look of mingled terror and sadness in the large brown eyes, such as might cloud the eyes of a child who has witnessed, and partly understood atrocious violences, degrading scenes.

But, as it happened, in Paola's eyes the terror prevailed over the sadness; for though she loved her lover, Sir Edward Morvan, and grieved miserably because she was deprived of his sweet company, still, as she was not one of those deep-natured, high-souled women who entangle their fate with one man, and losing him lose all, she might have consoled herself in happier circumstances even for that loss; whereas from her terror of the old man her husband there was no escape, and no consolation to modify it. Besides its very real action, increased daily by a thousand artifices, it remained with her always imaginatively, a prolongation of the sort of fear—but how much intensified! which had haunted her for a few hours in her happy childhood when she had seen a painting of the flames striking the feet of the lost let down into Hell.

To her, now, as she stood in the waning light, a black calash drawn over her head beneath which her brown eyes looked forth so mournfully, a vellum-bound volume of Petrarch she had carried out in the early afternoon clasped in her fragile long-fingered hand, was borne faintly the voices of the tenants as they plodded homeward after the rent-paying; a laugh breaking forth now and then, or a child's playful cry, as she listened enviously—the bewitched young lady whom the country folk hardly ever saw, and spoke of under their breaths—trying to decide herself to go indoors and face the desolation, the appalling shadows, the night.

And with a sickening of heart, she pictured what awaited her: the evening meal in the long half-lit room which she was forced to eat, not only in the presence of her husband, but of the odious one-eyed droll his steward, who was now grown so great with Verschoyle that he must sit at table with his master. All the time that the supper lasted, Verschoyle would pour out a stream of truculent wit directed against all the neighbourhood; the one-eyed wretch, who was himself pretty often the butt, chuckling and sweating and choking with obsequious laughter. Then, the supper over, Mr. Verschoyle and this mean fellow would sit down by the fire in the dark hall to a game of gleek; but if upon these dispositions Paola offered to retire, she was loudly bidden to remain.

"My lady's windows look towards Sir Edward Morvan's house which is known to be unwholesome, is it not?" he would ask with a meaning laugh of the one-eyed steward, who would of course set up another sniggering laugh of acquiescence.

That man had not always been one-eyed: Paola would sob in the wildest fear when she recalled the monstrous deed which had deprived him of sight. One night, when she had been married but a few months, they were eating their meal, after the manner just described, in the gloomy panelled room. All seemed to be going no worse than usual, when Mr. Verschoyle suddenly fell silent, and after a minute brusquely ordered the servants out of the room. Then he pitched back his chair with a clatter, and towering in his immense size, menacing and formidable, he seized the weazened little steward by the ear and dragged him from his place.

"Here, you!" he said. "You eat your victuals with me without a due sense of what you are about. You lack virtue, sirrah; you have need of a congruent gymnastic to keep your mind in humility. Begin your pious exercises. Kneel down and pray to me. I am God."

The poor mean fellow, taken utterly aback by this command, fumbled pitifully. It was more than he dared to do.

"Come sir," cries Verschoyle in a loud authoritative voice, "leave off your fooling and pray as you are desired. Pray, sing a hymn in my honour, you prick-eared rascal: 'tis all that will serve your turn in this world or the next. My lady had a Puritan to her father and is an Italian papist herself, and Sir Edward Morvan, they say, is a good State-Protestant. Shew her a new form to take up with in our pleasant home. Give her a chance to hear your cackle. Out with our Turnbull Street litany and the canticles of the Pict-Hatch fornicators, where you was bred, you *caitiff*. Come, begin down on your knees!"

But the man was recalcitrant: it was too much. His spirit was not as yet quite broken by Verschoyle, and certain rests of religion, or at all events of superstition, made him recoil from the blasphemy. And in effect, though he stood there trembling all over, he had the courage to stammer out a refusal. But he had scarcely time to get the words out of his mouth, before his master snatched up a candlestick and laid open his face, cutting into the nerve of the eye so that he was blinded.

Paola, standing meanwhile with her back against the wainscot, her hands spread out, her eyes dilated, heard his lamentable squeal as he sunk to the ground; and then the lights flashed and wheeled, the chamber rocked, and she saw no more. But before many days the steward, his head craftily swathed, was again at his work, closeted mysteriously with the tyrant, and more devoted to his interests than ever.

Such were her painful reveries as she stood at dusk, uncertain, in the gardens. It was cold and dreary; the moisture dropped from the trees; she shivered, drew her cloak about her, and decided. But as she went strolling reluctantly towards the house, she saw her husband suddenly a few paces in front of her as if he had surged out of the ground—coming on her, in fact, as he always did, noiselessly, before she was aware. He had laid aside his indecent foolish hat and charlatan's robe, and stood there, with his bare skull unscreened from the wintry airs and his ragged beard blowing over his shoulder, huge and black and sinister, threatening somehow, though he was smiling, ominous, presaging disaster. He had a letter in his hand, and as he came up to her—"My sweet chuck," he cried with a horrid shew of affection which made her wince, "here comes Ned Morvan home."

The blood fluttered into her face and fell away again, like the light of a candle that is carried past a window. She remained silent.

"This is his letter," said Mr. Verschoyle waving it. "He comes home from the king's armies under a pass of the prince, and doubtless one from the Parliament too, so he may lie snug. A brave lad, Ned Morvan, and a whiteboy wherever he goes. He will be truly welcome here. Perhaps he means to diet with us now he is home", he added, and peered through the dusk to see how this stroke took.

He did not think it necessary to explain that he was afraid to shew Morvan the cold shoulder and forbid him the house, lest the other might turn it into an affront to his cause and bring down a cavalier troop. Besides, he had heard a rumour that Morvan had the king's warrant to search out all those in that part of the country whose loyalty was equivocal or flaccid, and to put the estates of those who refused to contribute to the royal cause at the mercy of the soldiers. After a pause, finding that his wife did not speak, he thought it worthwhile to drop carelessly the news that Morvan had been wounded in a skirmish.

"Wounded?" she breathed, looking at him with startled eyes.

"Who knows but he may have lost an arm or a leg?" said old Verschoyle considering her with his cruel eyes, and enjoying her dismay. "Nay, Ned used to be a pretty sprig enough, but if a musket shot has removed his nose——"

His quick ear had caught the sound of a footbeat advancing from the house. "As you see, he is even now coming towards us, so his wound must be of the slightest", said Mr. Verschoyle. And lowering his voice—"'Tis a wound in the left side, I misdoubt me," he added with malevolent intention.

Then peering through the dark towards the house, where Paola could see nothing, "Ned, Ned, you come in pudding-time!" he shouted heartily.

Even as he spoke a pale young man who limped slightly, apparently between twenty-five and thirty years old, wearing his hair long, as most gentlemen did of both parties, and dressed elegantly in a habit trimmed with gold, with silver points and buttons, stepped out of the pleached alley hard by where they were standing, and greeted them debonairly with gay laughter.

2

The spring was early that year, and Sir Edward Morvan, riding light-heartedly, often with a song on his lips, to and fro between Verschoyle's house and his own, a journey he was making four or five times a week, might see the new-dropt lambs in the meadows, and innumerable violets on the roadside bank penetrating with their cool fragrance the mild air. Ah, how good it was to be in this secluded land, when all over the country men were battling and marching, lying hard at nights, risking their lives! That had been his own life till a few weeks since; later on, in a few days, a few weeks, some vague time always drawing near and always pushed farther off, that would have to be his life again.

But not just yet; if the gods were kind, not yet. And as he rode thinking of all that, he would feel his wound, perfectly healed by this time save for a little superficial soreness, to excuse his slackness. Because, for once, Mr. Verschoyle had got hold of a wrong story: Morvan had no warrant from the king to raise money in the country, nor any business whatever there beyond the healing of his wound. And he had certainly exaggerated its severity in his letters to the Newark garrison—nay, he was quite equal to opening the wound afresh if the governor, impatient as he well might be of this prolonged furlough, had threatened to send a surgeon to report on his condition.

But the governor did nothing of the kind; on the contrary, Morvan seemed to be utterly neglected and forgotten at headquarters; and to the letters he so laboriously composed (Paola sometimes aiding him with the intelligence and fineness of a woman in love) he received no reply at all. This was unusual, even when large free allowance was made for the hindering of messengers, and to one of another character might have seemed disquieting and suspicious; but Morvan was never a man to split straws or ponder might-be's, and lazily took it for granted that the governor was satisfied with those elaborate reasons he had put forward for not joining.

And thus, day after day went by him flowingly, hazily, as a man lounging half-asleep on a hot day might watch the ripples and eddies of running water. There was a dreaming ecstasy in every hour of this wonderful spring, the most wonderful, Morvan thought, certainly the most delightful he had ever lived. To see Paola, the woman whom he loved with a great consuming love which left no room for anything but itself, and who had been stolen from him by machinations the most nefarious—to see her not once or twice, which was the limit of his hope when he first came home, but every day without restraint for long sweet spells—that was an astonishing happiness against which, if the old legends were true, some great retributive punishment must be rolling up.

Well, he would face that with equanimity, come when it would, take it without murmuring, even welcome it and think himself all the same the gainer, if it were the penalty exacted from him in exchange for the present smile of her face in his, and the touch of her hand. In the meanwhile, it was enough for his life that every night his pillow was gladdened by the thought that he was going to see her in the morning.

And the strange part was that they were left, as I have said, as untroubled, as much to themselves, as lovers could desire, Mr. Verschoyle appearing but seldom, and then only to ask with marked concern after Morvan's wound, and to bestow his benediction—it actually seemed like that—upon the pair; afterwards vanishing—well, by magic! hiding himself for days and days so inscrutably that none in the house knew where to look for him, and yet revealing himself in disquieting apparitions, now to a lonely passenger over a windy heath, and then, almost at the same hour, as those colleaguing at the ale-house painfully took note, to a woman miles and miles away, as if he indeed possessed the receipt of fern-seed, and walked invisible by the aid of those black arts he was supposed to have at command.

Beyond question, Sir Edward Morvan regarded Mr. Verschoyle with infinite rancour and hatred: he had come home prepared for the worst reprisals if the other should give him the shadow of an excuse to take offence: but seeing now the old man's complaisances and loose ways his stronger feelings were almost extinguished by contempt. A miserable old dotard (so he thought), who by the long-continued practice of debaucheries dozed in his understanding, and he lamented more than ever the sacrifice of his beautiful Paola.

3

But if Morvan had known what Verschoyle was about while he was dallying, he would have changed his tune more than a little. Sir Richard Willis, who had lately succeeded Byron as Governor of Newark, amazed and furious at Morvan's long desertion of the shaken and sore-pressed garrison, without any excuse offered for his dilatoriness, had finally complained bitterly to the newly-appointed Commander-in-chief of the King's forces. In accordance with that, two letters desiring Morvan to return to his duty, one written chidingly, but the other couched in very peremptory terms, were despatched from Prince Rupert's headquarters; but they were carefully intercepted by Verschoyle, who was plotting nothing less than to ruin the cavalier with his own party, and had up to this managed to stop all expresses riding between Sir Edward and the army.

Some weeks before the time we are now arrived at, Morvan being

rather anxious, notwithstanding his insouciance, at the failure of letters from Newark, had himself applied directly to Prince Rupert for
an extension of his furlough, using in the business a safe man, one his
father, who in his time had been involved in some delicate affairs, had
often employed. This man came up with Prince Rupert at Beeston
Castle, and having delivered his master's letters, which were treated
as mere rigmaroles and feignings, he was entrusted with a very angry
letter written by the prince himself, in which Sir Edward was commanded upon his loyalty to join without delay, under pain of being esteemed a renegade and punished as such. The man carried also a very
strong message from Morvan's closest friend, acquainting him with
the bad odour he had fallen into, wondering at his supineness, and
urging him to loose all that held him and return suddenly to his place.

The messenger made good speed, and coming skilfully into his own
country congratulated himself on having passed through the area occupied by soldiery. As he journeyed along the familiar road, not more
than five miles now from home, riding at a smart trot, sitting loosely
in the saddle, and not paying much attention, suddenly he made out
in front of him on the bleak unsheltered road three horsemen halted,
whose steel he could see gleaming in the late afternoon sun.

He thought a moment, chagrined and weary, studying his mount,
and then decided to run for it; but as he wheeled his horse, he found
that he must have ridden past two more who were lying concealed in
the dyke-side, and who, once he was passed, had scrambled on to the
road to bar his way. Here was an end to the hope of flight; for the wide
dyke bordering the road on either side without any "take-off" made
a rush across country impossible. But alert and resourceful, he covered
his wheel about by acting as if his horse had shied, and pulling up to
a foot-pace he approached the main band with an open look, smiling, thinking he might by free manners and effrontery win through
without question.

The men were every one well-armed, but only the leader, a one-
eyed man in whom Sir Edward's servant after some hesitation and
with infinite astonishment recognised Mr. Verschoyle's steward, was
equipped like a soldier. This droll had furnished himself out with an
old buff coat, and an iron back and breast, and had clapped a "pot" or
headpiece on his skull which being too big for him hung awkwardly
askew. He had further girded on an extravagantly long sword which,
even on the mild old nag he bestrode, was more than he could handle.
Altogether, he presented an appearance something between a bully of

Alsatia and a guy ready for Bartholomew Fair.

He it was who summoning up a terrible voice, imitated from his master, ordered the oncomer to stand, and then demanded whither he was bound. The messenger answered, to Sir Edward Morvan's, adding carelessly that he had been to attend the market of a distant town. But the other frowning prodigiously began to vapour and talk big, saying that Sir Edward was a foul malignant, full of factious designs and immodesty, whom well-affected men were about to purge from that honest part of England, since he was naught but a riotous and drunken cavalier and dammy, lewd and a swearer, a man vastly insufficient and scandalous, who lacked healing and savoury counsel. When he had harangued in this style for some minutes, he suddenly threw up his arm, whereupon the two men behind came down the road at a canter, and the messenger found himself hemmed in.

"Give up what you are carrying", snarled the leader seizing the servant's bridle. "Expand, produce, cough it up. In the market you come from there's a king sitting on rotten eggs. The man Morvan is one of them, and you are even now carrying to him messages for the disordering of this peaceable country, which I command you in the Parliament's name to surrender."

The intrepid messenger protested that he carried nothing; and seeing that he must fight, he suddenly pressed his knees on his horse and rode smash against a big hulking fellow, whose small pole-axe, which hung in a ribbon tied about the wrist, he snatched before the other could recover from the shock, and then turning about he reached the one-eyed leader such a swinging blow on the pate that if it had not been for the steel cap he wore his head must have been cleft. As it was, the knock fetched him off his horse into the mud. Seeing one of them down, the messenger laid about him with such fury that had the road been wider, as he was so much a better horseman than any of his assailants, he might have got clean off.

But the narrowness of the road and the wide stream on each side gave them the advantage, and after a sharp tussle, in which one got a desperate wound in the side, they closed up and secured the messenger, whom they succeeded in mastering at last only by their numbers and the bad ground. Seeing that the fight was over, the one-eyed captain, who had meanwhile been sitting ruefully by the waterside bathing his head and trying to collect his wits, hoisted himself into the saddle and gave the order to march.

And as they marched, what must the worthy captain do to hearten them after the conflict but break out into various prayers and ejaculations, of the kind used by the precisians, for the mercy vouchsafed; and then struck up a psalm which he sang violently through the nose; all by way of convincing the prisoner, if by any chance he should escape, that he had been captured by one who belonged to the party of the Saints in the Parliament Army; though in truth the other was far too shrewd to be taken in by this impudent travesty of those stern and godly men.

After a sufficiently long march, variegated by this kind of thing, and by halts while the pious captain drank freely of strong waters to keep, as he explained, his head from swimming with obscene vapours, they drew up to a cottage, standing very lonely in a wood, which the prisoner, who knew every yard of the country, recognized as being on that old estate of Sir Thomas Foulkes which now of course belonged to Mr. Verschoyle through his wife. The house was uninhabited and almost bare; but the captain, kicking the door open, swaggered in with a great bustle, sat himself on the only stool, and clapping his sword on the table glared round him ferociously, while two men brought in the prisoner and the others laid the fellow who had been hurt in a corner.

Then, after telling the captive, whom he kept standing before him sorely bound, that he had a mind to hang him up forthwith, he once more ordered him to declare where he came from, and to give up the letters he carried. The man however persisted in denying that he carried papers, and immediately they began to search him; but nothing at all could be found. Matters being thus at a stand, Mr. Verschoyle's captain shouted that he was too old a bird to be cozened, and directed that the prisoner's fingers should be burnt with match. But the messenger, although he suffered atrocious pain, held dauntlessly to what he had said.

The captain seeing him thus firm, and being terrified to return home empty-handed, fell into a miserable blasphemous passion strangely at variance with his late psalm-singing, and roared out to twist a rope tight round the prisoner's head, swearing that he was resolved to make him know his master, and what he might trust to if he did not speedily confess. Then at last, after holding out till he was utterly crushed by pain and almost delirious, the messenger shewed where the letters were cunningly hid in a double lining of his sleeve; but no sooner had the agony ceased than he seemed ashamed of what he had done, and though they renewed the match-burning twice, and also tortured him abominably with water, not all the threats in the world could force him to give any further information.

So, after spending some time at this business, the captain finally was fain to be satisfied with what he had got, and rode off in the darkness, leaving the messenger in charge of two louts who sat all night sotting together, but always wide awake enough to prevent any move to escape, even if the prisoner, who lay half dead, had been in any condition to attempt it. And before the next day was over, the man had been carried miles and miles to the north, and the letters were safe in Verschoyle's hands, who used them to elaborate his snares.

4

This very morning, the most perfect of that perfect season, Morvan riding along heedlessly, now singing, now smiling out good-humouredly at the fair-lighted day, passed over, all unsuspecting, that part of the road where his messenger had been waylaid some weeks before. He was annoyed, as much as he could be in his beatific state—lying, as it were, dulled by love's drowsy medicine—about the messenger's miscarriage, and grumbled now and then without conviction at the stupidity which he supposed had led the man to be taken by the Roundheads.

But he had fallen of late, as we have seen, into such a contempt of Mr. Verschoyle that it never came into his mind to look for that hand in the business. He did not perceive, he was really perhaps with all his handsome audacity and physical gifts too stupid to perceive, that Verschoyle was not at all a man like himself, or governed by the motives of his generation; but rather a survival from the reign of Elizabeth and the early years of James, with all the peculiar subtilties, refinings, and roundabout methods of those times.

A man too having in him the spirit of that large body of men in Elizabeth's time whose horror of the violent sins—murder, ravage, piracy—was perfunctory and as it were spectacular; while in their breasts was a very real ferocity, in its essence barbaric and of the Middle Age, though softened and polished in a thousand ways and subdued to the ends in view: and with that, an almost complete freedom from harassing trammels of conscience, and a distinct preference for considering the fortunes of the soul as vague and matter for scholastic disputation, while the fortunes of the body were to be zealously pursued with unrelenting activity.

Had Sir Edward estimated Verschoyle aright, he would have kept his eye upon all sorts of covers expecting him to emerge: he would

143

have been most on his guard when he found the other vacant, senile, mildly foolish. But Verschoyle had always been taken by Morvan for a frantic beast who tore from people whatever of theirs he wanted; yet one whose roar you might hear, and whom you might descry so to speak afar off bounding on his prey, however little you could do to arrest the onset. At present, none too soon! the teeth of the beast seemed to have fallen, his fire dying, almost extinct; the frantic beast was become, in fact, now happily at last so insignificant, so little to be reckoned with, that Morvan as he turned in at the gate today, perceiving the gaunt black figure prowling in the churchyard, waved a recognition with an air of scornful tolerance.

It is so hard for the young to rate at their due value the powers of the old! Morvan, seeing the old man so weary, so unwary, so trembling and incurious, had almost allayed even the fears of Paola, who, however, as she owed them to numberless stronger experiences, could not be induced entirely to forget. Still, for all that, she was happy now and content with an immense wide happiness she had not known since her marriage; and when Sir Edward, his horse comfortably stalled, strolled out of the house on to the long lawn, his heart followed his eyes and lingered upon the exquisite picture she made in the distance as she stood under a blossoming almond tree, wearing a painted calico gown and white hood—graciously lovely, buoyant, full of laughter, fragrant, delicate, and young as the primroses, hyacinths, daffodils, blue violets she cherished there.

These long white days, veritable holidays, which she watched drop into darkness one by one as threaded crystals into well-water, she had arrived never to regret;—looking forward rather with a child-like expectation of indefinite felicity, and welcoming the gleam of the new jewel ere the ripple of the one just sunk had quite died away. Were not these hours today more suave, the sunshine over there on the old wall against which the flowers were opening more genial, than at the same time yesterday? And tomorrow surely would be fairer still. Anyhow, the blessed sweetness of wandering there together—yes, literally hand in hand, lingering over trifles, looking for nests in the hedges, playing a thousand childish pranks in mere youthful folly and high spirits— what was better in life than that?

The shadow of age seemed exorcised from the garden, leaving nothing old save the grey old house which looked blandly on this spectacle of young love, as though it gathered a warmth from youthful merriment, blitheness, and frolic, of which it had seen so little. And the tyrant, the ogre, the demon, where was he? Banished too by some good fairy; perhaps still prowling coldly in the place of graves.

But the long happy day of love was over. The sun fell; the wind, rising, blew chill from the Wolds; the birds, tired of their loves and quarrels, sought the nest; it was time to go in. They passed through the broad shadows, cast by the last rays of the sun upon the fine-shorn lawn, round to the front of the house, and passing through the empty hall where a great fire blazed, made their way to a small wainscotted parlour which overlooked the terrace. Here too a fire was set, but the logs fallen together gave but a red glow on the hearth; and while they stood warming themselves the day gradually died from the windows, leaving the old room in that tender light when afternoon merges into evening.

Then, after they had talked a little at random, saying tumultuously they knew not what, they fell into an intense silence, holding hands, gazing pensively into the fire. What was the use of speech? But Sir Edward, noticing a theorbolute leaning against a chair, took it up, and after preluding a little, sang these verses, which he had made in the time of their separation, to a sweet and plaintive air, composed probably by Henry Lawes, though it is not be found in his *Ayres and Dialogues*:—

I wonder if the lovers of old time
Like me upon the smoke of love were fed;
When in their lady's praise they made a rhyme
Were they so drear and little comforted?
Absence and sighings are my palmer's share:
Love that sees not the lover is despair.

I pay with scorns the heat of the clear sun
Since that it falls in groves where she is not,
Young quires make music, but I will have none,
Since by them all her name hath been forgot.
Days wind to months, and months creep into years
But all my portion is disgusts and fears.

If the one hour that brings the patient moon
To hang in Heaven its little silver crook
I could but see her, then the nights were soon,
The days were early after that one look.
'Tis now the lover's anguish and complaint,
Which if endured for God would make a saint.

And then in a dying fall he sang low over again the melancholy cadence:—

Absence and sighings are my palmer's share:
Love that sees not the lover is despair.

His voice was indistinct, trembling with love. As the last note fainted and failed, he put down the lute and bending over Paola took her head between his hands and kissed her on the mouth. She rose with an indraw of breath like a sob, naive, pale; and in a burst of tenderness, of despairing passion, threw herself against him, pliant, powerless, mad with happiness, with adoration. He seized that delicate head which drooped upon him like a too-heavy flower; he breathed the odour of her hair, stammering meanwhile some words, feverish and incoherent. But as they clung together in a disordered insatiable embrace, losing themselves utterly, suddenly they heard a cough in the room.

They started apart and stared into the darkness. Who was it? The door was fast closed with a stock-lock, and they must have noticed anyone coming from outside. However, before they could speak, they heard a great clapping of hands together, with the voice of Mr. Verschoyle calling loudly for lights; and as the servant entered, there was revealed the old husband seated at a table, a velvet skull-cap on his head, and holding to his face a pomander-ball over which his eyes glittered on the two before him, who, amazed, were asking themselves uneasily how he had got in, and how long he had been there.

"That was a good song, Edward", he called out cheerily, "a sweet ditty and well sung. Living here retired in a poor country-house, 'tis seldom our ears are refreshed with carols. There was parson", he went on, broadening his accent like a rustic, "he used to give us a stave o'nights. But a's gone, dead and gone; a was took off at Christian-tide come two years. A is a main loss is parson, a main sad loss; but a was not a man of God. There was no fervent prayer and savoury conference about parson. Should's ha' heard him read the Book of Sports in church o'Sundays afore the war came.

"He owed much to me which he forgot: till I put him here he was an old curate living on ten pound a year and unlawful marriages. A weak man, Edward, weak and deboshed, vastly lewd, given over to wenching and the devil. A had more bastards to his charge than any man in parish. He used to say he made a scruple about the ring-marriage, like a nonconformist divine. But like yourself, a was a rare hand at a song and talking bawdy, Edward—that he was; thof his songs had none of your fantastical French turns about them, and suited better with a tavern or play-house than a godly abode. Was't not so, madam?" he asked, looking straight as his wife.

She stood resting her elbow on the shelf above the fireplace, leaning her head on her hand, her other slim hand lying against her skirt, with that admirable dignity and unruffled demeanour she had always in reserve for trying situations.

"Sooth, sir," she answered, "my little knowledge of these matters I owe to you."

She said it in such a fine grave way that anyone else but Verschoyle must have been disconcerted, and even he judged it convenient to give over his odious clowning and laments for a man whom all the country knew he had plagued out of existence. He called Morvan's attention to the pace of a horse led up and down on the terrace.

"Why dost leave us so early, Ned?" he cried hospitably. "The nights be warm and thou knowest the road. Here 'tis uncommon trist at night after you go. I wax old and am only good for the chimney-side, and my wife sighs and mutters charms and passes Popish stones through her fingers to put the black spot on us; and I go all of a dither, what with fear of Sathanas, and the ultimate fire, and the end of a life of sin, which must ever afflict the old age of the saints; thof your secure and sensual sinners may carouse to their coffin, and make a health of perdition. So, we continue till the night is near spent. We have conduct, but we lack revelry and songs. Why not tarry yet a little?"

Old as the man was, Morvan felt like knocking him down. In the few minutes this scene had been transacting, he had made up his mind that he must contrive, at whatever cost, the escape of Paola from the house of this monster, and fly with her overseas. But now, angry and bewildered, he could find f or Verschoyle's question only a dull reply.

"Because, sir", he said fiercely, "I am resolved never to tarry in any man's house who considers me an intruder."

"Faith, then", replied Mr. Verschoyle with a loud laugh, "I'm thinking you'll deprive many of your company!" And with that, as he saw Sir Edward was bowing formally to Paola, he reached down a candle-branch from the sconce and preceded his guest to the courtyard, whither the horse had been led in. Morvan followed him in a passion of anger and hatred: wounded vanity never forgives, and the speech last uttered was the key, as it were, which locked finally from the outside the door of the chamber wherein all the injuries he had entertained from the same source were heaped up. His host stood on the threshold watching him while he mounted.

"It looks like a storm in the sky tonight", he said. "God grant thee a good home-coming, Edward". And as Sir Edward rode off without any reply, or even goodnight, he turned back into the house singing in a strong trolling voice, most weird in so ancient a man:

Absence and sighings are my palmer's share:
Love that sees not the lover is despair.

5

The wind was rising as Morvan rode forth, clouds were rolling together, and some drops of rain began to fall. Once on the road, he started homeward at a brisk trot, pressing his animal a little so as to put as many miles as he could behind him ere the wind, which always in storms swept with great fury across that open land, had risen to its full force. But he had barely covered two miles when he noticed his horse grow sluggish under him, and with some dismay found that it was running lame. He dismounted, and felt tenderly all round the lame leg to discover where the mischief lay and if it might be remedied; but the horse, as he found, had picked up nothing in the hoof, and for anything less simple it was as good as useless to waste time in the darkness.

What he did ascertain after a minute was that the horse, between its hurt and the wind and darkness, was grown too nervous to go forward unless it were led; so, as he cared not to return to Verschoyle's house for hospitality after his malevolent parting of just now with the squire, he resigned himself as cheerfully as he could to trudge the twelve miles and more which lay between him and home. He made, however, but poor headway; and what with leaning against the wind, and trying to soothe the horse which started and shied at the least noise, he ran some risk, well as he knew the road, of breaking his neck in the obscurity, or at least of tumbling into one or other of the ditches full of water which bordered a good part of the route. Thus hindered, it was close on midnight when he drew near to the park gates.

For some miles he had observed a glare in the sky without giving himself much concern about it: some barn, doubtless, carelessly ordered, where a spark falling had been blown into flame by the great wind. But now that he was almost on the skirts of his park, he made out that the fire must be pretty near his own house: a heavy smoke mingled with the scudding clouds, which were reddened by a great light whereof the palpitating centre seemed to be the mansion itself: the eastern lodge, perhaps, where a keeper dwelt, was in flames, or worse still! the stables.

He would learn all about it, of course, when he reached a cottage hard by which served as a kind of gatehouse, where he was used upon his return from journeys to hand over his horse. But when he did actually come up to the cottage, hoping to shelter there for a little, he found to his great astonishment that it was deserted, though the gates near at hand stood wide open. Somebody would pay for that, by Heaven!—that was the last straw of an awkward day. And it was in a rousing temper that Sir Edward, wet, footsore, thirsty, his arm nearly wrenched off by holding a jibbing horse, tramped up the avenue, the boughs over his head soughing and moaning in the storm.

The avenue was over a mile long. Morvan had advanced about two hundred yards when something white rushed at him from the bushes.

"Oh, Sir Edward! Sir Edward! Lo, now, Sir Edward!"—and the words dwindled to an incoherent wail.

He thought he recognised a maid-servant from the house, and inquired petulantly what was the matter with her.

"Oh, Sir Edward, sir, 'tis the soldiers, please you sir. Mr. Bates stood me here, and cautioned me not to let your honour go up to the house, for the soldiers were there all burning and firing."

"Nay, clear thy noddle, thou silly little fool!" cried Morvan impatiently. "What soldiers? Are they the Roundheads?"

But this was more than the maid could say, and when she fell once more to "Oh, Sir Edward, please you, Sir Edward!" he brushed by her and went striding up towards the house whence there came now to his ears, notwithstanding the gale, a great noise of voices. He was pushing on rapidly, when at a bend of the avenue he ran sharp against Will Bates, his faithful body-servant, a sturdy man who had attended him to the war. Bates was now moving cautiously towards the gate, followed by a stable-lad leading two horses on the grass border of the path.

"How is this, Bates?" exclaimed Morvan peremptorily. "Wherefore is all this noise?"

But Bates himself seemed alarmed. "For God's sake, Sir Edward", he said in a whisper, "get you to horse and let us be gone. 'Tis a party of dragoons from the King's army. They summoned the house towards eight o'clock, and finding you was away, entered with great shouts and went about pillaging and firing, their officers never quelling them that I did see, but triumphing and rejoicing, and calling you a damnable traitor. So that all's ruined. But they said 'twas your honour they was after, and when they catched you they would slaughter you, for that you was worse than the rebels, and served with the king to steal his secrets and then deserted, and that you was a what y'call and traitor.

"And I said that you was none, and they took me prisoner saying they would hang me up with my master, and so they put me in the little room over the stable, not knowing the trap in the floor. But I got out, and found Jock here, and took the two bays in the grass field and lay here to stop you, sir, for 'tis plain they mean your life."

Morvan grew paler and paler as he listened. "I am no traitor", he said sternly, "and I am going up to face them. Come you with me. Who is their commander?"

"Sir, I do not know. But two of their officers talking a little apart together under the window of the stable, I heard them say they had all their informations from old Mr. Verschoyle, and they took it ill he had given them the wrong hour for your homecoming—Don't go up to the house, Sir Edward", said Bates imploringly; "prithee, let us be gone. 'Twill serve nothing to go up."

"Rot thee!" shouted Morvan furiously. "Get thee gone, with a murrain! Save thyself, trembler! Thou art as pitiful a coward as yon poor wench. Am I to see my house burn and stand here idle?"

But Bates never moved. "For my life, I value it no more than another man", he said simply. "If Sir Edward goes up, I will go too. But 'tis useless; all's one ruin. Tomorrow, they mean to fell the trees, and fetch the horses and cattle away. When I came down, they were drinking and tobacconing in the stables; but they think you are on the road, and now as they have waited so long, they will be spreading out to seize you. Mount now, Sir Edward, in God's name! or 'twill be too late. Nothing can be saved by your going up," said honest Bates, and took the freedom to push his master towards the horses. "There will be no persuasion, they'll not listen, they are mad to slaughter you. One of them swore they would cut yourself down afore they cut down your trees. Nay, sir, they may have missed me by this time, which will set them running; for they mean to hang me tonight, and only waited till they catched you to finish us together."

While he was talking, he had passed the bridle of the lame horse to the boy, and twisting a lock of his own horse's mane round his finger, stood looking anxiously at his master, ready to jump into the saddle when Sir Edward had led the way. But Sir Edward was reluctant, and stood without moving. He trusted Bates; he knew that if Bates turned his back on a burning house and assaulting soldiers affairs must be indeed at a desperate pass. But to stand by while his wide fair house was plundered and burned without striking a blow, to be branded shamefully as a traitor to the king in whose cause he had been wounded, to run away from the doom of a traitor without defending himself, without ramming the charge back in their teeth—ah, no, his nature revolted against that. But even while he stood there deliberating, the trample of horses, the clang of accoutrements, and the sharp words of command were heard further up the avenue.

"Blood, Sir Edward, His too late!" whispered Bates lamentably. "Here they come!"

By instinct Morvan swung himself into the saddle. From the very first he had felt in his heart that the game was up. He breathed a deep malediction against the destroyers of his father's house, and the greybeard fiend whose machinations had rendered him homeless.

"Lead on, Will", he said. "Ride where you can".

The two horses moved with little noise over the turf, and then swerving out of the avenue struck into the plantations, guided by their riders without the least embarrassment or uncertainty through the tangle. Bates led and did all the marking and listening, for Sir Edward was so stunned and furious that he could bestow no care on the passages of his escape; and it was only the long-trained hand of the fine horseman, the rider of the great horse, apt at all the graces of *manège*, acting now as it were by habit, distinct from the rider's will, which cleverly steered the fretting mare over the rough ground.

The soldiers, however, were already beating the plantations; one or two of them who had got drunk were calling out ribaldries against Sir Edward; and just as Bates skilfully brought up against a little opening in the hedge, the fugitives were detected by some troopers posted hard by. These immediately ordered them to halt and give the word, and getting no answer, fired almost at random into the darkness, calling loudly meanwhile for their mates to bring up a lantern, and railing out against Judas Iscariot, and the Puritanical traitor.

But while they were groping, baffled by the thick night, Sir Edward and his man had pushed through the hedge, and taking the open, tore along blindly at a free gallop. The soldiers had no chance over that difficult country in the black night against two riders who had known every field from childhood. They followed gallantly; several plunged horse and man into the dykes; three at least, encumbered with their heavy fighting gear, were drowned. A few more shouts were heard, a few more scattered shots, and then the pursuit was abandoned; and the two flying rode on unhindered till the dawn broke upon their haggard faces. A little after sunrise they arrived at a hut standing lonely on the moors in a hollow between hills. This was the end of the journey.

While Bates dismounted and set about making a fire, Sir Edward still sat his horse, overwhelmed, as it seemed, by his misfortunes. He knew he was guilty of no treason; yet here he was a runaway, proclaimed up and down England as a traitor, his goods seized, his house burned, and miles and miles from Paola, with all hope gone of rescuing her. As he thought of these things, he turned in his saddle and childishly shook his fist in the direction of Verschoyle's house.

"From today there is no quarter between you and me", he muttered. "Ten years if need be, I'll pursue you, but I shall have you at last, God aid me!"

For the moment, however, there was nothing more exciting to be done than to lie concealed, and send Bates out to forage, who might pick up by the way some trustworthy information concerning the destruction which had fallen. And in effect before long Bates had cunningly established communications here and there, and from the news he brought in Sir Edward was able to piece together a story.

There could be no doubt he had been ruined by Mr. Verschoyle. The prince, finding his orders neglected and his letters unnoticed, was become angry and suspicious; and Mr. Verschoyle had succeeded, not only in conveying damaging reports to His Highnesses ears, but had also fastened on Morvan many imprecise and black discredits, contrived to blast his integrity with Lord Digby, Legge, Ashburnham, Warwick, and others who were in the private counsels of the king. But there was one letter, above all else, which definitely lost Sir Edward with the Royalists.

In this letter, written in cypher by Sir Richard Willis a few weeks after Morvan first came into the country, the writer, while strictly enjoining his correspondent to delay not his return to Newark, at the same time, very unfortunately as it turned out for the other, gave some tactical details of a sally which he was planning. Now this letter, having been warily trapped by Verschoyle's servants, and the express riding with it persuaded he had delivered the paper to none other than Sir Edward Morvan himself, was presently carried to a division of the Parliament Army under Massey, together with the key of the cypher, which Morvan in the mazedness and insouciance of those blissful days had left lying about, and a servant in Verschoyle's pay had purloined.

When Rupert defeated Massey's force at Ledbury, these papers among others found their way to the commander-in-chief's own hands. The prince disliked Sir Edward already, and was prepared to find in him all sorts of treacheries since he knew him to be a friend of the Lords Goring and Wilmot, and of Daniel O'Neil; and when he reached Oxford early in May he did not measure his words in passionately denouncing Morvan before the king. The upshot was that a troop was detached to carry fire and sword against the traitor. It is said (*Memoirs relating to the Family of Morvan*, vol. II), that the commander of the party had orders to put Morvan to death on the place, and having taken his informations timed his attack for the hour when that one was usually returned home.

So, if his horse had not gone lame, he would now be dead of a shameful death, and unavenged. His ruin, as he gathered from the report of Bates, was well-nigh complete: the soldiers had carried away everything; his tenants had been intimidated and ordered not to pay their landlord any more rent; altogether, he was undone and his two sisters—fortunately with their aunt in Yorkshire when the soldiers came—were likely to beg their bread. Morvan, as he brooded over this disaster, was filled with rage against the prince and the king's other advisers in this business, for their readiness to condemn him unheard.

True, Morvan had been of the party amongst the king's followers against Prince Rupert, whom he regarded as a young foreigner battling mainly for his own hand; a soldier of fortune whose methods of warfare were questionable, and who had on his side all the broken rakes, the men of prey, and the low-fortuned nobility and gentry of the country,—in fact all those disorderly and refractory persons who brought dishonour on the king's arms and made the name of cavalier a byword for lewdness, and rapine, and swearing. He even went so far as to suspect the prince of hiding a design to shoulder out the old king and set himself up instead.

These opinions upon His Highness he had expressed pretty freely up and down, and Rupert was no doubt acquainted with them; hence it was reasonable enough that when the opportunity offered the king's nephew should shew no reluctance to rid himself of an avowed enemy. That was as far as Prince Rupert went; but leaving him aside, Morvan had been loyal to King Charles and his cause to the full measure. He had not only served at his own charge, but at the first setting up of the Royal standard he had brought a strong company into the field which as the war went on had been gradually dispersed.

In common with many another man of his level serving in the

Royal Army, Sir Edward had taken the king's side more from sentiment than from any strong convictions as to the righteousness of the cause; and like many another man at all stages of the world, he found the justice of the cause strangely diminished by the harsh treatment he had suffered in his own person from its upholders. Still, for that cause he had fought even to shedding his blood: he might have got leave to travel, as many did at the beginning of the troubles; but he had remained and taken the brunt, and now this was his reward!

As a matter of fact, he had almost as many friends out for the Parliament as riding for the king; and in his present desperate fortunes, with his eagerness to get even, to assuage his soreness, to counteract his ruin, and above all, to lay a heavy retributive hand on that old vile rat and sorcerer Verschoyle, he was vastly disposed to revise his convictions, and to throw in his lot with those whom he no longer hesitated to consider as the honest party in the State.

Ultimately, that is what he made up his mind to do. Having first sounded some of his friends on the Parliament side to ascertain what welcome he might expect within their lines, he set forth one night attended by Bates, and notwithstanding some dangers and hindrances made a rapid journey to Oxford, which the New Model under Fairfax was at that time investing.

When he presented himself at headquarters, being very sensitive to slights after his late trials and because of his present equivocal position, he found himself irritated and baffled by the general's reserved, frigid demeanour, wherein he seemed to detect a note of irony. But one or two of his friends who stood by during the interview assured him that his impression was wrong, that those dry sombre manners were ordinary with 'Black Tom', and that on the whole he had been received very honourably. Anyhow, whether that was the truth or not, Fairfax must at least have thought well of his qualities as a soldier, for he had not been many days with the army before he was appointed to a rather important post. A few weeks later he drew his sword against the king in person at Naseby.

6

In the *Manuscript* of Sir John Holdershaw which we follow, at that part corresponding to the place we have now reached are inserted various excerpts from the Royalist News-letters, *Mercuries*, and pamphlets, which leave no doubt that Sir Edward Morvan's defection was deeply resented by that party. Ever since Marston there had been a pretty constant trickling of officers and soldiers from the king to the Parliament, and the lapse of a man of Morvan's standing could hardly fail to draw many waverers in its wake.

Beyond that, his action must have the worst effect upon those little squires and men of middling estate up and down the country, ostensibly for the king, but who watched the wind, and whose *lâchetés* have been covered over for us of a later day by the noble unswerving loyalty of the greatest part of the Cavaliers; just as on the opposite side the unquestionable religious fervour and conviction of a section of the Parliament Army stands forth so conspicuously, that some of us are led to attribute to that army as a whole a higher credit for godliness than perhaps it deserved.

But the writers against Morvan, to say the truth, somewhat overreached themselves; for though their evident game was to prove that they were well rid of him, their violence revealed their mortification. They did not regulate their attacks by any sense of decency, but rather fell on with a brutal freedom, fleshing their pens, and howling. The result, as might be expected, is a body of writing incredibly scurrilous, noisy, and confused, floundering in all that bad taste and licentiousness of vituperation which really seem often the only things that count in political writings and speeches.

Here, however, it is purposed to pluck but few weeds from all this garbage; basing ourselves upon the opinion of a gentleman who himself served the king without flinching to the end:—That to write invectives is more criminal than to err in eulogies. Our one great difficulty is the almost impossibility we are in to select among these indecencies so as to avoid shocking a fastidious age; and we take leave to premise that the specimens offered have been chosen rather because they are the least offensive than because they are the most witty—wit, alas! not being always inseparable from propriety, but on the contrary too often flourishing amid filth, as fair plants use to spring from the dung laid about their roots.

Nay, so far are we here from the spirit of true wit, that perhaps the most regrettable feature of those examples we are permitted by the aforesaid considerations to lay before the reader, is a dull, barbarous mood of contumely, fatal to those lighter graces which alone can render a malign way of writing tolerable.

For instance, one author, after railing scandalously at 'That notable hee-whore, who by his lewd embracements and chamberings with the rebels, hath dared, as we may say, to make the royal cause a cuckold',—thus bursts forth:

> *Temples of Venus fall apart!*
> *Ye bordelloes fall down!*
> *The bawds have given up their trade*
> *Since Morvan's on the town.*

Another delivers a laboured assault in a long dull pamphlet entitled, *God's Deliverance from the Lousy; Exemplifyed in the Filthy, Accursed, and Poysonous Seditions and Treachery of Sir Ed. Morvan, Kt.* From this wearisome compilation, which is full of lies, and among other fictions relates that Sir Edward, upon his reception by the Parliament forces, was stricken with a loathly disease, "Whereby his nose by God's mercy is now clene gon", we take the following lines, in which all point seems to be sacrificed to heavy ferocity and dirtyness:

> *That part which holds his wit and grace*
> *Is Morvan's only pride;*
> *Lest we might think it was his face,*
> *He shewed us his backside.*

The best of them perhaps is a long catch called *Morvan's*—," written, it is alleged, by "A Person of Honour now with His Ma...tie." It is too gross to repeat. The reader, we are sure, has been holding his nose over this noisome paragraph, which nothing but a scrupulousness to present this narrative impartially could have persuaded us to pen.

But Mr. Verschoyle himself with equal fervour, if more decorously, drew a grave and sober pen against Sir Edward, writing, as soon as he was possessed of the particulars, with great secrecy to Sir Edward Nicholas who had long stood his friend:—

Much Honored Frend,

The Pleasure I gain from writing to you is dulled and tarnished by the heavy matter I treat of which a poysonous wind hath presently blown into mine eares. Sir the newes of Sir Edward Morvan's defection, who was my neighbour, with tyes of kindred to my wife, has panged those hid and vital parts which truely I did think naught but the cold hand of death himself could reach to. For I do conceive that those who from the first stirring of these troubles have stood with the Parliament, should end by rangeing openly in the field against the king, is what our sad occasions (though bitterly) have learned us to endure: But that one who did enlist himselfe under the king's standard, and as it were under the very shado and countenance of Maiestie, should now unsheath the swoard against his anointed lord and sovraine, is what i can find no mate of in blacknesse since this most cruel unnatural war, and doth drap in herse-like weeds the pen of, Sir,

> Your most affectionat frend and humblest servaunt
> Simon Verschoyle.

And when he considered his neighbourhood and familiarity with Sir Edward, and how that one had unhinged all his cunningly laid plans by stepping over to the Roundheads, instead of being taken and killed in his own house; when he reflected upon Morvan's constant visits of late, and how promptly and terribly the king's troops had come down; he thought it wisest to allay any suspicion which might be reflected from Morvan on himself, and to nullify any pretext the Royalists might seize from this affair to plunder him in the same way. Accordingly he departed from the neutral and temporising policy he had hitherto pursued so far as to add to the foregoing letter this post-script:—

Sir, I ask you to represent to His Maiestie's Favour (tho' God knows I am not beforehand in my Fortune) that 3 sound hors goe with these to the army, and monyes for the comfort and maintenance of the cause: Also 3 lusty fellowes goe. Sir I pray your frendship to stand me in a fayre light before His Maiestie.

But he had favourable relations with both parties: raging as he was at Morvan's escape, he thought it convenient to throw a plank between the knight's legs in the camp of his new friends; and so, within a few days he wrote as follows to the Speaker of the House of Commons:

Right Honourable,
One I am ashamed to call my cosen and neighbour, Sir Ed. Morvan I meane, hath of late so insinuated himself as to be carried to your armies. Sir, be vigilant lest ye be by him ensnared. Truely I doe think he is a spye. He hath been entertained in Yorks by Mr. Perigal, a most fierce papist and malignant, who is his oncle, and careth not for staid company, but lewd and roaring boys. I confesse I would be loath to see you receive a foyle by this deboshed drinking Cavalier, who for all his white eies and feignings is a true Castilian at hart. Sir he strangely loves

the bottle, and I misdoubt me will join in your army with certain merrie roysterers (being a prime favourite among such, the same who have contrived his putting over to the Parliament) and thus sow poysonous tares of unrighteousness among the Godly field of your army.—Were my occasions to serve you matcht with my desires, I must be even more than now I am

Your Honour's truely Grateful Humble Servaunt

Simon Verschoyle.

7

What precise effect these letters had, or if they had any, cannot now be determined. But it is certain that Morvan was regarded unamiably by many of the Puritans: there are two letters of Whalley's, for instance, in which he is unmistakeably aimed at in bitter and discrediting terms. Still, for all that, he continued to serve with the New Model, and appears to have more than once distinguished himself, till the flight of the king and the capitulation of Oxford put an end to the war. In the troubled times that followed he took an active, though of course very subordinate part, and made himself useful to that party in the State with which certain of his friends, Sir Harry Vane amongst others, were identified.

But he had never influence enough to get himself compensated out of the sequestered estates for the loss of his house, or—what he wanted much more—to obtain legal authority for the rooting out of old Verschoyle. In those days he lived very hard and meanly; for the king's troops had not only burned his house, but had ruined many holdings on the estate, and the tenants, being encouraged by Mr. Verschoyle, who worked among them with a thousand wiles, gladly availed themselves of the excuse, which the unsettled state of the country made a sufficient one, that having been forbidden by the king to pay rent to Sir Edward Morvan they were no longer sure to whom rent should be paid.

They ended by paying nobody. And it is doubtless on account of his extreme poverty that the movements of Sir Edward about this time are so clouded. We lose sight of him more than once in the months that passed between the surrender of the king by the Scots and the outbreak of the second war. He seems to have had a lodging, or at least an address, in Milk Street, over against Maudlin Church; but we do not find in his obscure and tormented history any fact worth noticing till near the end of 1647, when he was a principal in a peculiarly unhappy sort of duel, the circumstances of which seem odd enough to deserve some particular relation in this place.

As he was seated one evening in an Ordinary, there entered a young gentleman who had been his greatest friend at the University, and who was now become one of those wild and dissolute spirits in the king's party whose exploits left that party as a whole accessible to the worst accusations of its enemies. This gentleman, perceiving Morvan, planted himself directly in face, called for wine, and began staring insolently, and making a thousand offensive gestures studied to affront the other opposite, who for his part paid but little heed to these antics. When the wine was brought, the newcomer turns to a precise serious clergyman near him who was attentively reading in some papers, and "By your leave, Doctor," he calls out, "determine me by the Synod of Dort whether it is the greater sin to sit in a room colleaguing with Judas Iscariot, or to. . . ."

The clergyman, seeing that a disturbance was in the air, answered drily, and gathering up his papers left the house. Upon this the Cavalier, not to be baulked of his quarrel, rose with a clatter so as to draw the eyes of all men in the room, and strolling over to where Morvan was seated, he cocks his hat at him, calls him a cuckoldy ass, and asked him what he meant by sitting down while his betters were standing? Without waiting for more, Morvan got slowly to his feet and hit the speaker a damned blow in the mouth. And in their frenzy, they were going to a bout of fisticuffs on the spot; but the drawers and some of the company pulling them apart, they caught up their cloaks and swords and stepped into the street, none offering to stay them, though all guessed the fierceness of the business they went upon.

Once outside, the two made their way doggedly and sullenly to the fields beyond the Pest-house. It was a rainy night, with a tearing wind, and a full moon, which shining forth at intervals through the tumultuous clouds gleamed on the pools and wet grass of the place. And, in effect, it was probably owing to the condition of the ground that the contest after all was so brief, which otherwise might have been prolonged and hardly fought, for Morvan was no better at sword play than his opponent; who, however, unhappily slipping in the mud, almost fell on Morvan's point which pierced him through.

When he found himself down, with Morvan clumsily bending over him, the wounded man raised himself on his hands and looked at the other very tenderly. "Buss me, Ned", says the poor heedless wretch, "for I think thou hast hurt me, lad, and I swear to God, I loved thee better than anyone all the time." Whereupon Morvan, weeping like a silly big child, careless of the danger he ran, took his friend up on his shoulders intending to make for his own lodging; but ere he had covered half the distance he was arrested with his dismal burthen.

Whether the stricken cavalier recovered is uncertain; but from the somewhat considerable efforts which St. John, who was Morvan's friend over this matter, apparently had to make, notwithstanding his influence, ere he could extricate his client, it is to be feared that the poor foolish gentleman died. Still, it is evident that this affair, however rigorously it may have been judged by some of the Puritans, did not stand in the way of Morvan's employment when the war broke out afresh, for he was undeniably in the field as a horse-captain under his old leader Fairfax at the capture of Maidstone.

Meanwhile, during those broken times, Mr. Verschoyle had dwelt on his lands perfectly unmolested. He gathered his rents as usual; he was regular in paying his taxes; he had taken the Covenant, and laboriously improved his relations with the Parliament. Sheltered by the Presbyterians, and looked on with a certain favour even by the Independents in London, at home he grew more close, more mysterious, and on occasions more truculent than ever. To his wife he would guard a moody taciturnity for weeks together; though he did not choose to spare her his company at these seasons, but would sit with her sometimes for hours, glowering, and frowning, and mumbling, and harshly rebuking her if she tried to leave the chamber.

At other times, with that fury which always possessed him because of his foiled vengeance upon Morvan, he would turn against his wife and cover her with insults which were no less stinging because they were indirect and veiled. He had a favourite song, beginning "*I am a cuckold bold*," full of low jests, and this he and his one-eyed steward would sit together bawling solemnly for half-an-hour on end, shewing a wonderful ingenuity in twisting Sir Edward's name into the verses, and appealing to Paola to applaud, as it were, the hits. The unfortunate lady gradually became such a slave to her fears that she was never able to pass a moment with him free from trepidation.

If he spoke, she awaited some reproach; every morsel that she ate she knew not but it was poisoned. One day when he had been extremely violent and sour, wishing at length to draw his watch from his pocket to regulate his time, his wife thought he was going to pull out a pistol to kill her, and fell from her chair fainting. When he was abroad, she could only sit for hours with a book on her lap which she would not even open, so discouraged was she! —wan, motionless, gazing afar off with a blank stare, holding a quaint flower to her cheek languidly. She went no more into the garden, neither in summer nor at autumn-tide, shrinking plaintively from that scene of her intensest joys and bitter sorrow.

8

The extraordinary and lamentable situation of Paola was not known to Morvan in all its details, but he knew more about it than Mr. Verschoyle suspected. Though he could not come into the country himself, he had trusty spies and sure intelligence. But rage as he might at what he heard, he could compass nothing against his enemy: Mr. Verschoyle was too strongly supported in London for Sir Edward's necessarily vague charges to prevail, and such charges, advanced as they had to be without any direct proof, did Morvan more harm than good. He would have been sensible of this himself, had not every new report of Paola's sad condition put all else out of his head save an iron purpose to deliver her by a bloody and punitive deliverance, no matter what the consequences might be, so long as she was delivered. For he feared that Paola might even die between the cruel hands of her gaoler, like a young bird panting out its life in the clumsy grasp of a boy.

But at last, when despairing and maddened he had almost made up his mind to desert and attempt Verschoyle's house single-handed, he obtained, by a singular piece of good-luck, or rather, if we recollect the methods by which his own integrity had been blasted before the king, by a kind of wild justice, the very thing he needed to assist his aim. This was nothing less effective than the letter given some pages back which was written by Mr. Verschoyle to Sir Edward Nicholas, and which, having been sent by Nicholas to a certain nobleman, was again passed on, and was at last forgotten with other papers in a house in Wales, hurriedly abandoned, to fall into the hands of a Parliament troop commanded by a friend of Morvan's, who knew partly what Morvan had suffered from Verschoyle, his soreness and rancour, his restless impatience to be avenged.

It was by the postscript of the letter that Verschoyle was undone: in face of such irrefutable evidence of malignancy there could be no more hesitation to prosecute the writer, who moreover added to his malignancy a particularly detestable kind of double-dealing. Nevertheless, there was still some delay; for Morvan, who was bent upon attacking Verschoyle's house in person, could not be spared from the blockade of Colchester, where he was indefatigable during the sick and rainy summer; and at last, it was the day after the town fell that Fairfax, whose good opinion he had secured by various acts of gallantry and discipline, gave him leave to detach half a troop, at the head of which he set forth grimly on his errand. It so happened that although Morvan, like Fairfax himself, for the rest, was of a "rational" temper, as it was called, most of the soldiers riding with him were zealots and fanatics of one kind or another, transported by various wild fancies, seraphical and notional, and full of a stubborn religious arrogance and intolerance.

It was on the fine afternoon of one of the earliest days of September that he drew near the familiar, and in spite of all! well-loved place. He was ready to forget the stern work he had come to do, as he gazed from a turn of the road at the house he had always preferred to his own or any other, standing now russet-toned and grey, so venerable, so sweetly quiet, so ineffably serene in the clear thin light. Just at the moment that the troopers wheeled in at the gate, Mr. Verschoyle was sitting down to dinner, finding himself today in an excellent humour with the world.

He was cordial, even conciliating to Paola, with debonair gracious manners, engaging enough when he chose to give them play; and he awed into cringing silence the one-eyed knave who usually at this hour had a loose rein. But scarcely had they begun the repast, than a young man, excited and panic-stricken, stood on the threshold.

Without interrupting himself in what he was saying to his wife, who attended dejectedly, Mr. Verschoyle made a sign to the steward to rise and learn the youth's message. The two whispered a minute at the end of the room, and then the steward came up to Verschoyle's chair, shewing a countenance perturbed and sallow.

"How now, whey-cheeks?" sang out his master, noticing his fearful look. "Why, what a troublesome thing is guilt! Have they come for thee at last?"

"May't please your honour", stammered the other, all of a shake, "'tis the soldiers in your noble honour's gate. 'Tis the soldiers that— 'tis the soldiers—"

"'Tis the soldiers, 'tis the soldiers" repeated Mr. Verschoyle, mocking him. "They will surely hang thee, Abraham; that is in no doubt at all. Thou art the last of thy noble race. Sure (he went on scoffingly) I have heard thee talk sedition and hold most damnable invective speeches: I have heard them and I'll say them. I'll betray thee, Abraham,—yes, I'll give thee up. I have heard thee say thou didst hope to see the Roundheads tumbling in their blood, when some of their money should chink in thy pockets. Was it not so?—Nay, the truth is thou hast been at the wine. Where are these soldiers save in thy drunken fancy and yon fool's?"

"Nay, so please you sir, even as I speak you may hear them". And in effect the trampling of many horses and the clatter of accoutrements were coming in plainly through the open windows.

Perceiving that he was for some reason or other evidently besieged, Mr. Verschoyle rose gravely from the table. "Since the soldiers encompass us", he said, "let us go forth to meet them."

But as he was passing down the room the steward in a frenzy of terror flung himself at his master's feet.

"Save me, save me!" he yelled. "Only you can save me. I have been an evil man, I have colleagued, I have had commerce with the devil, I have lain embraced by harlots. Here comes my last breathing hour, God ha' mercy! They will hang me if you'll not protect me, sir; they will tear out my bowels—yea, truly, they will rip me up."

Mr. Verschoyle spurned him with his foot as he might a whelp. "Get thee hence", he said contemptuously. And turning to Paola as they passed into the hall he added: "'Tis but an hour's madness in that poor mean fellow. He is no coward for the things of this world, but he sees hell-fire in a farthing rushlight. He was bred a Puritan."

By now some of the soldiers had entered the grassy court, and the great bell clanged harshly. This being followed by loud peremptory knocks, Mr. Verschoyle, who could not have offered any effectual resistance even if he had wished, ordered the doors to be thrown open. No sooner was this done, than Morvan at once stepped into the hall. Completely armed, he had his steel cap on his head, and it was easy to see he had come there to bring trouble. But Mr. Verschoyle, standing large and gaunt and black before the hearth, chose to ignore his implacable demeanour.

"Welcome, Ned!" he cried with an emphatic cordiality, "thou art returned home at last. We have heard of thy prowesses. No part of the earth but is full of thy labours. What battles thou hast seen, what signal victories!"

For all answer Morvan bowed low to Paola, noting with grief and anger as he did so her emaciated frame and the almost spectral paleness of her visage. She on her side spoke no word, but merely bent her head slightly in acknowledgement of his salutation, and remained seated in a high-backed chair, resting her head upon her fragile hand.

Morvan then looked straight at Verschoyle.

"My business, sir", he observed coldly, "is of an unpleasant nature, at least for you. My orders are to inform you that you are suspected to be a dangerous malignant, and to search your house. For that, I warrant you," he added insultingly, for he could hardly control his rage, "I'll not ask your leave—only taking care", said he, again looking at Paola to reassure her, "that the innocent shall not be confounded with the guilty."

About half-a-dozen troopers had by this time followed their captain into the hall. Mr. Verschoyle stared at them a moment with a kind of bland wonder, rocking himself up and down in his big shoes. Then he blew a long whistling breath through his teeth.

"Hoity-toity, these be fine words", he said; "vastly fine words. I protest I do love a round speech, sonorous and musical. But thou hast improved thyself in the army, Ned; thou hast plied thy book, man! How have they transformed thee? The next ignorant, sottish, ill-licked, impudent cub that I meet who's no good but to shamble about and make eyes at the women, I'll send him to the army. Truly, 'tis a better school for dunces than a university—that I see, that I see. Hast thy search-warrant, lad?"

Morvan, outraged and indignant, curtly handed him the document. Mr. Verschoyle glancing through it saw that he was accused of sending horses and money to the Royal Army, and otherwise comforting those in arms against the Parliament; his servants and tenants too were said to be deeply engaged. He saw further, that he was charged circumstantially with playing the traitor to the Parliament, and that Morvan was empowered to bring him in custody to London. There could be no doubt that the warrant was genuine; and with a feeling of uneasiness which he disguised perfectly he gave the paper back to Morvan.

"I question your authority", he said boldly. "But that can stand over till later. There is naught of treachery here; no, nor hidden either. Begin your search; I am small afraid."

Paying little attention to what he said, Morvan gave a few sharp orders, and the troopers scattered about the house striking their swords and the butts of their pistols against the wainscotting to discover monies or compromising papers concealed. Morvan left the hall to control the search, for it was not in the least his intention to have the house wrecked and plundered. Mr. Verschoyle too mounted the stairs and sat himself in the embrasure of a great window on the wide landing where the staircase turned, keeping always on his face a smile false and terrible. And Paola still remained moveless in the hall, resting her head on her hand.

While matters were at this tension, suddenly there arose a doleful wail or ululation which drifted in from the terrace, and softened by the walls, filled the rooms and corridors with sobs and miserable cries. It seemed as if the spirit of the place, rudely disturbed after peaceful years, and presaging some tremendous misfortune and downfall, was wandering disconsolate through the building with laments and long moans. But as a matter of fact, the disquieting rumour was due to the soldiers stationed outside, who, finding the waiting heavy, had started a religious service.

Most of these men were Straddlingites, or as they were more commonly named, "Oh-Ho's", one of those numberless petty sects which flourished at the period and found their most favourable ground in the army. Originally called by its popular name simply from a physical defect of the founder, Know-the-Lord Straddling, one of Harrison's captains—a defect which forced him when he rose to preach or pray at first to emit certain involuntary ejaculations, and cry out many times "Oh-ho, oh-ho!" accompanied by uncouth writhings, the popular name indicated in a measure the ritual of the sect; for the cries and contortions of the afflicted man would after a while so disturb the nerves of his listeners that they could not do otherwise than fall to imitating him sympathetically, and wail "Oh-ho, oh-ho!" in their turn with all their might. And this was the ominous and melancholy sound which was now wafted in and floated sadly through the house, while Morvan's troopers relentlessly searched, and Mr. Verschoyle sat smiling, smiling, gazing blankly out of the window.

After about half-an-hour, Sir Edward tramped down the stairs. He was ghastly pale, but his eyes gleamed, and on his face was a look of unshakeable resolution. Mr. Verschoyle rose to meet him, gathering together all his formidable powers of intimidation.

"Well, honest soldier," he began jeeringly, "gallant Hector, noble swashbuckler, runaway Ned, brave warrior on women and the aged, have you nosed out any treason lurking in my walls?"

"No", answered Morvan briefly, "we have found nothing". Then seeing that the other was going to speak, "You took good care of that", he added as an afterthought. "However, we know enough."

"All you can know, Edward", returned Mr. Verschoyle, speaking deliberately for the ears of the soldiers who now had gathered behind their leader up the stairs and on the first floor, "all you can know to my discredit is that I am a poor old man, bowed with age, who live here with no other wish than to finish out my few harmless dusty years in peace, far from all state tumults, and to be laid in a quiet grave."

"Ay, we'll give you that, brother", retorted Morvan grimly, "even as we gave it to Sir Charles Lucas a few days since. I mean to have you shot."

Mr. Verschoyle made a slight convulsive movement with his shoulder as if indeed a bullet had just struck him there, but otherwise he betrayed no surprise nor any emotion. "No, Edward", he said with sorrowful dignity, "you will not do that. You will not slay an unarmed, defenceless, and grey man, who has offered no resistance to your search. I knew your father, Edward, and your grandfather; I knew you when you were a little boy. If you command this most bloodthirsty and unnatural act, I tell you solemnly you will rue it all the days of your life. Observe, the deed will not be on the heads of these honest fellows here whom you order to fire the shot (and I heartily forgive them!) but you will be the horrible murderer yourself—yea, as truly as if you sheathed your sword in my vitals. Think well on it, Edward; commit not this black and horrid murder of a helpless old man".

He might as well have called to the east wind to blow softlier. "You burned my house", answered Morvan sombrely; "you scandalised me before the king. You have betrayed the dearest pledges; you have fired and harried. You have hunted the poor man like a partridge on the mountains. You have brought about the ruin and loss of many lives. You are an execrable and satanical cozener. Your lusts stink, your magics and bedevilments cry to Heaven. My conscience is clear for what I now do, and God judge between you and me. Not this country only, but all England will bless me for ridding it of such a monster." And turning, he called the soldiers to attention.

But the corporal, leveller, fanatic, preacher and Straddlingite as he was, a man who had been some time before chosen an Agitator for his uncompromising root-and-branch principles, on this occasion took the freedom to interpose.

"Stay, sir", he said familiarly to Morvan, "balance well what you do. Our warrant goes not to the spilling of this blood. Sooth, I know that this greybeard is a son of Belial, spuing forth rottenness from his mouth, and given over pertinently to destruction; but oh, consider you that he is old, his sojournings with rogues and strumpets termed, his toyings with his painted young concubine below stairs soured, his days of iniquity nigh ended. For what says Paul? Paul says, That which decayeth and waxeth old is ready to vanish away. Not of all malignants do I speak as one who would spare them nay, rather should they be smote with the edge of the sword, their kings utterly destroyed, and their hellish dunghill of filthy, beastly, Babylonish priests consumed by fire. But this malignant man is old, and old blood should have a dry death. Oh, if this man's days be evil, they are soon done; if his nights unruly, they are soon one black; and verily his latter end will be bitterness".

This harangue, cast in the language, and spoken, or rather preached, in the tone they delighted in, had a marked effect on the soldiers. Sir Edward, noticing this, and fearing the scruples of the soldiers might even provoke them to mutiny, and his prey escape after his careful toils, endeavoured with considerable readiness of wit to move them in a contrary sense by a vivid appeal to their prejudices.

"Seize the sorcerer!" he shouted, "he has bewitched our worthy corporal. Now he casts his Popish spells on us. The change is about to reach us all; soon we shall be turned into mice and rats if he be not presently slain. All the country knows this miscreant puts on the shape of a bloody beast at night, and has devoured two-and-twenty children in that form. Would you have the devil among you in the shape of a large wolf, raging and tearing? I tell you he is a wizard, and a Papist, and an atheist. Out into the courtyard with him ere worse befall! See!" yelled Morvan pointing excitedly, "Oh, God. see!—he is even now changing to a grey wolf.

The soldiers stared with dilated eyes, and thought they did really see some frightful transformation in progress. Recklessly brave in the field, they were slaves to their terror of Popish spells, and witchcraft, and magical receipts. Willingly, and even eagerly they formed up under Macron's order to drag Mr. Verschoyle forth.

But he, stepping up to the corporal who stood between him and Morvan, laid his hand on the trooper's shoulder. "Stand by, friend", he said gently; "I am no drunkard and carnal man as thou dost fancy, but a precisian even as thyself, who follows and sermons and prays in my family. The gentlewoman below stairs is indeed young, but of godly carriage, and truly my wife. I do set my face against the wicked railers and swearers and other lewd persons who persecute me for righteousness even"—he said, raising his voice and pushing the corporal aside, "yea, even as this swearing, cursing, Scottish knight of the blade here now."

And with that, fetching a spring swift and lithe as a tiger's, he leaped upon Morvan, with a force amazing in such an ancient man, and bore him to the ground—seizing him by the throat and face and throttling him with has great powerful hands. The soldiers threw themselves on him, and with immense difficulty mastered the terrible frantic creature who had now cast off all self-control and struggled with them, striking and ravening, to get once more at Morvan, the hatred of years boiling in his head.

"What!" he roared, "You would slay me, and then steal my house and marry my wife? Ah no!—before God, no! Not till I have torn the false tongue from your throat. What Verschoyle has Verschoyle holds. I will not leave the earth till I have seen you dead."

The soldiers dragged him downstairs, struggling furiously. But Morvan, gasping for breath, outraged and shamed, was taken with such a devilish frenzy of passion that he thought if he did not now kill Verschoyle with his own hand, he would be cheated after all of the sweets of revenge. He ran down the stairs, and reaching across the shoulders of the troopers, clapped the nose of his pistol against the old man's breast. But the weapon snapped without exploding, whereupon he brought the butt down with a smash on Verschoyle's face, "I will lie in Hell for an eternity to be even with you", he said,

A soldier threw open the door leading out from the hall; and there was the court, placidly green and silver in the kind afternoon sun. Mr. Verschoyle, since he had taken the blow, had ceased to struggle, and stood amid his guards gaunt, sinister and inscrutable, with his bleeding face raised to the sky, or perhaps only to a stone set high near the roof on which had been carved long ago the punning motto: *Verschoyle's Keep Verschoyle Keeps.* Sir Edward and another officer handed their carbines to a couple of troopers; and as it happened, Morvan being still too strangled with fury and excitement to get his voice, it was the cornet at last who gave the word. The soldiers fired and the old man fell lifeless.

How much of these dreadful scenes Paola had witnessed no one can tell. When Morvan went in search of her, he found her still seated in the hall with her head resting on her hand, but she had swooned.

9

In the event, when at length she was able to realise the sane wide spaces these harsh doings had opened about her life on all sides, it was not, astonishingly enough! relief that was her principal sensation. She felt gratefully, indeed, that the immediate stifling pressure of the tyrant was removed; that she was now able to breathe freely where before she had been suffocating; that she could go and come when she liked; that she was young and rich and free; but these pleasant impressions were blurred by the haunting conviction that her new state was unreal, that her terrible husband had but withdrawn himself for a little while, and would certainly come back whenever it suited his ends.

This insensate fear invested all her actions with a certain indecision; upon everything she did there was an air of the makeshift and temporary; she recoiled from any step decided and permanent, shadowed as she was by the dread of that gaunt irresistible form returning to take possession, to demand an account. Her very sleep was afflicted by shocking dreams in which he was constantly before her: now in the clinging cerements of the grave; *anon* in his habit as he lived, but with a green wound in his breast still bleeding; and always towering, threatening, terrifying, standing over her with a diabolic majesty, then crushing her down with his hands; till at last she would start up strangling, covered with sweat, feeling even after she was broad awake that the old man was there actually in the room, at her bedside.

Such dreams as these, the intensified prolongations of her waking reveries, took away from her all desire to stir abroad and see the world, or otherwise to taste the advantages of her freedom. Any attempt at pleasure, she felt, would not come off happily; would be cursed, so to speak, in advance. Far better to stay at home, to change nothing in her mode of life, to traverse none of the old orders and measures—not to beat, in fine, against that still powerful and implacable will, but just to rest quiet and wait.

Morvan tried to disengage her from these gloomy apprehensions, but it was long ere his exertions met with any response; and in fact, it may be said that never at any time did he succeed in quelling them altogether. Although towards the spring of 1650 she at last consented to marry him, that too was still with the consciousness of an act provisional, desultory, an idle and temerarious catching at happiness which the unseen, horror-striking watcher did not approve of, and might at any time bring to a harrowing termination. It was not, either, that Paola regarded the circumstances of her husband's death with compunction, or instinctively shrank from Morvan as a guilty and blood-stained man.

As far as her knowledge of the affair went, Mr. Verschoyle's house had been attacked by soldiery; he had resisted, perhaps slain one or two, and had been slain himself in turn. Such events were become too common in England of late years to cause any special wonder. She thought of her husband's end as she might have thought had he fallen in the field of battle, and of Morvan's part in it as if he had commanded a regiment which had but done its duty and come off victorious. Sir Edward took every precaution not to disabuse her mind in its imperfect apprehension of those events, and never spoke with any particularity of the attack on the house.

Abating these clouds, which were wont indeed since their marriage to dwindle to a thin sun-coloured haze, the wedded pair ought to have been happy; the world smiled before them almost genially. Young, and lovers who, long separated, were now fortunately joined in the suavity of wedded love, rich, seated in one of the fairest estates in England, truly it seemed as if Fortune, having plagued them so long, had of late grown ashamed of her persecutions, and turning benignant, was remorsefully loading them with compensating favours. The troubles which were shaking the country passed them by.

Sir Edward was looked upon with favour by the leading spirits of the Republic, and was outside of all suspicion because of his prowesses against the Royalist Armies, and his signal unkennelling of that notorious malignant and plotter old Mr. Verschoyle, of whose death he had rendered an acceptable account, which was perhaps the more eagerly received as there were more than one or two in the House who would have found themselves strangely embarrassed and uneasy if the old schemer had been carried alive to London. Vane the younger and Haslerig were special friends to Morvan, and willingly looked after his interests.

To be sure he had his enemies, and he was disliked, among others, by Cromwell, who, it is said, distrusted him. for changing his coat and gulping down the Covenant with such suspicious readiness, and who, after he became supreme, persistently refused to employ him in business of state; but for all that his credit was so good at the Protector's Council-table, that when, in time, the Major-Generals were let loose to fine and otherwise harass the country gentlemen whose loyalty to the government was questionable, he was left unmolested.

Yes, they had every reason to be happy, and no doubt in a measure they were so. The husband certainly was happier than he had ever been in his life. And Paola too would throw herself desperately on waves of love for days and days together, letting herself be drifted and swayed and lulled till her obsession, waning then and almost dying out, seemed to her as foolish as it did to her husband, and she arrived almost to forget the old man in his grave. For whatever her fancy might suggest, he was in his grave, deep down in the cold earth; of that there could be no question at all.

The huge ugly body had been buried as that of a Popish and atheistical villain, not in the churchyard, but by Morvan's orders under a tree which stood at some distance from the consecrated plot. And at present inside the house there was little to remind one of its former owner. All those servants employed indoors and out who had clung to Mr. Verschoyle, and who had even borne a kind of love for him, or at least took a sort of low pride and delight in his brutalities and powers of chicane and strangely enough! they made a good number had fled to the four winds on that day of their master's downfall. None offered to stay these panic-stricken wretches; but Sir Edward beat the country relentlessly for the one-eyed steward whom he would have hanged up with pleasure had he caught him.

That one, however, had taken to his heels at the first bruit of violence, and by the time Mr. Verschoyle had been laid in earth, and the soldiers began to look round for the fugitive, he had put a good many miles betwixt himself and the house. After various and surprising adventures, which probably would not interest and certainly would not edify the reader, he came at last to a town in Berkshire, where he settled ostensibly to the trade of a tailor, under the name of Everard.

Now in the town where he found himself dwelt one Dr. Pordage, a man of beard and severity, the chiefest then in England of that sect known as the Behmenists. Into the sober family of the doctor did our Everard force himself, pretending that he desired to be of their communion, and setting up a claim to rival Dr. Pordage himself in discerning spirits by the smell, with divers other deceptions of the sort. But in the end, he embroiled the doctor most lamentably by his pranks, bringing the reverend man to be accused of wantonness and familiarity with devils. For in truth, as the doctor soon found to his dismay, Everard was nothing less than a most wily speller and sorcerer, who held active conversation with extremely savage dragons and devils.

Besides that, he most heinously endeavoured to seduce and terrify the good doctor by his damnable arts, appearing to him, it is credibly related, at one time as a fiery dragon as big as a room, and then suddenly changing to a pernicious fly or gnat which buzzed about the doctor's face for above an hour, thus constraining him from learned meditations. Nor was this all. One morning the Pordage family were horrified to discover on the chimney-piece of their parlour the impression of a coach drawn by tigers and lions, and seated in the coach a figure, a very lively image of the reverend doctor himself, taking tobacco and embracing a madam; all obviously the handiwork of Satan.

This, though alarming enough, might yet have been endured; but what was far graver, by his magic and snares Everard gradually turned the good doctor to all manner of abominations, so that the excellent man's house became, while the spell worked, a harbourage for many of the deboshed sort to sit tippling, while he himself turned into an ordinary gamester at cards, sitting up and burning lights in the company of this Everard till two or three o'clock in the morning, to the intense scandal of the township. And one night in particular, the doctor, having sat many hours with the nigromancer engaged in drinking wine, and playing mine host and the good fellow in a very beastly and disgusting fashion which suited not at all with his reverend hairs, must now, if you please, when the night was near done, begin to roar most lewdly, singing carnal songs and setting up to be one of your blades, which brought upon him a remarkable, and fearful judgment.

For he suddenly found himself in his bed without any knowledge of how he got there, all clothed, and having on a pair of boots with spurs which belonged to no one else but Everard; whose face, the light being now come, the doctor, as he afterwards testified, descried nine times at his window, which was raised many feet from the ground, pulling his forelock at him, and making various low and disparaging signs with his fingers. Upon these monstrous events, and the consequent indignation of the doctor's wife, Everard was driven forth from the town, none heeding his contention that the doctor in his cups had insisted upon trying on the boots and could not get them off again; and it is attested that after his departure the excellent doctor at once regained the ways of decorum, to the great contentment of his pious family.

As for the steward, his subsequent fortunes are uncertain; one can only form the blackest conjectures touching his occupations; but there is reason to believe he was among the riff-raff who joined the expedition of Venables to the West Indies and died of a flux in Jamaica.

But though Morvan had the luck to find his house itself cleared of those servants who might have proved hostile, or by their presence recalled unhappy memories, the peasants, on the other hand, rapidly became very irregular and troublesome. By a singular piece of misfortune, the death of Mr. Verschoyle was followed within a few weeks by an outbreak of fever in the cottages, by mortality among the cattle, by all those ills from which for years the estate had been free. In face of this distress the peasants turned mulish and unruly, and fervently wished their old landlord back again, whose death they confounded with that of King Charles, and held Sir Edward Morvan responsible for both.

They would lounge in the ale-house, or hang about the church-yard on Sundays, telling over with a sheepish pride Mr. Verschoyle's most dastardly exploits, and drawing malevolent and disloyal compari-sons with the present owner. And the legend, the inevitable legend, began to gather about the old man's name. It was reported that on the night of his death, and for some nights after, the moon was covered with a shroud of a dismal and fearful texture, while a pool near the house where he used to be seen at twilight in converse with spirits stood three days the colour of blood to the amazement and terror of many. The sober and godly minister who (upheld by Morvan) now performed the duties of that parish, had a most difficult time of it. In vain he preached elaborate and learned discourses against Antinomi-anism; in vain he uprose searchingly against astrologers and witchcraft: his hearty words fell against stubborn and preoccupied ears.

His parishioners had got it into their heads that old Mr. Verschoyle had been opposed to all clergy, and they had done better by following his ways than they ever expected to do again. As a matter of fact, Mor-van was a far more liberal and easy landlord than Mr. Verschoyle had ever been; he had them tended in their sickness; he sent them wine and food and fire; but when all was done he found that his charities were accepted more as a compensation than a benefaction. The more he did for them the more they hated him.

It would seem as if there were a secret method to govern these people, and having that secret you might trample on them, you might treat them like dogs, and yet preserve their respect, obedience, and perhaps their affection; whereas, lacking the secret, though you low-ered their rents, though you improved their holdings, though you covered them with favours, you would find in the end the same in-gratitude, derision, and sullen implacability. For some time after his marriage Morvan used to make kindly visits to his tenants, bringing them gifts, and sitting patiently with those in pain. But he was not wanted; the sickness and misery increasing, notwithstanding his ef-forts, he was supposed to bring bad luck; and as he rode through the villages he was met with scowls and mutters, while a few of the most desperate would threateningly lay stones in their hands.

And as frequently happens, those people, especially those women, who had been the worst treated by Mr. Verschoyle were now his boldest partisans. Even the gentle Paola, whose heart was wrung by the sufferings of these poor folk, going abroad on an errand of mercy, was not spared some insults; and a strapping black-eyed wench called Lizzie Mend, who was said to have lent herself to the old man's embraces, and—as Heaven knows Mr. Verschoyle never made any scruple of defrauding the labourer of the wages of sin—had gained little more by her complaisance than a rough mouth and a wet jacket—well, what must this quean do but frighten Paola almost to death by daringly calling out in her pillory voice the words "Murderess" and Adulteress".

The groom rode back and laid about him with his heavy whip which soon brought Lizzie Mend to her tears; and upon his return, being closely questioned by his master who had noticed his wife's perturbed air, the man with many apologies and begging-of-pardons told the whole story. Morvan was naturally enraged, and the happy-go-lucky damsel would have been dragged before the justice and whipped almost to death, had not this measure reached Paola's ears, who commanded that nothing of the kind should be done. But she went forth among the tenantry no more.

Lizzie Mend, on the other hand, became a sort of popular heroine, and perambulated the country shewing her weals, which she maintained my lady herself had inflicted on her with a foreignlike scourge simply for calling out "God's rest to Mr. Verschoyle!" This lie took all the more because it had by this time become one of the grievances of the common people that Mr. Verschoyle's body had been cast rudely under a tree by soldiers instead of being laid in consecrated ground, and the unredressed injury to his corpse was reckoned against his widow. The idol of a people is sometimes made out of the most unpromising materials: it would have astonished Mr. Verschoyle himself more than anyone else to learn the reverence and affection with which his memory was cherished.

His name was now become a defiant banner, which rallied the most various and extravagant complaints. Had the silly people but known it, they might have done far better, they could have been far happier, with brighter opportunities and encouragement, under the government of Morvan than under their old landlord; but they would make no effort. Believing themselves under a curse, they became churlish and slovenly and unclean, and thus aggravated the evils which pressed upon them so sorely.

All their energies were spent in railing against the present family; and if we make due allowance for the narrow circle of his fame, it can truly be said that in that age of unpopular men there was not a more unpopular man in England than Sir Edward Morvan. And what made the situation immensely worse, Morvan's own estate, the estate he had inherited from his father, having lacked for some years the direction of his own hand and lain open to Mr. Verschoyle's potent wiles and cajoleries, was become infected with the heresies of the neighbouring one.

Often Sir Edward longed to go away and leave these perverse and ungrateful people to the unchained mercies of bailiff and steward; but since Cromwell's troopers had plucked the Parliament men out of their House, and especially after Cromwell himself became Protector, Morvan's hopes of state employment were shattered, and from a political point of view it became in the highest degree expedient for him to rest quietly on his lands.

To these grievous annoyances, and to the unnatural narrowness of life, the restrictions and seclusion which grew out of them, should doubtless be ascribed the singular mental condition which Sir Edward Morvan developed about this time—manifesting itself by an inclination to choose for his favourite resting-place out of doors the tree just out of the churchyard at the roots of which Mr. Verschoyle's body had been laid.

This habit, adopted at first perhaps in a mere angry spirit of bravado, provoked in him by hearing his old enemy's name and powers dinned constantly in his ears, and by the widespread belief that the dead man would not be content to rest there quietly and cold on his back while another sat in his place and watched his fire, became ere many months an uncontrollable impulse, a necessity of his very being; and he would linger for hours under the tree strangely entranced. It really seemed sometimes as if he were drawn there against his will, and even without his knowledge; for he would often start up from his meals, or in the middle of cheerful talk with his wife, and wander dreamily to the door; but no sooner did Paola lay her hand gently on his arm, and ask him with her fond smile on what business he went, than he would turn round with a sigh, apparently shake himself free from some hallucination, and forthwith returning to his place continue the talk as though it had not been broken off.

But as time went on this melancholy obsession grew more and more marked, and the unhappy lady could not fail to consider it now with the greatest distress. He would steal from her side at night, and go forth to stand by that unblessed grave for hours of wind and storm. What strange fascination led him there? It broke his sleep; he ate but little; he would answer vaguely with far-away looks: his spirit, one might think, was always by the tree even when his body was elsewhere. From a practical, healthy man, a soldier and sportsman, a man of good spirits and the open air, he had turned in a few months into a hesitating, haunted-looking dreamer, moody and distracted.

Oddly enough, the tree itself, sere and thunder-blasted as it was, quite dead long since as all supposed, began about this time to put forth blossoms and leaves, flourishing at first indeed only at the top; but as Morvan yielded more and more to his mournful fancy, and lengthened his stations by its side, it felt increasingly life slipping through all its boughs, and in less than six months it was completely robed with a dense and poisonous-looking foliage which fell not when the autumn winds stripped the other trees nearby.

Of course, there must always have been some life remaining in the tree which the disturbance of the earth at its roots when the grave was dug had invigorated; but what had the worst effect on the superstitious peasants, and what is indeed inexplicable, was the uncommon—nay, unknown species of leaves wherewith it had covered itself in this resuscitation. Large, round, spongy, velvety leaves, thick, clammy and soft to the touch, and when pressed or broken giving forth a putrid odour—such was the unfamiliar vesture of the tree, at which the peasants standing at a distance would gaze as long as they dared, and at the lonely figure so often beneath it.

And the terrors daily increased. Zilpah Green, a woman of conduct, reported that she had seen between lights a huge unmistakable hand reach out of the clay and move gropingly, as if it searched for someone whom it meant to pull down with it into the grave. Ere long the opinion grew that the tree was bewitched and brought the direst misfortunes upon those who loitered near it; and once that opinion had taken hold, Sir Edward's sad musings were no longer spied upon even by the hardiest. But he, careless whether he were observed or not, used to stand by that ominous tree for hours in all weathers, till his patient wife, shaken with anxiety, would at length go out and lead him in from the damps of the graveside and the dank umbrage of the tree, to the warm house and her warm embrace.

On top of all this there fell out towards the autumn of 1655 an extraordinary incident, which might well have been taken for a warning of the immense evils in store for that house. It chanced one evening as Sir Edward and his wife were at supper that her glance fell on his hand, whereupon she recoiled in horror.

"Where did you find that ring?" she exclaimed breathlessly, moved to the soul.

"What ring?"—Even as he spoke he looked down carelessly and incuriously at his fingers, and turned very pale.

There was a ring on his finger, and it was old Mr. Verschoyle's signet-ring. The ring was unmistakable. It was an unusual stone, carven with magical symbols, and had been given to Mr. Verschoyle by his "son", the youthful Elias Ashmole, out of gratitude for some instruction in divining by the Mosaical rods, and especially for the communication of secrets in the Rosycrucian faculty. Morvan gazed in a stupor at the ring for a minute, and then tried to pull it off; but it was as fast to his finger as though it had been moulded there.

"It must have been lying about the house and I slipped it on unawares", he said at last.

Paola assented, but neither of them believed this explanation. She knew that Mr. Verschoyle never laid by that ring, attributing to it various potent influences; while he remembered that it was still on the dead man's hand when he was laid in the grave, for a soldier had offered to remove it and had by Morvan himself been forbidden. Besides, how came it that a ring which fitted the thick finger of Verschoyle clung so tight to the slim finger of Morvan? The two looked heavily into each other's eyes with these unuttered thoughts, shaken by terror of the unknown, the inevitable.

"O my love, whatever happens I have you—you, your own self"! cried Paola at length with a burst of tears, and they clasped each other in a long embrace of intolerable sadness and anguish. Nevertheless, even in face of this ghastly and harrowing accident, he could not resist stealing forth in the course of the night to keep his station by the grave.

The next day, after many trials, he found that the ring was so deeply imbedded in the flesh that if he would have it displaced the finger itself must be sacrificed. Henceforward he concealed his hand as if it bore some disgraceful stain, and he and his wife in their talks together were sedulous to avoid all allusion to the ring. But it fell out with them as may be observed in an affectionate family whereof one of the members is stricken with a lingering and fatal disease, when, although, each takes infinite care to shun that subject, still the conversation against the will of all is constantly circling about the forbidden topic: each knows what the other is thinking as if he were speaking aloud, the sick person as well as the rest, and she and all are oppressed by abominable dolours, the more poignant because they are stifled.

But though the ring was ever in their thoughts, giving them the disquieting sensation that they were watched and threatened, and perhaps at the mercy of some pitiless invisible spirit, still, in the two or three months which followed its appearance they tasted intenser joys than any they had known since their marriage.

The offence which was common to both, and assured them that the menace hung over both alike; the conviction that if one were struck the other would fall too; the fear always lurking in their breasts when they sought their bed that they would never again see the day, or else see it in incalculable conditions of misery and prostration:—all this induced in them a pathetic mutual dependence, a dread of being separated or distinguished even in their sufferings; as two prisoners who have been taken and tried and sentenced together might come at last to feel, as they were being carted to the place of execution, all other hopes and fears swamped now in the ultimate great fear that ere their agony was ended one of them might be reprieved in spite of himself, and they would be cheated of dying together.

These feelings, and an instinct which told them that their lives were blighted, that such happiness as they might snatch would be of the briefest, and some tremendous price of despair and tears exacted for it, led them to open their hearts to the transports of love with an abandon hardly to be understood by those whose lives are regular and content. Though it is true that Morvan still persisted in his visits to the grave, and that by the tyranny of this habit they were for some precious hours of each day necessarily separated, yet it falls to be remarked, that once his dismal watch completed, he emerged so to speak out of a cloud, shook off the morbid ugly fancies with the damp from his hair, and came to Paola with the utterance and smile of a lover.

The two grew so enhardied by this enduring tranquillity that they no longer thought seriously of going away: they were almost quite happy where they had always dreamed of being happy. The calamitous ring, even, lost some of its terrors in this time of, passion and caress, and Morvan no longer troubled to conceal his hand when he was with Paola.—One lingers with complaisance over the last peaceable moments which were granted to this unhappy pair, and contemplates with especial assuagement any feeble and transient gleams of light which lay across the dusky life of the gentle and kind Paola, whose sufferings were so out of proportion to any faults she had committed during her brief, joyless, and baffled existence. The last days of the winter saw burst forth the germ of the evils which remain to be related, and in the procession of which there was never to be another interval of ease.

On a bleak and desolate evening in the beginning of March 1656, Paola was standing by the fire in that little wainscotted parlour where Sir Edward long ago had sung to her his love-song. The snow had been falling heavily for two days, and when her husband, whom she awaited, at last came in, his clothes and hair were covered with snow. He had been standing knee-deep by the grave; his eyes were not yet steady in the shine of the room; and there was a certain trembling indecision in his step. Warm and beautiful in the soft glow, Paola, glancing but carelessly from where she stood, laughed out some gay reproof for his tardiness, and with her wonderfully graceful gesture held out her arms. Upon this, all snowy as he was, he drew near and bent over her, but just as he did that, he saw the smile swept out of her eyes and face, and leaping up in its place an unmistakable look of repulsion and terror.

Morvan drew back, stung to the heart. "I should have shaken off the snow—" And he was going on.

"Oh, no, no!" cried his wife. She rested her elbow on the chimney-piece and covered her eyes with her hand. "It is nothing, nothing at all", she said, breathing hard. "A stupid fancy. I thought—I was reminded—O God!" she broke off, slapping her hand down on the wood, "why am I so tormented?"

He thought she was unreasonable and capricious and rather childish; and as the look still rankled, he turned on his heel and left the room without more words, and mounted the stairs to his own closet. This chamber had two steps down to it placed inside the door, the door itself not being so high as some other ones in the house, but still quite high enough for a man of the average height to pass through it without stooping. Morvan himself had always gone in and out without taking heed, but tonight his forehead struck against the lintel.

"How extraordinary!" he thought, rubbing his forehead ruefully, yet with some amusement. 'I must be growing taller.'

And as soon as he had shifted his habit—his little flick of ill-temper now quite gone—he hastened downstairs, eager to relate this comical accident to his wife, and promising himself they would laugh merrily upon it. So, standing in the hall, he called with cheery intention: "Paola, Paola, come hither, sweetheart."

Something in the sound of his voice sent the blood running cold through his veins. Whose voice was that? Where had he heard it before?

Into the hall came his wife slowly and wearily, supporting herself as she moved against the wall, and shewing a countenance deadly white and panic-stricken. She gave a quick oblique glance at her husband, and then drew from her heart a sigh or rather groan of relief, though the suspicious and terrified look still clouded in her eyes.

"I thought I heard *him* call", she said faintly, almost in a whisper.

"Whose voice did you think you heard, dearest one?" He meant to ask this question soothingly, as you might question a feverish child about its fancies, but it came out so harsh, so arrogant, with such a note of devilish raillery comprehended in the sound of it, that he stood thunderstruck.

"Ah, I knew, I knew! Yes, it is his voice!" cried Paola, and with that she flung herself down at full length in a perfect ecstasy of fear and despair, and beat her head against the floor.

Morvan heard a servant stirring at his work in a room near at hand, and hastening there, while he was still in the little dark passage which led to it, he called to the man to run for my lady's waiting-woman. With a clang, the servant dropped the vessel he was holding, and stared in the wildest amazement towards the passage whence the voice had come. Thereupon Morvan stepped out into the light, and the servant, recognising the well-known figure, hastened away.

"I saw Sir Edward right enough", he said to the others when he had given his message, "but I could have sworn to God it was old Mr. Verschoyle that called me".

10

Alas, the change thus observed in the master of the house was no delusion of the senses, but the bitterest reality, miserable and appalling, and that night only at its beginning. As the months ran, the features and presence of the fated Morvan gradually changed by slow, but salient and terrible stages, to the appearance of the dead old man. Morvan's handsome face became sallow and leathery and wrinkled; his hair fell, leaving only some grey locks straggling to his shoulders; his hands grew large and coarse, and his frame increased in size.

And what was infinitely disquieting, and even disgusting, these loathsome changes attacked his body sporadically: for several weeks he carried one hand large and thick, and the other his own slender hand—watching this day by day as it inflated; for over two months he stood on his own well-shaped foot, and on another much larger and broader; for nearly a year he found when he undressed himself, on one side of the body from the neck to the waist the flesh sane and firm, while on the other it was dry and shrivelled, coated with white hairs. Picture his emotions as he studied day by day the stealthy progress of his affliction!

Perhaps the most perturbing detail of all, was the long white beard which swept over his breast. At first Morvan, loathing this abominable ensign more than almost all other changes, used to shave his face closely many times a day; but in a few hours, in the course of sleep, the white thing would grow and again be hanging down, till at last the punished man resigned himself to let it grow as might.

Indeed, the struggles of the poor stricken wretch against his fate were as terrible and pathetic as the fate itself. By a refinement of torture, his character and mental attributes were not altered with his body; his soul was mercilessly enabled to stand by, as it were, and mark the ravages of the change; and Morvan would sit for hours, leaning Verschoyle's face on Verschoyle's hands and moaning in Verschoyle's voice that he was still Morvan. No, he was not Verschoyle, he would insist to himself vehemently all day—he was utterly different; he was not domineering, rapacious, tyrannical; he had no dealings with the devil; he was cheerful, merciful, eager for love and light, willing to give men their dues.

And perhaps his character did in truth assert itself, and his mind regain somewhat of its health under its shameful housing; for when the bodily transformation declared itself more rigorously, he relinquished his visits to the graveside. Strangely enough, about this time too the tree began to die, as if that which nourished it was passing elsewhere—perishing slowly in its rank luxuriance from the top.

He took the custom to go to Paola's room when it was dark, when his figure would be obscured, although he knew that she shrank from his presence in excruciating anguish and dismay; and there he would utter to the half-fainting woman in Verschoyle's voice words which came from his own soul making passionate appeals, begging her not to flee from him, to let him stay near her, for he was cold and lonely; imploring her to believe that, sick and weary and bewitched as he was, her lover was still there; endeavouring, in fact, to make the true accents of his soul heard from out of its monstrous prison of flesh.

But for her, only that dread figure remained from which she recoiled in unutterable horror and woe, as she witnessed it speaking her husband's thoughts and particular phrases with the voice, the inflexion, the gesture of the dead. No, this was not her brave kind husband who sat now in the room, but a phantom agenced by the powers of evil: those old bones long buried had disinterred themselves and stolen from their sepulchre. The sickness and revolts she experienced at his appearance would throw her into long fits, from which she would emerge haggard-eyed, undone, with flecks of blood upon her lips. The afflicted Morvan, fearing for her life, was fain at last to bend his head under the scourge, and perceiving that it was the will of the inexorable Fates that in his calamities he should be desolate, he put himself in her presence no more.

From that accursed house the servants aghast stole away on various pretences, and never returned. There were left but an Italian woman who had nursed the lady Paola and loved her as her own child, and an old, half-witted, dumb man who shuffled about the sinister corridors till nightfall, and then betook himself to the stable; —for even he rebelled when it came to a question of sleeping in the house. And the beautiful place, sorely neglected, took gradually an air of isolation and ruin. The stalls stood empty, for there was no one to care for the horses; the garden was become a wilderness; while within doors the rooms where the sun never entered waxed dusty and dank and sombre.

For by this time neither Morvan nor his wife could bear the glare of day, and the few rooms in use had lights burning in them at all hours. A waft of decay and anxiety, of death—nay, of a death beyond the familiar corporal death, as if Death himself had come to preside and be housekeeper there, exuded from the walls and tainted the atmosphere. For hours long a heavy stillness weighed on the house which seemed uninfluenced by sense or space or time, an illimitable stillness to which sound was not merely an antithesis, but in which any chance sound seemed indescribably single, alien, arising out of nothing, and having neither origin nor consequence in that underworld; and instead of falling, as sounds do, disturbingly through stillness, seemed here outside, beating against a burnished wall.

If you can imagine a tower which has never a bell, standing in an arid, void, and sterile plain uninhabited for centuries, and that suddenly, in a minute lying amid the centuries, a bell tolls slowly thrice in the tower, reverberates, and expires in the waste; if you can imagine a ship moving through an enchanted sea which washes round her keel and bows and deck without wetting them; if you can imagine how the voices of the living sound to the listening dead: then you can form some idea of the suddenness, distinctness, the isolation of any noise in the vacant air of that house.

So, at intervals would strike dully against the silence a symptom of life, as detached from the general vacuity as to a man suspended by vindictive gods just outside this globe of earth might come the cries of those at work or play upon it—a pathetic ditty crooned in a voice that vainly tried to be steady: it was the nurse who thus endeavoured to soothe Paola with a song she used to sing to her little child in the cradle. And one who might have wandered about the house day and night would have seen in a lower chamber, dusty and unkept, a white-bearded man, gloomy, and muttering to himself a crazy litany of curses and prayers, or resting his old wrinkled head exhausted and throbbing in his arms on the table; and above stairs a pale lady lying spent and still and nearly lifeless, or else torn with a passion of weeping.

Why did she tarry in that doomed, forsaken dwelling? Surely there were still for her, if not for the scourged and hedged-in man, the air, the birds, the sea; and far from here, Italy lay flowery and basking in the pleasant sun. Ah, pity her! She ever longed for her dear lost husband, and hoped the magic spells might yet be broken, and that suddenly, all in a minute! he would be there once more with his brave face to love her and to assuage her after these intolerable sorrows.

And that old man who sat always in the house, who infected the house, and whose hand she felt as a physical weight on her breast, would be hurried out into the night and tempest and cold. No, she could not travel away and forget: how could she forget, wherever she might wander, that the old man was seated in the house poisoning the sweet familiar chambers, while her poor lonely husband was creeping outside in the chill airs, longing to be at home by her side, and beating with vain hands at the doors. In the feverish dreams which thronged her broken sleep he would resurge, and solemnly enjoin her to wait for him.

Therefore, she lay there courageously and patiently, settled in her vague hopes, which after all kept her from dying of mere heart-break, and that chill sense of finality, of termination, of the outlets to life unredeemably beset and barred, which kills so many finely tempered spirits, so lamentably! And her hopes, after all, were not more monstrous and unreasonable than the calamity which gave them cause.—There came one night when as she lay on her bed, she was so sure she heard his hands on the casements, and his voice outside crying to her to let him in, that she flung a white robe about her and descended.

But as she entered the hall, suddenly she descried lurking in the shadows that gaunt black figure of the old man, whom she had escaped now for some months, and who began to cry out, "O Paola, my wife Paola, have pity—listen to me!"—words obviously of tenderness, but so deformed in the speaking that they seemed a mockery and jeer. The figure drew nearer, and Paola, sick and faint to the soul, frantically alarmed, dropped the lamp she held and fled away in the darkness with an unutterable panic and loathing, hearing as she regained her apartment a long, desolate, heartrending wail from below which filled her ears for many a day afterwards, and spoiled her few pauses of perfectly restful sleep. And she realised that there were things in life more fearful and unnerving than death: the dead, after all, might hope to lie untroubled in their desolate places. But if *That* came loverly to her bedside?

Meanwhile, out in the sun-coloured world Oliver Protector ruled and died, and his battle-worn corpse was at length entombed with sumptuous if unimpressive pageantry. Now, his son carried without conviction an uneasy sovereignty. Already the clanging echoes of the war were dying out of earshot; already by alert listeners the bright scoffing laughter and gaillardise of the next court might be heard faintly chiming in the distance. But intelligence of these events hardly penetrated the walls of that house, which once would have been so patently stirred by the like; neither could stirring rumours lift the heavy shadows which encompassed the building, wafting out from their folds a cold noxious breath of mortality.

However, one visitor forced a way through those repelling shadows. In the beginning of 1659 that sickness known as the New Disease, which had been prowling for some time to and fro in England, came at last into that part of the country, broke into the house, and laid its blighting hand upon Paola's tired brow. Tended only by her loving nurse, she lay in a kind of trance, wasting away, longing exceedingly for death. Her few years had been so bitter for the young, gentle soul, and she was miserable, and haunted, and weary. Her hold on life, so frail already and uncertain, she felt now soothingly—by what blessed drowsy physic?—becoming as the hours passed looser and more nerveless.

About the same time, the old creature who lived hidden among the shadows, and wandered from room to room at the other side of the house, was likewise stricken, and kept his bed.

The chamber he occupied had long ago been put into deep mourning, to compliment, as the usage was, a certain honourable guest bereaved of a wife or child; and by some insouciance this melancholy furniture had never been changed. The walls were hung with black draperies which fell from the ceiling to the oaken floor, and as they vacillated in the gusts of wind seemed agitated by hands behind them. The bed was an immense construction of ebony, with black covers and hangings—a lugubrious funeral couch of a kind common enough at the period among families of importance; and the chairs, antique, outworn, and incommode, were shrouded in black.

The sombre effect was increased by the almost complete exclusion of daylight, which filtered with difficulty through a window of stained glass. All these dismal trappings had been left to rot, and some of them were falling to pieces from long neglect; and it was doubtless owing to this, and to the absence of wholesome light, that there lingered in the room a sickening odour of decay and corruption.

Here, then, the old man lay suffering and forlorn. He was abandoned by all. Lacking Morvan's bodily features, he could not attract, excite sympathy; lacking Verschoyle's brutal, indomitable spirit, he could not compel attendance through terror. The dumb servitor would come in the morning and cast down a parcel of faggots on the hearth; and then, as if the sadness and harrowing chill of the room struck intolerably even into his dull senses, he would shuffle away and return no more. And tossing wearily from dawn till evening, and through the long night waiting anxiously for the comfortless dawn, the friendless Morvan lay alone there in his loathed and hideous casing, lost and forsaken, with what thoughts to pass the hours! Feeble and racked with cough, he supplied the needs of his old body as he could, but most of the time he lay covered in the dark bed.

One night about eleven o'clock, when he had been sick like this for four days, with increasing weakness every day, he was sitting up gaunt and wretched in his bed supping a posset he had made shift to warm. As he sat there holding the bowl in his shrivelled hands, his ear caught the tramp of a horse on the terrace, and then the court bell rang with a loud reverberating peal, as bells are wont to echo in empty houses. By whose hand? To that silent accursed house, where no one ever came, what visitor had the hardihood to venture at that

185

dead hour?

Now the hands were on the great door; he could hear it creak open on its long disused hinges; and presently he distinguished a footstep on the stairs coming in the direction of his room. Yes, there could be no doubt of that; and the old man lay with wildly beating heart, marking the steps draw nearer and nearer. They moved slowly and as if with difficulty; now and then there would be a pause, and then they would come on again; and to the old man there was something strangely familiar in the tread.

At last, the steps came up to the very door, and there was another pause. But not for long! The door opened, and into that hearse-like chamber, in front of the old man watching the door with dilated eyes, there stepped the young Sir Edward Morvan. He carried a short riding-sword, and was dressed very elegantly, wearing a deep lace collar over which his fair hair fell in curls; but his eyes were hollow, his visage cadaverous, and on his breast was a great stain of blood as though he had been shot there. Watching this visitor from his bed in terror and bewilderment, Morvan (as we must call him) when his eyes lighted on the crimson splash, recalled from all the wounds he had seen where he had seen a stain just like that before: it was on Mr. Verschoyle's black robe, the day when he lay dead in the sunlight with his face to the sky.

The apparition glided noiselessly to the foot of the bed and stood there looking at the old man, not in anger, but rather with compassion and a great yearning. After they had regarded each other a little space—"What brings you to this fatal house after so many years?" asked the old man; and if his accents had indicated the turmoil of his mind the words would have come out tremblingly and broken. But the voice, as usual, travestied the mental state, and the question actually sounded sardonic, unfriendly, and combative.

The figure stretched out his arm. "Mr. Verschoyle", he said, "I have come for my soul". His tone was soft and mournful and even appealing, and stayed a little on the air after the words had fallen, like the vibration of a harp when the musician is departed.

"I am not Verschoyle", clamoured the other frantically; "I tell you I am not Verschoyle. Do you not know? Verschoyle was shot to death and laid beneath the tree. I know it—I know it—I saw him put in the ground—I have said it to myself a thousand times. I am not Verschoyle. Why do you vex the night with your unhallowed pacings? 'Tis you who are Verschoyle, and you stole my body and hid it away in the earth. I am Edward Morvan."

Again, his voice belied his heart, turning these eager feverish words to derision and the bitterest irony. But the figure neither assented nor denied, nor shewed surprise or any emotion; only again raised his hand and repeated in his gentle tones:

"Mr. Verschoyle, I have come for my soul".

As these words were spoken, there was heard a little noise of hands feebly groping about the door of the chamber and striving to open it. The two in the room appeared to be listening intently, but neither stirred. On the young face was a look of tranquil, even happy expectation; on the old, an indefinable minglement of hope, trepidation, and despair. Then the heavy door slowly fell open, and on the threshold stood Paola, holding a small carven silver lamp above her head. She was clothed in white, and her face, which bore the marks of long illness, gleamed strange and pale amid the black hair rolling loosely over her shoulders to her waist.

No sooner did her eyes fall on the figure of the young man, than she put down the lamp and held out her hands with a wide amiable gesture, as if welcoming a long desired and long expected friend and lover, harnessed for her enlargement; and like a sudden light flashing across her shadowed and wasted features, came a look of wonder and content. She hastened her faltering steps through the wide room, till she stood by the side of the young man at the foot of the bed.

But he, though his look upon her was kind and friendly, did not respond to her welcome otherwise than by a quaint frail smile, as people sometimes smile in dreams.

The old man on the bed regarded them meanwhile with a perturbed and lowering countenance. He was breathing hard, as the dying are seen to do in the supreme hour when the soul is struggling to go forth. And he began to speak.

"Stay with me, Paola", he said. "Go not down with yon dead man. Can you not see that he is dead? Ay, he has been long dead, long in the mould, ever since the old king's time. He exists no more. Tis I who shelter under time, and marshal the order of existence. I have the hours and years at my beck. But he his limbs have been buried and are powerless; time and the agitation of the world are but like water poured over his hands. He is naught and gone, but I live—I am I", he repeated, and peered at her with his tired and blunted eyes.

"Ah, not you!" she answered, weeping dreadfully. "You have pressed too hard on me. Life has been too wretched!" And thereupon she turned to the young man with the air of making at that minute a deliberate and final choice, and threw her arms about him, and shadowed him with her hair. But that one responded to her caress in no wise, save with the same thin and friendly smile.

"You are cold, my dear", she murmured, "and we have been apart a long time. The day is at hand. Let us hasten to be gone, while yet the moon shines."

And with a countenance wrapped in dream, not quite happy, indeed, and yet far from grief-stricken and hopeless, she drew gently her companion towards a little door in the wainscot which opened upon a flight of steps built, just there, into the outside wall. But even as they moved, the form on the bed was shaken with an appalling convulsion, as if it were spending itself in a struggle with the spirit it held imprisoned; and then the old body rolled out of the bed and stood there confronting them.

It seemed as if those three were a last time in presence, and engaged in an ultimate wrestle for mastery. For a minute they stood and gazed: then the old man, his face trembling with evil, advanced upon the two. But even as he came, they passed through the door out of his sight; and he was left staring with haggard eyes, triumphant, yet somehow broken and defeated, from the top of the steps into the darkness below.

★★★★★★★★★★★★★★★★

The next morning the body of Paola, half covered with snow, was found by her faithful nurse at the foot of the steps. It was supposed that she had wandered to the dark room in her delirium, and having opened the little door, her senseless eyes had not noticed the void, and she had fallen headlong. But the woman was astonished to find, clasped tightly in the small dead hand, a lock of gold-like hair which she had never seen among the trinkets and keepsakes of her mistress.

By the orders of him who was called her husband, whose sickness, as it appeared, had suddenly left him, her grave was dug underneath the tree; for it was comely, he said, that she should be buried in the same enclosure as her husband, Sir Edward Morvan. Those who heard him—the waiting woman and the dumb man—refrained from questioning this curious speech, judging it to be some folded utterance of one who was scarcely human and who spoke to them out of another world.

With some difficulty a certain reckless man who lived far off was found to assist the old servant: in the twilight, between a crimson winter sun and the moon already up in the penitential evening sky, they bore her quickly; and at length the thin piteous body, which had

been so vexed and tormented, was hidden out of sight in the earth—
her hard fate, in the end, relenting so far as to spare her the vanity of
mourners' tears, and the grisly pomps of sepulture.

Sir Edward Morvan—or Mr. Verschoyle, as some in that country,
seeing the terror he inspired, preferred to call him—survived in great
seclusion till near the end of Charles the Second's reign, disappearing
at last with his house in one of those frequent devastating fires which
swept away so many stately houses of the Seventeenth century.

When I Was Dead

(*A.k.a. Revenge of the Soul*)

"And yet my heart
Will not confess he owes the malady
That doth my life besiege."
—*All's Well that Ends Well.*

That was the worst of Ravenel Hall. The passages were long and gloomy, the rooms were musty and dull, even the pictures were sombre and their subjects dire. On an autumn evening, when the wind soughed and wailed through the trees in the park, and the dead leaves whistled and chattered, while the rain clamoured at the windows, small wonder that folk with gentle nerves went a-straying in their wits! An acute nervous system is a grievous burthen on the deck of a yacht under sunlit skies: at Ravenel the chain of nerves was prone to clash and jangle a funeral march. Nerves must be pampered in a tea-drinking community; and the ghost that your grandfather, with a skinful of port, could face and never tremble, sets you, in your sobriety, sweating and shivering; or, becoming scared (poor ghost!) of your bulged eyes and dropped jaw, he quenches expectation by not appearing at all.

So, I am left to conclude that it was tea which made my acquaintance afraid to stay at Ravenel. Even Wilvern gave over; and as he is in the Guards, and a polo player, his nerves ought to be strong enough. On the night before he went, I was explaining to him my theory, that if you place some drops of human blood near you, and then concentrate your thoughts, you will after a while see before you a man or a woman who will stay with you during long hours of the night, and even meet you at unexpected places during the day, I was explaining this theory, I repeat, when he interrupted me with words, senseless enough, which sent me fencing and parrying strangers,—on my guard,

"I say, Alistair, my dear chap!" he began, "you ought to get out of this place, and go up to town and knock about a bit—you really ought, you know."

"Yes," I replied, "and get poisoned at the hotels by bad food, and at the clubs by bad talk, I suppose. No, thank you: and let me say that your care for my health enervates me."

"Well, you can do as you like," says he, rapping with his feet on the floor; "I'm hanged if I stay here after tomorrow—I'll be staring mad if I do!"

He was my last visitor. Some weeks after his departure I was sitting in the library with my drops of blood by me. I had got my theory nearly perfect by this time; but there was one difficulty.

The figure which I had ever before me, was a figure of an old woman with her hair divided in the middle; and her hair fell to her shoulders, white on one side and black on the other. She was a very complete old woman; but, alas! she was eyeless, and when I tried to construct the eyes she would shrivel and rot in my sight. But tonight, I was thinking, thinking, as I had never thought before, and the eyes were just creeping into the head, when I heard a terrible crash outside as if some heavy substance had fallen. Of a sudden the door was flung open, and two maid-servants entered. They glanced at the rug under my chair, and at that they turned a sick white, cried on God, and huddled out.

"How dare you enter the library in this manner?" I demanded, sternly. No answer came back from them, so I started in pursuit. I found all the servants of the house gathered in a knot at the end of the passage.

"Mrs. Pebble," I said smartly, to the housekeeper, "I want those two women discharged tomorrow. It's an outrage! You ought to be more careful."

But she was not attending to me. Her face was distorted with terror.

"Ah dear, ah dear!" she went, "We had better all go to the library together," says she to the others.

"Am I still master of my own house, Mrs. Pebble?" I inquired, bringing my knuckles down with a bang on a table.

None of them seemed to see me or hear me: I might as well have been shrieking in a desert. I followed them down the passage, and forbade them with strong words to enter the library. But they trooped past me, and stood with a clutter round the hearth-rug. Then three or four of them began dragging and lifting, as if they were lifting a help-less body, and stumbled with their imaginary burthen over to a sofa. Old Soames, the butler, stood near.

"Poor young gentleman!" he said, with a sob; "I've knowed him since he was a baby. And to think of him being dead like this—and so young too!"

I crossed the room. "What's all this, Soames?" I cried, shaking him roughly by the shoulders. "I'm not dead, I'm here—here!"

As he did not stir, I got a little scared. "Soames, old friend," I called, "don't you know me? Don't you know the little boy you used to play with? Say I'm not dead, Soames, please, Soames!"

He stooped down and kissed the sofa. "I think one of the men ought to ride over to the village for the doctor, Mr. Soames," says Mrs. Pebble, and he shuffled out to give the order.

Now, this doctor was an ignorant dog, whom I had been forced to exclude from the house, because he went about proclaiming his belief in a saving God, at the same time that he proclaimed himself a man of science. He, I was resolved, should never cross my threshold, and I followed Mrs. Pebble through the house, screaming out prohibition. But I did not catch even a groan from her, not a nod of the head nor cast of the eye, to shew that she had heard.

I met the doctor at the door of the library. "Well!" I sneered, throwing my hand in his face, "have you come to teach me some new prayers?"

He brushed by me as if he had not felt the blow, and knelt down by the sofa.

"Rupture of a vessel on the brain, I think," he says to Soames and Mrs. Pebble after a moment. "He has been dead some hours. Poor fellow! You had better telegraph for his sister, and I will send up the undertaker to arrange the body."

"You liar!" I yelled, "You whining liar! How have you the inso-lence to tell my servants that I am dead, when you see me here face to face?"

He was far in the passage, with Soames and Mrs. Pebble at his heels, ere I had ended, and not one of the three turned round.

All that night I sat in the library. Strangely enough, I had no wish to sleep, nor, during the time that followed, had I any craving to eat. In the morning the men came, and although I ordered them out, they proceeded to minister about something I could not see. So, all day I stayed in the library or wandered about the house, and at night the men came again, bringing with them a coffin. Then, in my humour, thinking it shame that so fine a coffin should be empty, I lay the night in it, and slept a soft, dreamless sleep—the softest sleep I have ever slept. And when the men came the next day, I rested still, and the undertaker shaved me. A strange valet!

On the evening after that, I was coming downstairs, when I noted some luggage in the hall, and so learned that my sister had arrived. I had not seen this woman since her marriage, and I loathed her more than I loathed any creature in this ill-organised world. She was very beautiful I think—tall, and dark, and straight as a ram-rod—and she had an unruly passion for scandal and dress. I suppose the reason I disliked her so intensely was, that she had a habit of making one aware of her presence when she was several yards off. At half-past nine o'clock my sister came down to the library in a very charming wrap, and I soon found that she was as insensible to my presence as the others. I trembled with rage to see her kneel down by the coffin—my coffin; but when she bent over to kiss the pillow, I threw away control.

A knife which had been used to cut string was lying on a table: I seized it and drove it into her neck. She fled from the room screaming.

"Come, come!" she cried, her voice quivering with anguish, "the corpse is bleeding from the nose."

Then I cursed her.

On the morning of the third day there was a heavy fall of snow. About eleven o'clock I observed that the house was filled with blacks, and mutes, and folk of the county, who came for the obsequies. I went into the library and sat still, and waited. Soon came the men, and they closed the lid of the coffin and bore it out on their shoulders. And yet I sat, feeling rather sadly that something of mine had been taken away: I could not quite think what. For half an hour perhaps—dreaming— dreaming: and then I glided to the hall door. There was no trace left of the funeral but after a while I sighted a black thread winding slowly across the white plain.

"I'm not dead," I moaned, and rubbed my face in the pure snow and tossed it on my neck and hair, "Sweet God, I am not dead."

The Houses of Sin

The street lay tremulous in yellow light
Which mingled with the blackness of the night;
Soft murmured laughter sounded everywhere,
And sobs like laughter glided on the air;
While on the steps, grouped round each open door,
Sweet persons stood and gazed on Heaven's floor.
Then, as a perfumed wind came glancing by
And kissed me with its melancholy sigh,
And wooed me to its lair
Of flower-haunted rooms: "Would you go there?"
A voice said low, and charmed my willing ear.
"Would you take part with those who give the cheer
In yon gay scene, and look on those who lie
'Neath every incense-freighted canopy?"
Ah ! well I knew
That only to escape the horrid crew
Of daily tiresome deeds, the noisome crowd
Of those who seek themselves and seek aloud,
Who think austerity a prick of pin,
And folly call, to dignify it, sin,
I had all-hailed the Infamous! Then "Yes,"
I said to him who soothed my loneliness,
And looked upon his face.
He was a man on whom some strange disgrace
Had settled in the morning of his years,
And bowed him to a life of shame and tears;
Pride and humility mingled in his mien—
The servant of the servant of a queen.
"Come, let us go!" he cried, and passed along
With hasty steps between the mighty throng:
Onward we pressed through crowds with laughter lit,
Till at a house where *Avarice* was writ

In scarlet letters, he said: "Get you in!
This is the first house in the street of Sin."
An ancient dame was sitting at a wheel
With which she spun the gold threads of her reel,
And all her threads she twined in little rolls
Around her bodkins, which were human souls.
"Here all is peace," quoth she; "but you descry
Just opposite a house of revelry:
There doth she dwell for whom I eat the dust—
My ever good and constant neighbour *Lust*"
"Quick!" spoke my friend, "the revels now begin."
And lo! we sought the second house of Sin.

Throughout that night we passed from door to door
And saw all men on earth, as on the shore
Of various lands a traveller may see
Wreckage cast up by one great shuddering sea.
Now when the moon was highest, I descried
The state and splendour of the house of *Pride*,
And sought the gracious hostess, in whose eyes
A man looks once, then serves her till he dies.
And when the moon was waning, and the night
Was yielding to the day's encroaching light,
Haggard and bowed we dragged our way within
The portals of the final house of Sin.
Here two dark sisters did their arms entwine:
"My name *Anger*" "*Jealousy* is mine."
A banquet of strange dishes was outspread—
A banquet served by unforgotten dead
With wild entreating eyes
Which begged a respite from men's memories.
When I had tasted of a subtile dish
At this grave feast, behold! I had no wish
Left in my heart, but grew as one asleep
Amongst the dead, whose passions strong and deep
Are merged in longed-for, unexpected peace,
And give them ease.
So full of joy I cried out to my friend:
"Come, join this deathly feast and so make end!"
He wailed: "I dare not—dare not gather near!"
Then hung his head and wept: "My name is *Fear*."

The Interval

Mrs. Wilton passed through a little alley leading from one of the gates which are around Regent's Park, and came out on the wide and quiet street. She walked along slowly, peering anxiously from side to side so as not to overlook the number. She pulled her furs closer round her; after her years in India this London damp seemed very harsh. Still, it was not a fog today. A dense haze, grey and tinged ruddy, lay between the houses, sometimes blowing with a little wet kiss against the face. Mrs. Wilton's hair and eyelashes and her furs were powdered with tiny drops. But there was nothing in the weather to blur the sight; she could see the faces of people some distance off and read the signs on the shops.

Before the door of a dealer in antiques and second-hand furniture she paused and looked through the shabby uncleaned window at an unassorted heap of things, many of them of great value. She read the Polish name fastened on the pane in white letters.

"Yes; this is the place."

She opened the door, which met her entrance with an ill-tempered jangle. From somewhere in the black depths of the shop the dealer came forward, he had a clammy white face, with a sparse black beard, and wore a skull cap and spectacles. Mrs. Wilton spoke to him in a low voice.

A look of complicity, of cunning, perhaps of irony, passed through the dealer's cynical and sad eyes. But he bowed gravely and respectfully.

"Yes, she is here, madam. Whether she will see you or not I do not know. She is not always well; she has her moods. And then, we have to be so careful. The police—Not that they would touch a lady like you. But the poor alien has not much chance these days."

Mrs. Wilton followed him to the back of the shop, where there was a winding staircase. She knocked over a few things in her passage and stooped to pick them up, but the dealer kept muttering, "It does not matter—surely it does not matter." He lit a candle.

"You must go up these stairs. They are very dark; be careful. When you come to a door, open it and go straight in."

He stood at the foot of the stairs holding the light high above his head as she ascended.

The room was not very large, and it seemed very ordinary. There were some flimsy, uncomfortable chairs in gilt and red. Two large palms were in corners. Under a glass cover on the table was a view of Rome. The room had not a business-like look, thought Mrs. Wilton; there was no suggestion of the office or waiting-room where people came and went all day; yet you would not say that it was a private room which was lived in. There were no books or papers about; every chair was in the place it had been placed when the room was last swept; there was no fire and it was very cold.

To the right of the window was a door covered with a plush curtain. Mrs. Wilton sat down near the table and watched this door. She thought it must be through it that the soothsayer would come forth. She laid her hands listlessly one on top of the other on the table. This must be the tenth seer she had consulted since Hugh had been killed. She thought them over. No, this must be the eleventh. She had forgotten that frightening man in Paris who said he had been a priest. Yet of them all it was only he who had told her anything definite. But even he could do no more than tell the past. He told of her marriage; he even had the duration of it right—twenty-one months. He told too of their time in India—at least, he knew that her husband had been a soldier, and said he had been on service in the "colonies."

On the whole, though, he had been as unsatisfactory as the others. None of them had given her the consolation she sought. She did not want to be told of the past. If Hugh was gone forever, then with him had gone all her love of living, her courage, all her better self. She wanted to be lifted out of the despair, the dazed aimless drifting from day to day, longing at night for the morning, and in the morning for the fall of night, which had been her life since his death. If somebody could assure her that it was not all over, that he was somewhere, not too far away, unchanged from what he had been here, with his crisp hair and rather slow smile and lean brown face, that he saw her sometimes, that he had not forgotten her. . . .

"Oh, Hugh, darling!"

When she looked up again the woman was sitting there before her.

Mrs. Wilton had not heard her come in. With her experience, wide enough now, of seers and fortune-tellers of all kinds, she saw at once that this woman was different from the others. She was used to the quick appraising look, the attempts, sometimes clumsy, but often cleverly disguised, to collect some fragments of information whereupon to erect a plausible vision. But this woman looked as if she took it out of herself.

Not that her appearance suggested intercourse with the spiritual world more than the others had done; it suggested that, in fact, considerably less. Some of the others were frail, yearning, evaporated creatures, and the ex-priest in Paris had something terrible and condemned in his look. He might well sup with the devil, that man, and probably did in some way or other.

But this was a little fat, weary-faced woman about fifty, who only did not look like a cook because she looked more like a sempstress. Her black dress was all covered with white threads. Mrs. Wilton looked at her with some embarrassment. It seemed more reasonable to be asking a woman like this about altering a gown than about intercourse with the dead. That seemed even absurd in such a very commonplace presence.

The woman seemed timid and oppressed; she breathed heavily and kept rubbing her dingy hands, which looked moist, one over the other; she was always wetting her lips, and coughed with a little dry cough. But in her these signs of nervous exhaustion suggested overwork in a close atmosphere, bending too close over the sewing-machine. Her uninteresting hair, like a rat's pelt, was eked out with a false addition of another colour. Some threads had got into her hair too.

Her harried, uneasy look caused Mrs. Wilton to ask compassionately: "Are you much worried by the police?"

"Oh, the police! Why don't they leave us alone? You never know who comes to see you. Why don't they leave me alone? I'm a good woman. I only think. What I do is no harm to anyone." . . .

She continued in an uneven querulous voice, always rubbing her hands together nervously. She seemed to the visitor to be talking at random, just gabbling, like children do sometimes before they fall asleep.

"I wanted to explain—" hesitated Mrs. Wilton.

But the woman, with her head pressed close against the back of the chair, was staring beyond her at the wall. Her face had lost whatever little expression it had; it was blank and stupid. When she spoke, it was very slowly and her voice was guttural.

"Can't you see him? It seems strange to me that you can't see him. He is so near you. He is passing his arm round your shoulders."

This was a frequent gesture of Hugh's. And indeed, at that moment she felt that somebody was very near her, bending over her. She was enveloped in tenderness. Only a very thin veil, she felt, prevented her from seeing. But the woman saw. She was describing Hugh minutely, even the little things like the burn on his right hand.

"Is he happy? Oh, ask him does he love me?"

The result was so far beyond anything she had hoped for that she was stunned. She could only stammer the first thing that came into her head. "Does he love me?"

"He loves you. He won't answer, but he loves you. He wants me to make you see him; he is disappointed, I think, because I can't. But I can't unless you do it yourself."

After a while she said:

"I think you will see him again. You think of nothing else. He is very close to us now."

Then she collapsed, and fell into a heavy sleep and lay there motionless, hardly breathing. Mrs. Wilton put some notes on the table and stole out on tiptoe.

She seemed to remember that downstairs in the dark shop the dealer with the waxen face detained her to shew some old silver and jewellery and such like. But she did not come to herself, she had no precise recollection of anything, till she found herself entering a church near Portland Place. It was an unlikely act in her normal moments. Why did she go in there? She acted like one walking in her sleep.

The church was old and dim, with high black pews. There was nobody there. Mrs. Wilton sat down in one of the pews and bent forward with her face in her hands.

After a few minutes she saw that a soldier had come in noiselessly and placed himself about half-a-dozen rows ahead of her. He never turned round; but presently she was struck by something familiar in the figure. First, she thought vaguely that the soldier looked like her Hugh. Then, when he put up his hand, she saw who it was.

She hurried out of the pew and ran towards him. "Oh, Hugh, Hugh, have you come back?"

He looked round with a smile. He had not been killed. It was all a mistake. He was going to speak. . . .

Footsteps sounded hollow in the empty church. She turned and glanced down the dim aisle.

It was an old sexton or verger who approached. "I thought I heard you call," he said.

"I was speaking to my husband." But Hugh was nowhere to be seen.

"He was here a moment ago." She looked about in anguish. "He must have gone to the door."

"There's nobody here," said the old man gently. "Only you and me. Ladies are often taken funny since the war. There was one in here yesterday afternoon said she was married in this church and her husband had promised to meet her here. Perhaps you were married here?"

"No," said Mrs. Wilton, desolately. "I was married in India."

It might have been two or three days after that, when she went into a small Italian restaurant in the Bayswater district. She often went out for her meals now: she had developed an exhausting cough, and she found that it somehow became less troublesome when she was in a public, place looking at strange faces. In her flat there were all the things that Hugh had used; the trunks and bags still had his name on them with the labels of places where they had been together. They were like stabs. In the restaurant, people came and went, many soldiers too among them, just glancing at her in her corner.

This day, as it chanced, she was rather late and there was nobody there. She was very tired. She nibbled at the food they brought her. She could almost have cried from tiredness and loneliness and the ache in her heart.

Then suddenly he was before her, sitting there opposite at the table. It was as it was in the days of their engagement, when they used sometimes to lunch at restaurants. He was not in uniform. He smiled at her and urged her to eat, just as he used in those days. . . .

I met her that afternoon as she was crossing Kensington Gardens, and she told me about it.

"I have been with Hugh." She seemed most happy.

"Did he say anything?"

"N-no. Yes. I think he did, but I could not quite hear. My head was so very tired. The next time—"

I did not see her for some time after that. She found, I think, that by going to places where she had once seen him—the old church, the little restaurant—she was more certain to see him again. She never saw him at home. But in the street or the park he would often walk along beside her. Once he saved her from being run over. She said she actually felt his hand grabbing her arm, suddenly, when the car was nearly upon her.

She had given me the address of the clairvoyant; and it is through that strange woman that I know—or seem to know—what followed.

Mrs. Wilton was not exactly ill last winter, not so ill, at least, as to keep to her bedroom. But she was very thin, and her great handsome eyes always seemed to be staring at some point beyond, searching. There was a look in them that seamen's eyes sometimes have when they are drawing on a coast of which they are not very certain. She lived almost in solitude: she hardly ever saw anybody except when they sought her out. To those who were anxious about her she laughed and said she was very well.

One sunny morning she was lying awake, waiting for the maid to bring her tea. The shy London sunlight peeped through the blinds. The room had a fresh and happy look.

When she heard the door open, she thought that the maid had come in. Then she saw that Hugh was standing at the foot of the bed. He was in uniform this time, and looked as he had looked the day he went away.

"Oh, Hugh, speak to me! Will you not say just one word?"

He smiled and threw back his head, just as he used to in the old days at her mother's house when he wanted to call her out of the room without attracting the attention of the others. He moved towards the door, still signing to her to follow him. He picked up her slippers on his way and held them out to her as if he wanted her to put them on. She slipped out of bed hastily. . . .

It is strange that when they came to look through her things after her death the slippers could never be found.

202

The Verge

Now midnight tolls, and up the stair
Creep the wild visions of despair—
Sin and Sorrow, Sin and Sorrow,
Creep to meet the trembling morrow:
Now midnight tolls from ancient clocks
Whose rusty strokes, like muffled knocks,
Fall on the heart, and frighten it,
Of one who mournfully doth sit
In a dark chamber dimly lit,
Surrounded by the violet breath
And glamour of approaching Death.

Like a white horse, which rushes past
The watcher and divides the blast,
On a bleak night on some wild shore
Where the strong breakers' massive roar
Drowns the resounding of its feet;
So terribly, so almost sweet,
Beside the dull and bitter sea
Of man's life passes silently
A sheeted ghost whose face is hid.
But never—never shall man rid
Himself from thinking of that face—
What its strange pallor, what its grace,
When the unveiling doth take place.
Can Heaven lie hid in grave-cold eyes?

Ah, at the midnight one man tries
To gather near, to lift the veil
And read upon that face its tale;
To gather near that dread and holy
Figure, and his melancholy

Shatter by a wild caress
In the all sombre silentness.

The face of her the lately dead,
New wandering from her little bed—
Shall it be as it once has been,
Or grey and horribly serene?
The eyes which he has closed, alas!
Have light, or stare like painted glass?
Her hair—oh! of her wilderness
Of hair, shall there be left one tress?

But lo, a hand has thrust aside
The veil—as when the moon doth ride
In Heaven she parts the blinding clouds
And scatters them in flying shrouds.
A filmy figure, almost air,
Bends slowly o'er the mourner's chair;
A sacred figure, grave and dim,
Seeks for his face and kisses him:

And at that kiss, from off the wall
The ghastly taunting shadows fall—
Writhe and expire there as they fall.
He dreams: a hush floats down the air—
Is this her mellow glorious hair?
He dreams: then leaps from clutching years,
And sees her eyes are bright with tears.

The Next Room

July 14.—I moved into the house this afternoon.

Now that I am settled, let me set down exactly the events which have brought me here. This diary-keeping habit of mine is an immense aid, I find, to clear thinking. And it is more necessary for me than for most men to keep my thoughts absolutely clear—to think and observe *precisely*, without any intermixture of drama or romance or sentiment.

A few days ago, then, it being Sunday, I was strolling along a street in one of the older parts of the Brooklyn district of New York. It was growing towards evening, the end of a day that had been terribly oppressive. Now and then lightning flickered over the sky. How still some of those streets in Brooklyn are!—for all the world as still and plaintive as the streets of a small New England town. Trees border the street; a footfall sounds afar off. Yet not a quarter of a mile away is a street of roaring traffic, and only a few blocks down nearer the river a noisy tenement district of Italians.

There was nobody, I think in the street. Many of the people in this quarter are well-to-do, and close their houses in the summer. No doubt a fear of the storm had kept the usual Sunday promenaders indoors, or they were elsewhere—down at the sea-beaches or in the park. My footsteps sounded. Far off a bell for evening prayer tolled heavily.

Now as I came down the street I noticed a horse-drawn cab of the kind called a *coupé* standing in front of a house. Why should his have struck me as strange? Of course, horse-drawn cabs are becoming rather an unusual sight in any district of New York, except for pleasure; and people do not take a closed cab on a very hot evening for pleasure. But it was not that. It was the cab taken in relation to the house.

It was a low wooden house, which had been left over from the first settlement of Brooklyn. On one side of it was a row of comparatively modern stone houses. On the other side was a vacant lot closed from the street by a high fence. The house itself looked shabby and dismal. The boards needed painting. Dingy green shutters were closed on all the windows, and tied together with pieces of rag to keep them from blowing open. It looked like a house that had been given over to poor folk till it could be pulled down.

I stood on the opposite side of the way looking at it. The street-door was standing about a quarter open. The cab driver had got off his box and was sitting on the steps bare-headed and in his shirt sleeves. He had a rather long beard, and otherwise did not look much like a coachman. I could not have been standing there more than half a minute before some words which I did not catch were spoken to the driver from within the house, and the door closed with a bang. The man got up and stationed himself at his horse's head, eying me with distrust and defiance.

"Go a few blocks down," he called out offensively, "and you'll have the boats and the river to look at. What do you want here anyhow?"

There was nothing for it but to walk away. As I strolled along, I turned to have another look at the house. Two of the upper floor windows looked upon the empty lot. They were shuttered like the others, but through the chinks of the shutters I could see a crimson light in the back room—not the white light of gas or electricity—a crimson light. It was now quite dusk, and the light was plain.

I came to where the street ended, and I had to turn right or left. Half-an-hour later I came back through the street. The cab was gone; the house was in darkness. There was an atmosphere about it such as we see sometimes, though very exceptionally, perceive, without being able to analyse it, around certain men—I have never observed it in women—an atmosphere of isolation, of loneliness and fatality, of being under a curse. Some secret lodged inside the shell and discomposed the features, as a dread secret in the heart sometimes ravages the human face.

During the next two days I could think of little else. What was the cab doing before such a house? Cabs are expensive I New York, and the house looked as if the kind of people it might shelter in the normal course of life would not be in the habit of taking cabs. Why was the door partly open, and then shut as soon as those inside saw they were being watched? And what was the meaning of the crimson light?

On Wednesday I could not resist an impulse to see the house again. A board had been put saying it was to let, and the address of an agent was given. At once I was seized by a desire to live in the house. I was sure it had a mystery; perhaps I might fathom it. Besides I had not been at all comfortable in the New York boarding house which had been my abode since I arrived here from my engineering works in Mexico. The people were hostile and suspicious. I have never spoken at any length to any of them. I could tell by their looks and their veiled remarks that they thought I had been guilty of some atrocity. If you are different from the rest of the flock, they bite you. What a joy, I thought, to live in this little house away from the faces and voices so unfriendly and exterior.

Yesterday I went to see the agent. The rent is exceptionally low. It seems they are only waiting to fine a purchase of the land before they tear down the old house. I took the house for three months, and paid in advance. I tried to find out something about the owner of the house and why he desired to let it but the agent was evasive.

"He has only just vacated the house—last Saturday in fact."

"Saturday?"

"Yes. He brought us the keys." He added: "You will find the house sufficiently furnished. I don't say it is well furnished but all that is necessary is there."

And here I am. I have arranged with a woman to come in a few times a week to set things in order. She comes early in the morning and stays about half-an-hour. What food I want I can prepare myself, or go to some restaurant near at hand. What a relief to be free from the chatter of the boarding house table!

July 17.—I am very happy here. There is nothing at all strange about the house—or only one thing. The house is vey poorly furnished with dilapidated furniture. The carpets are colourless and threadbare. The only sight of the former tenants is a pile of medical journals and some surgical bandages in the room at the back downstairs, and a pair of women's stockings, left over the back of a chair in the front bedroom upstairs which I occupy.

There is a telephone apparatus downstairs, but the wire has been cut. The strange thing—it *is* a little odd—is that the back room next to me bedroom is locked. There is not a key in the house which will open the door. I thought of notifying the agent; then I decided to let it be. After all I cannot use the room

July 26—It has been terribly hot these last days, a thick crushing heat under a sky tinged ruddy. Hardly any sunlight. I have been a few times in the street. Just below a dead cat lay for hours rotting under a swarm of flies.

There is certainly something unusual about this house. When night falls, and I am sitting in the back-room downstairs, I feel—I *know* that there is something alive in the house beside myself. Last night I placed W. J. Loudon's *Treatise on Rigid Dynamics* closed on the table, and went out of the room. When I returned the book was open and a leaf torn across. How did that happen? It may have been lack of attention on my part. Perhaps I did it myself inadvertently? That is most likely. And yet I cannot escape the impression that it was done by somebody who is in the house and wants to attract my attention.

There is no corner where anybody could possibly be concealed except the locked room. I could almost take my oath that I have heard footsteps up above and, on the stairs—light footsteps and not sequential. This very night at twenty minutes past eleven a door upstairs banged. I hurried upstairs. My bedroom door stood open as usual. I tried the door of the next room. It was locked.

Several of the houses nearby are empty. There are people living in the house two doors above. As I came in the other evening, they were sitting on the steps taking the air. Their dog got between my legs, and by accident I trod on its paw. The dog yelped, and the woman on the steps violently accused me of kicking her dog. I noticed the singular hostility of the whole lot.

As I entered my door, they were saying objectionable things about me. Is it possible they know or suspect something against the former tenants, and identify me with them? In any case, a vague idea of calling on my neighbours with a view to finding something out about the history of the house and its owner had now been extinguished.

July 28—I am persuaded that there must be somebody or something living in the locked room. Last night about one o'clock occurred a great thunderstorm. While it was at its height I, being in my bedroom, heard low cries on the other side of the wall. I rapped on the wall two or three times. Then the cries ceased; but it seemed to me that I could hear light footsteps in the next room.

I lay awake the best part of the night. About four o'clock I thought I heard a cry again, and knocked on the wall; but there was no response.

This morning I made my way into the vacant lot which, as have said, lies on the left side of the house. It is a dank, ugly place, into which cans, bottles and other refuse have been cast. I found the shutters of the back room closed, just as they were the night, I saw the crimson light behind them; but by standing in a far corner of the lot one can get a glimpse of the windowpane. I thought I saw a woman's face. It is difficult to say; perhaps my tired eyes played me a trick. Perhaps the sounds I heard last night are but imagination. Yet I was not used to be imaginative. And I can sketch the woman's face.

But if a woman is really in the room, why does she not make some sign? She knows I am in the house: why does she not cry aloud for help? All I have heard up to this are moans so low and incoherent that I can scarcely be sure now that I did hear them. And how can she get food? If she gets any, it must be passed up to her window from the lot. But I have never heard a sound at the window. Is it possible that she is here voluntarily—that she is staying locked in a room, for some purpose of her own, or concerted with others.

July 29.—I heard the sounds again last night. There were the same low cries; and then the knocks came in reply to mine for a little, but soon ceased. This morning I asked the woman, whom I have hardly set eyes on since I have been here, whether she could find a key for the locked door. But she said she knew nothing about the house: she had never been inside it till I came to live here.

I could easily break down the door with an axe, but the noise would be heard in this quiet street and draw the attention of the ill-natured neighbours, who would doubtless send the police to annoy me. Since the affair of the anarchist shells four years ago, I don't want any more of that kind of attention. Still, if the sounds continue, I must end by breaking in the door. I try the handle at least twenty times a day. It is a strong door and a strong lock.

July 30.—The terrible silence which replaces your thoughts, which is more terrible than anything *active*. The expectancy of what is going to happen. The imminent thing, unconditioned and appalling, perhaps atrocious. Whisperings.

July 31.—Last night or rather this morning about two o'clock, I was lying awake in the darkness, with my ears strained to catch any sound in the next room. All day I had remained in my bedroom, sitting close up to the wall, or standing close to the locked door, lest I should miss the least movement. At one time I went out into the lot, and through the gap in the shutters I saw distinctly a head and shoulders. I could see no more than the back of the head., with a glimpse of the neck and shoulders, but enough to make out that it was a figure of utter desolation. It was as if she was standing with her face bent forward into her hands, in grief and hopelessness. For all the time I was there the figure never stirred, and I cannot say how this moveless-ness awed me.

But I heard no sound from the room all day or all night till two o'clock—2.14 to be precise—this morning.

I had just struck a match to look at my watch, and the match was still in my hand when I heard the street door being opened and then closed. It was done without haste, but very softly. Then somebody began to creep up the stairs, slowly, with infinite precautions. I could hear each stair creak, and then a long pause before another step was taken.

During this time, I thought of nothing but the plain fact. Some-body had entered the house: he was coming upstairs to enter my room or the next room. To open the door and shout would be to ask for death. In New York a man who breaks into a house by night has made up his mind to kill if necessary.

That was all I could think of at the moment. Meanwhile the steps arrived at the landing, and I heard the door of the next room being unlocked.

With the utmost care, calculating each movement, arranging be-forehand where I was going to put my foot and my hand, I got out of bed and place myself full length on the floor beside the wall. I was like a man who has just got a blow on the head. Whatever worry or torments may be harassing him, he can think of nothing else but the blow. I thought: he will certainly come in and kill me. In a little while I shall be lying here stabbed. If I open the window and cry out, he will stab me and then escape. I am in a trap. Why did I take the damned house?

It may have been only a few minutes, but it seemed to me like an hour that I lay waiting for the man to come in.

Then voices on the other side of the wall reached my ears. Perhaps they had been talking all the time, and that I had now grown calmer and recovered my powers of attention. I could not distinguish the words. The woman's voice seemed to plead. The man's was emphatic and intense. He was evidently trying to persuade her to some action. As I listened, I forgot my fears of being robbed and murdered. I took sides with the woman. At the first cry of distress, I would rush to the next room and take my chance. Something bound me to her—the fact that we were living in the same house together, as likely as not, and that I had seen her weary face.

What happened to me I cannot say. The man must have been with her a considerable time, and yet it seemed not long till I heard him open the door. I heard him going downstairs. I had the impulse to open my door and look at him. But no sooner had I thought that than I decided it would be better to wait till he came again, when I should be prepared. I heard the street door closed quietly.

I might have seen him by opening the shutters and looking out, but my first thought was about the woman. Had he left her alive? I knocked hard at the wall. There was no answering knock. Then I went out on the landing and rapped on the door of the next room and called.

Nothing.

I turned the handle, but the door was locked as usual. Dawn was just breaking in the sky.

August 1.—I stayed in the house all day yesterday. In the afternoon I went into the lot, and once more I thought I saw her near the window in the attitude of affliction I have described; but I am not sure. Last night I lay awake listening intently, but the man did not come. In the dead of night, I heard her crying.

August 2.—This afternoon, about three o'clock, the doorbell rang, and I opened it to a florid, well-looking, middle-aged woman, almost fashionably dressed, who asked for Mrs Purves. I said that Purves was the name of the owner of the house, but the house had been let to me. She seemed completely taken aback, and, as it were, stupefied at this news, and hurried away. No sooner was she in the street than she looked back with dismay at the house and began to weep.

Last night the cries came again. I hammered on the wall, and several times the wall was rapped in answer. I went to the door and called out: "Will you not speak to me? Do you want anything? Shall I break down the door?" Distinctly I heard a low voice say, "No." So I passed the night.

August 3.—I have been to see the agent. I complained that there was a room shut off from the rest of the house.

"Oh, yes," he said. "I ought to have mentioned it before you signed the lease. The owner stipulated that one room was to be reserved. It is not an unusual clause in letting houses of any size. As you told me you were going to live in the house by yourself, I supposed that with the rest of the house at your disposal you would have no objection."

"I should not," I said, "in an ordinary case." I hesitated, for I did not wish to tell him everything—I wished to find out how much he knew. I don't want to use the room, but it seems to me that some very curious sounds come from there."

I could see that his face changed. He looked defiant and cunning, trying to spy out where I was. He began to shuffle some papers on his desk, pretending he was busy.

"You look as if you need sleep. Perhaps this hot weather in the city does not agree with you. Why not pack your bag and go down to the near beaches for a few days? Long Beach—there's a fine sea there. Fine place to rest up."

I smiled at him compassionately. Poor fool! Did he think to deceive me with his clumsy fencing? I could see that he knew something that he did not want to tell. Go away indeed, and leave her alone for all the devilish machinations to do their worst to her!

I bought a revolver on my way back to the house, and it is in my hand as I write this.

11 o'clock in the evening.—I have not slept for a long time, and it is as much as I can do to keep my eyes open. But I dare not go to sleep, lest while I sleep the man should come in. I am firmly resolved, whether she wishes it or not, to face him, and if possible, to get her out of his hands. She must be starving unless food is passed up to her through the window, at night or while I am out.

1 o'clock in the morning.—To keep myself awake, I have been writing an account of these happenings to a friend in Massachusetts. I shall have his reply in two or three days, and be guided by his opinion as to whether I should force the door or not.

I have just been to the door and called out to her: "Shall I bring you some food?" She replied with the same moaning "No" as before. "Speak to me, for God's sake!" I said. I heard her crying.

3.25 a.m.—Have I been asleep? I was awakened by a loud cry. *He* is with her. He is torturing her in some way.

I am writing this deliberately. It may be the last entry I shall ever make. I am calm. I have put the time in the margin. In ten minutes, if he does not come out. I will blow off the lock of the door with my revolver.

The ten minutes are up.

NOW.

Note:

My poor friend, George Manders, was by profession a mining engineer. He returned about a year and a half ago from Mexico, where he had been working for some time. When he was found dead in the old wooden house he had rented in Brooklyn, I was sent for, because there was a letter on his table addressed to me. Early in the morning of August 4, his body was discovered by the woman who did the housework, lying face downward on the floor of the back room upstairs. He had shot through the lock of the door. A revolver with only one chamber emptied was found near him. He did not bear the mark of any wound. The room looked like a common place bedroom without special character. I was told that the owner of the house, a Dr. Purves, desired to keep it shut because his wife had died in it only a few weeks before.

Children of Wrath

Last night I wandered in the Devil's close,
Crushed by the aching agony of those
Who know strange secrets which they must disclose.

I found him seated in a herbless plain
On two large stones, nor with him any train
Of courtiers, or throng of souls in pain.

Across the muffled sky wild lightning broke,
And ever through the air the acrid croak
Of ravens fell: then drawing near I spoke.

"Almighty Master, thou whose name is feared
Throughout the sick world, and whose heart is cheered
By suitors, why alone?" The Devil leered.

"Look round this land!" he cried; "let your eyes scan
Till they go blind this desert—in its span
You shall not find the footprint of a man."

I answered: "There is one. Behold! I kneel
To whisper shameful things, that I may feel
Thy dread praise for the horror I reveal."

Then Satan: "Rise! If you would serve me, keep
Your sins locked in your heart as herds fold sheep
At fall of night: sin silently and deep!

"Walk armoured as a saint in open day;
Blaspheme me, and the Sacred Office say:
My servitors to God the loudest pray.

"I love the virtue of the fools who lie
Besotted with celestial vanity—
Who think they cannot sin, and shall not die.

"To them I ever murmur: 'You do well;

The Holy Spirit in your soul doth dwell!'
For them I keep alight the fire of Hell."

I wailed: "O Master, thou whose name is feared
Throughout the sick world, and whose heart is cheered
By suitors, spare the people scorched and seared!"

The Lonely Women

The lonely women wist not of the hours
Which make the burthen of their dim despair,
Nor know they if the years bring sweets or sours:
As Sorrow's path grows broader in their hair
The lonely women wist not of the hours.

The lonely women twist and twine a wreath
Of bloodstained flowers which decked them in their youth,
And see not Terror with his gleaming teeth,
And never see the pearl-eyed face of Truth.
The lonely women twist and twine a wreath.

Around them move the phantoms of the dead
Who close their ears to words, and in the street
Tis not the crowd they gaze at, but the head
Of one to whom their lips were erstwhile sweet:
Around them move the phantoms of the dead.

And bitter pleasures which they never share
Press tepid kisses odorous of the tomb;
For on their grey, cold feast-days they prepare
A welcome for the ghosts that throng the gloom,
And bitter pleasures which they never share.

No wine-soaked sponge your constant torture lulls
Ye martyrs! as through life you bear your cross,
And reel beneath it to a place of skulls;
And there, when on a grievous bed you toss,
No wine-soaked sponge your constant torture lulls.

O lonely women, I have looked on you
And seen the pain of your unheeded sighs,
And marked the grief you struggled to subdue;
Yea, when forgotten tears were in your eyes
O lonely women, I have looked on you!

Yield

(Propoundeth the Fruit of Seed)

It was when the summer afternoon was most pleasant, about four o'clock, that a young man—a farm labourer with sun-browned face and brown toil-marked hands—rounded a corner of the road and came to a stand in the village street. It was delightful to pause, and rest there, with the bees murmuring softly, the trees waving, and the splash of a far-off stream just touching his ears. The stream's noise, after a while, the warble of it, its cool song, made him thirsty—some dust of the sunny lanes had got into his throat—and he moved slowly towards the "Nag's Head," his cap in his hand, letting the breeze soothe him, and the quietude of the peaceful neighbourhood.

He entered the inn, nodding freely, with a large smile which shewed his white teeth, at the three or four rustics who were seated in the tap-room drinking mugs of ale, talking heavily with slow words; then when he was comfortable, placed in a corner, a mug of sile before him too, he joined in the talk. Yes, he had come from a distance: he "belonged" actually to a town some leagues away, but he had been working in the fields during the summer, passing from farm to farm, hardly knowing where he would be the next week. The season had been so bad: even today, fine as it was, had a certain film in the atmosphere, a torpor which boded more rain.

The others grew confidential: they liked this young fellow who had somewhat the flavour of an adventurer, a toiler in perilous unknown places; and a farmer's trap drawn by a brown cob, which, in good time, drove up to the door, hardly damped a familiar conversation. The farmer alighted, leaving a pretty, youthful woman in the trap—his wife, he called her to the landlady with whom he entered the tap-room: a burly man, with a whip in his hand, about forty, wearing a low white felt hat, talking loudly, tossing easy salutations. He sat down at the table with the labourers, taking the strange labourer too

219

into his favour, bestowing his patronage on him as on the rest.

But for him, this strange labourer, the presence of the newcomer was gravely disturbing. He who felt kindly to all men, found himself, of a sudden, torn by an inexplicable hatred of this prosperous, amiable person. Surely he was crazed!—the sun with one of its thin penetrating darts had, in his long journey under it, struck him mad. His great loathing of this man he had never seen before—he felt too, in part, as one feels in a disturbed dream, that he had some wrong to avenge—his loathing and abomination of the man was come quite suddenly, ere the farmer had even spoken.

How was it that he felt himself, thickly yet tumultuously, to be in an open space—a churchyard perhaps—with the rain and darkness around, harried by an angry crowd, bruised by a stone flung by someone—by that one over there! How was it? This corner—was it not too hot? Yes, that was it—he would move—soon. Well? No! No! he must not! The picture on the wall over there—it was so curious, so interesting—why was it upside down? Why was it—and then with a shout he had sprung into the middle of the room and seized the farmer by the throat.

The woman in the trap outside, hearing a tumult, leaped to the ground and rushed in. What she saw was the farmer with a man at his feet whom he was lashing unmercifully with his driving-whip—lashing brutally, as though he would beat him to death—and the others standing open-mouthed, frightened, gazing.

"Harry!" she cried.

Her cry seemed to pierce the head of the man on the floor—he had been so gay that morning!—seemed to cut his head in two. Clumsily he got to his feet and stood staring idiotically at the company, rolling vacant, senseless eyes, not wiping the blood from his face. Then he went back to his corner happily, and sat down there, and began to play childishly with the mugs on the table.

The Hour of Ghosts

When the wind blows and stirs their earth-worn faces,
Sometimes they wake and rise up from their places,
Seeking each other's looks
In sad wise;
Sad, sad they gaze at the buffeted elms,
And shew the vague dismay that overwhelms
(Scaring the crazy rooks)
Their tired eyes.

Wistfully then they strive to touch each other,
Yearning for life. One murmurs: "Lo! my brother,
See you in yonder field
The red kine?
They and that small white farmhouse with the gable,
The garden, and the brown horse in the stable,
All that and all its yield—
All was mine!

"Now as I laboured on the brightling sward
I thought that life beneath the sun was hard,
That to lie here were peace,
Sleep, and death:
In yon square barn I took a rope one morn
And hanged myself amid the amber corn,
And swung till came full cease
To my breath.

"I had a red-haired woman for my wife;
A year past, when she saw me void of life,
Her weary strangling sobs
Bewildered me:
Now behind those lit windows she delights,

221

While I must lie here till the end of nights
Listing to the dull throbs
Of the sea."

Thus, these old ghosts make converse in their woe,
While the day thickens and bats whir and go,
And in the twilight dream
Lad and lass:
Birds droop; the drowsy church-bell tolls for bed;
'Tis bedtime too for the forgotten dead,
Who in the light's last gleam
Sigh "Alas!"

Will

1

Have the dead still power after they are laid in the earth? Do they rule us, by the power of the dead, from their awful thrones? Do their closed eyes become menacing beacons, and their paralyzed hands reach out to scourge our feet into the paths which they have marked out? Ah, surely when the dead are given to the dust, their power crumbles into the dust!

Often during the long summer afternoons, as they sat together in a deep window looking out at the Park of the Sombre Fountains, he thought of these things. For it was at the hour of sundown, when the gloomy house was splashed with crimson, that he most hated his wife. They had been together for some months now; and their days were always spent in the same manner—seated in the window of a great room with dark oak furniture, heavy tapestry, and rich purple hangings, in which a curious decaying scent of lavender ever lingered.

For an hour at a time, he would stare at her intensely as she sat before him—tall, and pale, and fragile, with her raven hair sweeping about her neck, and her languid hands turning over the leaves of an illuminated missal—and then he would look once more at the Park of the Sombre Fountains, where the river lay, like a silver dream, at the end. At sunset the river became for him turbulent and boding—a pool of blood; and the trees, clad in scarlet, brandished flaming swords. For long days they sat in that room, always silent, watching the shadows turn from steel to crimson, from crimson to grey, from grey to black. If by rare chance they wandered abroad, and moved beyond the gates of the Park of the Sombre Fountains, he might hear one passenger say to another, "How beautiful she is!" And then his hatred of his wife increased a hundredfold.

So, he was poisoning her surely and lingeringly—with a poison more wily and subtile than that of Caesar Borgia's ring— with a poison distilled in his eyes. He was drawing out her life as he gazed at her; draining her veins, grudging the beats of her heart. He felt no need of the slow poisons which wither the flesh, of the dread poisons which set fire to the brain; for his hate was a poison which he poured over her white body, till it would no longer have the strength to hold back: the escaping soul.

With exultation he watched her growing weaker and weaker as the summer glided by: hot a day, not an hour passed that she did not pay toll to his eyes; and when in the autumn there came upon her two long faints which resembled catalepsy, he fortified his will to hate, for he felt that the end was at hand.

At length one evening, when the sky was grey in a winter sunset, she lay on a couch in the dark room, and he knew she was dying. The doctors had gone away with death on their lips, and they were left, for the moment, alone. Then she called him to her side from the deep window where he was seated looking out over the Park of the Sombre Fountains.

"You have your will," she said. "I am dying."

"My will?" he murmured, waving his hands.

"Hush!" she moaned. "Do you think I do not know? For days and months, I have felt you drawing the life of my body into your life, that you might spill my soul on the ground. For days and months as I have sat with you, as I have walked by your side, you have seen me imploring pity. But you relented not, and you have your will; for I am going down to death. You have your will, and my body is dead; but my soul cannot die. No!" she cried, raising herself a little on the pillows: "my soul shall not die, but live, and sway an all-touching sceptre lighted at the stars."

"My wife!"

"You have thought to live without me, but you will never be without me. Through long nights when the moon is hid, through dreary days when the sun is dulled, I shall be at your side. In the deepest chaos illumined by lightning, on the loftiest mountain-top, do not seek to escape me. You are my bond-man: for this is the compact I have made with the Cardinals of Death."

At the noon of night, she died; and two days later they carried her to a burying-place set about a ruined abbey, and there they laid her in the grave. When he had seen her buried, he left the Park of the Sombre Fountains and travelled to distant lands. He penetrated the most unknown and difficult countries; he lived for months amid Arctic seas;

he took part in tragic and barbarous scenes. He used himself to sights of cruelty and terror: to the anguish of women and children, to the agony and fear of men. And when he returned after years of adventure, he went to live in a house the windows of which overlooked the ruined abbey and the grave of his wife, even as the window where they had erewhile sat together overlooked the Park of the Sombre Fountains.

And here he spent dreaming days and sleepless nights—nights painted with monstrous and tumultuous pictures, and moved by waking dreams. Phantoms haggard and ghastly swept before him; ruined cities covered with a cold light edified themselves in his room; while in his ears resounded the trample of retreating and advancing armies, the clangour of squadrons, and noise of breaking war. He was haunted by women who prayed him to have mercy, stretching out beseeching hands—always women—and sometimes they were dead.

And when the day came at last, and his tired eyes reverted to the lonely grave, he would soothe himself with some eastern drug, and let the hours slumber by as he fell into long reveries, murmuring at times to himself the rich, sonorous, lulling cadences of the poems in prose of Baudelaire, or dim meditative phrases, laden with the mysteries of the inner rooms of life and death, from the pages of Sir Thomas Browne.

On a night, which was the last of the moon, he heard a singular scraping noise at his window, and upon throwing open the casement he smelt the heavy odour which clings to vaults and catacombs where the dead are entombed. Then he saw that a beetle—a beetle, enormous and unreal—had crept up the wall of his house from the graveyard, and was now crawling across the floor of his room. With marvellous swiftness it climbed on a table placed near a couch on which he was used to lie, and as he approached, shuddering with loathing and disgust, he perceived to his horror that it had two red eyes like spots of blood.

Sick with hatred of the thing as he was, those eyes fascinated him—held him like teeth. That night his other visions left him, but the beetle never let him go—nay! compelled him, as he sat weeping and helpless, to study its hideous conformation, to dwell upon its fangs, to ponder on its food. All through the night that was like a century—all through the pulsing hours—did he sit oppressed with horror gazing at that unutterable, slimy vermin. At the first streak of dawn, it glided away, leaving in its trail the same smell of the charnel-house; but to him the day brought no rest, for his dreams were haunted by the abominable thing.

All day in his ears a music sounded—a music thronged with passion and wailing of defeat, funereal and full of great alarums; all day he felt that he was engaged in a conflict with one in armour, while he himself was unharnessed and defenceless—all day, till the dark night came, when he observed the abhorred monster crawling slowly from the ruined abbey, and the calm, neglected Golgotha which lay there in his sight. Calm outwardly; but beneath perhaps—how disturbed, how swept by tempest!

With trepidation, with a feeling of inexpiable guilt, he awaited the worm—the messenger of the dead. And this night and day were the type of nights and days to come. From the night of the new moon, indeed, till the night when it began to wane, the beetle remained in the grave; but so awful was the relief of those hours, the transition so poignant, that he could do nothing but shudder in a, depression as of madness. And his circumstances were not merely those of physical horror and disgust: clouds of spiritual fear enveloped him: he felt that this abortion, this unspeakable visitor, was really an agent that claimed his life, and the flesh fell from his bones. So did he pass each day looking forward with anguish to the night; and then, at length, came the distorted night full of overwhelming anxiety and pain.

2

At dawn, when the dew was still heavy on the grass, he would go forth into the graveyard and stand before the iron gates of the vault in which his wife was laid. And as he stood there, repeating wild litanies of supplication, he would cast into the vault things of priceless value: skins of man-eating tigers and of leopards; skins of beasts that drank from the Ganges, and of beasts that wallowed in the mud of the Nile; gems that were the ornament of the Pharaohs; tusks of elephants, and corals that men had given their lives to obtain. Then holding up his arms, in a voice that raged against heaven he would cry: "Take these, O avenging soul, and leave me in quiet! Are not these enough?"

And after some weeks he came to the vault again bringing with him a consecrated chalice studded with jewels which had been used by a priest at Mass, and a ciborium of the purest gold. These he filled with the rare wine of a lost vintage, and placing them within the vault he called in a voice of storm: "Take these, O implacable soul, and spare thy bond-man! Are not these enough?"

And last he brought with him the bracelets of the woman he loved, whose heart he had broken by parting with her to propitiate the dead. He brought a long strand of her hair, and a handkerchief damp with her tears. And the vault was filled with the misery of his heart-quaking whisper: "O my wife, are not *these* enough?"

But it became plain to those who were about him that he had come to the end of his life. His hatred of death, his fear of its unyielding caress, gave him strength; and he seemed to be resisting with his thin hands some palpable assailant. Plainer and more deeply coloured than the visions of delirium, he saw the company which advanced to combat him: in the strongest light he contemplated the scenery which surrounds the portals of dissolution. And at the supreme moment, it was with a struggle far greater than that of the miser who is forcibly parted from his gold, with an anguish far more intense than that of the lover who is torn from his mistress, that he gave up his soul.

On a shrewd, grey evening in the autumn they carried him down to bury him in the vault by the side of his wife. This he had desired; for he thought that in no other vault however dark, would the darkness be quite still; in no other resting-place would he be allowed to repose. As they carried him, they intoned a majestic threnody—a chaunt which had the deep tramp and surge of a triumphant march, which rode on the winds, and sobbed through the boughs of ancient trees. And having come to the vault they gave him to the grave, and knelt on the ground to pray for the ease of his spirit. *Requiem aeternam dona ei, Domine!*

But as they prepared to leave the precincts of the ruined abbey, a dialogue began within the vault—a dialogue so wonderful, so terrible, in its nature, its cause, that as they hearkened they gazed at one another in the twilight with wry and pallid faces.

And first a woman's voice.

"You are come."

"Yes, I am come," said the voice of a man. "I yield myself to you—the conqueror."

"Long have I awaited you," said the woman's voice. "For years I have lain here while the rain soaked through the stones, and snow was heavy on my breast. For years while the sun danced over the earth, and the moon smiled her mellow smile upon gardens and pleasant things. I have lain here in the company of the worm, and I have leagued with the worm. You did nothing but what I willed; you were the toy of my dead hands. Ah, you stole my body from me, but I have stolen your soul from you!"

227

"And is there peace for me—now—at the last?"

The woman's voice became louder, and rang through the vault like a proclaiming trumpet. "Peace is not mine! You and I are at last together in the city of one who queens it over a mighty empire. Now shall we tremble before the queen of Death."

The watchers flung aside the gates of the vault and struck open two coffins. In a mouldy coffin they found the body of a woman having the countenance and warmth of one who has just died. But the body of the man was corrupt and most horrid, like a corpse that has lain for years in a place of graves.

For the End

As sweetly comes to those this world calls mad
The thought of calm worlds without scream or cry,
So is it unto man when he is sad
Pleasant to think that he shall surely die.

The sick and throbbing child upon its bed
Murmurs of streams, and for the sea doth rave;
So, on this fevered earth, my thoughts are led
To dwell upon the coolness of the grave.

Out of the Cloud

That fiend who tricked out like a saint
Did haunt a most unhappy youth,
And wall it in, and coarsely taint
Its whiteness with the lees of truth,

And choose for instruments the fools
Who prate of duty to themselves,
Who fish for virtue in cess-pools,
And line with lies their mental shelves,—

He is not dead, though Youth is dead,
And Age, Youth's weary son, has smashed
The walls which held his sire and fled!—
He hunts the thing he erewhile lashed.

A scowling ghost with scorching breath
He follows hard, and shall not cease
Till God speaks through the mouth of Death
And smites the sombre silences.

The Voice of the Winds

Warm wind, whispering high and low,
Tell me which way did my lost love go.
(*Hear the south wind sighing far out to sea!*)
"Oh, I passed o'er a land where soft voices say
A sad 'Dona Pacem' for dead folk alway:
'Mid a countless host thy lost love was there,
With pure white stars in her shining hair;
And she smiled at me,
As one who is free
From grief and strife and all misery."
(*So, the south wind sighed from the sounding sea.*)

Warm wind, whispering high and low,
Tell me which way did my lost love go.
(*Hear the west wind wailing far out to sea!*)
"I come from the court of a glorious king,
Where a choir of maidens doth sweetly sing:
Amongst the brightest she brightest shone,
But eyes were sad, and she seemed alone:
Then she looked at me
And she bent her knee,
And I heard her prayer and it was for thee."
(*So, the west wind wailed from the restless sea.*)

Wild wind wandering to and fro,
Tell me which way did my lost love go.
(*Hear the east wind shrieking far out to sea!*)
"I come from a region deserted and drear,
Where spectres shudder in frenzied fear:
'Mid those phantom forms thy love in the frost
Wrung her hands and wept like a soul that is lost,
While she cried to me,

'O wind, that we
Might be as free as the wind is free!'"
(*So, the east wind shrieked from the cruel sea.*)

Wild wind, wandering to and fro,
Shew me how I to my love can go.
(*Ho, the north wind howleth far out to sea!*)
"In cheerless churchyard by crumbling tomb—
Dank and heavy and fraught with gloom—
She stands, and knows that when life is sped,
With its flame and fever, all hope is dead.
'Hope not for me—
I shall never be free,'
Is the message she charged me to bring to thee."
(*So, the north wind howled from the sobbing sea.*)

The Bars of the Pit

And where is now my hope? as for my hope
who shall see it? They shall go down to the bars of the pit.
Job XVII. 15, 16.

When the last notes of the opera had sounded, and the curtain slowly came down, the plaudits and huzzaings were so loud and prolonged that it seemed to me the whole of Vienna must have been let loose to bellow its approbation. I had heard of what they call popular ovations for great composers, but this was the only one I had ever seen which truly merited the description.

Even those there who had little or no genuine feeling for music or any other art, who must of course form the largest body of spectators in gatherings of this kind, were carried away by that well-known contagion to which those who make up a crowd are exposed, and perhaps shouted the loudest. I must confess it was impressive enough to see that great theatre filled with brilliant and beautiful people as mad with enthusiasm for one old man who had appealed to them with no vulgar state or parade, as they might have been for a great king, or a great conqueror. It was the first performance of a new opera by the celebrated Russian composer who died nearly three years ago. Written in his seventieth year, it proved to be his last work, and by many it is esteemed his best.

A party of us, amongst whom was L——, the poet, whose poem the composer had chosen for his opera, went across to Sacher's restaurant for supper. We had a private room; and the Master, who had been obliged to linger while he received the compliments of the *Kaiser*, or the archdukes, or I don't know who, had promised to join us as soon as he could get free.

Meanwhile we asked L——, who had seen him just after that storm of applause at the end of the last act, how the old man had taken it. It was easy to see how L—— himself had taken it: he was flushed and radiant.

"He didn't seem much moved", answered L——; "in fact I don't think he was moved at all. Or at least except in one point I noticed which seems absurd, and may well have been in my imagination:—I was excited enough to imagine the theatre was on fire if anyone had suggested it. Anyhow, as he talked to me, through that melancholy, that kind of terror which is always about him, I thought I made out a strange look—something new—in his eyes. The applause had hardly died away in the theatre, and I thought I saw in his eyes—not contempt exactly—no, it wasn't that—it was more a look of hatred, of rage, of vengeance—and you may laugh if you like—I swear it seemed to me a look of unsatisfied vengeance—a vengeance only half appeased."

We took this up and discussed it with more or less eagerness: the Master was one of those mysterious men about whom, as in the case of ghosts, people are always willing to discuss any proposition thrown out, because they feel certain they are not even on the skirts of truth. We fell back upon this atmosphere of melancholy, and as L—— had said, this species of terror which constantly enveloped him. Yes, we agreed, there was no doubt that he was uncanny. We were all fairly intelligent, I think; we made due allowance for the difference between the genius, the madman, and ordinary humanity; but after that we wandered whither we would—rather wildly, I'm afraid.

Some attributed his character to the struggles and obscurity of his young years; some esteemed that the number of years he had gone unrecognised had embittered him; some accounted for the whole matter by heredity:—the son of obscure Russians flung into new and artificial conditions, and the conditions perhaps reacting on him. There was not wanting even the commonplace suggestion in cases of this nature of thwarted and unfortunate love.

We were hard at it when the door was thrown open and the Master himself came in. I picture him still as he walked through the room in the odour of flowers and cigarette smoke, his tall thin figure hardly bent at all with age, his neat white hair just touching his velvet coat, and above all that unforgettable face, not in the least of the blunt Slav type, but rather with a clear-cut fineness almost eastern, the whole suffused by a subtilty, and dreaminess, and sombreness commingled which you found at once attractive and yet somehow repulsive, but at any rate unusual.

In his youth he must have been singularly handsome, and even in his age he had conserved in his features traces of that terrible sensitiveness for which the possessor pays, till he becomes hardened by age, or insane, with such bitter hours. Nor would his portrait be complete without some mention of his wonderful hands, now indeed somewhat crabbed and dry from age, but still of incredible daintiness—made to touch flowers, and fragile porcelain, and precious stones. It was said he preferred the violin to all other instruments, and it was not difficult to realise that with a hand of that kind he could do more with a bow than with a keyboard.

We all examined him pretty closely, as well we might: it was the night of his triumph and he seemed to expect our scrutiny. But the envy, or at least the little half-sighs of desire which often accompany such looks at a celebrated personage, were in this case, I am sure, absent. There was something about the Master which extinguished envy. Each of us felt that he would not take to himself the gnawing serpents of anxiety and wretchedness which lurked in that man's mind, for all the laurels in the world.

He sat down, broke a piece of bread, and drank half a glass of wine. He seemed rather fatigued, but not otherwise disturbed. He jested pleasantly enough about a man of his age coming to a supper party at that hour of night. His age indeed seemed very present with him at the moment, and he kept coming back to it in his talk.

"It is all very well for L—— here," he said, putting his hand on the poet's shoulder, "who has youth, and fire, and courage, to go out and gather his smiles on the highways. But as for me—" He made a little pout of disgust. "What a ridiculously giddy old thing I must seem to all you young people. I feel that I haven't a shred of character left. I paint my face, and wear a wig and too many jewels. Seriously, the dignified thing for me to have done would have been to have waited at home in silence for the traditional telegram. Instead of that, I expect I shall finish my youthful frolic tonight by breaking the shopwindows in the Graben."

"But surely, *cher maître*, if you *will* think of your age, it must make you very happy when you look back over so many years and see the steps and struggles and hard work which have made you the great master you are." It was the pretty little Mme. W——. who found herself there, and who ventures such things, who said that. Some of us gave her a look of thanks: we found his insistence upon his age a little excessive.

The Master put his elbows on the table, took his face between his hands, and glanced round at the company. "I wonder," he said slowly, to Mme. W——, "I wonder when you ask me to do that, if you really have the slightest inkling of the kind of torture you suggest I should go in for. And yet," he added, "I have a good mind to do it—yes, I will. I am excited; this is an occasion which will never recur. Tonight, I feel, is the culminating point in my career; let me celebrate it by getting some perilous stuff off my heart. It has lain there so long that it hates to be disturbed. It is almost wrenching nature to disturb it. And really in telling now in this gay company what I have never uttered to a soul in solitude, I feel like a man going naked through a busy street. You say you owe me some trifling pleasure from this evening," he said with a little bow; "you can easily repay me by listening to an old man's tale.

1

"I was thirty years old. Here in this very city of Vienna I was living, not in actual physical wretchedness, for I had always enough to eat, but still in deplorable conditions. From my twenty-fifth year I had drifted through no fault of my own into a backwater of life: not only was I without real friends, but I was without the acquaintance who in a measure make up for the lack of friends. I knew nobody to speak to: I knew nobody even to write to. All my pains and disappointments had to be eaten up in my own bosom. Add, that I had singularly little power of exciting sympathy, that, either through pride or shyness, I would have found myself at the last extremity ere I had asked for any being's sympathy or society, and you will easily enough understand that even with the people of the house where I lodged I had very little intercourse.

"If they saw me well they took it for granted, if they saw me ill they were not unquiet so long as the rent was paid. No doubt I could have picked up companions of a sort by sitting in the beer-gardens and drinking with the first comer; but I was fastidious in my way, and if I couldn't have good companionship I preferred to go without any. Possibly some of you here think you know what solitude is: you have gone to some remote place in the Alps or Pyrenees and you have lived more or less alone for three or four months, with all the time the conviction that your exile was voluntary, and a comfortable consciousness at the back of your head of the express train which you might step into from day to day and which in a few hours would land you among your clubs, and your friends, and your usual life.

"Well, let me assure you that you know nothing about solitude. In the days I speak of, when I chanced to read in a book an author's complacent description of his solitude, I used nearly to go mad with rage and scorn. Whatever is voluntary cannot be altogether painful: my solitude was involuntary. Besides, your solitary, I have found, is seldom quite alone; he has struck up a friendship with the brave fisherman, or the honest blacksmith, upon whom he sheds his wisdom. Now I have known what it is to go for a year without speaking a word to any soul, except just those few words which the obscurest existence makes necessary, and do not take up two minutes all together in a week.

"I have known what it is to feel a few casual sentences exchanged at random, which one leading a normal life would not think of twice—I have known that to become an event in my life, and give me matter for speculation to last a month. I have known what it is to move about a great city with no sense of making one with the crowd, with no sentiment of human solidarity, feeling on the contrary a helpless piece of wreckage absolutely at the mercy of the human sea, as I drifted through the streets gazing fearfully yet wistfully at the passers, even as a spectre" exiled from another world might gaze; hating them too because I feared them, and feeling in my turn that I was hated by them because I was different.

"This kind of life signally hindered my poor fortunes. On the few occasions when I came in contact with men of the world to discuss affairs, they found me stupid, and unready, and disagreeable; and I have no doubt they were right. For them a conversation such as they had with me was an every-day affair, or rather a ten-times-a-day affair, to which they attached little or no importance and never gave a thought before or after; for me, on the other hand, it was an abnormal event, filled with a thousand dangers and ruses, to be prepared for by endless precautions.

"Add to this, that as human intercourse had no part in my existence, my normal state was to be silent, and even in the most ordinary conversation I felt myself in the regions of the unreal; that I was acting, and I placed my words, so to speak, with an eye to a foreseen effect;—that my interlocutor, in a word, stood in the same relation to me as an audience to a playwright; and you will get some notion of the sorry result. How often have I gone over a conversation days afterwards word for word in my head, correcting it with abominable sensitiveness, as one might correct a proof! No wonder people found that I lacked spontaneity; a man of the present age in a suit of mediaeval armour we should not find spontaneous.

"In one matter, however, I saw clearly. I felt that the law, which had its origin in the desire of the weak for protection against the oppressor, had become from various causes and by various accretions a kind of oppressor itself—that is to say, a blind machine of terrible power, pretending to be worked by accurate science, but with no trace of scientific precision in its action. I reminded myself that while the law is a protection for groups of citizens, before it the individual is generally in the wrong.

"If the individual be lonely, and friendless, and powerless, for such an one it is pitiless: before it he is certainly in the wrong. At its core the law is rotted by obsequiousness. The policeman who is a protection for the noble and the banker, is a perpetual menace for the weak and obscure. For the entirely powerless, for the social outcast, for the pariah dog, such as I (however blameless) was become, he is a sombre dread and terror, and takes the aspect of a malignant arbitrary god who may at any moment, if the whim seizes him, lay his heavy hand on your shoulder and ruin the rest of your days. The number of cases which we read of daily in the newspapers of all lands where the testimony of the prisoner goes for nothing against some tainted evidence the police have raked up, or even against the policeman's unsupported word, does nothing to weaken this belief.

"I resolved, therefore, seeing myself a mere shred and feather in the world without a scrap of importance of any kind, without a hope of protection on any side—nay, with no claims or qualifications whatever which I could think would weigh for a moment with any judge against the testimony of a man almost certainly prejudiced, and possibly ignorant and malevolent into the bargain; a man whom society at the same time as it gave him a uniform invested mystically with omniscience, the most rigid veracity, the impossibility to fall into error—seeing all this, I resolved, I say, to live in such a manner that the hand of this monster might never have cause to touch me, either to crush, or what was almost as terrible, to help, I did my best to occupy my mean little life as one is supposed to occupy an apartment in Paris—*bourgeoisement*.

"Many an injustice have I let go by unnoticed to keep to my resolution;—a strange enough result if one ever really hoped for justice from Justice. Many an hour have I sat trembling, lest my will being overpowered by some sudden freak of insanity, I might be betrayed into some act which would cast me between those iron hands by which I should be most infallibly ground to powder without reflexion or mercy. I came to shrink from the most harmless frequentations, torturing myself to carry forward all situations from their actual circumstances towards purely hypothetical ones which were unlikely to come about, which it was most improbable would come about, but which still might possibly come about—such circumstances, I mean, as would suggest to a policeman to interfere. My constant feeling of the impression of this tyrant put such disorder in my spirits, that whenever I heard the law or courts or criminals mentioned, so great a confusion would at once shew itself in my countenance that many people must have thought I had something to conceal and was afraid of the police—which indeed I was, but not in the sense they meant.

"By way of getting a living I copied music—a badly paid trade, but taken with a little store of my own it enabled me to live. I tried giving lessons, but I found them insupportable, and the employers I fell in with, mostly of the small-burgess class, were rude and exigent, with a vanity to have *Mademoiselle* play the piano. I am rather sorry now I did not seriously try to get lessons amongst the important families here: I might have interested one or two, and they might have helped me in the wild night and darkness. But would they have helped, after all? I wonder. I confess I doubt it.

"One of the publishers I copied for thought I had some talent. One day when I called as usual at his shop, he told me of a place of choir-master at Munich which was sure to suit me. I was delighted, and determined to start for Munich at once. There was nothing to make me tarry at Vienna, and accordingly I set out the following day. Towards evening I came to Salzburg, where I lay the night. True to my principle never to put my foot into any lodging which might possibly be suspect, or where suspicious people might gather with whom the law would not hesitate to confound the innocent, I descended at a very decent, even expensive inn by the Residenz Platz. You could catch sight of Mozart's statue from the windows.

"All this is forty years ago, and the hotel may now have disappeared. I ate my supper, went out, looked at Mozart, looked at the fountain before the cathedral, penetrated through an archway to the river, stood on the bridge a while watching the lights and the rapid water, thought of my choirmastership, strolled slowly back and went to bed. The next morning after breakfast, having a couple of hours on my hands before the train started, I went out again, roamed about a little in the great bare cathedral, crossed the river, mounted up past the stations of the Cross to the height of the Capuzinerberg, and then, when I thought it was time, returned to my inn, went to my room, and called for my reckoning.

"Now as I stood waiting in the little room, I noticed on the floor near the bed a spot of wet blood. It was not much bigger than a five-crown silver piece. Except that I hate the sight of blood in itself, I was not otherwise startled: so far as I thought about it at all, I thought that the man who had carried down my trunk had fallen a-bleeding from the nose, or had cut his finger. That was all.

"And yet the sight must have had a deeper effect than it seemed at the moment to have; for all the time of my journey to Munich I was besieged by vague presentiments of evil. At Munich I repaired to another decent inn near the Frauenkirche: I mention this because I have never since been able to hear any bells, the sound of which resembles the dismal toll of the clock of the Frauenkirche, without a sensation of faintness. I was tired; I lay fully dressed on my bed; soon I fell asleep. Had God been merciful I should have died while I slept.

"I was rudely awakened by a heavy knock and a loud voice summoning me to open the door which I had fastened. I started up, but half awake. Two policemen followed by the landlord came into the room. I was shocked almost out of my senses; but at the same time, I must add that these terrible men coming into my room without my leave did not in itself surprise me as it might any of you: I was nothing, whereas their power was absolute: as well might the blade of grass expostulate with the boot that crushes it. They explained gruffly that they had instructions from Salzburg to arrest me on a charge of murder committed at an inn in that town.

"I stammered some sentences in my pitiful broken German; but I don't think I shewed any passion. Remember that I had not the habit of fluent speech; remember too that I regarded the human race acting thus concretely as something incredibly powerful, malicious, and pitiless. Now that it had risen against me, I abandoned all hope. If there are any of you here whose minds are so moulded by traditions and prejudice that it is impossible for you to think except by the formulas and systems which generations hand down one to another, you will say that such is not the attitude of an innocent man.

"All I can reply is, that such was my attitude, and that I was innocent. Indeed, what I think did me considerable harm in the estimation of these functionaries, formed in a groove, rigorously drilled in traditions which they could no more dispense with conveniently than they could with their breath—was that I did not in effect shew all the surprise to be looked for if their arrival had been totally unexpected. No, I did not shew an immense surprise, for let me avow that their visit did not in truth come altogether without warning. All my vague fears had crystallized since a moment; I knew now that this horrible thing which had just happened was what I had apprehended since I had seen the blood stain on the floor.

"Ah, truly, judges should be selected, not from the sober pedants learned in precedents and punishments, not from the ample discoursers, the rotund orators, not from the fox-like knaves who in the name of justice set their trained wits to befog and befool some unhappy, unready, ignorant wretch in the witness-box—no, not among them should we seek the judge, but rather among the subtlest and profoundest students of the thousand variations and aberrations of the poor human brain.

"I was to be returned to Salzburg. One took me by each arm, and I was led ignominiously through the streets to the station. Oh, my friends, with what words can I bring home to you the anguish, the sickening of heart of that ruining moment! To estimate aright its poignancy, you must recall that no nun cloistered from the world had kept clearer of offences, including those which the law pretends not to interfere with, than I had. Remember again, that I was abnormally sensitive, that I had a power of feeling and imagination a thousand times more acute than the average prisoner.

"Moreover, one thing I had always cherished above all—my personal liberty; the power to go and come at my own will. This feeling was as strong in me as it was in Rousseau; it was in fact the spring of all that sedulous care I took to keep my life clear and disentangled. Judge then my horror, my prostration, as I put it to myself that by no means in the world could I stay in Munich, could I stay anywhere or go anywhere except just to the gaol at Salzburg.

"And as if these tortures were not sufficient, there was another bar still in the gridiron. You will have gathered that I have little or no faith in the protection afforded by justice administered through law. But beyond that, I have never been able to convince myself either from history or observation that mankind at large is naturally just. I have never had reason to believe that before a pitiable and humiliated brother the instincts of men lead them to act nobly.

"I have therefore always had a peculiar dread, a physical loathing and shrinking from all situations where men might be tempted to be malevolent and brutal, because I have felt certain they would yield to the temptation. I have been sure from my earliest youth that whatever rarities I may possess would be no match whatever as against man acting upon the impulses of his corporal strength directed by his dwarfed and malignant mind. The man-brute had always filled me with more repulsion and horror than anything else in creation, because I knew what his ferocity would be if he were once unchained. Alas, what I now experienced gave me no ground to modify this conviction.

"Against the criminal real or supposed—anyhow against the luckless individual whom the machine has sucked in, the whole of humanity is unchained. My captors were of course domineering and brutal enough; but after all that was part of their profession, and besides they were brutal in a half-mocking, almost good-humoured manner, as men congratulating themselves on having done a sharp turn in collaring a dangerous felon before he had got clean away. But never shall I forget the hateful fiendish looks—a minglement of mean cowardice, of suspicion, of self-righteousness, contempt and triumph, which were cast upon me by the men who looked at me in the street, and at the station who passed by the windows of the train.

"Such looks do cringing cowardly slaves cast at their fellow-slave when the master has felled him to the ground. At Rosenheim, where we had to change the train, a few women gazed at me with a certain tenderness; and those were the only glances of pity I saw till the end. The great scene which was transacted on Calvary is typical in all its superb details: was it not women who followed the prisoner weeping?

"But you will ask, what was the crime? That is what I myself kept asking my captors all the dreary way to Salzburg, and for all reply they threw me bits of answers in the sarcastic tone of one who conveys to another information which he thinks the questioner is only pretending not to know. At Salzburg, however, I gathered the following facts.—A farmer of the hill-country having come down to Salzburg for the market, had lodged in the room next to mine at the inn. His affairs were known to have prospered, and on the night we both spent at the inn it was certain he had a rather large sum of money in his possession.

"About an hour after I left the inn his murdered body was discovered in my room under my bed. There was no money in his clothes beyond a few pence. But I had paid at the railway station for my ticket to Munich with a fifty-crown note bearing a number which a Salzburg banker stated he had issued to the farmer the day before. In those days the press of travel was not nearly so great as it is now, and the railway clerk easily remembered who had tendered a fifty-crown note for a ticket to Munich. All this was recited to me, and I could only reply that I knew I had had a fifty-crown note, though I had never noticed its number; that I had had it when I arrived at the inn; that I had paid with it for my journey to Munich; and that I certainly not had taken it from the farmer. The magistrate told me he believed that I lied; he had evidently made up his mind I was the last of men; and after a summary examination which he contrived to render more atrocious by a thousand insolences, I was sent to prison."

"But didn't you protest, didn't you threaten to appeal to some-one—to the *Kaiser?*" exclaimed Mme. W——, whose eyes were very bright and who looked feverish and excited.

"Appeal? protest?" repeated the Master, glancing round the table very drearily. "Threaten?" he repeated. "Ah, yes, it is very well for all of you here, people of assured positions, flanked by affectionate, or at least assiduous relatives and friends, backed by Ambassadors and con-sulates, to talk of threats and appeals and *Kaisers.* That is just the sort of thing that would first come into the head of people with power and the means to use it—people who have never been humbled. But it is precisely the people with power who scarcely ever find themselves in such positions. The law and police avoid people with power as if they brought bad luck.

"Look at myself. I know that if the body of a man was discovered under my bed tonight, they would send to the confines of the world for the culprit before they would suspect me. Am I not honoured with the friendship of the *Kaiser*, of statesmen and princes? But as I was then, at the most awful moment of my life—ah, my dear friends, that was a different song, I assure you. What was a poor solitary wretch, a foreigner without friends, lacking even acquaintances of the least importance, who had never seen an ambassador, and would have been kicked by the ambassador's lackeys if he had tried to, who had never been at a Consulate except to get his passport *visa-ed* by a clerk behind a grill with what confidence could such a one threaten an honourable judge supported by all the weight of the state and public opinion?

"Would not his protest degenerate into a mean swagger, pitiful to bring tears to the eyes? Ah, my brothers, why do we laugh so harshly when we see a poor devil trying to ape his betters—'to play the gen-tleman', as they say? Is there not rather something infinitely moving in the sight, is he not after all trying through his imagination for just a little of that power which will help him against injustice in his day of need? Anyhow, that is how it seems to me. The powerful man has no idea to what extent the powerless man feels powerless.

"And even if I had decided to protest, who would have listened, who would have believed? Besides, I had always borne myself so meek, I had so continually effaced myself, my spirit and self-respect had been so ruined by numberless degradations and insults suffered in silence during years, that I was become the unfittest person in the world to defend myself. I knew what I wanted to say, I knew what I should say, and when I opened my mouth, it came out shambling, the merest shadow of what I had intended. That is why I dwelt a while ago on the solitude in which I had lived, that you might realise to what extent I had lost the use of man's natural weapon, speech.

"But while we are upon appeals and protests, I will add that I did think of writing a statement of my case to one or two of those gentleman in Paris and elsewhere who are called Socialists, and who have written beautiful books against the injustice which crushes down the outcast man. Well, upon reflexion I refrained, and I will tell you why. I considered that all of these gentleman were men of reputation, not only in their immediate circle, but in the world generally; fashionable people went to hear them speak, their books were found in fashionable houses.

"Now, I reasoned that these men, sprung for the most part from families of the lower middle-class which had been coerced for generations by the police, however strong-minded and kind-hearted they might be, must still have enough of the rags of heredity hanging about them to shy at the letter of a foreigner lying in a far-off gaol on a capital charge; must still be subject to their surroundings so far as to argue somewhat as follows: 'After all, when the police get hold of a man and put him in prison there must be something in it. The police don't often make mistakes. I had better not interfere: I may get myself into trouble, or make trouble with a foreign government. Besides, this may well be a plausible scoundrel.' And, to strengthen him in these prudent resolutions, even if upon a thousand chances he was disposed for more generous action, there would always be a wife, I thought, to counsel him at breakfast: 'Don't mix yourself up in it, Antoine; if you do, and it makes a smash, the Senator's wife will stop coming on my Tuesdays.'

"Looking back, with forty years' added experience of men, I still think that my reasoning was sound. Those who know the eighteenth century say that Voltaire did not move in the case of Calas till he was sure of a backing. And Calas, after all, was rather important, what the devil!—a Protestant, a religious man, almost a gentleman:—not at all the same thing as entangling yourself in questionable relations with an obscure foreign worm accused of murder. Let us recollect that, however you look at it, one owes something to society, one has a reputation to keep up!

"Once indeed the spell was broken, and I did speak really and truly from the depths of my tortured heart. The lawyer appointed to defend me was a genial, almost a jovial personage. He spoke to me softly, even kindly; he seemed amiable. Abandoned by all, thrown upon myself, yearning for some support, for some sympathy, I was at the mercy of the first person who shewed—no, I will not say pity; but who at any rate appeared to regard me otherwise than as something vile and noxious. One day with this lawyer I did indeed shift the burthen: I told him my story just as I have told it now, only with how much more fire, more vigour, more conviction!

"Then I was pleading for my very existence: now I am not pleading for anything; I am relating. We were alone, and by a miracle all my awkwardness, my timidity, my false shame fell from me. There on the floor of my dungeon with what passion, what abandon I was delivering up my miserable soul, when all at once I happened to glance at the lawyer and I perceived a kind of smirk lurking on the thick lips. 'Repeat that in the assize-court,' he said, 'and by Heaven, we may get you off. I find it very well done.'

"At that terrible word the black waters surged over me. That was the end. In my simplicity I had thought to convince this man; I had torn away the bandages which habit had made almost part of my nature and shewn him my green wounds bleeding, and he took me for a comedian.

"So, without encouragement or hope I lay in gaol and waited for the trial. When the trial did come on, it must have appeared to all but myself a very simple, even uninteresting affair. The judges, I could see, were decided against me in advance; my lawyer made a long and vivid harangue which won general applause and could not fail to raise him in the eyes of his profession; and the upshot was that I was condemned to die.

"Yes, I was condemned to die. Shall I tell you which anguish, of the thousand anguishes I endured through those hours of trial, put its head above the rest and bit the sorest? It was to hear people during the brief recesses which occurred two or three times—it was to hear even the warders in the hot, stuffy court-room discussing their plans for that evening, for tomorrow, for next week. All of them were free when the court rose to turn to the right or to the left; I alone must go down into the dark and never return.

"I was taken back to prison and waited for death. I lay in expectation of that numbing of the senses, that sullenness of despair, which I had read of as falling upon prisoners without hope; but my nature refused me such relief. I think I might be as brave as another in any situation calling for courage where the cause was worthy and noble; but before the disgraceful and miserable end which attended me but a few days off, I will not deny that I trembled. You must reflect that my nerve was broken by my isolation, by the absence of any support or pity from outside: even the ruffians who went rollicking to Tyburn had their doxies; *Macheath* had his *Lucy* and *Polly*; but for me there was nobody in the wide land to care, or to say a prayer for my soul.

"Add to this that I was torn to pieces by paroxysms of powerless raging against the heinousness of this crime the law was committing; by the reflexion that even if it discovered its error after my death it would be scarcely moved, and would certainly profit not at all, but continue to stumble on self-satisfied in its blind way; and that even if the police did one day discover the truth, they would be so afraid of the scandal, of the public indignation, of the dishonour, of the hatred they would arouse, (for a case like mine would strike home to every man's egoism, since he might himself be the next victim), that they would simply stifle all investigation:—figure to yourselves that these and a thousand other torturing reflexions haunted me day and night, and you cannot fail to form some kind of dim picture of my state, though far enough from the real thing. I lay in gaol, trodden down and abandoned by mankind, and waited to die.

2

"Well, it is obvious that I did not die, since here I am speaking to you tonight. I was redeemed by one of those extraordinary interpositions which, though they do sometimes happen, yet happen so rarely that they encourage us to believe that the Eternal Being does really glance from time to time at this planet, and puts out His finger occasionally, and negligently stirs the pieces here and there, when the little animals on its surface are planning a deed more than usually abominable and monstrous.

"Two days before I was to die, a man-servant of the inn was walking along a by-street when he came upon a bull guided by a drover with the aid of a heavy whip. The bull was tethered from the horn to the fore leg, as is the custom in those parts; but maddened by the hot dust and flies, and the shouts, and the whip, it managed to snap the tether and ran free. The bull found the servant directly in its road, and it gored him fatally. When the servant regained consciousness, he was told that his life could not be saved, and thereupon he asked for a priest and gasped out the truth of the mystery at the inn.

"This man had had entire charge of the rooms in which the farmer and I were lodged. Now upon entering the farmer's room early in the morning to rouse him, he found that the traveller had died in the night. Astonished and confounded, his first thought was to call up the house; but observing a good sum of money on the table his cupidity was excited, and he determined by all means to make it his own. Following his plan, he left the room silently, locked the door, and waited till the house was astir and the lodgers had gone upon their affairs. The farmer was a heavy drinker, and as it was his custom to lie late after a market day, nobody thought it worthwhile to notice that he was not yet abroad.

"The servant meantime had determined to make me the scapegoat. Under pretence of brushing my coat whilst I was half asleep, he searched in the pockets, found a fifty-crown note, and substituted for it one from the hoard of the farmer. Then, when he had seen me go out, knowing himself perfectly unwatched, he re-entered the farmer's room, transported the corpse into my room, and there did not hesitate to stab the dead body brutally with a long knife—such a stab as no living man could have survived. Knowing that I would return to the room, he removed, as he thought, all traces of his deed, went downstairs, kept with the others, and observed that the farmer slept late.

"While I was waiting upstairs for someone to carry down my trunk, he had to be haled from a table where he was drinking a pot with some cronies, and was sharply reprimanded by the landlord for being out of the house all the morning. Then, when he knew that the train for Munich had left, he remarked generally that he would go up and clean my room, and at the same time cursed the farmer for lying a-bed so late. A minute or two after, he roared out to the house that he had found the farmer murdered under my bed. I don't think that when he did this, he saw the results clearly to an end: he told the priest that he thought they would never find me: he was a low type of man, of stunted understanding, and he believed that once a man was out of Salzburg he was in a wilderness where he could never be tracked.

When he saw me brought back, he was afraid to open his mouth; and what is more, he was afraid to spend a penny of his ill-gotten money which was all found under a board in his room. Such was his story. He died soon after.

"I was at once set free, with the frigid apologies customary in such cases—without a stain on my character, as the phrase is. What good were their apologies to me? Even for the poor, brutalised, labouring man in like case, whom they think it will help to find work, it doesn't meet the situation; for most people jib at a man who has been in prison though he be declared innocent fifty times over. But for me, sensitive beyond the run of men, with my health ruined, my brain un-hinged, physically broken, and morally degraded, with not an ounce of self-respect left, afraid to look men in the eyes for fear they would read I was a gaol-bird, with in fact all the sneaking manner, half-deprecatory, half -insolent, of the ticket-of-leave man—what could their apologies do to heal my maimed life, to restore to me a sense of dignity, of equality, of freedom? As well may a man in a motorcar apologise and send a bottle of *eau-de-Cologne* to a youth whose legs he has crushed. I had lain down by the machine; I had done my best to keep free of it, to guard against its strokes; and lo, it had sucked me in as though I had slept.

"I hurried into Italy. I did not dare to change my name for fear they would make that a crime. The terror was upon me; I felt their eyes in every street, in every room; I dreaded that at any moment their claws might be outstretched to drag me into the dungeon. No protection, no justice, was to be looked for. Almost I was afraid to breathe; literally, I was afraid to move out of my room: to walk in the street might by some subtilty be twisted into a crime. At last, one day as I was slouching meanly by the side of the pillars under the arcade in Milan, so as to be on the far side away from the shops, something buzzed in my head and I fell down. When next I knew anything, I was in an asylum for the crazy.

"There is little more to relate. One of the doctors who visited there was interested in music; he conversed with me frequently; and when they deemed that I was more or less normal and let me go, he helped to start me anew. He is dead long since. He was as near a friend as I have ever had, and yet—will you believe it?—great as the relief would have been to pour into his ear my doleful history, every time I was tempted to do so, I refrained. Why? Because good as he was, high-minded as he was, yet I was not certain that he was so far removed from the generality of men as to restrain himself from shaking his head and saying, or at least thinking: It may have been a mistake, but still when a man has been in the hands of the police, there must be something, something.

"In like manner, I have never mentioned my catastrophe to any man or woman whatever, because, with the best faith in the world, and the firmest intention to guard the secret, still, you know, the facts might just happen to leak out, and then it would be: 'O yes, what's-his-name, the composer: he has had rather a stormy life; he was mixed up in a murder case in Austria when he was young.' No! since I bore the stigmata of the machine, I determined to keep them covered. And yet tonight, at length, I am blabbing it all here at a supper-table.

"Again, you may ask, why. Well, because this is perhaps the most important night of my life, because I am excited, because you are—are you not?—my friends and well-wishers, but chiefly," added the Master with a sombre smile, "because I am seventy years old, I cannot possibly live much longer, my life is over, and consequently I have nothing left to fear from the malice and treachery of mankind."

He paused, sipped some wine, and then concluded.

"Many hard words have been broken upon the Anarchists, and no doubt they are in great part deserved. Still, it is necessary to recollect when we give way to our indignation, that the motive of the Anarchist is always noble. The usual imputation of a craving for notoriety is only twaddle invented by the newspapers hard up for invective, and has been discredited long ago. The Anarchist, viewing the transitoriness and discontinuity of man's existence, is sickened by the contemplation of the thousand evils which society has wantonly created to make man suffer with a poignancy so out of proportion to the length of his days.

"And so, when he flings his bomb, he considers he is advancing the destruction of this nefarious society, and bringing nearer the time when all the old being destroyed and levelled, a better system will have room to arise in the untainted air. In thus reasoning he may possibly be right: personally, I do not think so, and I care little. Evils such as the one by which I was crushed have their cause not so much in the usurpation of some and the submission of others, as in the fact that man is what he is, in the constitution of society itself.

"Whether this will ever alter, and how, is to me of small impor-tance: my concern is with the hopeless position of the individual as opposed to the group—I care not whether a group of outdoor la-

251

bourers, whisking tradesmen, lawyers and doctors, authors and college-professors, merchants and bankers, soldiers and nobles. I have no rose-water notions, I am sure, about the superiority of one class over another; about the superior virtue of the poor and ignorant, or the superior generosity and insight of the rich and educated. I see no reason to believe that what goes by the name of education will ameliorate the former, or that vague slumming and ostentatious charity will make the other more gracious and merciful.

"All classes are equally formidable to the individual: they will even sink their angers and jealousies to make common cause against him. The only essential difference my experience leads me to draw in this matter is that the lower the class, the more disposed it is to be vindictive and persecuting, because it has stronger desires, and more rancour to get rid of. It is not the rich and educated who follow the poor prisoner through the streets hooting. But all classes without exception supply oil to the machine, and gloat when an individual is sucked in.

"Considering these things, shall I be forgiven if I say I am so far one with the Anarchist, that if I had thought tonight that by throwing a bomb over there just now among the brilliant audience, I should have dislocated one joint of the machine, and so brought nearer by an hour its utter annihilation, then would I have thrown the bomb, and gladly have suffered death amid the general ruin."

Fear at Night

Beside the crying river
Where night is cold and pale,
And gaunt trees groan and shiver
In the shrewd autumn gale,
I ever hear it wail.

It pauses when I pause,
Then moves distraught and wild;
I follow it because
It cries like a sick child
Whose soul is good and mild.

Its hands explore the ground
All night while dark winds rave,
And heap a little mound.
It has a corpse to save:
It digs a shallow grave.

O God, let me awaken
If this Thing is a dream;
Or let yon soul be shaken
Into the shadowy stream,
And hush its boding scream.

Or on this foul alarm
I'll steal with stealthy pace,
And hold it in my arm,
And feel its breath a space—
Then see it face to face!

A Silken Ladder

1

The lights within the little distant town
Come out like evening plants at eventide,
And struggle with the dusk, as from the side
Of starry Heaven God lets the darkness down;
The moist breath of the sweet drenched earth is blown
Across my face, and oh, tonight I ride
Upon that breath, and watch, when day has died,
The darkness add a glory to your crown.

O Love, these first steps in the drowsy lane,
These magic moments—whither do they tend?
Tomorrow shall the morn be grey with rain,
Or sunlight with the fragrant pathway blend?
You leave me half in gladness, half in pain,
Like weary pilgrims at their journey's end.

2

I sometimes have this fancy in the rain:
I think the soothing rain those poignant tears
Wept silently beside the troubled biers
Of strange dead hopes, which, flying in their pain

Skyward, drop gloomily to earth again,
And, like forgotten words of flouted seers,
Bring back the buried terror of old fears,
And rust a cherished treasure with their stain.

Still, when on dreary days I see you part
From sheltering house, and leave the dainty trace
Of your thin foot in muddy lanes, and dart
Laughing through showers with mountain-maiden's grace,

I, looking from the prison of my heart,
Rejoice to know my tears shall kiss your face.

3

Methought I was a prisoner lying dead
In a close room of some grave citadel,
Where no white gleam did penetrate to tell
Of day outside and sunny hours that sped;
But horrid dark was there, and round my head
Strange vermin crawled: when sudden in the cell
A warm light broke; the damp walls shook and fell;
Around my feet the hushed grass carpet spread.

My fantasy was mated in this wise:
Sullen I paced the noisome yelping street
Hating its breath, when for a dear surprise
You, wrapped in gracious musing, I did meet!
I met you and looked deeply in your eyes,
And lo! I felt the town was strangely sweet.

4

Like the assaulting sea with fury shod
Hurling grey breakers on an iron coast,
Or like the passionate music of the host
Of large-eyed youths who stand on Heaven's sod
Chaunting before the bannered towers of God—
To these I liken the strange power of lost
Delicious memories, and stronger boast
Than these the strength of love's all-touching rod.

A wondrous night still holds me with its spell!
Alone you walked the garden, the hot air
Hung heavily: enchaunted by the smell
Of witching flowers, you dipped your fair
And star-bathed bosom in their dewy well,
While the fond lilies kissed your gloomy hair.

5

As youthful playmates gambolling in joy
Spring suddenly from rapture to dull hate,
And glaring madly snap the bond of fate,
Not knowing man is fashioned by the boy,

And toss their passion like a broken toy,
 (Each striving fierce with his afflicted mate,)
Bite hard and gibe, until they find too late
That stings which come in hours, for years annoy

So, all the holidays we once thought sweet,
And all the festivals we once held dear,
Are mowed by grief as fields the reapers mow;
And when I hail your shadow glinting fleet,
We touch hands for a breath in icy fear—
Two passing phantoms trembling in the snow.

LEONAUR

ALSO FROM LEONAUR

AVAILABLE IN SOFTCOVER OR HARDCOVER WITH DUST JACKET

MR MUKERJI'S GHOSTS *by S. Mukerji*—Supernatural tales from the British Raj period by India's Ghost story collector.

KIPLINGS GHOSTS *by Rudyard Kipling*—Twelve stories of Ghosts, Hauntings, Curses, Werewolves & Magic.

THE COLLECTED SUPERNATURAL AND WEIRD FICTION OF WASHINGTON IRVING: VOLUME 1 *by Washington Irving*—Including one novel 'A History of New York', and nine short stories of the Strange and Unusual.

THE COLLECTED SUPERNATURAL AND WEIRD FICTION OF WASHINGTON IRVING: VOLUME 2 *by Washington Irving*—Including three novelettes 'The Legend of the Sleepy Hollow', 'Dolph Heyliger', 'The Adventure of the Black Fisherman' and thirty-two short stories of the Strange and Unusual.

THE COLLECTED SUPERNATURAL AND WEIRD FICTION OF JOHN KENDRICK BANGS: VOLUME 1 *by John Kendrick Bangs*—Including one novel 'Toppleton's Client or A Spirit in Exile', and ten short stories of the Strange and Unusual.

THE COLLECTED SUPERNATURAL AND WEIRD FICTION OF JOHN KENDRICK BANGS: VOLUME 2 *by John Kendrick Bangs*—Including four novellas 'A House-Boat on the Styx', 'The Pursuit of the House-Boat', 'The Enchanted Typewriter' and 'Mr. Munchausen' of the Strange and Unusual.

THE COLLECTED SUPERNATURAL AND WEIRD FICTION OF JOHN KENDRICK BANGS: VOLUME 3 *by John Kendrick Bangs*—Including twor novellas 'Olympian Nights', 'Roger Camerden: A Strange Story', and ten short stories of the Strange and Unusual.

THE COLLECTED SUPERNATURAL AND WEIRD FICTION OF MARY SHELLEY: VOLUME 1 *by Mary Shelley*—Including one novel 'Frankenstein or the Modern Prometheus', and fourteen short stories of the Strange and Unusual.

THE COLLECTED SUPERNATURAL AND WEIRD FICTION OF MARY SHELLEY: VOLUME 2 *by Mary Shelley*—Including one novel 'The Last Man', and three short stories of the Strange and Unusual.

THE COLLECTED SUPERNATURAL AND WEIRD FICTION OF AMELIA B. EDWARDS *by Amelia B. Edwards*—Contains two novelettes 'Monsieur Maurice', and 'The Discovery of the Treasure Isles', one ballad 'A Legend of Boisguilbert'and seventeen short stories to cill the blood.

www.ingramcontent.com/pod-product-compliance
Lightning Source LLC
Chambersburg PA
CBHW031120030726
47496CB00002BA/613